A SEASON OF SECRETS

Sweeping from the Great War, through to the 1940s, this unforgettable tale follows the lives of the Fentons, an aristocratic family from Yorkshire. Thea, the eldest daughter of Viscount Gilbert Fenton flouts all the unwritten rules of her class, embarking on a love affair with the son of one of her father's tenant farmers. Olivia, the middle Fenton sister, follows a more conventional path, forging friendships with the British royal family and attending finishing school in Germany. While Violet, the youngest is reckless and dreams of becoming an actress in Hollywood, unaware her life will be filled with more drama than any part she will ever play.

A SEASON OF SECRETS

A SEASON OF SECRETS

by

Margaret Pemberton

Magna Large Print Books
Long Preston, North Yorkshire,
BD23 4ND, England.

British Library Cataloguing in Publication Data.

Pemberton, Margaret
    A season of secrets.

    A catalogue record of this book is
    available from the British Library

    ISBN   978-0-7505-4190-9

First published in Great Britain in 2015 by Pan Books
an imprint of Pan Macmillan,
a division of Macmillan Publishers Limited

Cover illustration © Bernd Tshakert by arrangement with
Arcangel Images

Published in Large Print 2016 by arrangement with
Pan Macmillan General Books

Magna Large Print is an imprint of Library Magna Books Ltd.

Printed and bound in Great Britain by
T.J. (International) Ltd., Cornwall, PL28 8RW

For my niece, Gemma Steele

Mega thanks are due to my publisher, Wayne Brookes, and to my editor, Catherine Richards, both of whom have been tremendously supportive and encouraging. Thanks are also due to the rest of the formidable Pan Macmillan team and I particularly want to thank copy-editor Mandy Greenfield and editorial manager Ali Blackburn. At Curtis Brown my agent, Sheila Crowley, has been as indefatigable – and as much fun – as always, and also to be thanked are Rebecca Ritchie and Katie McGowan. Thanks are due to many friends, not least Oliver Smith, for help with German.

Chapter One

AUGUST 1915

It was early morning and eight-year-old Carrie Thornton sat on a sheep-studded hillside, her arms hugging her knees, her face wet with tears. Below her, in one of the loveliest valleys North Yorkshire possessed, a river curved. On its far bank, beyond an ancient three-arched stone bridge, lay a Georgian mansion sheltered by trees.

With blurred vision and deeply apprehensive, Carrie stared down at it. Gorton Hall was the home of the Fenton family. Carrie was familiar with stories about the Fentons, for when Viscount Fenton had been a child, her granny had been his nanny. Not only that, but when her widowed father had marched off to war, a little over a year ago, his company commander had been Lord Fenton, and Lord Fenton had still been his senior commanding officer when, three short weeks ago at the battle of Hooge, German shellfire had ended his life.

The tears Carrie was now shedding were for the father who had been loving and kind and had always had time for her. The apprehension she felt was because of the letter Lord Fenton had written to his wife, suggesting it might help the granddaughter of his old nanny get over her grief if, for the remainder of the summer, she were to spend a little time each day at Gorton with their daughters, two of whom were close to Carrie in age.

Ever since her mother had died of diphtheria her granny had said that when she was old enough – twelve or thirteen – there could be no better training for her than to be taken on as a tweeny at Gorton, and when the news of Lord Fenton's suggestion had been broken to her, Carrie had said, not understanding, 'But I'm too young to be a tweeny, Granny.'

Her granny had hugged her close to her ample bosom. 'You're not going there to work, silly-billy – and won't be doing so for a long time yet. You're going there to be company for Miss Thea and Miss Olivia.'

Carrie had frowned, still deeply puzzled. She had known Thea and Olivia ever since she could remember, for whenever the family were at Gorton, and not at their London town house, Lady Fenton would call on her husband's nanny for a cosy chat, a cup of tea and a slice of home-made ginger cake. When she did so she nearly always brought Thea and Olivia, and sometimes their younger sister, Violet, with her. Not only that, but the Fentons' current nanny often walked Thea and Olivia into the village so that they could spend their pocket-money on butter-scotch at the village shop.

'But why do I have to be company for them at the big house?' she'd asked, not liking the way it would set her apart from her friends. 'Why can't they come down to Outhwaite to play?'

'Because that wouldn't be at all proper,' her

granny had said briskly. 'Now stop asking questions and just think what a lucky little girl you are, being invited to play in such a wonderful house.'

Not feeling at all lucky, Carrie wiped the last of her tears away, pushed wheat-coloured plaits back over her shoulders and rose glumly to her feet. Until now, she had never set foot inside the house and had never expected to until the day when, if she fulfilled her granny's plans for her, she would begin working there.

Hal was a year older than Carrie, and his father was one of Lord Fenton's tenant farmers. Hal had told her quite bluntly what he thought of her being invited to Gorton to be a playmate for Thea and Olivia. 'It's going to muck things up,' he'd said grimly, wiping his nose on the sleeve of a shabby jacket. 'How can you spend time wi' them and still spend time wi' me? You can't. You're not going to be able to do any bilberry-picking, and you're not going to be able to watch the vole pups take to the water – and seein' as how it's August, it'll be the last litter this year.'

'Perhaps Miss Thea and Miss Olivia will want to bilberry-pick and see the vole pups as well,' she'd said.

Hal had laughed so much he'd had to hug his tummy. 'Not in a million years, daft idiot!' Suddenly he'd straightened up. Pushing a tumble of coal-black curls away from his forehead, he'd said fiercely, 'And if you're playmates, don't call them *Miss* Thea and *Miss* Olivia. Not unless they call you *Miss* Caroline.' And at this unlikelihood he'd begun laughing again, this time so hard that

Carrie had thought he was going to be sick.

'Hello, Carrie,' Blanche Fenton's voice was low-pitched and full of reassurance as, still holding her granny's hand, Carrie faced her in the intimidating surroundings of a room stuffed with gilt-framed paintings, silver-framed photographs and small tables crammed with ornaments. 'Thea and Olivia are very much looking forward to you spending time with them.'

Despite her nervousness, Carrie was glad to discover that Lady Fenton was just as nice and approachable within the walls of her home as she had always seemed to be outside it. She had a cloud of dark hair that she wore caught in a loose knot on the top of her head and, wherever she went, she carried the faint scent of roses with her. Though she seemed old to Carrie, her granny had told her that Lady Fenton was only twenty-nine, which, she had said, wasn't old at all.

'And Gilbert is only thirty,' she had added, forgetting her rule always to refer to her former charge as either 'Lord Fenton' or 'his lordship'. 'They were scarcely old enough to be out in society when they married, and neither of them has any side whatsoever.'

Carrie had been mystified by the word 'side' until her granny had explained it meant that Lord and Lady Fenton weren't pretentious. 'Which means they behave in exactly the same way to absolutely everyone, no matter who they are,' she had added when Carrie had continued to look bewildered.

'Please don't worry about anything, Nanny

Thornton,' Blanche Fenton said now. 'I'm sure this arrangement is going to work beautifully.' She took hold of Carrie's free hand. 'Jim Crosby will collect Carrie every morning in the pony-trap and bring her home in it every teatime.'

Carrie felt a flash of alarm. As well as being the general handyman at Gorton Hall, Jim Crosby was Hal's uncle, and Carrie didn't think he'd take kindly to ferrying her back and forth every day. He'd think she was getting ideas far above her station in life – as would her friends in the village when they got to hear about it.

Foreseeing all kinds of difficulties ahead, she said a reluctant goodbye to her granny and allowed herself to be led from the room.

'Thea and Olivia are in the playroom,' Blanche said encouragingly. 'Violet doesn't visit it much, as she is still in the nursery and spends most of her time with Nanny Eskdale.'

They were walking down a royal-blue carpeted corridor lined with marble busts set on fluted pedestals. Through an open doorway Carrie saw a maid busily dusting. The room looked to be a smaller version of the room they had just left and she wondered how many other such rooms there were, and how the Fentons decided which room it was they wanted to spend time in.

Another maid, a smart black dress skimming neat buttoned boots and wearing a snowy lace apron and cap, walked down the corridor towards them. She stood to one side as they passed, giving Blanche a respectful little bob and shooting Carrie a look of curiosity.

Together, Blanche and Carrie turned a corner

17

and began climbing a balustraded staircase carpeted in the same dazzling blue. At the top, on a spacious landing, it divided into two.

'This is the main staircase of the house,' Blanche said. 'I'm taking you this way so that we can look at a few family portraits together.'

The portrait looking down on them as they approached the landing was of a robust-looking gentleman with a shock of silver hair.

'This portrait is of Samuel George Fenton, Lord Fenton's grandfather,' Blanche said as they came to a halt in front of it. 'He was a Yorkshire wool baron, a Member of Parliament and the first Viscount Fenton.'

They turned and began to mount the left-hand flight of stairs.

'This portrait,' she said, referring to the first painting they came to, 'is of his wife, Isabella May.'

Isabella May's stout figure was encased in purple silk. She was heavy-featured and stern-faced, her thin lips set in a line as tight as a trap. Carrie didn't like the look of her, but knew it would be bad manners to say so.

There were several more portraits. One was of the present viscount's late father who, Blanche told her, had spent his early years in India, an officer in the British Army. Carrie liked the dashing red of his uniform and the wonderful sword at his side.

By the time they reached the next landing, where the royal-blue carpet gave way to carpeting a lot less dazzling, Carrie knew that, where Lady Fenton was concerned, she had never met any adult she thought more wonderful.

'The playroom is up here on the third floor, so that noisy games can be played without the rest of the house being disturbed,' Blanche said. 'The schoolroom is on the second floor of the east wing and easier to get to.'

'The schoolroom?' Carrie had never before given any thought as to how Thea and Olivia were educated. All she knew was that they certainly didn't go to Outhwaite elementary school where, clutching slates and chalk, everyone sat in rows on uncomfortable benches and only their teacher, Miss Calvert, had a desk.

They were outside the playroom door now, but Blanche didn't open it. Until now she had never had any doubt that inviting Carrie to spend time with Thea and Olivia was, under the circumstances, the right thing to do. It wasn't as if Carrie was just any village child. As Gilbert's nanny, Ivy Thornton had played an important part in his childhood and his affection for her was deep. When he had outgrown the nursery, Ivy had become nanny to one of his young cousins and then, later, nanny to a whole string of his nieces and nephews. Now in her seventies and comfortably pensioned off by him, she lived rent-free in one of Gorton's tied cottages.

Knowing her husband as she did, Blanche was certain that, like her, he would have assumed any grandchild of Ivy's would be reasonably well educated. Now, seeing how startled Carrie was by the word 'schoolroom', she was no longer so sure.

'Can you read and write, Carrie?' she asked,

trying not to let her concern show in her voice.

Carrie looked even more surprised at this.

'Yes.' She tried not to show how affronted she was by the question. 'My granny taught me to read and write – and how to do numbers – long before I went to school.'

Blanche breathed a sigh of relief. If Carrie could read and write, it made things easier. She would feel less awkward with Thea and Olivia and might even be able to join them in their lessons when Miss Cumberbatch, their governess, returned from her summer leave.

Hoping that Thea and Olivia would be immediately friendly towards Carrie – especially as she had explained to them the manner in which Carrie had been orphaned – Blanche opened the playroom door.

With butterflies dancing in her tummy, Carrie followed her into the room. What she had been expecting she didn't quite know, but certainly it wasn't the sight of Thea garbed in a trailing cloak of gold-coloured velvet, a cardboard crown crammed on a waterfall of glossy chestnut ringlets.

'I'm King Cophetua,' she said, looking exceedingly cross. 'Olivia is supposed to be the beggar-maid, only she refuses to take off her shoes and stockings and she won't wear anything raggedy out of the dressing-up box.'

Olivia, her marmalade-coloured hair held away from her face by a floppy brown bow, skipped up to them, unrepentant. 'That's because Thea always takes the grand parts and never lets me wear the crown. Would you like to be the beggar-maid, Carrie? Or have we to play at being pirates instead?'

Blanche, grateful that Ivy Thornton wouldn't now have to be told by Carrie that on her first day at Gorton she'd been asked to dress in rags, said, 'Being pirates sounds far more interesting than being King Cophetua and his beggar-maid.'

Thea, still trailing a river of gold-coloured velvet behind her, came over to stand next to Olivia. Blanche, aware that her daughters were patiently waiting for her to go, blew them a kiss and, certain they would now take good care of Carrie, closed the door behind her.

Thea swept her late grandmother's opera cloak up and over her shoulder, toga-like. 'What is it like to be an orphan?' she asked bluntly as the sound of her mother's footsteps receded. 'Is it very hideous?'

'Yes.' Carrie felt it was a stupid question, but as she hadn't yet got the measure of Thea, didn't tell her so. 'And I'm only an orphan because my father was killed fighting in Flanders. How would you feel if it had been your father?'

Thea, who was a year older than Carrie and Olivia, regarded her with eyes that were very narrow, very green and very bright. She'd been happy at the thought of having Carrie as a temporary playmate and was quite prepared to be condescendingly nice to her, but she wasn't happy about a village girl being uppity with her.

As she tried to think of a suitably crushing retort, Olivia took hold of Carrie's hand and began leading her towards a huge wicker hamper that was the dressing-up box. 'Papa isn't going to be killed. Mama gave him a little silver crucifix that used to hang on one of her necklace chains,

21

and he carries it with him all the time.'

There was such happy trust in Olivia's voice that Carrie hadn't the heart to express doubt as to whether the crucifix would stop bullets, bayonets and murderous shellfire.

'Are you wearing a black pinafore dress because you're in mourning?' Olivia asked. 'I saw you in a pretty red gingham dress once. We don't have any gingham dresses. All our dresses have pin-tucked bodices and big sashes that are always coming undone.'

'Yes,' Carrie said to the question. 'And the red gingham is my Sunday-best dress. Granny made it.'

The flowered linen smocks Thea and Olivia were wearing now were far from being either pin-tucked or sashed and were not the kind of clothes Carrie had expected them to be wearing. Thea even had a hole in one of her white stockings. That she was so obviously unembarrassed by it impressed Carrie. Aiming for self-confidence herself, she liked to see it in other people.

Thea, aware that the moment for saying something crushing to Carrie had passed, said impatiently, 'If we're going to be pirates, let's find something pirate-like to wear.'

Energetically she began rummaging in the hamper, tossing things in Olivia's direction. Carrie didn't help in the search. Instead she looked around her.

The room was large and packed with things she itched to take a closer look at. There was a huge rocking horse with flaring nostrils and a long swishy mane and tail in one corner. In another was the largest doll's house she had ever seen. There was a long shelf stacked higgledy-piggledy with books, including one she recognized because she had been given the same book, *The Wind in the Willows*, as a present two Christmases ago. On other shelves there were jigsaw puzzles and board games and on the bottom shelf was a row of beautifully dressed dolls. Beneath the dolls was a gaily painted wooden box crammed with toys. Spilling out of it were a train, a spinning top, a musical box and a monkey-up-a-stick.

Just as she was about to go and have a closer look at the monkey-up-a-stick, Thea said, 'I think we have enough stuff now to be going on with, but as I could only find one pair of breeches, you and Olivia will have to be lady pirates.' She stuffed a pile of garments into Carrie's arms. 'There's a red-spotted scarf you can tie around your head like a bandana, a striped shirt, a fringed orange sash for tying round your waist and an eye-patch that belonged to Mama's Uncle Walter.'

Olivia was already clambering into an outlandish selection of garments, and Carrie, beginning to get into the spirit of the thing, pulled the man's shirt over her head, anchoring it around her waist with the sash.

Olivia giggled. 'You look first-rate, Carrie. All you need now is a big black moustache. There's a stick of burnt cork somewhere. Let's see if we can find it.'

'So we drew moustaches on our faces with the burnt cork,' she said to Hal, much later in the day. 'And we had enormous fun jumping from the table onto a chair and then onto other chairs, pretending the floor was the sea and that we would drown if we touched it.'

Hal made the kind of sound in his throat that he always made when he wasn't impressed. 'Doesn't sound like much of a game ter me.' He scowled so hard his eyebrows almost met in the middle. He was herding his father's cows in for their evening milking and bad-temperedly switched the rump of the animal nearest to him. 'Aren't you going to do 'owt else this summer but go ter Gorton? The vole pups were out this afternoon, but it weren't much fun watching 'em all on me own.'

Carrie tried to feel sorry about not having been with him, but she'd enjoyed herself so much she couldn't quite manage it.

'Before I came home Lady Fenton introduced me to Mr Heaton,' she said as the cows headed up the narrow tree-lined track towards the farm buildings and the summer sky now smoked to dusk. 'Mr Heaton is the butler. She told him I was Miss Caroline Thornton, that I was a guest of Miss Thea and Miss Olivia and that I would be at Gorton Hall every day until mid-September.'

Instead of being impressed, Hal forgot about his bad mood and hooted with laughter.

Carrie punched his shoulder. 'What's so funny?' she demanded hotly. 'Mr Heaton was very nice to me. *Everyone* was very nice to me – apart from Thea, but that was only in the beginning. And Lady Fenton is like the Good Queen in a fairy story. She's...' Carrie struggled to find words that would do Blanche Fenton justice. 'She smells of

24

roses, and she talked to me as if I was a grown-up. Apart from Granny, I think she's the most special person in the whole wide world.'

'You're barmy.' Still chuckling, Hal fastened a rusting iron gate behind them so that if the cows decided to head back to the meadow they wouldn't get very far. 'And you're not the only one. My Uncle Jim says Lady Fenton isn't right in the head, and that her having you up at Gorton every day is proof of it. I know you don't want to go there, getting above yourself, because you told me you didn't.'

It was true. She had. But that had been yesterday. It had been before she'd fallen under Lady Fenton's spell, and before she'd known she was going to be best friends with Olivia and possibly a friend of Thea's, too. It had been before she'd sensed that, where the Fenton family was concerned, she had started on a long and very special journey.

Chapter Two

'I knew Lady Fenton would look after you,' Ivy said, undoing Carrie's plaits by candlelight. 'She has a kind heart for such a young woman.'

Carrie, kneeling with her back to her, twisted her head around. 'Don't young women usually have kind hearts, Granny?' She was wearing a nightdress that had been made out of one of Ivy's old ones, her hands cupped around a beaker of warm milk.

Realizing she had spoken without thinking and not wanting to give Carrie a gloomy view of human nature, Ivy said hastily, 'I'm sure they do, pet lamb. It's just more noticeable when they are as high-born as Lady Fenton.'

'You mean when they are a viscountess?'

Ivy began brushing Carrie's hair. 'Lady Fenton wasn't born a viscountess, Carrie. Her father is the Earl of Shibden and so, where the hierarchy of the peerage is concerned, she married beneath herself when she married a viscount.'

That anyone could be regarded as having married beneath them when marrying a viscount was beyond Carrie's understanding.

Seeing her bewilderment, Ivy laid the brush down. 'Let me explain, lovey. Top of the pile, after royalty, are dukes and duchesses – and there aren't a lot of those. A degree lower in rank are marquesses and marchionesses. A degree lower still are earls, and an earl's wife is called a countess.'

'And then there are viscounts and viscountesses?'

Ivy nodded. 'All those ranks, including that of baron, who is a rank below viscount, are peers of the realm and sit in the House of Lords – or can if they wish. It's something you should know, if you are going to go into service – and I'd far prefer to see you in service with Lord and Lady Fenton than working in a Bradford woollen mill or,' she added, 'working on a farm.'

Carrie, sensing a slur on Hal, said defensively, 'Hal is very clever, Granny. Even though he misses a lot of school when his dad needs him to help on the farm, he always makes up for the time he's missed, and he's always top of his class. Miss Calvert has told him that if he works really hard, he could win a scholarship to a grammar school.'

'Has she indeed? If he went to a grammar school he'd have to speak a lot differently than he does now – and how would the Crosbys be able to kit him out with suitable clothes?'

She spoke crossly and that was because she was cross, though not with Carrie, but with Miss Calvert. As far as she was concerned, putting an unobtainable idea into a child's head was a cruelty. Though Hal Crosby's parents were a step up from being agricultural labourers, their tenant farm wasn't the magnificent Home Farm, where all the fresh produce for Gorton came from, but a three-field farm on the edge of the estate that was, in Ivy's eyes, not much more than a glorified smallholding. Hal, a year older than Carrie, would in two or three years' time be required by his dad to work alongside him from sun-up to sun-down. Going to a grammar school was, for Hal, as remote as pigs flying.

The next morning Jim Crosby called for Carrie in the pony-trap. It was a blisteringly hot day and although there were lots of things she wanted to play with in the playroom, she hoped that today Thea and Olivia would want to play outside.

'How's tha getting on wi' yon posh lassies?' Jim asked as he clicked the reins and they trundled off down the lane in the direction of the road

27

leading out of Outhwaite towards Gorton. 'Did you 'ave your tea wi' 'em?'

'Yes.' Carrie only answered his second question, as she didn't think the first one was anything to do with him and, if she had answered it, she knew her answer would have been all round the village before the day was out.

Jim pushed a flat cap to the back of his head. He was still a young man and the hair that sprang free was as dark and as curly as Hal's.

'It's a rum do, you goin' every day, specially if you don't tek tea in t' kitchen. You can't be a tweeny there when you've bin treated as a ruddy guest!'

'I will be a tweeny. Granny's promised me.' Carrie wished Jim would keep his troubling opinions to himself and also that he wouldn't swear. When her father had been alive, he had never sworn in her presence. Her granny wouldn't have allowed it.

Jim shifted the lame leg that made him unfit for army service, yet didn't detract from gypsy-like good looks, into a more comfortable position. 'And 'ow long is this lah-di-dahing going to carry on for?'

They were almost out of the village now and the hedgerows were thick with the frothy white blossom of meadowsweet and late-flowering foxgloves.

Watching a bee busily gathering pollen, Carrie said, 'Till the harvest is in and school starts again. Granny said Lady Fenton, Miss Thea, Miss Olivia, their governess, Miss Violet and Miss Violet's nanny will be leaving for London at the end of

28

September and won't be back at Gorton until Christmas.'

'Did she?' Jim gave a crack of laughter that reminded Carrie of the way, Hal laughed. 'Well, for once your granny is wrong. Her ladyship won't be going back to London this year. Not wi' zeppelins raining bombs dahn on it. This year Lady Fenton is going ter be keeping Miss Thea, Miss Olivia and Miss Violet safe out of harm's way, up 'ere in God's own country.'

'God's own country' was the way Jim always referred to Yorkshire. It was an expression Carrie liked. It made her feel that being Yorkshire-born was something special and something to be proud of.

As the horse continued to trot along the lane Carrie wondered if Jim was right about Lady Fenton and her children not leaving Gorton Hall at the end of September, as they usually did; and if he were, if it meant her visits there would continue right up until Christmas and possibly into the New Year.

As the river came in sight Jim said, 'If they do stay on, not much'll be 'appening at Gorton, not even at Christmas.'

'Why not?' It seemed to Carrie that though Jim was only an odd-job man, he knew far more about the goings-on at Gorton than her granny did.

'Because there can't be weekend parties and such when there's no valets or footmen to tek care o' folk. Even the gardeners are in Flanders now, fighting for King and country.'

'Doesn't it bother you, that you aren't with

29

them?' she asked curiously.

His face darkened. 'Have you bin listening to village talk, Carrie Thornton?'

Though Outhwaite had plenty to say about Jim Crosby, the only talk Carrie ever heard was from her granny, who quite often said Jim was like all Crosby men, in that he was too good-looking for his own good. To Carrie this sounded like a compliment, but she knew it wasn't, because of the way her granny said it.

Deciding it was safest not to tell Jim her granny's opinion of him, she said, 'No, I haven't. And Granny won't have either, because she doesn't like gossip and, if she ever hears any, she never repeats it.'

'Then she's the only woman in Outhwaite who doesn't.'

He still sounded bitter and, knowing she had somehow put him in a bad mood, Carrie stayed quiet.

Jim stayed quiet too, but as they neared the bridge he said suddenly, 'There's folk who don't believe being born lame is any reason not to be fighting, but what's a chap to do, when the War Office don't agree wi' 'em? They say I'd be an 'andicap to the rest o' the lads, and though I've told 'em I'm as nimble as any bloke wi' two legs the same length, they won't wear it. They won't tek me, and there's an end o' it.'

Wishing she hadn't asked her innocently thoughtless question, Carrie said, 'I'm sorry, Jim. I didn't know that if you were lame you couldn't be a soldier.'

Jim shrugged. He wasn't particularly tall or

broad-shouldered, but he was whippy and strong, and all his life he'd never been shy of joining in any fight that was going – as many pub landlords, clearing up after a fracas in which he had been involved, knew to their cost. That he couldn't now take part in the biggest fight in all history, but had to stay home with elderly men – and men like Armitage, Lady Fenton's pacifist chauffeur – was something that rankled so deeply there were times when he could hardly breathe for humiliation and disappointment.

Aware that Jim was no longer in a talkative mood, Carrie concentrated on enjoying the novelty of riding in the pony-trap, which was far more comfortable – and far sweeter-smelling – than Hal's father's donkey-cart.

To her surprise Jim didn't take her to Gorton the way they had gone the previous morning, when he had reined in at a side-entrance close to the front of the house. Instead he approached the house from the rear, reining the horse in at a far less impressive entrance.

'I don't think this is the right door, Jim.' Her voice was uncertain. 'There won't be anyone to meet me here...'

'This is where I was told to drop you, so forget about being little-miss Lady Muck and be on your way.'

Still feeling doubtful about it, but not seeing any other option, Carrie jumped down from the trap.

As she did so the door flew open and Olivia, her lion's mane of hair flying around her shoulders, came hurtling out to meet her, her eyes alight with welcome. 'I've been waiting *ages* for you,' she said, grabbing hold of Carrie's hand. 'If you and I decide now on what we want to do today, Thea will have to agree to it, because two against one always wins.'

'If you say so, Olivia.' Carrie's voice was full of laughter as Olivia began pulling her at a run towards the house. And then, remembering she hadn't said goodbye to Jim, she turned her head in order to do so and was rewarded by the sight of him staring after her wide-eyed.

Knowing his bewilderment was because she hadn't addressed Olivia as Miss Olivia, and because Olivia had so clearly not expected her to, giggles fizzed in Carrie's throat. Not many people took Jim Crosby by surprise, and that she had done pleased her enormously.

'I'd like to do something completely different today,' Olivia said, hurrying her along a grey-carpeted corridor. 'Something Thea and I have never done.'

Carrie waited for her to tell her what that might be, but Olivia simply said, 'So what shall we do, Carrie?'

'I don't know.' For once Carrie was at a loss. 'I don't know what it is you've never done. What is it you would like to do?'

They were climbing some stairs now. It was a narrower staircase than the royal-blue carpeted staircase, but the walls on either side were still hung with lots of different-sized paintings in heavy gilt frames.

'I'd like to do what you would be doing if you weren't here.'

Carrie thought for a moment and then said, 'That's easy. I'd be with Hal and we'd be bilberry-picking or watching the vole pups.'

'Who is Hal?'

'Hal's my friend.'

As they began climbing a second flight of stairs Olivia said, 'And what are voles?'

Slightly breathless, Carrie said, 'Voles are tiny furry animals with chubby faces. They live in burrows in the river-bank.'

As they reached the top step she could see the playroom door. Remembering how long the corridors she'd walked down yesterday had been to reach it, she appreciated the less-splendid route Olivia had taken.

Before they reached it the door flew open and Thea stepped out into the corridor, saying imperiously, 'I've decided what it is we're going to do. We're going to do what Rozalind does. We're going to take photographs.'

'Rozalind is our cousin,' Olivia said to Carrie. 'She's American and lives in New York. When she last visited she took lots and lots of photographs, and Papa rigged up a darkroom so that she could develop them.'

'And I've found the Box Brownie she left behind.' Thea looked very pleased with herself. 'And so we're going to do the same thing.'

'No, we're not.' Olivia both looked and sounded mulish. 'Today we're going to do what Carrie and I want to do. Today we're going to look for vole pups.'

Thea sucked in her breath, her eyes flashing fire.

Aware that a row was about to take place, Carrie said pacifyingly, 'We could do both things. We could look for the vole pups and then photograph them. Think how special a photograph of vole pups would be – and these voles are water voles. I don't suppose anyone has ever taken a photograph of water voles before.'

Thea hesitated and Carrie knew she had caught her interest. Remembering the copy of *The Wind in the Willows* she had seen sitting on one of the playroom's bookshelves and hoping to clinch things, she said, 'I expect you know that Ratty in *The Wind in the Willows* isn't a rat, but a water vole. Think how wonderful it would be if we took a photograph of our very own Ratty. I bet even Rozalind would be impressed.'

'You've read *The Wind in the Willows?*' Having assumed Carrie to be illiterate – or nearly so – Thea was surprised.

'Yes, and I've read *The Railway Children, Black Beauty* and all of *A Child's History of England* by Charles Dickens.'

Forced into reassessing her opinion of Carrie, Thea said, 'The voles. Where would we find them?'

'There's a burrow in the river-bank, about a quarter of a mile down from the bridge where the water is slow. It's hard to spot, but Hal finds it straight away every time.'

'Hal?'

'Hal Crosby. He lives on a small farm this side of Outhwaite.'

Olivia and Thea looked at each other and Carrie was aware there was a problem. 'What's the matter?' she asked. 'Is it Hal? Do you not want him to come with us?'

'We're not allowed so far from the house un-accompanied.'

Carrie looked at Thea disbelievingly. The river was far further from her home in the village than it was from Gorton Hall, and yet she'd been playing on its banks and paddling in its shallows unaccompanied ever since she was six years old.

'Does that mean we can't go?' Olivia's dis-appointment was deep. 'I did so want to see the voles, Thea.'

'We could go if we could find anyone to take us. Tom would have been ideal, or William Beveridge.' Thea looked towards Carrie. 'Tom was a footman, and the last one of our footmen to enlist. William was one of the gardeners. The two of them enlisted together when the fighting began at Ypres.'

'There's Armitage,' Olivia suggested doubt-fully.

Thea gave a rude snort. 'Can you really see Armitage, in his dove-grey uniform and gaunt-leted gloves, escorting us a quarter of a mile down the river? Mama would never ask it of him. She'd know how insulted he'd be.'

'And it would have to be a man who came with us,' Olivia said to Carrie. 'Maids would be no use on a river-bank looking for voles.'

'Then let's ask your mother if Jim Crosby can take us.' To Carrie it was the perfect solution. 'He's Hal's uncle. Hal won't mind having Jim with us, and Jim won't mind spending his morning down by the river.'

Jim, who had been mucking out a horse box when he had been given his new instructions, hadn't minded at all. Over the last few months he'd become accustomed to doing jobs that weren't rightfully his. Stable-work was one instance. Gorton Hall's grooms and stable-boys were nearly all now with the 7th Battalion of the Yorkshire Regiment and the lad who should have been mucking out the horse box had been blown to kingdom-come three weeks ago in the same battle in which Carrie's father had lost his life.

Being good with horses, Jim enjoyed stable work, but he'd chuckled as he left the yard, more certain than ever that the gorgeous-looking Lady Fenton was barmy. Who'd ever heard of an odd-job man being asked to nursemaid the daughters of the house on a river-bank while they took photographs? Even barmier was that they were going to do so with Carrie Thornton and, if he could find him, his nephew Hal.

If Carrie had felt it a little odd having Jim ferrying her to Gorton and back every day, she found it downright disconcerting riding in the pony-trap alongside Thea and Olivia. It became even more disconcerting when Jim tracked Hal down and he, too, squeezed into the trap, carrying with him a distinct smell of cow, and with mud and bits of straw on his boots.

'So what's all this then?' he asked chattily, as if riding in the Fenton pony-trap was nothing out of the ordinary. 'Where are we jaunting to?'

Seeing Thea and Olivia were too dumbstruck by his grubby appearance to answer him, Carrie

36

said, 'We want you to take us to the burrow so that we can take photographs of the vole pups.'

Hal grinned cheekily across at Thea and, carefully not addressing her as Miss Thea, or even by name, said, 'Is that right? You 'ave a camera?'

Jim made a muffled sound that Carrie strongly suspected was one of suppressed mirth.

Thea, quite obviously wishing she'd never agreed to Hal accompanying them, said stiffly, 'Yes. I have.'

'Can I 'ave a look at it?'

'Certainly not!' Thea's outrage was so deep Carrie half-expected her to box Hal's ears. 'You're here to show us where the voles live, and that's all!'

Instead of being suitably apologetic, Hal laughed.

Jim made another muffled sound. Thea flushed a deep angry red. Olivia giggled. Carrie, exasperated beyond all endurance, punched Hal so hard he half-fell off the narrow seat.

Regaining his balance, he said in mock reproach, 'Steady on, Carrie, 'ow d'you expect me to find the burrow for you if you knock me into the middle o' next week?'

She glared at him, wishing she'd never thought his coming with them was a good idea.

The bridge was now a fair distance behind them and Jim said, 'Whereabouts d'you want dropping off, our Hal?'

Hal squinted across the wide expanse of rough meadowland separating the lane from the river. Looking back to the bridge to gauge the distance, he said, 'Anywhere here will be grand.'

As Jim reined in the horse and the trap rocked to a gentle halt, the girls looked at each other. Thea put into words what they had all suddenly realized. 'Mama thought Mr Crosby would be with us on the river-bank, but he can't be, can he? He can't leave the pony-trap unattended in the lane.'

'That don't matter.' Hal, oblivious to the conditions under which Thea and Olivia had been allowed their trip to the river, jumped down from the trap.

Olivia followed him.

Thea looked at Carrie, hesitated for a moment and then said, 'Come on, Carrie. Mr Crosby has a good view of the river from here. We'll be in sight all the time.'

She jumped down from the trap, the Box Brownie tucked under one arm. Carrie, not seeing that she had much choice, jumped down after her.

As they began walking through deep grass in Hal and Olivia's wake, Thea said disapprovingly, 'I know I thought it a good idea for your friend to come with us, but you didn't tell me how smelly he was, or that his jacket would have been used as a dog-bed.'

Carrie came to an abrupt halt, her face white. She knew that in giving Thea a piece of her mind she would ruin everything for herself; that afterwards she would never be invited to Gorton again, never again play in its wonderful playroom and, though she wouldn't miss Thea, she would miss Olivia. It was a lot to lose, but she didn't care.

'How *dare* you talk like that about Hal?' She

38

fought the urge to grab fistfuls of Thea's chestnut ringlets and tug on them hard. 'All Hal smells of are the cows he looks after for his dad. If *you* had to look after cows and only had cold water from a yard pump to wash in, *you'd* smell of cow! And his jacket is shabby because it's years old and wasn't new when he was given it!'

Angry tears scalded the backs of her eyes. 'Not everyone lives in a house as big as a palace with nannies and governesses and maids. Most Outhwaite children work in the fields before they go to school *and* afterwards – and often with nothing more than bread and dripping to eat!'

Knowing that she'd ended all hope of ever being invited to Gorton again, and had probably also ended all hope of one day being taken on as a tweeny, tears of another kind mixed with her tears of anger.

Not wanting Thea to see them, she began running after Olivia and Hal, knowing she'd have to tell them that their morning of vole pup-watching and photography was almost certainly not going to happen now.

Catching up with them, she said unhappily, 'Thea and I have fallen out. She didn't say so, but I don't think she's now coming to see the voles – and I don't think she'll be letting me travel back in the pony-trap, either.'

Hal raised his eyebrows. 'Are you telling us the two of you 'ave 'ad a barney?'

'Yes.' Carrie hadn't the faintest intention of telling him what the barney had been about. 'I don't like her, and she doesn't like me.'

'Doesn't mean to say the three of us can't

watch the voles. Olivia still wants to watch 'em, don't you 'livia?'

Olivia, who often fell out with Thea and didn't see anything odd in Carrie having done so, nodded her head. As if to show where her loyalties lay, she moved a little closer to Hal's side. From being initially alarmed by him, she now wanted to be friends with him. There was, though, Thea to think about. If Thea returned home without her, there was no telling what kind of explanation Thea might give their mother and it would probably be one that would get her into trouble.

She looked towards the pony-trap. Jim Crosby was leaning against the side of it, smoking a cigarette, one foot crossed carelessly over the other and Thea was striding towards him.

'Come on, 'livia,' Hal said impatiently. 'What are you waiting for?'

'I want to see if Thea is going to tell Mr Crosby she wants to go home and that he's not to wait for us.'

'She can tell 'im what she wants, but Uncle Jim takes 'is orders from your ma. He won't budge an inch until you're in the trap as well.'

All three of them looked towards the pony-trap. As Thea reached it, Jim nipped his cigarette out and put it behind his ear in order to give her a hand up. Though it was hard to tell from the distance they were at, it didn't look as if Thea said anything to him. She simply seated herself in the trap. Jim, lighting up his cigarette, once again leaned nonchalantly against it.

'There. See.' Hal clinked a couple of marbles

around in his jacket pocket. 'Now can we get goin'?'

Olivia nodded, eager to do so. She could never remember a more interesting morning. She was with two new friends – friends who, for the very first time, weren't family members. She was down by the river and unsupervised by an adult, for although Jim Crosby was keeping an eye on their safety, he couldn't be said to be supervising them. Best of all she wasn't just *pretending* to do something, as when she and Thea played at being pirates or princesses. She was really *doing* something. She was an explorer, about to see little creatures most people had probably never heard of.

Unlike Olivia, Carrie was far from happy. As all three walked quietly and carefully to the edge of the river, all she could think of was how disappointed her granny was going to be when she told her that she'd fallen out with Thea, and that Thea wouldn't want to see her any more.

Hal interrupted her thoughts by signalling for her to drop onto her tummy. She did so, pulling Olivia down with her. When they had all wriggled forward far enough to see over the thickly foliaged bank, they lay still and waited.

Seconds turned into minutes and then, just as Olivia felt she couldn't stay still a moment longer, there was movement.

Even though she had experienced the sight several times over the summer, Carrie felt her throat tighten as two bright little eyes peeped from a tangle of reeds a yard or so to their left. Beside her, Olivia gasped.

41

Carrie squeezed her hand, willing her to remain silent.

As the water vole emerged from the foliage covering the mouth of the burrow, to be followed by a troop of tiny pups, it was all too much for Olivia. 'Oh,' she whispered on a long drawn-out breath. 'Look at their pretty little faces, Carrie. Aren't they just the sweetest things you've ever seen?'

The pups scrambled and half-fell into the water and Carrie nodded, temporarily forgetting the huge disappointment she was feeling. Here, lying in the deep grass, with the hot sun on her back and the vole pups to watch, she was happy.

It was happiness that lasted until they finally rose to their feet and began heading back to the pony-trap. As they approached it, Jim, once again seated, picked up the reins. Thea didn't acknowledge any of them, not even Olivia, and as Carrie climbed into the trap her heart was heavy with the certainty that she was doing so for the last time.

Jim dropped Hal off at the bridge and then, with Olivia chattering about what a wonderful morning it had been and Thea still silent, they returned to Gorton.

When Jim reined the horse in, Carrie wondered what she ought to do. Should she just get out of the trap, as if nothing had happened between her and Thea? Should she stay in it and ask Jim if he would take her back to her granny's? Or should she get out of it, say goodbye to Olivia and begin walking home?

It was Thea, getting out of the trap first, who

solved the problem for her. 'Jim will take you home,' she said abruptly, standing on the gravel and looking up at her with an inscrutable expression in her narrow eyes. 'And then tomorrow we'll take a picnic with us when we go to see the voles. I hadn't understood about Hal, but I do now. I think he'd like a picnic. I'll ask Cook to make a seed cake.'

Chapter Three

OCTOBER 1917

Two years later Carrie wasn't only best friends with Thea and Olivia, but friends with Violet, as well. Violet, now eight, was as eager to be independent of Nanny Erskine as Thea and Olivia had been at the same age. Thea and Olivia, however, hated Violet tagging along with them, and whenever Violet escaped Nanny Erskine it was generally only Carrie who spent time with her.

On a mellow Saturday morning Carrie stepped out of Gorton Hall to find Violet sitting glumly on the magnificent flight of stone steps fronting it.

'Do you want to come down to the village with me to post the officers' mail?' she asked, coming to a halt beside her.

For more than a year Gorton Hall had served as a convalescent home for wounded officers, and Carrie – now regarded almost as family at

Gorton – had taken it upon herself to act as their postwoman.

Violet's pretty heart-shaped face brightened. 'Are you going in the pony-trap or are you bicycling?'

'Bicycling.'

'Goody!' Violet sprang to her feet.

Like Thea and Olivia she had red hair, but whereas Thea's hair was a deep chestnut and Olivia's was the colour of pale marmalade, Violet's tumble of waves and curls was a true fox-red.

'Just like Papa's hair,' Violet had once said to Carrie. 'And my eyes are the same colour as Papa's, too.'

Her eyes, a deep golden amber, were as distinctive as her hair, but Violet didn't mind being distinctive. Being distinctive was something she actively aimed for.

She said now, as they made the long walk round the side of the house to the bicycle shed, 'Papa is coming home on leave soon, did you know?'

Carrie moved the pile of envelopes she was carrying from one arm to the other. 'Yes. It's going to be a very special few days.'

A year ago, after suffering a wound on the Somme at Flers–Courcelette that had rendered his left arm near useless, Lord Fenton had been appointed to a staff job behind the lines. Until now his leaves had always been spent in London, and Blanche and the children had always joined him there at their town house in Mount Street, just off Park Lane. This time, though, Gilbert Fenton was going to be spending his short leave at Gorton. Carrie, who had only ever seen him

44

from a distance and then not since before the war, was looking forward to his arrival almost as much as his children.

Once in the bicycle shed, Carrie took the spare bicycle that had been bought with Roz in mind and put the letters into its pannier. Seconds later, with Violet close behind her, she was skimming down the long drive leading through Gorton Hall's parkland to its main gates and the lane beyond.

On the far side of the bridge the lane divided, one arm continuing south, following the line of the river, the other arm leading straight into Outhwaite.

Violet, oblivious that at eight years old she was enjoying a freedom her older sisters hadn't enjoyed until Carrie and Hal had become a part of their lives, was singing 'Tipperary' at the top of her lungs, the patriotic red, white and blue ribbons tied to her handlebars streaming in the breeze as she freewheeled down the hill into the centre of the village.

The post office served as a general meeting place and there was a small group of women outside it, most of them wearing shawls against the autumn nip in the air.

'Mornin', Carrie. Mornin', Miss Violet,' they said in unison as Carrie and Violet dismounted from their bikes. Someone else added that it was a lively morning – 'lively' being the local expression for the turn in the weather signifying that summer was well and truly over.

Inside there was a queue. Carrie, needing to buy stamps, joined it and immediately sensed an odd atmosphere. Instead of the usual buzz of friendly conversation, there was a tense silence.

The cause appeared to be a young man in the queue, to whom people were carefully not standing too close. With only a rear view of him, Carrie wasn't sure who he was, though she rather thought it was Charlie Hardwick, the son of a local cow-man.

The woman in front of Charlie – if it *was* Charlie – was being served, and Effie Mellor, the postmistress, was doing so tight-lipped, all the while shooting her next customer nervous, covert glances.

It occurred to Carrie that if the young man wasn't Charlie – Charlie had been one of the first of Outhwaite's young men to enlist – then he might be a pacifist. The women of Outhwaite were hard on pacifists. Armitage, Gorton Hall's chauffeur, rarely ran the risk of being publicly name-called by them and seldom ventured into the village. In contrast, the officers at Gorton kept what contempt they felt, if they felt it, to themselves.

The woman at Effie's counter turned away from it and was so disconcerted at having to pass the young man that she dropped her post-office book. It fell at his feet and, clearly hesitant because of her attitude towards him, he made no move to retrieve it. Because it would mean moving closer to him, neither did she.

Ever helpful, Violet darted forward, scooping the book up and handing it over. In doing so she bumped into the young man. With a sunny smile she turned to apologize.

Her smile froze. Her eyes widened in horror. Then she screamed, backing away from him so fast that she fell against the woman whose book she had retrieved.

It was as if a trigger had gone off.

'See what you've done, Charlie 'ardwick?' the woman with the post-book shrieked. 'You've scared little Miss Violet 'alf to death!'

'You should be in 'ospital!' someone else shouted. 'Somewhere you won't be able to frighten folk!'

Other voices gave the opinion that Charlie had no thought for others; that he should be wearing a balaclava.

Puzzled and alarmed, Carrie's immediate concern was for Violet and she grabbed hold of her by the hand, pulling her close.

Charlie's immediate concern was to be free of the cruel abuse. Heedless now of whatever it was that he had come into the post office for, he turned blunderingly away from the counter, desperate to escape.

Carrie sucked in her breath, her eyes widening, her jaw dropping. Charlie's face was a face no longer. Many of the officers recuperating at Gorton had facial burns and injuries. None came close to Charlie Hardwick's monstrous disfigurement. One eye was now much lower than the other, the eyelid distorted and puckered. He had no eyelashes. No eyebrows. His nose was missing and, on a face once pleasant and homely, every inch of skin was leprously white and shiny, the scarring so raised and tight that all facial expression was impossible.

47

For a fleeting instant his eyes met Carrie's, filled with an agony beyond all bearing. Then, with a low moan, he pushed past her and, as the woman who had said he should be wearing a balaclava hastily got out of his way, made a desperate dash for the door.

It banged behind him, and once again there was a clamour of voices.

'It would've been better for him if he'd bin killed.'

'He's no right walking the streets, giving folk nightmares.'

'He won't be doing so for much longer. He can't get work – and no wonder. First time I saw 'im I thought I was going to faint.'

With Violet clutching hold of her free hand tightly, Carrie bought stamps. Then, moving along the counter so that the woman behind her could be served, she stuck the stamps on the envelopes, her fingers unsteady, her legs like jelly. What she had seen had frightened her just as much as it had frightened Violet, but she didn't want Violet knowing that.

Taking her by the hand, Carrie led her outside to where a bright-red pillar-box stood. Normally posting the officer's mail was a happy occasion. Violet liked hearing the envelopes drop inside the letter-box, and Carrie enjoyed thinking of the pleasure with which the letters would be received. Today there was no joy in it for either of them. All both of them wanted was to get back to the normality of Gorton Hall.

As they straddled their bicycles Violet said in a stunned, scared voice, 'Will the monster-man

48

always be in the village, Carrie? Because if he is, I don't think I'll come with you to the post office any more. I don't want to see him again. He frightened me.'

With her foot down hard on a pedal, ready to push off, Carrie said, 'He isn't a monster-man, Violet.' Her voice was unsteady. 'He's Charlie Hardwick. He used to play in the village cricket team, and he once rescued Miss Mellor's cat when it had climbed a tree it couldn't get down from.'

She had been trying to make Violet feel better, but for some reason that she didn't understand her words only made her feel worse.

The minute they returned to Gorton, Violet fled in search of her mother.

Carrie went up to the playroom and was glad, when she got there, to find it empty. She didn't go in search of Thea and Olivia. Instead she pulled a chair up to the table that had once been used for jigsaws and was now covered by a huge map of Belgium and northern France.

The map had been Blanche Fenton's idea. Blue crayoned lines indicated the last-known British positions, red lines the German ones. To say that the lines gave only an overall general idea was an understatement, but the girls gleaned what information they could from newspaper reports and from information Lord Fenton gave Blanche whenever he had one of his all-too-rare leaves.

It wasn't often that any of the lines moved backwards or forwards more than an inch – an inch that invariably moved back to its original position immediately – but they lived in hope,

49

waiting for the day when the blue line would surge forward, heading victoriously towards Germany.

Carrie stared at the map unseeingly, unable to think of anything but the moment when Charlie Hardwick had turned around and his eyes, in a face scarcely recognizable as human, had fleetingly held hers.

She was still seated at the table when Blanche Fenton entered the playroom. Startled, Carrie scrambled to her feet, saying quickly, 'Thea and Olivia aren't here, Lady Fenton. I think they may be down on the courts, playing tennis.'

'I wasn't looking for them, Carrie.' Blanche's voice was full of concern. 'Violet has been telling me that when you went to the village there was a monster-man in the post office. She's so distressed I didn't want to question her about it, but I'd like to know who it was she had seen, and why she is describing him in such a way.'

Relief at the prospect of being able to talk with Lady Fenton about what she had seen and experienced flooded through Carrie. If anyone could make sense of it and make the world seem a happy place once again, Lady Fenton would be able to do so.

'He wasn't a real monster, though he looked like one, and that was why everyone in the queue shouted at him and was angry at him for being there.'

Blanche's concern deepened. 'Who was he, Carrie? Was he from the village?'

'It was Charlie Hardwick – though he only looked like Charlie from the back. His father is

50

the cow-man at High Top Farm.'

High Top was one of the few farms in the area not part of the Gorton estate and, though Blanche had never spoken to either Charlie or his father, she knew them by sight.

Aware of how unnerved Carrie still was, she said gently, 'What happened in the post office, Carrie?'

'Violet and I were standing behind Charlie, so we couldn't see his face. Other people in the post office had seen it, though, and because of what they began shouting out when Violet screamed, I think they had seen it before.'

Blanche's hands had been clasped lightly in her lap. Now they tightened.

Still keeping her voice carefully under control, she said, 'And what were they shouting, Carrie?'

Tears burned the backs of Carrie's eyes. 'Someone shouted at him that he'd scared Violet half to death; and someone else said he should be in a hospital, where he wouldn't be able to frighten anybody; and then someone else, the lady who had come in behind me, said that he should be wearing a balaclava.'

Blanche's knuckles shone white.

'After he had gone they said other things, too.' Carrie's voice trembled. 'They said it would have been better for him if he'd been killed, and that he had no right to be walking the streets, giving folk nightmares.'

Blanche struggled to master, her emotions. Charlie's unspeakable injuries had been suffered while fighting for his king and his country, yet women who had cheered him for enlisting had

51

shown no pity when he had paid for doing so with a ruined face and, because of it, a ruined life.

'He can't get work,' Carrie added. 'What will he do, Lady Fenton, if he can't get work?'

Blanche closed her eyes. Men who'd had a leg blown away – or, even worse, who'd had both legs blown away – sold matches on city streets, with trays of them around their necks as they stood with the aid of a crutch, or sat in small makeshift carts. How many people, though, would be compassionate enough to approach a man with his face blown away?

She opened her eyes and looked at Carrie, knowing that although she was only ten years old, Carrie would approach Charlie, and that for her the horror of the morning had been made worse by the hideousness of the remarks Charlie had met with.

When she could trust herself to speak she said, 'What happened to Charlie has happened because he fought for his country, Carrie. He is a hero and he deserves to be treated like one.'

She unclasped her hands and ran a fingertip across one of the blue lines on the map, wondering what it was that she should do; wondering what it was Gilbert would want her to do.

Her decision, when she came to it, was one she knew would not be popular. It would be hard on her children and hard, too, on her domestic staff. Even the nurses at Gorton now would probably have difficulties with it, as would perhaps some of their patients. If Charlie Hardwick was willing, it was, though, what she was going to do.

52

Her mind made up, she said, 'I'm going to pay a visit to the Hardwicks, Carrie. Would you come with me? Your presence will perhaps make Charlie feel more at ease.'

For a brief moment Carrie hesitated, wondering if she was brave enough to look at Charlie's face a second time. Then she remembered the fleeting moment when her eyes had met his. Even though one eye had not been where it should have been, his eyes had still been Charlie's eyes. If she looked only into his eyes, then she would be able to behave as she knew Lady Fenton expected her to.

'Yes,' she said, wondering what was going to happen when Lady Fenton arrived at the Hardwicks' tied cottage; wondering if Lady Fenton was truly prepared for the horror that awaited her there.

They left Gorton chauffeured by Armitage in Lady Fenton's Rolls-Royce Silver Ghost. It was the first time Carrie had ever ridden in a motor car and even though she wasn't looking forward to reaching their destination, she found the experience thrilling. They sped down the hill into Outhwaite, the breeze stinging their cheeks and tugging at the lilac gauze scarf that Blanche had tied over her hat to prevent it being blown away.

'How fast are we going, Lady Fenton?' she asked, knowing it was far faster than she had ever been able to go when riding downhill on Rozalind's bicycle.

Blanche leaned forward, touching the chauffeur lightly on his shoulder with the handle of her furled umbrella. 'Armitage?' Her voice was raised so that even against the breeze he would be able to hear her.

'Fifteen miles an hour, m'lady. Would you like me to slow down?'

'No, thank you. Carrie is enjoying the speed.'

Though Blanche couldn't see him doing so, Armitage clenched his teeth. He was having a bad morning. Carrie Thornton's near-constant presence at Gorton Hall had always mystified and offended him. Her granny might once have been Lord Fenton's nanny, but it didn't alter the fact that she was a village girl. Her riding alongside Jim Crosby in the pony-cart was one thing; her presence in the back of the Rolls-Royce that was his pride and joy was quite another.

Even worse were the directions Lady Fenton had given him. He was to take her to High Top Farm. What was a viscountess doing, paying a visit to a working farm? And what state was the Silver Ghost's highly polished aluminium bodywork going to be in, after he had driven it up a farm track? Lady Fenton had always had her eccentricities – treating Carrie Thornton as if she was quality being a major example – but as far as he was concerned, this latest eccentricity beggared belief.

High Top Farm lay on the edge of moorland, and the autumn heather was in full bloom. A sea of vivid purple, it stretched into the distance as far as the eye could see, filling the air with honey-sweet scent. Carrie drank in the sight of it. Despite her anxiety about the meeting that was shortly going to take place between Lady Fenton and Charlie, she couldn't help being happy. She

54

had always been told that Wensleydale was the most beautiful of all Yorkshire's dales and, as Armitage drew up outside the farmhouse and she looked around her, she knew, beyond a shadow of a doubt, that what was said was true.

At the sound of the car drawing up a middle-aged woman ran out of the farmhouse, her hands and arms covered in flour, her face a picture of incredulity.

'I'm sorry to disturb you,' Blanche said. 'I'm looking for Charlie Hardwick. I believe his father is your cow-man. If you could tell me where-abouts the Hardwicks live I'd be very grateful.'

The woman gaped at her. Carrie didn't blame her for being speechless. It wasn't every day that a farmer's wife opened her door to find in her farmyard a silver motor car and, seated in the back of it, a member of the aristocracy.

'The 'ardwicks, Your Ladyship?' she managed at last. 'They live over yonder.' With a beefy arm she pointed across a couple of fields to where a chimneystack peeped above a fringe of trees. 'But Your Ladyship won't be able to speak wi' Charlie. Charlie doesn't speak wi' anyone these days.'

'Thank you for telling me where I can find him, Mrs...?'

'Lumsden. Florence Lumsden.'

'Thank you, Mrs Lumsden.' Blanche turned to Armitage. 'As near to the cottage as you can get, Armitage.'

The cottage, when Armitage reluctantly reached it via a narrow, overgrown lane, was appallingly decrepit. Mrs Hardwick rushed from its dark interior to find out who on earth was coming to pay a call on her and then, on seeing who it was, fell against its door jamb in shock, causing a tile to fall from the roof.

Both Mrs Hardwick and Blanche ignored it.

'Good afternoon, Mrs Hardwick,' Blanche said, sending hens scattering as she walked across to her. 'I understand your son has returned from Flanders badly injured. I would like to have a few words with him, if I may?'

'Wi' our Charlie?' Mrs Hardwick stared at Blanche as if she had taken leave of her senses, something that Armitage, standing yards away beside the Silver Ghost, was convinced of. 'You can't see Charlie, m'lady. He isn't fit to be seen. Not by anyone.' She plucked agitatedly at the edge of an apron, which was as long as the shabby dress skimming her clogs.

'I know about Charlie's injuries, Mrs Hardwick.' Blanche's low, sweet voice was as reassuring as she could make it. 'They are why I am here.'

Mrs Hardwick's bewilderment was now total.

Aware of this, and also aware that Mrs Hardwick was far too overwhelmed by her title to think of inviting her into her home, Blanche went on, 'I want to help Charlie, Mrs Hardwick. Perhaps it would be best if we continued talking inside?'

Without waiting for Mrs Hardwick to agree, Blanche stepped past her, with Carrie still at her side.

The low-ceilinged stone-floored room they entered was dominated by a blackleaded kitchen range almost the height of the room. Though it was autumn it was a mild day and there was no

56

fire in the grate, or kettle on the long hook hanging above it. In one corner of the room was a cast-iron copper for heating water, in another was a well-scoured stone sink and in the centre of the room stood a heavy wooden table and two upright chairs.

Blanche seated herself on one of the chairs and Mrs Hardwick, with nervous glances towards a half-open door leading to a narrow curving staircase, seated herself on the other one. Carrie, mindful of her manners, remained near the door they had entered by.

'I understand Charlie is finding it difficult to earn a living, Mrs Hardwick,' Blanche said, her voice as friendly as if they had known each other for a long time, 'and I would like to give him employment at Gorton.'

Mrs Hardwick gasped.

Carrie heard a similar sound come from beyond the half-open staircase door.

Unsteadily Mrs Hardwick said, 'I think maybe you don't understand quite 'ow bad my Charlie is, m'lady. He frightens folks, you see.'

'Gorton Hall is a convalescent home for wounded officers, Mrs Hardwick. Charlie won't frighten them. Every one of them will know that what happened to him could easily have happened to them too, and other people at Gorton will take their example from me. What kind of work did Charlie do before he enlisted?'

As Mrs Hardwick hesitated before replying, a shadow fell across the last three steps of the staircase.

Seeing it, Carrie wondered if Blanche was

aware that someone was standing just out of sight on the stairs – and had now moved down them a tread or two in order not to miss anything being said.

Mrs Hardwick plucked again at her apron. 'Charlie was an agricultural worker, m'lady. Sometimes he worked for Mr Lumsden, sometimes he worked for Mr Benson at Sproggett Farm, and sometimes he worked for a vicar over at Nosborough.'

'A vicar?' Blanche's sleek, dark eyebrows rose. 'But why on earth did Nosborough's vicar require an agricultural labourer?'

Mrs Hardwick cast another nervous look towards the half-open door leading to the stairs. 'The vicar 'eard as 'ow Charlie was good wi' flowers – laying 'em out prettily like.' Almost apologetically she added, 'It's summat Charlie enjoys doing, m'lady.'

'And will the vicar want Charlie to continue gardening for him?'

Carrie, who had been shocked rigid by the revelation that Blanche intended offering Charlie employment at Gorton Hall, bit her lip, fervently hoping that Mrs Hardwick was going to say yes and that Blanche's offer – an offer that would surely terrify Violet out of her wits – wouldn't need to be taken up.

'No, m'lady. Not now everything's planted and blooming...'

From the staircase a voice raw with bitterness cut across hers. 'That's not the reason, Ma, and well you know it.' Still hidden from view, Charlie said, 'It was the vicar's wife who put paid to me

58

working on t' garden – and I could 'ave worked, for it's my face that's been burned away, not my 'ands. He said she was very sorry for me, but that I gave 'er a funny turn and that 'e couldn't 'ave 'er being taken ill on account o' me.'

Blanche rose to her feet and, facing the stairs but making no move towards them, said, 'I have Carrie Thornton with me, Charlie. She was in the post office this morning and told me what happened there. From what she said, I gather you haven't yet found work. If that is the case, I would greatly appreciate it if you would consider becoming an estate worker at Gorton Hall. The gardens and parkland have been virtually untended since Gorton's gardeners enlisted with the 7th Yorkshire Regiment. Mr Crosby – Jim Crosby – does his best, but he's also doing stable work and odd jobs, and a house as big as Gorton is never short of work needing doing to it.'

For a tense moment there was still no response and then Charlie said in an odd, abrupt voice, 'I'm very appreciative of your kindness, Lady Fenton, but you 'aven't seen me yet and might think twice when you do. I already scared Miss Violet 'alf to death this morning. I don't want to do so again.'

'Violet was scared because what has happened to you hadn't been explained to her, and because the sight of you was so unexpected. That won't be the case in the future, as it won't be the case with my other two daughters and with everyone else at Gorton, both household staff and nursing staff.'

There was another silence and then came the

59

moment Carrie had been dreading; the moment when Charlie walked down the last of the stair steps and entered the room.

Despite her fierce determination to show no outward sign of horror, Blanche sucked in her breath, shaken to the depths of her being, as everything she had imagined paled in comparison to the reality.

Charlie stood perfectly still, his eyes holding hers.

Carrie could hardly bear the tension as she watched and waited – and then Blanche dug kid-gloved fingers deep into her palms, saying in a voice that was only slightly unsteady, 'I'm very pleased to meet you, Charlie. I do hope you will become one of Gorton Hall's estate workers. A tied cottage goes with the position and, if you are agreeable, I will tell both Mr Heaton and Jim Crosby that you will be arriving tomorrow morning to take over the care of the Hall's gardens.'

'Thank you, m'lady.' There were tears in Charlie's eyes. 'I vow you'll never regret the asking – and if it's beautiful gardens Your Ladyship wants, I'll make gardens so beautiful they'll be the talk o' the county!'

Chapter Four

NOVEMBER 1918

On a misty day a little over a year after Blanche and Carrie's visit to the Hardwicks, Blanche burst into Thea and Olivia's schoolroom with news she had been praying for every day for four long years.

'The war is over!' Her face was radiant with joy. 'The Germans have signed an armistice!'

Hermione Cumberbatch had been writing on the blackboard. Tall, thin and angular, she dropped the chalk, clapped a hand over her mouth and then, when she could trust herself to speak, put her hands on either side of her pedestal desk, saying emotionally, 'Dear Thea and Olivia – remember this moment, for you are living through history. The most terrible war ever known is at an end. Years of unimaginable struggle, bloodshed and sacrifice are over. There will be no more grieving war widows and war-orphaned children. Today...' her voice surged with pride, 'today, we are a Christian nation seeing the dawning of a brave new world!'

She turned to Blanche and, in an action so unexpected both Thea and Olivia were never to forget it, the two women hugged each other tightly, tears of relief and joy streaming down their cheeks.

Aware that such momentous news could, with luck, mean no further lessons for the rest of the day, Thea pushed her chair away from her desk. 'Do the officers and the nursing staff know the war is over, Mama? If they don't, can I go and tell them?'

Laughing through her tears, Blanche broke away from Miss Cumberbatch's embrace. 'They already know, darling. Listen!'

By now the sound of jubilation was spreading through the house like wildfire.

'Then can I go and tell Hal, Mama?' Thea's voice was urgent. 'I do so want to be the first to tell someone.'

'And me, too, Mama.' Olivia was also now on her feet. 'I want to tell Carrie. And what about Mr Crosby and Charlie? Will they know yet? Can I tell them?'

Another sound merged with that of a score of convalescing men roaring out 'Rule, Britannia!' at the top of their lungs. Blanche ran across to the window and flung it open, letting in the distant sound of Outhwaite's church bells as they rang out peal after glorious peal.

'I think everyone knows by now, darlings,' she said, still laughing, so happy she thought she was going to burst with it. 'But as it is such an extra-ordinary, historic, wonderful moment, I'm sure Miss Cumberbatch will let you off lessons for the rest of the day.'

Miss Cumberbatch, who as a staunch Methodist was eager to hurry to the little Methodist chapel in Outhwaite's High Street in order to give thanks to her Maker for her country's deliverance from evil, gave an affirming nod of her head.

Gleefully Thea and Olivia scampered from the room. 'I'm going to find Hal,' Thea said as they raced upstairs to their bedroom for hats and coats. 'You go and tell Jim and Charlie.'

'But they'll already know! How could they not know? The singing and cheering the officers are making can probably be heard as far away as Richmond!'

'Doesn't matter.' Still running, they skirted around two housemaids who, with piles of clean linen in their arms, were dancing a jig and singing the national anthem. 'It's the being the first to share in the news with them that matters now.'

Once in the bedroom, Olivia hurled herself into a coat and crammed a beret on her head. It was a Monday, so Thea would be heading to the village school in order to find Hal – and if she found Hal in the school playground, it meant that, of the two of them, she would not only be the first to share the news with Hal, but she would also be the first to share the news with Carrie.

Without waiting for Thea, who was still hooking up the buttons on her winter boots, Olivia ran from the room. It was too bad that she wouldn't see Carrie before Thea did, but she would have the kudos of being the first of the two of them where Jim and Charlie were concerned.

The entire west wing of Gorton had been converted into wards and sitting rooms for convalescing soldiers, and as Olivia shot past the double doors of the main sitting room she could hear, above the singing and cheering, the sound of champagne corks popping. It was a sound that hadn't been heard at Gorton since before the start of the war, and that it should be heard now would, she knew, have been her mother's idea.

Once outside the house the sound of Outhwaite's church bells was clearer than ever. Olivia paused, breathless from running, wondering who she should seek out first. She knew where Charlie would be, because for the last month or so he had been busy building a walk-through rockery of large boulders and tree-ferns where the ground shelved down on the far side of the east wing's grand lawn. It was a project Jim sometimes helped him with, and she decided to head for the rockery-in-the-making in the hope that she would find not only Charlie there, but Jim as well.

Taking a deep breath and beginning to run once again, she headed for the east wing's grand lawn, reflecting on how odd it was that Charlie and Jim had become such good friends. Because Charlie had enlisted at the first opportunity and suffered such a horrendous legacy for having done so, and because Jim hadn't seen a day of fighting, everyone – even her mother – had expected that even if Jim was able to come to terms with Charlie's nightmarish disfigurement, Charlie would want nothing to do with him.

Olivia hadn't been there when her mother had taken it upon herself to make the potentially difficult introduction, but much later, when she had finally been able to be in Charlie's presence without shuddering and wanting to run away from him, he had told her how Jim had made things easy between the two of them right from the beginning.

'The instant folks see me, they can't hide their feelings, no matter how hard they try. And truth to tell, I don't know which of their feelings is the worst: horror, fear or pity.'

He had been taking a break from scything grass that hadn't been tended since the last of the gardeners had left for the front.

With his hands around a mug of steaming tea he'd said, 'There was shock on Jim's face, but nowt else. Then Jim said, "Holy hell, mate! But you well and truly copped it!" and he shook my hand and said he'd show me around so that I could get my bearings. It was the way he said "mate" that made things grand between us, right from the off. Jim might have a bit of a roving eye for the ladies, but he's a champion bloke and, if he could have enlisted, he would have.'

By the time she was only halfway across the great east lawn Olivia was too out of puff to continue running. She staggered to a halt, taking in great gulps of air. There was a smell of damp leaves and wood smoke, and the grass beneath her feet was rimed with the remainder of the previous night's frost. She set off again at a fast walk, beginning to hope that although Charlie would have realized the ringing of church bells meant good news, he might still be unaware it meant the war was finally over and that, if he was, she would be the one to break the news to him.

Ground at the far end of the lawn, where the rockery was being built, shelved down to a stream that eventually ran into Outhwaite's river. She found Charlie and Jim at the bottom of the dip and, though it was obvious they had been working, their shovels and pickaxes had been cast aside and Jim was sitting on one of the giant boulders while Charlie leaned against an adjacent one. Both of them had cigarettes between their fingers.

'It's over!' she shouted, holding onto her beret and slipping and sliding down the slope towards them. 'The war is over!'

Charlie nipped his cigarette out. 'We reckoned it was when the bells began ringing.' He smiled at her. 'It's kind of you to come and tell us, though.'

'I wanted to be the first to break the news to you.' She came to a breathless halt in front of them, confused by his lack of emotion. 'Why aren't you singing and cheering? Everyone at Gorton is.'

'Aye, well, they'll probably calm down a bit when they think on what's been achieved and at what cost.'

The expression in the one eye that was now visible – the other eye had long been covered by the black eye-patch from the dressing-up box – was bleak.

Seeing her confusion, Jim tossed the butt of his cigarette into the stream. 'It might be victory, but what's the prize? Millions dead, and God alone knows how many more millions wounded and maimed. And for what? You tell me, Olivia lass, because I'm jiggered if I know. Officers may be singing and cheering this morning, but it won't be long before they'll be remembering today as a

66

day of mourning – and you can't be jubilant when you're mourning.'

That wasn't how people were thinking of things yet in the centre of Outhwaite. It seemed that everyone was out in the streets sharing in the relief that at last the agony was over.

'No more knitting khaki socks!' one woman shouted elatedly as Thea bicycled past her. 'And no more black-edged telegrams!'

As the bells of Outhwaite's Anglican church continued to peal, another, far different bell could be heard. It was the school bell. The congestion in the main street grew worse as children, let off lessons for the rest of the day, began racing exuberantly down it.

Unable to make any further headway on the bike, Thea dismounted and began pushing it. Hal saw her before she saw him.

'We're over 'ere!' he shouted from the crowded pavement.

Carrie was with him and, as Thea began eagerly making her way towards them, Hal shouted, 'We've news I bet you 'aven't 'eard yet! The Kaiser 'as abdicated! Me and Carrie are off to buy a bag of sherbert lemons to celebrate. Are you coming wi' us?'

With Thea and Olivia both on their way – if they were fast enough – to spread the news that the war was over, and with Hermione Cumberbatch having declared her intention of walking into Outhwaite to join her friends at the Methodist chapel, and with Heaton in full control of organizing the bringing up of crates of champagne from the cellars so that officers and nursing staff could celebrate suitably, Blanche was able to turn her thoughts to the person who mattered most to her in the whole wide world. Gilbert.

She closed her eyes, thanking God that he had survived the war – and that he had survived it with distinction. In the autumn of 1916 he had led his men through the German front-line system of trenches, during which he had suffered the wound to his arm that had left it virtually useless. Despite being so severely wounded, he had remained in command and had gone on to mount a successful assault on the second objective, a strongly fortified village. Though wounded twice more, he had held the village throughout the day and the following night, and only when reinforcements had arrived had he finally left the line, even then having refused to do so before issuing final instructions.

For his gallantry he had been awarded the Distinguished Service Order. His citation for the award, published in the *London Gazette* a couple of months later, described the events and concluded with: *The personality, valour and utter contempt for danger on the part of this Officer enabled the lodgement of the most advanced objective of the Corps to be permanently held, and on this rallying point the line was eventually formed.*

Blanche had snipped the piece out of the paper and had pasted it to the back of the photograph of Gilbert that stood on her writing desk in the private sitting room adjoining her bedroom.

Looking at the photograph now, she thought of

the future. It was more than four years since they had all lived together as a family. Thea had been eight, Olivia seven and Violet four when the assassination of Archduke Franz Ferdinand in Sarajevo had plunged the world into the most terrible war ever known.

Since then Gilbert had only spent a handful of short, snatched days with their daughters and those days had been nearly always in London, for whenever he had leave he hectically caught up with as many of his friends in government as he possibly could. It meant he had no real knowledge of the huge changes that the Great War had wrought at Gorton Hall. Thea was now twelve, Olivia was eleven and Violet was nine. When they had last all been together at Gorton, Thea and Olivia had never left the gardens and parkland unless in the company of Hermione Cumberbatch, Nanny Erskine or herself. Now, outside the schoolroom and in the company of Hal and Carrie, they ran as wild and free as if they, too, were village children.

It hadn't seemed to do them any harm, and she doubted if Gilbert would object too strongly to the unusual amount of freedom their children now enjoyed. He had also not objected to her having employed Charlie Hardwick.

Tenderly she ran the tip of her finger over the silver frame of Gilbert's photograph. When he came home there would be much more to think about than the sometimes tricky management of her household staff. Though Gilbert loved Gorton with a deep passion, he had another passion too, and that passion was politics. He had written to her a week after arriving in Flanders:

When this ghastly murderous debacle is over, I intend becoming more active in the House of Lords. Where politics is concerned, Raymond is of the same mind and intends standing for Parliament. Only politics can ensure there will never again be a hell on Earth such as the one we are now enduring.

By Raymond, he had meant Raymond Asquith, whose father, at the time, had been the prime minister. Now David Lloyd George was prime minister, and Raymond, loved by everyone who knew him, had died in battle two years ago, at Ginchy, on the Somme.

A husband with a political life would mean far more time spent in London. It would also mean resuming the high-society social life they had enjoyed before the war. Blanche's heart beat a little faster as she thought of the dinner parties and supper parties – of all kinds of parties – of the theatre and opera. Before the war, balls were commonplace in all the great London houses. It was at one such ball, at Londonderry House, that she and Gilbert had first met.

Unlike the millions of women who had been widowed, she had a future to look forward to, with a husband she loved with all her heart. Thanking God for her many blessings, she seated herself at her desk, drew a sheet of pale-blue notepaper towards her and picked up her pen. Her eyes brimming with tears of thankfulness, she wrote:

My dearest darling,

We heard news of the Armistice an hour or so ago and I am mad with relief and joy. Outhwaite's church bells are ringing non-stop. The convalescing officers are toasting the news with champagne and their singing and, cheering are about to lift the roof off.

Thea is on her way to share the moment with Hal, and no doubt with Carrie as well. Olivia has hared off to give Jim Crosby and Charlie Hardwick the news. Violet was out for her morning walk with Nanny Erskine when the news came over the wireless. Wherever they are, they will have heard the church bells and so Violet, too, will know by now that her papa will be coming home soon – and coming home for good.

Those words are such magic to write, my darling. I can hardly believe that soon you will be in my arms again and there will be no more agonizing partings. For the rest of our lives, until we are both old and grey, we are going to be so happy, Gil. As I think of the future that is waiting for us my heart is full of the very deepest joy.

All my love, now and forever, your very own devoted Blanche

Chapter Five

APRIL 1919

As Hal walked across the yard to where his father's pigs were penned he could faintly hear the village school bell being rung. It was something he no longer needed to pay any heed to, for it was April and, ever since his thirteenth birthday in February, his schooldays had been behind him.

He had a heavy bucket of pig swill in either hand and put them down on the ground in order to open the gate of the pen. Though learning had always come easily to him, he hadn't been sorry to say goodbye to the long bench seats of the classroom and the slates and chalk – and it wasn't as if he'd stopped learning, for thanks to Miss Calvert he was now learning in earnest.

Every weekday evening, after he'd brought the cows in for their milking, he ran over the fields to Outhwaite for one-to-one lessons with Miss Calvert in her pin-neat little terraced home. She'd wanted him to sit for a grammar-school scholarship, but his dad hadn't been having any of it. 'He's needed on t' farm,' he'd said bluntly to her when, to Hal's embarrassment, she had come to their farmhouse to speak with him about the scholarship exam. 'Even if 'e weren't, no lad o' mine is going to a grammar school to 'ave fancy ideas put in 'is 'ead. Folks like us don't do things like that, and the sooner 'e realizes it, the 'appier we'll all be.'

Nothing Miss Calvert could say would change his dad's mind – and as Hal had known it wouldn't, he was neither surprised nor disappointed. Instead he was determined. Outhwaite might satisfy Carrie, who wanted nothing more than to be in service at Gorton Hall and to live the rest of her life in the Yorkshire Dales, but ever since he could remember he had known that a life in Outhwaite – or even in Yorkshire – was never going to be enough to satisfy him.

At the sight of the buckets, the pigs had begun stampeding towards him and he snatched the buckets off the ground, kicked the gate of the pen closed and barrelled a way between them to the trough.

'There, you greedy blighters,' he said, pouring the contents of the buckets into it. 'Get your mucky snouts into that.'

The pigs did so with gusto as Hal watched them. Miss Calvert was a good teacher, and he was a hard worker. Not being allowed to go to a grammar school wasn't going to hold him back. In another few years he wouldn't be milking cows and feeding pigs. Exactly what he would be doing he didn't know, but whatever it was would involve being a socialist and fighting to make the world a different place, one where the divisions of class ceased to exist.

It wasn't Miss Calvert who had taught him that only via politics could the world be changed. It had been Miss Cumberbatch.

For a long time after he had become friends with

Thea and Olivia he had known nothing about Miss Cumberbatch, other than that she was Thea and Olivia's governess. On the rare occasions he caught sight of her it was always when she had come into the village to do a little shopping, or to attend church.

He'd thought her an odd-looking woman, tall and thin and raw-boned, her mousy-coloured hair worn in a severe bun. Her nose, as thin as the rest of her face, was abnormally long and Olivia had told him it twitched whenever she became impassioned about the subject she was teaching – something that Olivia said happened often.

'She looks like a witch,' he'd said, and Olivia had giggled and said, 'She does a little bit and she can be awfully strict, but she's very fair. I like her, and so does Thea.'

It was only when Charlie Hardwick had begun working at Gorton and living on the estate that Hal had begun taking real notice of Miss Cumberbatch. He knew, via Thea and Olivia, that the reactions at Gorton to Lady Fenton's invitation to Charlie had been extreme.

Miss Cumberbatch's reaction hadn't been extreme, though. She had gone out of her way to run into him and to introduce herself to him. 'According to Charlie, she didn't even flinch when she first saw him. She simply told him she was pleased to meet him and that she hoped he would be as happy working at Gorton Hall as she was,' Olivia had said.

Hal had been impressed at Miss Cumberbatch's strength.

The pigs had finished jostling each other to get

at the food and, with the trough now empty, were barging at him, trying to get their heads into the buckets on the off-chance there was still something left in them.

He kneed them away, lifting the buckets out of their reach. Not only had Miss Cumberbatch made friends with Charlie herself, but by helping Thea and Olivia to overcome their revulsion at the way Charlie looked, she had paved the way for them to become friends with him as well. And his own Uncle Jim had also made a difference.

'You like me well enough, don't you, Hal?' he'd said, one arm thrown affectionately around Hal's shoulder. 'And you like being wi' me, don't you?'

It had been such a silly question that Hal hadn't even bothered replying to it.

Understanding the reason why he hadn't, Jim had said, 'If I'd 'ad two legs the same length and gone to Flanders, like Charlie did, and if what 'appened to Charlie 'ad 'appened to me, you wouldn't 'ave stopped wanting to spend time wi' me, would you? You wouldn't 'ave let me be all lonesome, would you?'

'Course I wouldn't,' he'd said stoutly.

'And why is that?' Jim had asked.

Hal had been flummoxed at first, and then he'd said, 'Because, though you'd look like a monster, you wouldn't be, would you? You'd still be Uncle Jim.'

Jim had hugged his shoulder. 'That's right, lad. And behind Charlie's monster-face, Charlie is still Charlie. I'm helping him wi' his gardening late this afternoon. Why don't you come and help the two of us out?'

He had, and it was via Charlie that he'd got to know Miss Cumberbatch – and Miss Cumberbatch had turned out to be a long-distance member of the Women's International League, and political to her fingertips.

He shut the pen's gate behind him, aware that he'd been dawdling and that when he joined his father, who was waiting in the fallow field for help with the ploughing, he'd be given a clout around the ear.

Carrie was also well on the way to being in trouble that morning, for she should have been on her way to school and instead she was on the doorstep of her granny's cottage, staring aghast at Thea, who had bicycled from Gorton to give her some news that wouldn't wait.

'You and Olivia aren't going to be taught by Miss Cumberbatch any more?' Carrie repeated dazedly. 'You're going away to school?'

'To St Ethelburga's near Norwich. It's so far from both Yorkshire and London it might as well be in France.'

Thea looked decidedly fed up, because although she'd been impatient to go to a proper school and be taught with other girls her age and not just with Olivia, she'd imagined it would be somewhere not too far from either Gorton Hall or Mount Street.

'What about Miss Cumberbatch?' Carrie's head was spinning. 'What is going to happen to her?'

Thea stopped looking fed up and grinned. 'Something absolutely dreadful. She's going to

76

join the household at Mount Street as Violet's governess.'

Carrie knew Thea was trying to make her laugh, but she couldn't do so. By now the school bell had stopped ringing and she knew she was going to be horrendously late for class. She didn't care. 'And your mother – as well as your father – is going to be living mainly in London?'

Thea, still straddling her bicycle, nodded. 'Mama loves Gorton, and she and Papa will be back every opportunity they have. Papa has hopes of becoming a junior minister, and if he becomes one there will be lots of weekend entertaining at Gorton. Other than that, and apart from the servants, no one else will be there. Not Mama and Papa, not me, not Olivia, and not Violet or Miss Cumberbatch.'

Carrie was carrying her school books in the crook of her arm and hitched them a little higher. 'I'll be there,' she said firmly. 'I'll be there, because I was twelve two weeks ago – and I'm now old enough to be a tweeny.'

Thea stared at her, trying to imagine what it would be like returning to a Gorton where Carrie was one of the servants. It would be extremely odd. How would they be able to spend time together as friends?

She said doubtfully, 'I'm not sure it would work, you being a tweeny when you've been coming in and out of the house as a friend for four years. I think it might be best for you to speak with Mama – but if you're going to do so, you'll have to be quick, as Armitage is driving Mama, Violet and Miss Cumberbatch to London the day after tomorrow. I'm going to be parcelled off with Olivia to St Ethelburga's the same day, and so if we're all going to be able to say a proper goodbye to each other it's going to have to be today or tomorrow. I vote we do it at the vole place tomorrow afternoon, when you come out of school.'

She hitched herself back onto the seat of her bicycle, a foot down hard on one pedal, her chestnut hair tumbling waist-length. 'I'm off to the farm now to tell Hal. D'you think St Ethelburga's will be like the boarding schools in Angela Brazil's books? All midnight feasts and jolly japes?'

Without waiting for an answer and no longer looking fed up, her cat-green eyes alight with anticipation at all the fun hopefully lying in store, she pushed off, heading in the direction of the lane that led to the Crosby farm.

Carrie watched her go, her emotions in tumult. Because her friendship with Thea and Olivia crossed a class divide they couldn't ever hope to overcome, her former friends at school had distanced themselves from her. Though Carrie had never wanted to be seen as being different from everyone else in Outhwaite, that was how she was now regarded. She would still have Hal as a friend, of course, but nowadays Hal had barely a minute of free time, for after a hard day's work on the farm he headed straight for Miss Calvert's house and a long evening of private tuition.

She bit the corner of her lip, knowing she was going to miss Thea and Olivia far more than they

78

were going to miss her. At St Ethelburga's they would have the novelty of a new experience and new friends.

She drew in a deep steadying breath. If she left school and began working as a tweeny at Gorton, she too would have the novelty of a new experience and she'd be able to make friends with the other maids, something she'd not been able to do until now. And Thea was right. It was something she needed to speak to Lady Fenton about immediately, for once Blanche left Gorton for Mount Street there was no telling how long it would be before she returned.

She stepped out into the street, closing the door behind her and then, uncaring of the explanation she was going to have to give later to Miss Calvert and her granny, she didn't run down the street towards the school. Instead she headed out of the village, towards the road leading to Gorton Hall.

Blanche was in Thea and Olivia's bedroom supervising the packing of two enormous tin trunks bearing St Ethelburga's address when the butler, Heaton, informed her that Carrie was at Gorton Hall and wished to speak with her.

As it was a school day and as Carrie should have been in school, Blanche was bewildered. It occurred to her, though, that Ivy Thornton might have been taken ill. 'Tell her I'll speak with her here,' she said to him and then, to the maid who was stowing a pile of navy serge tunics into the trunk marked with Olivia's name, she said, 'That's all for the moment, Helen. I'll ring for you when I've finished speaking with Carrie.'

'Yes, m'lady.' Helen almost ran in her eagerness to be back below stairs, where she could tell everyone that Carrie Thornton was having a private chat with her ladyship.

'Is anything wrong, Carrie?' Blanche said the instant Carrie entered the room. 'Is everything all right at home? Your granny isn't ill, is she?'

'Oh no, Lady Fenton.' Carrie was appalled at the thought of having caused Blanche even the slightest twinge of anxiety. 'Thea bicycled to Outhwaite this morning to tell me that she and Olivia are going away to school the day after tomorrow and that you are leaving Gorton Hall as well this week – and there's something very important I wanted to ask you before you left.'

Blanche regarded Carrie with affection. Her welcome of Carrie into the house four years ago as a playmate for Thea and Olivia had been an overwhelming success. Before her arrival Thea and Olivia had often squabbled, and picked on Violet. Since her arrival they did so far less, for Carrie was a natural-born peacemaker.

Blanche had been standing at the open door of Thea's wardrobe selecting dresses, as well as school clothes that had to be packed. Now, despite having very little time in which to finish organizing her daughters' departure for Norfolk, she sat down.

'What is it you wanted to ask me, Carrie?' she said, happy to spare a little time for this child she liked so much.

'I was twelve at the beginning of the month, Lady Fenton,' Carrie said sunnily, 'And I'd like to know, please, if I can begin working at Gorton Hall as a tweeny?'

Blanche stared at her, not knowing which aspect of Carrie's request appalled her the most; that she was cherishing an ambition to become a tweeny – and at Gorton – or that she thought she could leave school and become one now that she was twelve years old.

'I had no idea you had ambitions to go into service, Carrie.' Even as she said the words she was shocked at how naive she had been where Carrie was concerned. What had she thought Carrie was going to do on leaving school? When Thea and Olivia left St Ethelburga's they would most probably, like other girls of their class, go to a finishing school in Europe. Then, when they were eighteen, they would be presented to Their Majesties at court and, as debutantes, enjoy a London Season where, at countless parties, balls and high-society events, they would meet eligible young men of good family. After that, as night follows day, there would be engagements and high-society weddings at St Margaret's, Westminster.

It wouldn't be like that for Carrie.

When Carrie left school she would have to find work and, unless she wanted to leave Outhwaite, her choice was limited to either farm work or domestic service. And domestic service, for Outhwaite girls, meant Gorton Hall.

Oblivious that there could be a problem with her request, Carrie said confidingly, 'I've wanted to go into service for as long as I can remember, Lady Fenton. And as I love Gorton Hall so much

I wouldn't want to do so anywhere else. Besides, if I was in service anywhere else, I wouldn't be near to Granny – and I wouldn't like that, and neither would she.'

Blanche took a deep steadying breath. 'You can't become a tweeny yet, Carrie. Not anywhere. A law was passed several months ago that has raised the school leaving age to fourteen.'

Carrie looked stricken.

Blanche, knowing that she was now going to have to deal her an even worse blow, leaned towards her, taking Carrie's hands in hers. 'What I am going to say now, Carrie, is going to seem very unfair, but I want you to try and understand and not be too unhappy about it.'

She paused, searching for the right words. Not finding them, she said gently, 'Because you have been an almost daily guest at Gorton for so long now, it isn't going to be possible for you ever to work here as a servant. The rest of the staff would feel far too uncomfortable about it – and it would drastically alter your relationship with Thea and Olivia. What I would like to do is to speak to a friend of mine, Lady Markham. She has a country home at Richmond and I am certain that when you are fourteen, and if you still want to go into service, she would be delighted to employ you as a tweeny. Richmond is a not-too-far bus ride away. You will be able to see your granny quite easily whenever you have time off. Lady Markham has a reputation for being fair and generous with her household staff, and I think you would be happy at Monkswood.'

Carrie stared at her, struggling desperately for

understanding. How could she be a tweeny at a strange place called Monkswood, when all she had ever wanted was to be a tweeny at Gorton Hall? And why should the other staff at Gorton feel uncomfortable with her, when she had always exchanged cheery hellos and goodbyes with them? Another, even more terrible thought struck her.

With a face the colour of parchment she said tremulously, 'If I become a tweeny at Monkswood, will I have to stop coming to Gorton Hall?'

The question – and Carrie's distress – smote Blanche's heart. 'No,' she said firmly, closing her mind to the social difficulties that were quite obviously going to arise in the future. 'Absolutely not. Whenever we are at Gorton you will always be welcome here.' She squeezed Carrie's hands reassuringly. 'What you have to concentrate on now is your schoolwork. Will you promise me you will do that?'

Still so disappointed that she didn't quite know how she was going to bear it, Carrie nodded. With Thea and Olivia in Norfolk, Violet in London and Hal either working in Richmond or having lessons with Miss Calvert, there was going to be a lot of lonely time to fill and she knew now how she was going to fill it. She was going to make sure that she wasn't only sometimes at the top of her class, but always at the top of it.

From now until she left school at fourteen she was going to make Lady Fenton proud of her.

Later in the day, when Gilbert made his daily evening telephone call to her, Blanche said, 'Carrie came to see me this morning, and I do so wish she hadn't.'

'A strange sentiment coming from you, darling. I thought you found Carrie a delight.'

'I do. It was the reason she wanted to see me that wasn't delightful. She was twelve at the beginning of the month and thought she was old enough to become a tweeny – and that she could do so here, at Gorton. I had to explain to her why that would be impossible. It's such a modest ambition, Gil, and I did so hate disappointing her.'

'How did she take the news?' There was concern in his voice, for he was as fond of Carrie as she was.

'She looked bewildered – then devastated. I suggested that if she still wants to go into service when she is fourteen, Monkswood would be a good idea. I'm sure that if I had a word with Lydia there would be no problem, and Richmond is near enough to Outhwaite for Carrie not to feel isolated.'

'True. I'm glad you thought of it. I wouldn't like Carrie working hundreds of miles away and unable to keep in contact with Thea and Olivia when she has time off.' He paused and then said, a different note in his voice, 'I have some news, Blanche. It involves Charlie. I want you to ask him if he'll be willing to come with you to London – and, if he is, I want you to tell him to bring enough clothes for a long stay.'

'You want me to bring Charlie to Mount Street?' Blanche's incredulity was total. 'But he'll hate it at Mount Street, Gil! It will mean lots of people he's never met before, staring at him and talking about him. And what will he do? There will be no outdoor work for him.'

Gilbert Fenton chuckled. 'If he's agreeable, he isn't going to be at Mount Street. He's going to be at Queen Mary's Hospital at Sidcup, which is close to London, in Kent. A pioneering surgeon by the name of Harold Gillies has set up a unit there expressly for treating soldiers and sailors whose faces have been destroyed by explosives and shrapnel. Gillies is achieving miracles, Blanche. When I described Charlie's injuries to him, he said he thought he would be able to create a new nose for him and he showed me before-and-after photographs of a badly injured sailor for whom he's done just that. Can you imagine what it will be like for Charlie, if Gillies can do the same thing for him? It will transform his life.'

'It will be ... a miracle.' Blanche could hardly speak, her throat was so tight with emotion.

'And before I forget, Rozalind and her mother are sailing on the *Mauretania* in the first week of June and will be with us until the end of August, and the general consensus of opinion is that I'm going to be made a junior minister. So all in all, life looks good – and the very, very best thing about it, my dearest darling wife, is that you are soon going to be here with me in London.'

Chapter Six

In late August, wearing well-worn country tweeds and with two cocker spaniels at his side, Gilbert Fenton walked down off the moor towards Gorton Hall a happy man. The sun was hot, the air heavy with the fragrance of heather and the sound of bees. It was only the second time he'd been back to Gorton since having been given a junior ministerial appointment and, with Parliament now in recess until mid-September, he had every intention of enjoying as much of that time in Yorkshire, with his family, as he possibly could.

Politically the last few months had been momentous and the chance to reflect on things was welcome. In Paris the Peace Conference, in which a treaty between twenty-seven Allies and associated powers had been drawn up and signed, had finally ended, but nobody – not even the French – thought it had ended satisfactorily.

Lloyd George had promised to 'squeeze the German lemon until the pips squeak', but even he had been aghast at the demands made by France. Not all of them had been acceded to. Together with Great Britain, America had baulked at the French demand that Germany be partitioned and a separate peace made without Prussia. France had still carried the day, though, on lots of other issues and the end result was a Germany impoverished, humiliated and burning with bitterness.

Gilbert's longtime friend Winston Churchill, who, as Britain's Minister for War and Air, had attended the talks at Versailles, had said grimly to him when congratulating him on his new appointment, 'Instead of seeking Germany's utter ruin, our watchword should be magnanimity in victory and, in peace, goodwill. If cripplingly excessive war reparations are demanded of Germany, her working classes will be reduced to conditions of sweated labour and servitude – and the result will be another war in twenty or twenty-five years' time.'

Winston's opinion hadn't carried any sway. The terms finally agreed – and which the Germans had had no choice but to sign – stipulated a provisional compensation payment from Germany of billions of gold marks, with the final reparation figure to be decided later, and a stripping-away of all her territories.

Gilbert brushed past a clump of gorse, sending a cloud of yellow petals scattering. Ahead of him Caesar and Pluto, his two spaniels, were fruitlessly chasing a rabbit.

Still deep in thought and with his hands in his pockets, he continued walking in the direction of the river and the bridge. Gloomy though he felt the results of the Paris Peace Conference had been, there was a ray of light where world politics were concerned, and that ray of light was the newly formed League of Nations. The League had been dreamed up by President Woodrow Wilson, its purpose to sort out international disputes, as and when they occurred. In this way – and by sanctions – world peace would be maintained. It was an idea that fired Gilbert's imagination and he couldn't understand why Lloyd George was so lukewarm about it.

Now on the bridge, he paused, leaning against the moss-covered stonework, staring down into the water. Lloyd George was a Liberal, as had been the former prime minister, Herbert Asquith, and the present government was a coalition of Liberals and Conservatives. As a Conservative, Gilbert had issues with many Liberal policies, but nothing disappointed him more than the prime minister's lack of fervent enthusiasm for President Wilson's great vision.

The water below him flowed down towards the village, gin-clear. A fish leapt in a flashing silver arc. A dragonfly darted low, skimming the surface.

Watching it, he turned his mind from the League of Nations to the latest death-by-influenza figures, which showed that the Spanish-flu pandemic – which had taken nearly as many lives as had been lost in the war – was now officially over, and without ever having touched Outhwaite.

It was something to be deeply grateful for, but the thing he was most deeply grateful for was the news Blanche had given him earlier that morning. 'I'm pregnant, Gil darling!' she had said, her face radiant. 'And I'm sure it's a boy. Isn't it wonderful? Isn't it just unbelievably splendid?'

It was so unbelievably splendid that as he thought of it now he felt dizzy with joy. Even if the new baby wasn't a boy, it would mean a fourth daughter, who would be as loved and cherished as his other three daughters; and, if it *was* a boy, it would mean the continuance of his family name and an heir for his ancestral home.

For a moment he felt dizzy at his good fortune. Even sending Thea and Olivia to St Ethelburga's had turned out to be inspired, for they had both settled down there without a beat of homesickness and had come home for the long summer holidays full of new slang expressions and bursting with happy chatter about new friends.

'Georgiana Middleton, Olivia's class monitor, is an absolute *screech*,' Thea had said to him and, slightly more alarmingly, Olivia had assured him that, 'Our French teacher, Mademoiselle Moreau, is *divine*, Papa. Simply *everyone* is in love with her!'

St Ethelburga's was close enough to the sea for them to be taken swimming once a week. As well as tennis, they were also playing lacrosse. All in all, he was very satisfied with St Ethelburga's – and with his daughters' ability to adapt easily to new circumstances.

Other things had also gone well. For several months after the war had ended wounded officers had continued to convalesce at Gorton. The last of them had left in May and since then, under Blanche's careful direction, the wing of the house that had been given over in its entirety to them had been restored to its former use, and Gorton Hall was now ready for as many weekend house-parties as he cared to give. Or would be, once it again had a full complement of staff.

In the aftermath of the war the servant problem had become acute. Where butlers, footmen, chauffeurs and gardeners were concerned, the problem was to be expected, for they had gone off en masse to fight for their country and far too few of them had returned – and of those who had returned, far too many were permanently disabled. What hadn't been expected, though, was the acute shortage of female domestic staff.

With men away at the front, many of the jobs done by them had been taken over by women. They had acted as tram conductors, as postmen. In factories they had manned lathes, made weapons and in a whole host of industries had proved they were as capable as men. After enjoying that kind of freedom – and wages – few of them wanted to return to domestic service, where they had no choice but to live in, the pay left a lot to be desired, the hours were long and they were at the beck and call of an often tyrannical housekeeper or butler.

Tyranny wasn't, of course, an issue at Gorton Hall, and neither were excessively long hours or pathetically poor pay. Because of this, although they were short-staffed where maids were concerned, they were managing.

It was male staff that presented the difficulty. Heaton the butler was elderly, and had intimated to Gilbert that in the not-too-distant future he would like to retire and go and live with a married daughter at Bridlington. Their two former footmen had died of wounds at Ypres and so far, despite several classified advertisements in *The Lady*, had not been replaced. Under Charlie's direction, two jobbing gardeners were doing their best with the flowerbeds closest to the house, but their three former gardeners had all been killed at

90

the front.

Thinking of them, and of the ultimate sacrifice they had made, Gilbert reached into the pocket of his tweed jacket for his pipe and tobacco pouch. The first thing he had done, on returning home from France, had been to fund the erecting of a war memorial to Outhwaite's dead.

The memorial, made of Yorkshire stone, stood on the corner of the village green and among the names inscribed on it were those of Tom Bailey and Dick Wilkinson, his former footmen, and William Beveridge, Colin Graham and Albert Dixon, his former gardeners.

He tamped tobacco into the bowl of his pipe and lit it. Not one of the five had been over twenty-one. They had been fine young men with all of their lives before them.

His free hand clenched so tightly that his knuckles were bloodless and then, as Caesar and Pluto skittered around him restlessly, he blew a cloud of blue smoke into the air and, keeping the dogs happy, resumed his walk.

On reaching Gorton he approached the house across the east lawn, and Violet, who had been playing a lone game of hopscotch on the terrace, hurtled down the wide shallow steps and across the grass to meet him.

'Papa!' she called out, racing towards him. 'Where have you been? Why didn't you take me with you? A tinker-lady woman came to the kitchen door this morning, selling pegs. Mrs Hiscox was ever so cross when she found out. She said she didn't know what the world was coming to!'

Mrs Hiscox was Gorton's housekeeper and, as Violet collapsed breathlessly against him, he put an arm around her and hugged her close.

'Thea and Olivia have taken Rozalind into Outhwaite to meet Carrie,' she said, the sun making a burning bush of her fox-red hair. 'I could have gone with them, but I wanted to try and catch up with the tinker-lady so that I could have my palm read.'

'And did you?' There was alarm in his voice.

Violet shook her head. 'No. I hadn't even got as far as the lane before Jim came after me and brought me back. I don't think he had any right to, do you?'

'Yes,' he said emphatically. 'If he hadn't, you could have found yourself in Lancashire, selling pegs alongside her!'

Violet was tempted to say that selling pegs in Lancashire sounded like good fun, but there had been such strength of feeling in her father's voice that she thought better of it. Only hours ago she'd heard Cook telling Mr Heaton about a moving-picture show that her daughter had seen in Richmond. It had starred Charlie Chaplin and was called *The Vagabond*. The only person she could think of who would take her to see it was Hal, and she was going to ask him to do so. She would have to persuade him to keep it a secret, though, for she knew without asking that her father would be appalled at the thought of her jaunting off to Richmond to sit in the dark watching Charlie Chaplin.

To take her father's mind off the tinker-lady she said chattily as they neared the house, 'Is Mr

Hardwick happy in the hospital, Papa? Has he got his new face yet?'

'I don't think he's happy being so far away from Yorkshire.' Gilbert saw no reason why he shouldn't be absolutely truthful. 'Whenever I've visited him he's said how much he misses all his friends at Gorton.'

'I expect he means Jim and Hal and Miss Cumberbatch.' With her hand in his, she skipped along at his side. 'And us, as well. He does miss us as well, doesn't he, Papa?'

'I'm sure he does, Violet. As for his new face, he's undergone one operation, but he's going to have to have many further operations. He won't be back in Yorkshire this year, but hopefully he'll be back sometime next year.'

Gilbert wondered if he should prepare Violet for the fact that, however skilled Mr Gillies's surgery, Charlie was never going to look as he had once looked, but that he would look a whole lot less scary. He decided to leave it for the moment. Next year, before Charlie returned to Gorton and when Violet would be a year older, would be time enough for such a forewarning.

Violet cut across his thoughts. 'And then Charlie can ask Miss Cumberbatch to marry him, Papa. I know he wants to.' Unaware of what a thunderbolt she had dropped, she skipped off, intent on heading at the first opportunity for the Crosby farm, and Hal.

'Why do we have to walk all this way down the river-bank to meet this friend of yours?' Buttercups brushed the hem of Rozalind's linen smock.

'It would have been much easier to have met her at the bridge.'

'The bridge isn't our meeting place.' Olivia swatted a bee away. 'The vole place is where we meet. It's our secret place,' she added helpfully.

Rozalind rolled her eyes. A year older than Olivia, she thought meeting at 'secret places' pathetically childish.

'It's a breeding place for voles,' Thea said, having seen Rozalind's exasperated look towards heaven. 'And it's somewhere Hal can meet us.'

Rozalind still hadn't met Hal – and saw no reason why she should. 'I don't understand these friendships you've made since I was last at Gorton. Why would you make friends with a village girl and a boy who is a farm labourer? I'm not surprised Uncle Gilbert and Aunt Blanche object, and that you have to meet out of sight of the house.'

Instead of being indignant, as Olivia expected her to be, Thea burst out laughing.

'It's not like that at all, Roz. When Papa was a little boy, Carrie's granny was his nanny, and when Carrie's father was killed in Flanders, it was Papa's idea that Carrie spend time with us at Gorton. She's one of the family now. As for Hal, you'll like him when you meet him, and neither Mama nor Papa objects to our being friends with him.'

Rozalind was intrigued. As a small girl she had always enjoyed her visits to her English cousins, and after an interval of nearly five years she was enjoying this visit just as much as she had her earlier ones. Her parents were divorced and, compared to Gorton Hall, the Fifth Avenue mansion she lived in with her mother and stepfather was lifeless and dull, her mother being too busy with her social life ever to spend time with her.

At Gorton Hall things were very different. There her Aunt Blanche, with her husky voice and gentle smile, was the centre of everything; always interested in whatever it was that her daughters – and Rozalind – were doing. She would picnic with them, ride out on the moors with them, and was the very best audience when they plundered the dressing-up box to put on a theatrical perform-ance.

Only the previous evening they had acted out one of the funniest scenes from *Twelfth Night*. She had been Malvolio, wearing yellow stockings cross-gartered in red. Thea had been Maria, Olivia had been Olivia (having refused to be anyone else) and Violet had been Sir Toby Belch, with a pillow stuffed up her smock to give her a middle-aged paunch.

By the time the scene was over, her uncle had tears of laughter streaming down his face and her aunt was giggling so much she had hiccups. Afterwards Rozalind and her cousins had gone down to the kitchen, and Cook had made them mugs of hot milky cocoa and given them toasted crumpets slathered with butter.

Back home in New York she didn't even know where the kitchen was, and the cosy, loving jollity of the previous evening was something quite unknown.

'There's Carrie,' Olivia said suddenly to her. She broke into a run, shouting at the top of her voice, *'Carrie! Carrie!'*

A hundred yards or so away a girl who had been sitting on the river-bank rose to her feet. Even from a distance Rozalind could see that she wasn't wearing her hair down, but in a waist-length thick plait. As they drew nearer she couldn't decide whether the rope of hair made her look older than her years – like Olivia, Carrie was twelve – or younger.

Close to, she saw that Carrie had a sprinkling of light freckles across the bridge of her nose and that her eyes were a clear blue and held the same kind of frank curiosity about their meeting as she was feeling.

Carrie shot her a wide smile. 'Hello,' she said with disarming friendliness. 'I hope you don't mind, but when it was the war and you couldn't visit I used to ride the bicycle that was yours.'

'Until it got too small for her,' Olivia said, ever helpful. 'We've all got new bicycles now – and so have you. We could go down to the village on them this afternoon, if you like.'

'Of course I don't mind that you rode my bicycle, Carrie.' And to Olivia she said, 'Does the village shop still sell butterscotch?'

'Of course it does. And it now sells sherbert lemons too. You can get a big paper cone of them for tuppence.'

'First, though, we're going to show you the voles.' Thea linked her arm in Rozalind's. 'We've been watching them every summer for years now. Hal showed us where to find them.'

As they walked towards the part of the bank where Carrie had been sitting, Rozalind said to

Thea, 'When will I get to meet Hal?'

'Sunday probably. He has a little free time then, but not much. There's never any free time when you live on a farm. There's always too much work to do.'

'And on an evening,' Olivia said, 'when he's finished bringing the cows in for milking, he has lessons with Miss Calvert.'

Rosalind's eyebrows rose questioningly.

'She's the village schoolmistress.' There was a note in Thea's voice that Carrie had never heard before. Pride on Hal's behalf. 'Hal could have gone to a grammar school,' Thea continued. 'Miss Calvert is the village schoolmistress and she said he would easily have won a scholarship, only his father wouldn't let him sit for one. He said a grammar school would put fancy ideas in Hal's head.'

'And would it have?' They had reached the vole spot now.

'Not ideas that we think are fancy,' Olivia chipped in stoutly. 'Last week he applied for a job on the *Richmond Times*.' They flopped down into deep grass.

'As an office boy?'

Olivia giggled. 'He might have to be an office boy to start with, but Hal intends to become a journalist – and after he's worked as a journalist in Richmond he's going to go to London, to be a journalist on a national newspaper.'

It was such pie-in-the-sky moonshine that it took all Rozalind's self-control not to raise her eyes to heaven again. She said drily, 'That's a bit of a big ambition for a farmboy, don't you think?'

Thea's cat-eyes narrowed. 'Not really, Roz. Hal's ultimate ambition is to be not just any journalist, but a political journalist reporting on parliamentary affairs.'

Carrie sucked in her breath. If it was, he had never told her about it – and she had always assumed Hal told her everything.

For the first time it occurred to her that perhaps she wasn't his closest friend any longer, and that perhaps now Thea was. The thought gave her an odd feeling in her tummy. Until now she had always thought that the four of them were all friends together, with Hal perhaps being an extra bit closer to her than he was to Thea and Olivia, and that if he was a little *less* close to anyone, that he was a little less close to Thea on account of how annoyingly bossy she could be. Now it seemed she had got things wrong – and she didn't know how she felt about that.

'And what do you want to be when you leave school?' Rozalind suddenly asked her, wondering if, like Hal, Carrie also had high-flown ideas as a result of her friendship with the Fentons.

Carrie put her complicated feelings about Hal and Thea to one side and gave Rozalind a sunny smile. 'I'm going to go into service.'

It wasn't the answer that Rozalind had been expecting, but it certainly proved one thing. Carrie wasn't the least bit uppity. A little later, when they had said goodbye to Carrie and were walking back along the river-bank towards the bridge, she said to Olivia, 'I like Carrie Thornton. I can see why you're friends with her.'

'Goody.' Olivia hugged Rozalind's arm. 'That

means we'll be a circle of five, not four.'

Rozalind was fairly sure she wasn't going to feel the same way about Hal as she did about Carrie, but decided that Hal was a subject she was going to leave well alone until she had met him. Instead she said, 'Your maths are out, kiddo. When you include Violet you already are a circle of five.'

'We never do include Violet.' Olivia wondered if she could start using American slang. 'Kiddo' would be a great word to use at St Ethelburga's when she was with anyone younger than herself.

She shielded her eyes, looking to where a motor car was speeding from the direction of Outhwaite towards the bridge. 'I think that's Dr Todd's car,' she said to Thea. 'He's going very fast, isn't he? He must be on his way to an emergency.'

Knee-deep in buttercups, they all came to a standstill, watching to see if, after it had crossed the bridge – which it did at ferocious speed – the car would continue on the road or turn in at the entrance to Gorton Hall.

In a cloud of dust it turned in between the pillared gates.

Rozalind sucked in her breath.

Olivia said uncertainly, 'I expect one of the maids has had a fall and hurt herself. Or maybe one of the new gardeners has injured himself with a scythe or a billhook.'

'But maybe they haven't.' Beneath her turbulent chestnut hair Thea's face was very pale. 'Maybe something has happened to Mama, or Papa – or to Violet.'

For a brief second they were all frozen into immobility – and then they began to run, racing

99

up the grassy slope that led to the bridge; pounding over the bridge's ancient cobbles. Then, not following the road and approaching Gorton via its long elm-lined drive, they cut across its parkland, running with wings on their heels and a premonition of fear in their hearts.

Chapter Seven

MAY 1924

The Fentons' London town house was *en fête* with flowers sent down from Gorton. In the marble-floored hallway silver hanging baskets overflowed with frilled white roses. Pink peonies decorated the grand staircase, weaving with heady fragrance in and out of its wrought-iron balustrades. Pale-lilac anemones with indigo hearts massed the fireplaces. Hothouse freesias, sharply yellow, decorated beautifully laid supper tables. On every available surface were vases of wax-white orchids and bowls of carnations and lilies-of-the-valley.

Thea stood in the hall, breathing in the perfumed air, appreciative of all the effort that had been made.

'Charlie must have had his gardeners working night and day to ensure everything was in bloom at the same time,' Rozalind said, reading her thoughts.

Thea didn't reply. She was thinking how much her mother would have loved the sight of the peony-festooned balustrades. 'Mama always loved flowers,' she said, not trusting herself to look towards Rozalind for fear that, if their eyes met, she would no longer be able to check the tears that were threatening to fall. 'And she would have loved presenting me at court.'

Rozalind said nothing. For once, speech was beyond her. It was now almost five years since Blanche and the baby she had been carrying had died, and time was still not working its magic on those who had loved her. When it had come to Thea's presentation at court, her Aunt Hilda had presented Thea to Their Majesties, King George and Queen Mary. To say it had not been the same as if Blanche had done so was a major under-statement. Today, with the Mount Street house beautifully prepared for Thea's coming-out ball, the prospect of Blanche not being with Gilbert and Thea at the head of the stairs, welcoming the hundred or so guests, was a reality so monstrous that Rozalind wasn't sure how any of them were going to cope with it.

With legs that felt suddenly weak, she crossed the hall and sat down on one of the staircase's lower treads, the sheer suddenness of her Aunt Blanche's death jackknifing through her once again.

It had been such a lovely morning the day her aunt had died. Blanche hadn't been down for breakfast, but that was nothing unusual, for she always had breakfast in bed. Her Uncle Gilbert had been at the breakfast table, though, and breakfast had been the happily noisy occasion it usually was, when she had just arrived at Gorton for a long vacation and there was so much news for them all to catch up on.

When her Uncle Gilbert had finally risen from the table he'd said teasingly, 'I can see the only way I'm going to find peace and quiet today is by taking the dogs for a long moorland ramble.'

Then, his hands in his pockets and whistling for Caesar and Pluto, he'd left the room, unaware that within hours his life would change irrevocably.

Rozalind's plans for the day had already been made, for almost the first thing Thea had said to her when she arrived at Gorton the previous evening was that she simply had to meet Carrie. First, though, they had started off the morning as they always did, by haring up the stairs and running along the corridor to her Aunt Blanche's bedroom.

The minute they had tumbled into the room Blanche had set what looked to be a still untouched breakfast tray aside, so that the three of them could perch on her wide bed with its coronet of delicate muslin drapery.

'What are the three of you going to do today?' Blanche had asked, her flawless ivory complexion unusually flushed. 'Is it going to be a day on ponies or a day on bicycles?'

'Neither.' As usual Thea had answered before anyone else could. 'We're going to walk down to the river, where we're meeting with Carrie. Then I'm not sure what we're going to do.'

'Then off you go, darlings. And don't kiss me goodbye. I've got a headache and I'm beginning to feel shivery. A summer cold, I expect.'

They had left her and had walked in hot sunshine down to the river-bank and had spent the next few hours with Carrie. Then, on their way home, they had seen Dr Todd's car speeding towards Gorton Hall. Premonition, well founded, had seized them.

'Shortly after you left the house this morning her ladyship's ear began bleeding,' a white-faced Heaton had said to them when they had arrived at Gorton, breathless and alarmed. 'It's a major first symptom of Spanish flu, and the minute I was told of it I telephoned for the doctor.'

'Can we see Mama? Where's Papa? And where's Violet? Mama is going to be all right, isn't she?' Thea, who never, ever cried, had looked close to tears.

'Dr Todd has quarantined your mama in her bedroom. Your papa is with her, as is her maid and Dr Todd, but no one else is to be allowed in the room until the worst is over and your mama is on the road to recovery. Miss Cumberbatch has taken Miss Violet to Richmond for the day. A house of sickness is no place for a young child.'

At the words 'the road to recovery' Olivia had looked reassured.

Rozalind hadn't been reassured, though, and she doubted that Thea was. The death rate from Spanish flu was viciously high. Whole communities, worldwide, had been wiped out by it. In the last days of the previous year more soldiers had died from it than they had from the carnage of the war. It killed with mind-numbing swiftness; victims who were healthy in the morning were often dead by the evening.

All through the autumn of the previous year, when the pandemic had been at its height, Outhwaite had been spared. In the early spring, when the pandemic had peaked, there had still been no deaths from it in their part of the Dales, and by the summer the pandemic had seemed to be over. That being the case, how had her aunt fallen victim to it?

'She visited Effie Mellor's mother,' Cook had said grimly when, not knowing where else to go or what to do, they had made their way to the kitchen. 'She suffers terrible with arthritis, and her ladyship likes to keep an eye on her and take her a basket of whatever there's a glut of at the Home Farm. When Dr Todd asked Heaton who her ladyship had been in contact with over the last ten days or so, he told him about her visit to old mother Mellor. It turns out that Effie's sister, who lives in Manchester, was visiting. She's gone back there now, but Manchester was still recording deaths from influenza right up until the end of April. Dr Todd told Heaton he reckoned Effie's sister was carrying the infection.'

'And is she dead now? And is Effie's mother and Effie dead now?' Olivia's eyes had been wide and dark with fear.

'Effie's mother and Effie aren't dead. There's no telling as to Effie's sister.'

'Then Mama won't die, either. And neither will we.' The relief in Olivia's voice had been vast.

Cook had made them comforting mugs of milky cocoa and given them warm scones sandwiched with raspberry jam. Then, not knowing what else to do, they had sat outside on Gorton

Hall's wide pillared steps, waiting for the moment when Dr Todd would emerge en route to his car and tell them that the person they loved most in all the world was well on the road to recovery.

Twilight had fallen.

Evening had come.

When the door had finally opened, it hadn't been Dr Todd who had emerged into the moonlit darkness. It had been Heaton. One look at his face had been enough for them to know the news he was bringing.

Olivia had screamed and jumped to her feet.

Thea had stood up slowly, her face as still and set as if it had been carved from stone.

Rozalind hadn't moved. She couldn't. Movement had been beyond her.

When finally she had followed Thea and Olivia into the house, it had been to the sight of her uncle walking down the grand curving staircase to meet them. Beneath the burning red of his hair, his face had been grey. He was a man who had been poleaxed; a man who simply couldn't believe what he was living through was real.

'I want you to be very brave,' he had said when he had reached the foot of the stairs and enfolded Thea and Olivia in his arms. 'Mama would expect it of you.'

Olivia had sobbed uncontrollably.

Thea had said with steel in her voice: 'I want to see Mama. I want to say goodbye to her.'

'You can all come and say goodbye to her,' he had said, 'but you mustn't kiss her. You mustn't run any risk of catching the infection.' He had

105

looked over Thea's head to Rozalind. 'Violet is in the drawing room with Miss Cumberbatch. Would you ask her to join us, Rozalind? And please tell Miss Cumberbatch the reason why.'

She had nodded, her throat too tight for speech, unable to envisage Gorton Hall without her aunt. Unable even to begin envisaging the effect her aunt's death was going to have on her uncle and cousins.

Roz was brought sharply back to the present moment by Thea springing to her feet and saying fiercely, 'I wish Carrie was here, Roz! It's so hateful having a friend who can't be with you when you need her to be. If she has to be in service, why does it have to be with Lady Markham? Why can't she be in service at Gorton and here?'

It was a rhetorical question. They all knew exactly why Carrie could never be in service at Gorton.

As Thea walked up the curving staircase with Rozalind she said, 'Carrie and I have a plan,' her cat-green eyes narrowing as they always did when she was stubbornly determined on anything. 'She has already worked her way up from being a tweeny, via being a housemaid, to being a parlourmaid – which isn't surprising when you think how capable and hard-working Carrie is. Her next aim is to be promoted from parlourmaid to chambermaid duties – and because, thanks to us and when she wants to, she can speak without a Yorkshire accent and is so presentable, that's bound to happen before very long. Who would you like to have in and out of your bedroom? Carrie, or some of

106

the horrors that our housekeeper at Gorton has employed over the last five years?'

Rozalind didn't trouble to answer Thea's question. Instead, as they made their way to the ballroom to see how the flowers there had been put to good use, she said, 'And then what? How is Carrie one day being a chambermaid going to help us see more of her?'

They sidestepped two footmen laden with piles of starched white table linen.

'Because her final aim is to be a lady's maid. Lady Markham's maid has been with her forever, so there won't be an opening for such a position at Monkswood, but if Lydia Markham's maid is allowed to train Carrie – and I'll make sure Papa asks her if she will permit that – then Carrie can become my lady's maid. Lady's maids hold a senior position. There won't be any trouble at Gorton – or here – from other members of staff And Carrie will be with me nearly every minute of the day.'

They paused at the open double doors to the ballroom. Inside, footmen were setting up music stands for the orchestra that would be arriving in a few hours' time. A professional florist was supervising the arranging of the Gorton-grown white roses over and around enormous gilt-framed mirrors. Crystal chandeliers, taken down for cleaning, were now being laboriously winched back into position.

'And Hal?' Rozalind asked. 'How is Hal going to feel about Carrie fetching and carrying, and doing your hair and caring for your clothes?'

Thea avoided Rozalind's eyes. 'He'll understand. He'll have to. How else are any of us ever going to get to spend time with Carrie? Besides, Carrie doesn't see being in service the same way Hal sees it. He thinks it's demeaning and that it reinforces the kind of class differences he hates. Carrie doesn't think of it that way. She doesn't want to man the barricades and become a socialist and change the world. She wants what she has always wanted. She wants to be in service – and she wants to be in service at Gorton Hall.'

Rozalind was sure Thea was right about Carrie, but she didn't think she was right in assuming that Hal would be understanding if Carrie one day became her maid. Far from being understanding, Rozalind was quite certain Hal would be absolutely furious, and she thought it typical of Thea not to realize this. Whenever Rozalind visited Gorton, which was for a couple of months every summer, the only spats that ever took place between the five of them were always between Thea and Hal. Though if Carrie went into service at Gorton as Thea's personal maid, it wouldn't just be a spat that would take place between them, it would be an all-out blistering row – the kind of row that could well put an end to their friendship.

Mindful that it was a very special day for Thea, Rozalind didn't think it a good time to point this out. Instead she said, 'Hal is going to be here tonight, isn't he? Reporting on the ball for the *Richmond Times?*'

Thea, who had seen enough of what was happening in the ballroom to know that it was going

108

to look splendid that evening, turned away from the open double doors.

'Yes.' Her voice was taut. 'It wasn't my idea – and it certainly wasn't Hal's. Papa thought that if Hal attended my coming-out ball in order to cover it, it would be a scoop for Hal and would help his career. Without a word to me – or to Hal – he put the idea to Hal's editor, who leapt at it. Why wouldn't he, when so many of Papa's governmental friends are going to be in attendance, and when the Duke and Duchess of York are the guests of honour?'

At the bitterness in her voice, Rozalind's eyes widened.

Thea stamped her foot. 'Don't look at me like that, Roz! It's taken Hal three years to move from reporting weddings, funerals and lost dogs to reporting on Richmond city-council matters and now, thanks to Papa, he's likely to lose his local-politics slot and be given frivolous high-society events instead!'

Appalled at Thea's depth of feeling, Rozalind sought something to say that would put Thea in a mood appropriate for the specialness of the day. Before inspiration came, Violet, on roller-skates and undeterred by the carpet underfoot, came whizzing down the wide corridor towards them.

'Oh, *God!*' Thea said with deep passion. 'Keep that wretched child out of my hair, Roz. And if anyone asks where I am, say I've gone for a walk.'

Without pausing to put on a hat, she marched off, hands clenched in the pockets of a mid-calf-length navy suit, the heels of her shoes high, her hair cut in the shortest, sleekest shingle that Rozalind had ever seen.

She headed straight out of the house and down the street in the direction of Park Lane and Hyde Park, the backs of her eyes burning with tears.

She needed to be alone. If she'd stayed another second with Rozalind she would have told her just what the true state of affairs between her and Hal was – and if she told Roz, then she would also have to tell Olivia and Carrie, and she had no idea how any of them would react.

She walked towards Hyde Park Corner, entering the park at the Achilles gate. Roz would probably take the news with more equanimity than Olivia or Carrie, but then Roz's relationship with Hal was far more uncomplicated than Olivia's and Carrie's because, unlike Olivia, Roz didn't have an embarrassingly obvious crush on him. As for Carrie...

Thea dug her hands even deeper into her pockets. Carrie and Hal were as close as brother and sister – but that didn't mean to say that Carrie didn't expect their relationship to change into something far different in the near future. It would be what people in Outhwaite, people like Jim and Charlie and Carrie's granny, were expecting to happen – and why not?

A marriage between Hal and Carrie would raise no eyebrows. There would be no class differences to overcome. True, if Hal hadn't worked so hard to better himself educationally, Carrie's granny might well have been unhappy at the thought of Carrie marrying him. Mrs Thornton had, after all, been a nanny in the household of a

110

peer of the realm and, in working-class hierarchy, that counted for a lot. She might well have been unhappy at the thought of her granddaughter marrying a man whose only prospect in life was to one day inherit a tied smallholding.

As it was, though, Hal had made it very clear that wasn't going to happen. Encouraged by Miss Calvert, he had become a cub-reporter on the *Richmond Times* when he was fifteen. Now, three years later, he spent most of his time in the council chamber of the town hall, reporting on local politics. As a husband for Carrie he would, in her granny's eyes, be ideal. And he'd probably be ideal in Carrie's eyes, too.

Deep in unhappy, complicated thoughts and, because of being hatless and unescorted in such a public place, attracting many curious glances, Thea strode on towards the Serpentine, her hands still rammed into the shallow pockets of her suit jacket. Did Carrie expect Hal to propose to her one day? And, if he didn't, would Carrie's heart be broken?'

Even more to the point, as Hal was adamant he was never going to ask anyone to marry him, was her own heart going to be broken as well?

The lake came into view, its surface glittering grey and green beneath the hot sun. Shaded by parasols, couples and families strolled along its banks. Having no desire to join them, Thea seated herself on an unoccupied park bench and, with her face raised to the sun and her eyes closed, considered her dilemma.

She was madly, passionately, violently in love with Hal. Though Hal had not yet admitted that

111

he felt the same way about her, it was, she was certain, only a matter of time before he did so. And then what would happen? How could they become engaged when the class gulf between them yawned as deep as a chasm and when marriage was something Hal didn't believe in?

'Marriage is as old hat as Liberalism,' he had once said when they were sitting on the riverbank, their arms clasped around their knees.

Olivia and Carrie had been out of earshot, paddling in the shallows with fishing nets, their skirts hitched high. When such moments occurred he would take full advantage of them, pulling her against him and kissing her swift and hard. They were moments that made her head spin and her heart race; moments when every atom of her being melted with longing. On this occasion, though, he had made no move towards her. Instead he had merely turned his head to hers, his blue-black curls tumbling low over his forehead, his gold-flecked eyes goadingly provocative, as he'd added, 'Why would any sane person want to commit to tying themselves to one person for life?'

She'd known then that he knew what her fantasy for their future was, and because he didn't share it – because he should have been stunned with grateful incredulity for what it was that she wanted for them both, and because he was so clearly neither grateful nor incredulous – her rage and hurt pride had been incandescent.

'They do it because that's what people who love each other do!' she'd stormed, springing to her feet, uncaring that Olivia and Carrie had stopped

112

trawling the water with their nets and were staring towards them in consternation. 'And if you don't understand that, Hal Crosby, then you're stupid beyond belief!'

Without even unclasping his hands from around his knees he'd cracked with laughter. Olivia and Carrie had begun noisily splashing their way towards the river-bank. Fearful of what explanation for her angry outburst Hal, in his present mood, might give, Thea had done the only thing she could think of in order to save her dignity. She'd stalked off, her head high, her nails digging deep into her palms.

Now, seated on one of Hyde Park's benches in the glittering afternoon sun, the thought of the endurance test lying ahead of her that evening aroused in her the same level of angry, frustrated impotence. That her well-meaning father had suggested to Hal's editor that Hal should attend her coming-out ball in order to write an exclusive account of it was bad enough. What was infinitely worse was Hal's editor thinking it a good idea. Coming-out balls, presentations to royalty and all the razzmatazz that went with being a debutante were a red rag to a bull, where Hal was concerned.

'A summer-long spree of champagne lunches, seven-course dinners, lavish parties and balls that cost a king's ransom is a flagrant example of the aristocracy with its feet in the trough,' he had said contemptuously.

It hadn't helped that until now she had always assured him that his views were hers. Trying to convince her father that she didn't want an official Season had, however, been impossible. Usually infinitely understanding, on the subject of her coming-out Gilbert had been immovable.

'I know that, thanks to your friendship with Hal, you like to think of yourself as being outrageously left-wing, Thea, but on this occasion I can't indulge you,' he had said gravely. 'For girls of your class being presented at court is a rite of passage. It is what Mama would have expected for you, and it is what I expect.'

She had been prepared to argue further, but he had then put a conciliatory arm around her shoulders, saying, 'Mama always intended that on your presentation you would wear the Prince of Wales's feathers that she wore when she was presented and, bearing her wishes in mind, I have kept them very carefully stored. With Mama's feathers in your hair and her pearls around your throat, I think, Thea darling, you will feel Mama is very close to you when you make your curtseys in front of Their Majesties.'

After that, of course, there could be no further argument and, for her father's sake, she had resolved to put her left-wing principles on a back burner for the duration of the Season. It hadn't been too hard to do. She'd enjoyed shopping for an extravagant new wardrobe of Parisian-designed clothes and anticipating a coming-out ball at which royalty would be present. It was enjoyment that had ended the moment she'd realized Hal was also going to be in attendance though only as an onlooker.

How was she ever going to convince him that the class difference between them didn't matter, after he had seen her in a gown that cost five times the annual salary of a working man, waltzing around the ballroom of her London family home in the arms of royalty or of men he disparagingly referred to as 'chinless wonders'?

A nanny, wheeling a perambulator and wearing a spruce brown-and-cream Norland uniform, walked up to the bench and, with a polite bob of her head to Thea, sat down. The baby, frustrated by the perambulator's sudden lack of movement, clenched its fists, went red in the face and began to bawl.

Wishing that she, too, could give vent to her feelings, Thea rose to her feet, not knowing which was worse: her distress that Hal was going to see her in a role she knew he would find contemptible, or the agonizing prospect of dancing until the early hours with partners she was indifferent to, when the person she longed to dance with was only there to write a report for a newspaper.

As she walked back through the park she was certain of one thing. Far from enjoying her coming-out ball, she was going to hate every single agonizing minute of it.

Chapter Eight

Hal stood outside a small cafe fronting the obelisk in Richmond's cobbled market place. His train for Darlington, from where he would catch a London-bound train, left in just over an hour's time and, as it was Carrie's day off, she had suggested they have a cup of tea together and that she walk to the station with him and wave him goodbye.

'I'm only going to London,' he had protested, shooting her a down-slanting smile, 'and I'll be back by tomorrow night.'

'So soon?' she had said ingenuously. 'Won't you be staying for a few days? I know Thea, Olivia and Roz won't be able to spend much time with you at the ball – there'll be too many grand people they'll have to be polite to – but they'll want to spend time with you once it's over.'

'Thea, Olivia and Roz won't be spending *any* time with me at the ball,' he'd said bluntly, exasperated by her naivety. 'And they won't be spending time with me when it's over, either. London isn't Outhwaite, Carrie. The Fenton girls may ignore the class difference that divides us when we're all at the vole place by the river, or up on the moors, but when it comes to London, there's not a cat in hell's chance of them being able to do so.'

He had seen her happiness at the thought of

116

him spending time in London with their friends extinguished, but he hadn't hated himself for having killed it. She had to learn that the friendship between the five of them couldn't endure for much longer in the same uncomplicated way it had endured until now. Not, he thought wryly as Carrie turned into the market place and began hurrying towards him, that his relationship with Thea had ever been truly uncomplicated. As far back as he could remember there had always been a clash of wills between them. For one thing she was far too bossy, and he'd never allowed himself to be bossed by anyone – and certainly not by a girl. Now, with the sexual tension sizzling between them, it was even more complicated, but Carrie didn't know that yet and, as far as he knew, nor did anyone else – which just went to show how blind people could be.

Carrie ran up to him breathlessly. 'I'm sorry I'm late,' she said sunnily, tucking her hand through his arm and giving it a hug. 'Have we still time for a cup of tea, or do you want to head straight for the station?'

'We've time for tea.'

At the nape of her neck and beneath a shallow-brimmed straw hat her long plait of hair was coiled into a chignon. A narrow band of mauve ribbon decorated her hat and there was a bunch of artificial violets pinned to the lapel of her summer coat. She looked neat and pretty and wonderfully wholesome. He wondered how long it would be before some young man asked her to walk out with him – and how he would feel about it when they did.

117

'What are the footmen like at Monkswood?' he asked when he had ordered a pot of tea for two from a waitress who couldn't keep her eyes off him.

'Some of them are very nice, and some of them think a little bit too much of themselves. As a chambermaid, I don't see as much of them as I did when I was a tweeny. Why do you ask?'

'Have any of them asked you if you'd walk out with them?'

'Of course they haven't!' She flushed rosily. 'What on earth put that idea into your head?'

The waitress served them their pot of tea, giving Hal a long, come-hither look as she did so. It fell on stony ground.

'Just that when someone likely asks to court you, I'd like to check him out before you let him,' he said as the waitress flounced away, disappointed that Hal should be more interested in a girl who looked like a Sunday-school teacher than he was in her. 'It's what your father would do if he was still alive, and it's what a brother would do, if you had one.'

Common sense told Carrie that such concern for her was a great compliment, but she didn't feel complimented. Instead, and for some reason She couldn't quite define, she felt exceedingly cross.

'That sort of thing doesn't happen in service,' she said, trying to keep the crossness out of her voice as she began pouring the tea. 'Romance between members of staff is a no-no everywhere. If anyone was to get a whisper of it, both people involved would immediately lose their positions.'

118

'Would they? Doesn't that make you angry, Carrie?'

'No. Why should it? It's a fact of life, and being angry about it isn't going to change anything. Are you still liking your lodgings in Richmond? Have you been back to Outhwaite since we last met up? Granny writes me a weekly letter, but her gossip is never about Jim and Charlie and Miss Calvert. Do you have any news of them?'

Twenty minutes later, as they walked past the obelisk and into the steeply cobbled street known as Frenchgate, they were still talking about their Outhwaite friends.

'Charlie never wears his mask now,' Hal said as they neared the turning into Station Road. 'He's still not the bonniest thing on two legs, but what his surgeon did for him is beyond belief.' Charlie's prosthetic mask, made for him when he first became a patient at Queen Mary's Hospital in far-away Kent, had become a talking point in Outhwaite – and for miles around. Made of silvered copper, it had been sculptured to resemble the shape of his face, before his face had been destroyed. Carrie had never liked it, but during the long years when his face had been being gradually and painfully reconstructed, Charlie had been deeply grateful for it. It had been something for him to hide behind; something at which people stared in morbid, fascinated curiosity, but which, unlike his face, they didn't recoil from in revulsion and horror.

She said, 'Lord Fenton says Mr Gillies should be knighted. He says he's saved Charlie's life.'

'Lord Fenton's right.' Usually Hal was disparaging when talking about anyone with a title before their name, but he always made an exception for Gilbert Fenton, who treated everyone from agricultural labourers to his fellow peers – with exactly the same kind of courtesy and respect. 'Gillies couldn't have done what he's done, though, if Gilbert Fenton hadn't been so determined to help Charlie and taken him to the other end of England in order to meet the surgeon.'

Carrie nodded her head in eager agreement. 'Lord Fenton is the handsomest, kindest man I know.'

'You find red hair handsome then, do you, Carrie?' he said teasingly as they began crossing the bridge over the Swale that led to the station. 'Is that why you don't fancy any of the lads at Monkswood? Is it because none of them are copper-knobs?'

'Don't be silly.' She flushed rosily again. 'And you like red hair, too. Think how much you like Olivia's hair.'

He made a non-committal sound in his throat, amazed that even Carrie, who knew him so well, didn't realize that it wasn't Olivia's waving marmalade-coloured hair that he ached to feel between his fingers and the palms of his hands, but Thea's deeply burnished, chestnut-red hair.

Olivia, of course, had had a crush on Hal ever since the day they had first met, and Carrie wasn't the only person to think it would be quite natural if her romantic feelings for him were returned. Certainly Hal's Uncle Jim and Charlie thought so, for whenever they made any sly remarks – and they made them often – they were always about him and Olivia, never him and Thea.

At the thought of Thea the muscles in his stomach clenched.

All morning he had been fighting against thinking of her and of how fiendishly difficult the next twenty-four hours were going to be, standing as an impotent bystander as other men – men of her own class – danced and flirted with her; men with whom he couldn't possibly compete when it came to status and wealth and eligibility.

As they entered the station a voice over the loudspeaker system announced that the ten o'clock train to Darlington was about to depart. Urgently Carrie grabbed hold of his arm. 'Run, Hal, or you'll miss it!'

There was nothing Hal would have liked better than to miss it, but if he did so, it would mean the end of his job on the *Richmond Times*.

He kissed her hastily on the cheek and ran for the already-moving train, clambering into a carriage with the help of a gentleman already inside it. As the door slammed behind him he leaned out of its window, waving an energetic goodbye.

Carrie waved in answer until the train had vanished from sight. Whenever she and Hal met up in Richmond, they never seemed to have enough time together, for her to chat to him as she would have liked to chat, and today had been no exception. She would have liked to have asked him about Miss Calvert, and whether Jim was still romancing the barmaid from the Pig and Whistle in Outhwaite's High Street. Now, chat about Jim and Miss Calvert would have to wait until she had time off from Monkswood that coincided again with time when Hal was free to meet up with her.

She always tried hard not to feel sad that the years when she and Hal had met almost daily with Thea and Olivia – and Roz, too, when she was visiting – were over. Though her friendly nature ensured she was on good terms with other members of the staff at Monkswood, there was no one there she had come close to, in the way she was close to Thea, Olivia and Roz.

She made her way back to the market place, her heart aching at being so cut off from them – and at being cut off from other friends at Outhwaite, friends such as Jim and Charlie. She paused on the bridge, biting her lip, telling herself how lucky she was to have a position in a house like Monkswood and, at seventeen, to have risen from being a tweeny to being a chambermaid. The tears that were threatening abated now, but her painful sense of isolation didn't. Though Monkswood was much grander than Gorton Hall, it wasn't Gorton, and Lady Markham wasn't Lord Fenton.

Something she had never admitted to anyone, not even Hal, was how much she missed the little exchanges of conversation that Lord Fenton had always had with her when he was at Gorton and she was a visitor there. With no father to watch over her and take an interest in her doings, knowing that Lord Fenton did so meant a lot to her.

She began walking again, thinking how proud Lord Fenton would be of Thea that evening and wishing that, like Hal, she could be at her coming-out ball, to see Thea become the centre of all attention in a fairytale white ballgown.

Thea viewed herself in a cheval-glass and liked what she saw. Her white silk and tulle Parisian-made ballgown was embroidered with tiny crystals that shimmered and shone with every tiny movement she made. Her mother's pearls glowed seductively at her throat and her delicately beautiful tiara was a Fenton family heirloom.

'You look sensational, honey,' Rozalind said truthfully from behind her. 'I guarantee you'll have a proposal of marriage before the ball is over.'

'A proposal of marriage, from any of my guests, is the last thing I want.'

'Catching a rich husband is what the Season is all about.' There was amusement in Rozalind's voice. 'And some of us are aiming even higher than merely rich.'

Thea pulled a long white glove high above her elbow. 'Explain yourself, Roz. D'you mean fabulously rich? Monumentally rich? *Stupendously* rich?'

Rozalind tucked a straying strand of blue-black hair back into her glossy chignon. 'I mean royally rich. Prince Edward is expected to make an appearance tonight, isn't he?'

'He's proposed himself.'

Rozalind looked mystified, and Thea reached for her other glove.

'The Prince of Wales is never directly invited to these kinds of social functions.' She smoothed the glove and reached for its partner. 'If he wishes to attend a particular ball or party, he proposes himself – and he's proposed himself this evening,

123

probably because his brother Bertie and his wife will be here.'

'That's the Duke and Duchess of York, right?'

'Right.'

The correct names and titles of Britain's royal family had never been Rozalind's strong point. Bertie's Christian name, for instance, was actually Albert and, until he'd married Elizabeth Bowes-Lyon a little over a year ago, he had been known as Prince Albert. The title of Duke of York had been given to him on his marriage, and Rozalind couldn't understand why. Being addressed as a prince seemed, to her, far superior to being addressed as a duke. Similarly confusing was that Prince Edward was known to family and close friends as David.

Thea turned away from the cheval-glass. 'There are thirty people invited to the pre-ball dinner, Roz, and it's time to show our faces.'

Violet burst into the room, saying as if on cue, 'Papa wants to know what on earth is keeping you!' Her cream lace and satin dress was tied with a childish sash around the waist, had no lavish ornamentation and, because she was still young, she wore no jewellery and her fiery red hair, crowned by a wreath of green leaves, streamed down her back in an unrestrained torrent of waves and curls. 'There are relatives in the dining room I've never even seen before – and most of them don't look to be any fun – plus you never told me your godfather was Chancellor of the Exchequer.'

'Is he? I didn't know. The last time I met him was when I was christened.'

As they all left the room Thea turned her

attention back to Rozalind. 'I think you're in for a crashing disappointment where Prince Edward is concerned, Roz. He's head-over-heels in love with Freda Dudley Ward.'

'And she is?'

'The very pretty and petite wife of William Dudley Ward, a Liberal MP.'

'Well, if she's married, she's not going to become Princess of Wales. When it comes to a wife, Prince Edward is going to have to look elsewhere – and so why not in my direction? I think it's about time the royal family stretched its wings and included an American.'

'You're too tall,' Violet said from behind them. 'You're at least five foot eight and the Prince is only five foot four. I heard Olivia say so. I'm never going to be too tall, though.' She skipped past them towards the dining room, saying as she did so, 'And when I become Princess Violet, you'll have to curtsey to me all the time!'

The obligatory pre-ball family dinner was just as boring as Thea had anticipated. Her late mother's cousins lived on the Welsh Borders and she barely knew them. Her godfather shook her hand, said it was a long time since they had last met, that it was very nice seeing her again and then turned his attention elsewhere.

Thea's attention had long been elsewhere. It was focused on Hal. When the dinner was over there would be a very small hiatus and then the guests to her coming-out ball would begin arriving, which meant Hal was in all probability somewhere in the house, ready to take note of distinguished

125

arrivals. But whereabouts in the house?

Her father would know. Seated on her left, he was deep in conversation with the person across from him at the table. She toyed with her chicken fricassee, waiting for a lull in their conversation. When it finally came she said, 'Has Hal arrived, Papa?'

'Most probably.' He turned towards her, a lump rising in his throat. She looked so very beautiful in her shimmering white ballgown and with her mother's pearls around her throat. With every atom of his being he wished Blanche was at his side, sharing in his joy and pride.

'Where will he be?'

He patted her hand. 'Don't worry about Hal, Thea. Broadbent has made sure he'll be looked after.'

Thea looked towards their butler, who was supervising the waiting at table, wondering just what arrangements he had made for Hal. Presumably, as he was there to report on the ball, Hall would be in the ballroom once the ball began, but what would he be wearing? He didn't possess a formal suit, and certainly didn't possess evening clothes. If the evening was going to be ghastly for her, it was going to be even more so for Hal. She dug her nails deep into her palms. Royalty was going to be present, and Hal would not have the slightest idea of the protocol this entailed and, even if he did know of it, would very likely ignore it.

She abandoned all pretence of eating and drinking. She had to find him. She had to ensure he didn't enter the ballroom, for all she could see

126

ahead, if he did, were disasters of the most horrific proportions.

Abruptly – and before a footman could do so for her – she pushed her chair away from the table.

'I'm sorry, Papa. Please make my excuses. I'll be back in a few minutes, I promise.'

He shot out a hand to restrain her, but she was too quick for him. Aware of her guests' startled bewilderment, she left the dining room as fast as her floor-length ballgown would allow, followed, as she had known she would be, by Broadbent.

As he closed the dining room's double doors behind him, and before he'd had time to ask how he could assist her, she said urgently: 'Papa has arranged for Mr Crosby of the *Richmond Times* to be in attendance this evening. Has he arrived yet? And if so, where can I find him?'

'If Mr Crosby has arrived in the last half-hour he will either be in the servants' hall, where a cold collation has been left in readiness for him, or in one of the attic rooms set aside for visiting valets.'

Broadbent's voice was as impassive as his face – and would be when, on his return to the dining room, he gave an account of their conversation to her father.

Thea, aware that he would be doing so and that though her father would be justifiably cross with her, he would at least be relieved she hadn't been taken ill, headed straight towards the nearest green baize door and the back stairs leading down to the basement and the servants' hall.

It was the room where the servants both ate

and relaxed, but with a dinner for thirty now well under way and 300 guests about to arrive for the ball, no one was relaxing in it now. There was, though, on the long deal table in the centre of the room, a covered plate and a place setting for one.

She paused in the doorway, her heart hammering. Did the untouched plate mean Hal hadn't arrived yet? Or had he arrived and gone straight to the room set aside for him? She bit her lip. Being found looking for Hal in the servants' hall was one thing. Looking for him in a part of the house where the footmen and other male servants slept was quite another.

Her hesitation lasted barely a second. She had to find him. She had to tell him he needn't suffer the embarrassment of the ball in order to write about it – she could give him all the information he'd need. That way, although he would still see her in her dress (there was absolutely no way of avoiding that now), he wouldn't see her in a setting that might well convince him that the class gulf between them was unbridgeable.

It didn't seem unbridgeable to her, because she wasn't going to allow it to be so. Politically she thought of herself as just as much a socialist as Hal was. He had taken her to Labour Party meetings in Richmond and, unknown to her father, she had continued attending them by herself in London. To her surprise, she'd discovered that she wasn't the only upper-class girl with socialist sympathies.

'We're known as ballroom pinks,' a girl who recognized her as a social equal had said when she had attended a meeting in Farringdon

Street's Memorial Hall. 'Quite a hoot, don't you think?'

Thea hadn't thought it a hoot. She'd thought the term both derisive and condescending and was certain that whoever had coined it had done so believing that girls of her class couldn't possibly be seriously committed to Labour Party principles.

As she ran once again in the direction of the back stairs she wondered if the expression was one Hal was familiar with. If it was, she was certain he would never apply it to her. He knew her too well to imagine that she would play-act about something so important.

She ran up the first two flights of stairs, remembering the world of working-class poverty to which Hal had opened her eyes. There had been the Tetley family in Richmond. Their oldest son, Wilfred, had been knocked down by a horse and cart. One of his legs had got stuck in the wheel spokes and, as the cart had moved forward, the rotation had twisted his leg so badly that it had had to be amputated.

'And now the lad's stump is festering, and Joe Tetley is unemployed and they can't afford the doctor,' Hal had told her, flinty-eyed. 'If you want to see real poverty, Thea, come wi' me and see what happens when folk like the Tetleys are still paying off the last doctor's bill and he won't come to 'em again before it's been paid – not even for a little lad who's lost his leg.'

She had gone. In a house with no sanitation and no running water she had seen Wilfred's father apply live maggots to his sobbing son's putrid stump. She had been there when the doctor's debt collector had made his weekly visit to collect payment off the bill they had incurred at the time of the amputation. And she was there when, with tears streaming down her face, Wilfred's mother had pleaded with the debt collector that he put in a word for them with the doctor, and he had curtly told her that he could do no such thing.

Halfway up the third flight of narrow stairs she paused to let a startled housemaid who was coming down them squeeze past her. Thanks to her father – who, when Thea had told him of the Tetleys' ghastly situation, had promptly paid off the doctor's previous bill and paid him for future visits – Wilfred had survived.

'But he can't do that for all the hundreds and thousands of other Wilfreds,' Hal had said grimly. 'Families like the Tetleys are caught in a trap of poverty they can't break free of. Things you take for granted – a doctor coming when you're ill – can't be taken for granted when you haven't the money to pay for one. That's why we need a Labour government. So that things will change. So that provision for the sick and infirm can be put in place, and the vileness of the workhouse can be done away with forever.'

She paused to get her breath on the small landing before the fifth and last flight of stairs. That conversation with Hal, and the incident with the Tetley family, had taken place three years ago. Just over four months ago King George had appointed James Ramsay MacDonald as Britain's first Labour prime minister. It was a minority government, reliant on Liberal goodwill for its survival, but already it had passed legislation on housing, education and social insurance.

She hurried up the stairs leading to the topmost floor. Set aside for male servants, it was somewhere Thea had absolutely no right to be. There weren't many bedrooms. Though extra footmen had been drafted in for the evening, only two footmen were Fenton regulars, and as they were at present in attendance in the dining room she knew she ran no risk of running into them.

Panting from her long, hurried climb up the stairs, and knowing that she had very little time – when her guests began arriving, she absolutely had to be standing next to her father in order to greet them – she hurried down the short corridor, giving an urgent rap on each door she passed. No one called out. No door opened. At the last door she didn't bother knocking; she simply yanked down on the handle and burst into the room.

'*Hellfire!*'

With water dripping from his hair, Hal spun round. He had been standing at the washbasin, bare-chested and with the braces of his trousers hanging loose.

As shocked by the sight of him semi-naked as he was by the sight of her in a ballgown, tiara and pearls, Thea fell back against the door.

'I had to find you.' She gasped the words, the breath tight in her chest as the door slammed shut.

She was aware of a small skylight window. And a bed, narrow and functional with a sheet and blanket tightly tucked in and clothes she recognized – a jacket and a waistcoat – flung down on top of it.

She was vaguely aware that she was leaning against other items of clothing: clothing that had been hung on the back of the door. Whoever it belonged to, she neither knew nor cared.

The last time she had seen Hal in nothing but his breeches had been when they had been children, playing in the river. She, Olivia and Carrie would scream and splash in the shallows, their skirts hitched high into their bloomers, while Hal would tear off his shirt and cavort in the deepest part of the river like a sea lion.

Seeing him in a state of undress then hadn't had the same effect as it was having on her now. Her knees were so weak that she put her hands behind her, digging her fingers into what felt like a gentleman's tailcoat, in an attempt to stay upright.

'Why did you need to find me?' he demanded explosively, his body taut with tension. 'This is a valet's bedroom, Thea! You can't be found in here!'

She wanted to say that she wasn't going to be found; that every servant in the house was on duty floors below them, but her mouth was too dry, her throat too tight. She couldn't even remember why she had needed to see him. She was too overcome with desire; so confounded by it that she was speechless.

He had been watering his hair, trying to tame his tight black curls into some kind of submission. Droplets of water dripped onto a chest that was olive-skinned, wide and firmly muscled.

She wanted to be crushed against it. She wanted to sink her teeth into the strong curve of his shoulder; to lick the drops of water away, to taste every part of him. So overcome with longing that she didn't know how she was remaining upright, she finally found herself capable of speech, but not in order to tell him why she was there.

'Kiss me, Hal!' Her voice was hoarse, desperate with need. 'Kiss me now! Please!'

Instead of moving towards her, he clenched his fists, his arm and shoulder muscles bulging. 'In a gown covered with diamonds and wearing a tiara? You might as well be carrying a placard saying, "Prohibited. Trespassers will be prosecuted."'

'They aren't diamonds. They're crystals.' There was a sob in her throat. 'As for this...' She ripped the tiara from her hair and tossed it on the bed on top of his jacket.

Her action unleashed a raging desire, which until now in their romance he had struggled to keep tightly checked. Moving so swiftly that she had no time to catch her breath, he pulled her into his arms, his mouth coming down violently on hers.

They had kissed passionately before, but never like this, with all restraint gone.

With a low moan she dug her fingers deep into the coarseness of his still-damp curls, her tongue sliding past his, her entire body ablaze with the need to be made love to.

And it was going to happen.

As she felt the urgent hardness of his body against hers, she knew it was going to happen – and she wanted it to happen. She wanted to lose her virginity there and then, more than she had ever wanted anything else, ever. The bed was a bare two feet away. The door was closed. No one would walk in on them. The occupants of the other rooms in the part of the house they were in were all on duty, anticipating the imminent arrival of 300 distinguished guests.

As Hal swung her up in his arms and turned with her towards the bed, she had a cataclysmic vision of her father standing without her at the head of the grand staircase. How would he explain her absence to her mother's family and his political friends? Even worse, what if she wasn't beside him when her royal guests arrived? She would be the talk of the Season, and her father's bewilderment would be total, his humiliation and bitter disappointment all-consuming.

Though she was aching with longing, desperate with every fibre of her being to take advantage of the little room and its neatly made bed, she knew she couldn't do so. Never in her life had her father embarrassed her, and he didn't deserve that she should embarrass him.

'Put me down, Hal!'

He sucked in his breath, took one look at the urgency in her eyes and abruptly did as she'd demanded.

For a brief, delicious second the flat of her palms pressed hard against his naked chest and then she spun away from him. How long had she been away from the dining room? Had the family dinner already ended, and were the ball guests already beginning to arrive?

As she snatched her tiara from the bed he said tautly, 'What the heck's the matter, Thea?'

'My guests!' She ran to the door. 'They'll be

here any minute and I have to greet them. For me not to do so would be just too shaming for Papa. I simply can't do that to him.'

'Then why did you run the risk of it? Why did you have to find me?'

She tugged the door open, saying in swift haste, 'I came to tell you not to go down to the ball-room. There's no need. I can tell you everything you need to know about the ball. Papa wasn't thinking of how uncomfortable you'll feel...'

He frowned, tilting his head questioningly to one side. 'Uncomfortable?'

'Not having the right clothes. Not knowing the correct etiquette. Oh God, I must go, Hal! If I'm not there when Prince Edward arrives, the world will cave in!' And she fled down the corridor as if the hounds of hell were at her heels.

He didn't move.

He heard her reach the end of the corridor; heard her begin to run down the stairs. A few seconds later there came the faint sound of a door opening and then rocking shut. And then nothing.

Still he didn't move. He couldn't move.

In just a few words she had ended everything there had ever been between them. Because Thea had said that she would – and could – move from her world into his, he had allowed himself to believe her. Where her politics were concerned she was, he knew, sincere. But it wasn't enough. When the chips were down, she cared too much for things he didn't care about at all. Things like having the right clothes and knowing the correct etiquette. And instead of being uncaring at the thought of him standing out like a sore thumb among her high-and-mighty guests, she had been horrified by it. So horrified that she had ordered him not to make his scheduled appearance in the ballroom.

He breathed in hard, knowing that both of them had been fools ever to think the class gulf between them could be bridged. Seeing her in her family's London town house – a house so palatial it possessed a full-sized ballroom – had slammed the realization home, even before she had burst in on him looking like a vision from a royal fairy tale.

In all their years of being first childhood friends and then secret sweethearts, he had never seen her dressed up – as common sense told him she would be dressed – for high society. He had only ever seen her in and around Outhwaite, where the clothes she wore were country clothes, barely distinguishable from those Carrie wore. The sight of her in a sumptuous ballgown and wearing a tiara as if it were a crown had robbed him of breath, first because she had looked so jaw-droppingly beautiful, and second because it had shown him that left-wing politics alone could never remove her from the class into which she had been born.

Whatever had been between them was over. Pain sliced into his heart as deeply as a knife wound. He gritted his teeth; he would get over her. There would be other girls. No doubt there would be lots of other girls.

And he was going to take no notice of her demand that he steer clear of the ballroom. He hadn't wanted the assignment he had been given, but by God, now that he was here, he was going to carry it out.

He stepped grim-faced towards the door and lifted down the formal evening clothes that had been left for him to change into.

Thirty minutes later, wearing a black tailcoat, black trousers, a stiffly starched dress-shirt and collar, a low-cut white waistcoat, a white bow-tie that he'd had a difficult battle with, black patent shoes and white kid gloves, he strolled into the flower-filled ballroom looking every inch a member of the class he so despised.

Chapter Nine

With spiralling excitement, Rozalind looked around the crowded ballroom. Her dance card was almost full. The hired swing orchestra was playing a foxtrot. The Duke and Duchess of York had arrived. Soon the Prince of Wales would be making his entrance. He would be duty-bound to dance with Thea, but might he also dance with her? She remembered Violet's remark about her height and for the first time in her life found herself wishing she was a petite five foot two, instead of a willowy five foot eight.

'The next dance is mine, I believe,' a chinless young man said affably, breaking into her thoughts.

He was Barty Luddesdon, eldest son of the 2nd

Marquess of Colesby, and someone with whom she had been partnered in a jolly treasure hunt at a party she had attended with Thea only a few days ago. He was not someone she would ever wish to be romantically involved with, but he was nice and knew enough about her passion – photography – to be able to talk intelligently about it.

'Why, so it is,' she said with a wide smile. She looked down at her dance card. 'And it's a quickstep, Barty. What fun!'

As the orchestra struck up with a fast-paced, upbeat melody, she said teasingly, 'I hope you're going to be up to all the syncopations, Barty. The quickstep has been a craze in New York far longer than it's been a craze here, and I'm pretty much an expert at it.'

'Don't you worry your pretty little head,' Barty said comfortably. 'They don't call me fast-as-greased-lightning-Luddesdon for nothing.' And he proved it by leading her off into a whole series of hops and runs that had her giggling in delight.

The next dance was a waltz and this time her partner wasn't so congenial. Rozalind made up for it by letting her attention drift, looking over his shoulder as they circled the room, trying to see if she could spot Thea.

She couldn't, but she did see a dreamy-eyed Olivia dancing with a blond-haired, blond-moustached Nordic-looking young man. As Olivia's seventeenth birthday wasn't for another few weeks, Rozalind was amused by how much Olivia was being allowed to get away with. Violet, of course, wasn't being allowed to dance with anyone other than close family members – and as she had no brothers or male cousins, this meant she was restricted to dancing only with her father and a handful of middle-aged and distantly related uncles.

As the waltz came to an end Rozalind wondered whether, if her stepbrother had been with her in London, he would have counted as close enough family for Violet to have danced with him. Kyle was twenty-two, head-turningly handsome and had just been accepted as a junior Foreign Service officer in the US Department of State in Washington. As children, even though Kyle had lived with his mother (her stepfather's first wife) in Illinois, they had still seen each other pretty regularly, for every school vacation he had visited his father in New York for at least a couple of days. He had never, though, been to England with her, and the Fentons, who were no blood relation to him, had never been of any interest to him, or he to them.

Lately, though, Rozalind had noticed Kyle begin asking questions about her uncle's political life in the House of Lords. 'It's a strange set-up, don't you think?' he had said the last time they had met. 'Members sitting in a second chamber by virtue of hereditary right?'

'It isn't something I've ever thought about,' she'd said. 'Come with me next time I visit England and talk it over with my uncle. I'd like you to meet my English family. They mean a lot to me.'

So far he hadn't made the trip, but that didn't mean he wouldn't one day do so. As she con-

139

tinued trying to avoid her partner's feet, she became aware of a frisson of excitement running through the ballroom.

'I think Prince Edward may have arrived,' she said, fascinated at the effect the prince had on even the most blue-blooded of the aristocracy.

'Does he have the adorable Mrs Dudley Ward with him?' her dancing partner asked, showing a rare spark of animation.

'I don't know. I haven't caught sight of him yet.' She turned her head as far to the left as their dance-hold would permit and, though she caught sight of someone who, from the back, looked remarkably like Hal (though as he was wearing a tailcoat it obviously wasn't Hal), she couldn't see the Prince.

'Freda's rather a corker. I'm not surprised HRH is smitten with her.'

Rozalind would have liked to have heard some more about Prince Edward's mistress, but the waltz came to an end and they dutifully parted company.

'There you are!' Olivia rushed up to her. 'Prince Edward has arrived! Do come and be presented.'

As Olivia seized hold of her hand, Rozalind went with her willingly, determined to make an impression on the future King of England and to dazzle as she had never dazzled before. He was standing with his equerry in the centre of a small group of people and there was no diminutive 'corker' anywhere in sight. Her uncle was to one side of him, Thea to the other.

'Remember your curtsey,' Olivia said as they approached. 'Left leg well back behind the right, back straight. No wobbling.'

Seconds later, praying for balance, Rozalind sank into a deep curtsey. Her first impression of the Prince was that although he was slightly built, he was handsome in the way that fairytale princes in storybooks were handsome. His pale-blond hair was slickly straight and glassily shiny. His eyes were a stunning azure-blue. Although he was thirty, he radiated boyish charm – a charm that won her over immediately.

As he asked which part of America she was from, Rozalind's uppermost thought was of how much she longed to photograph him.

'New York, sir,' she said, wondering if her Uncle Gilbert would make such a request for her; wondering what the protocol would be.

'That's splendid!' He looked genuinely de-lighted. 'I shall be in Canada in a couple of months' time, visiting a ranch I own in Alberta. I intend making a holiday of things and going from there to New York, staying with friends on Long Island in order to play polo and watch some of the international matches between Britain and America.'

He didn't turn away from her or give any indi-cation that their conversation was now at an end, and Rozalind was unsure what was expected of her. Uncle Gilbert had primed her on how she was to act when presented. 'Never, ever initiate any conversation,' he had said. 'It simply isn't done.'

'Not even for an American?' she'd asked mis-chievously.

'*Especially* for an American,' he'd said firmly.

141

Prince Edward, however, was obviously waiting for some kind of chatty response from her – and responding in a conversation wasn't the same as initiating a conversation. Remembering the almost hysterical welcome New York had given him when he had visited it four years before, she said in her naturally friendly manner, 'New Yorkers love you, sir. When you make your visit you will be given a wonderful welcome.'

She was aware of some quick intakes of breath – though not from the Prince.

He gave her a broad smile. 'Thank you, Miss Duveen. Where your fellow New Yorkers are concerned, it's a sentiment I fully reciprocate.'

This time the intonation in his voice told her that their conversation had come to a close – though Rozalind felt he had brought it to a close a little regretfully. Seconds later he was carrying out his duty dance with Thea.

'You spoke far too familiarly, Rozalind,' Gilbert said, looking unhappy. 'There was no need for you to make any comment. Especially not one about New Yorkers loving him!'

'Don't worry, Lord Fenton.' The military-looking equerry was unperturbed. 'Prince Edward won't. He likes Americans and finds their natural informality refreshing.'

Gilbert made a noise that indicated he wasn't convinced and Rozalind said, hastily changing the subject, 'Is Hal here, Uncle Gilbert? I can't see him anywhere.'

'He's here, Rozalind, but don't go seeking him out unnecessarily. Let him get on with the job he's here to do.'

142

He turned to say something further to the equerry and Olivia said to her in a whisper, 'I saw Hal a few minutes ago. He was out on the balcony, smoking a cigarette and talking to the chinless wonder you danced the quickstep with.'

'Barty Luddesdon? Why on earth would Hal be talking with Barty?' Another thought followed almost instantaneously. 'And how do you know the two of them are out on the balcony? Who were you out there with?'

Olivia blushed. 'Someone you don't know.' She flashed a glance towards her father, but he was deep in conversation with the equerry, his back now turned to them. 'I've just made my mind up about something very important, Roz.'

'And what's that?'

'I want to go to finishing school. I want to go to one in Germany; Berlin, to be precise.'

'Why on earth–?'

It was a sentence she never finished.

'My dance, I believe,' the brother of one of Thea's fellow debutantes said, having finally run her to earth. 'It may be half-over, but better late than never, what?'

Hiding her irritation, Rozalind smiled graciously. 'Swell! And it's a tango. Perhaps I should put a rose between my teeth?'

As they danced she did her best to catch a glimpse of Barty and Hal through the long windows giving out onto the balcony, but if they had been there a little while ago, they were there no longer. She wondered if Thea had managed to have a few words with Hal yet, and if Hal was the reason Thea had so suddenly and inexplicably

143

left the dining table earlier in the evening.

A giant red-and-white-striped marquee had been erected in the garden to act as a supper room, and it wasn't until Roz was in there, enjoying *chaud-froids* with truffle designs on them, that she again caught sight of Thea.

She weaved her way towards her through a throng of tiara-headed debutantes. 'This is a terrific coming-out ball, Thea. Having been presented to the Prince of Wales and having chatted with the Duke and Duchess of York, I'm now a fully committed, diehard royalist.'

Thea giggled, a near-empty glass of champagne in her hand. 'No, you're not. You're a dyed-in-the-wool Republican. Prince Edward is pretty dishy, though, isn't he? And the Yorks are sweethearts. The Duchess is only twenty-four, which isn't too much older than us. There's something very maternal about her. She spent ages chatting to Violet, and the Duke danced with her.'

'With whom? Violet?'

'The very one. Papa could hardly veto her dancing with royalty. He's sent her off to bed now. Two o'clock was curfew time for her – which is perhaps a good thing. Without it, we'd have run the risk of seeing her dancing with Prince Edward.' She drained the contents of her glass and placed it on a tray being carried by a passing waiter. 'I spoke to Hal before the guests arrived. He hasn't come into the ballroom because I told him there was no need. He can write his article without enduring something he would hate and being mortified into the bargain.'

'I don't know what you mean about being

mortified.' Rozalind wondered if Thea had drunk a little too much champagne. 'You're mistaken, though, in thinking he hasn't been in the ballroom. A couple of hours ago he was on the balcony with Barty Luddesdon. Olivia saw them together, talking.'

'She can't have done.'

Thea was emphatic, but then, as Rozalind knew from long experience, whenever Thea gave an opinion she nearly always was.

Rozalind shrugged, not finding the subject important enough to argue over, saying, 'If Barty has been in conversation with a socialist Yorkshireman this evening, it's an experience he'll have remembered. He's down on my card for another dance. A Charleston. I guess dancing it and talking at the same time won't be easy, but I'll give it a shot.'

She changed the subject to one she thought far more important. 'What are my chances of dancing with the Prince of Wales? Would your father dropping the suggestion in his equerry's ear do the trick?'

Thea gave a rude snort. 'Of course it wouldn't. I doubt Edward takes the slightest notice of his equerries. They are just there for form's sake. He dances with whomever he wants to dance with – and if he'd wanted to dance with you, he would have.' She changed the subject without pausing for breath. 'I'm off to have a word with Olivia. Saying she saw Hal when she didn't is just causing mischief.'

Rozalind didn't see what mischief could possibly be caused, but Thea's barb that Prince Edward would have already danced with her if he had wanted to had annoyed her. 'I thought I caught a glimpse of Hal earlier on,' she said. 'Only from the back, and he was wearing tails.'

'Tails?' Thea shot her a glance of blank astonishment and then, without another word, headed out of the marquee, weaving through the crush as fast as she possibly could.

Was that what she had felt behind her, on the back of the visiting valet's bedroom door? Had it been a set of evening clothes for Hal to change into? Now that supper was being served, the lamplit garden was nearly as full of people picnicking on quail's eggs, lobster and hothouse peaches as the marquee was. Instinct told her that this wasn't where she was going to find Hal. If Olivia and Rozalind were right in thinking they had seen Hal in the ballroom, then that was where he would still be, and with so many people now taking a break from the dancing, if he was there he would be relatively easy to find.

Thea saw him the minute she stepped into the room. He was standing near one of the ballroom's long windows, watching the dancers, most particularly her father, who, with what looked like a great deal of enjoyment, was waltzing with the very vivacious Duchess of York.

As if someone had punched her hard in the chest, she came to a sudden halt, more stunned by the sight of Hal in evening dress and in his present surroundings than she had been a few hours ago when she had walked into the valet's bedroom and seen him barefoot and bare-chested.

He looked so knock-down handsome she could hardly breathe. He also looked completely at ease.

146

Her relief was so vast that her legs felt weak. How could she have thought being at the ball would be a mortifying experience for him? She'd dreaded him being embarrassed – and of being embarrassed for him – but her fear had been groundless.

'Idiot!' she said of herself, full of pride in Hal's easy self-confidence.

With joy in her heart she began skirting the ballroom floor towards him. As she did so the waltz came to an end and her father escorted the former Elizabeth Bowes-Lyon off the floor only yards ahead of her.

While hurrying from the marquee to the ballroom Thea hadn't allowed herself to be waylaid into exchanging so much as a word with anyone, uncaring of how rude she appeared to be. She couldn't, though, be rude to royalty.

'Such a splendid evening,' the Duchess of York said with a smile so sweet that Thea didn't doubt her sincerity. 'I can't remember when I've enjoyed an evening more.'

As the Yorks had stayed at the ball far longer than had been expected – the Prince of Wales and his equerry had left before supper had been served – Thea knew her coming-out ball could be counted a huge success.

'Your sister, Violet, has utterly charmed Bertie.'

There was a gurgle of laughter in the Duchess's voice and Thea felt a rush of warmth towards her. She was someone it would be easy to become deeply fond of. She was also clearly bubbling over with the desire to have a friendly chat.

'The Duke and I have just moved out of White

Lodge and into Chesterfield House for the summer,' she said, as if a temporary move from White Lodge, Richmond Park, to Chesterfield House, Mayfair, was the most exciting thing in the world. 'We are having our first party there in a week's time. Do come. It's going to be such fun. Fred Astaire and his sister will be there. Don't you love the prospect of dancing with Fred?'

Thea did, and although she was impatient for the conversation to come to a close so that she could be with Hal for a little while, and so that they could arrange which cafe they were to meet in before he caught his train back to Yorkshire, she was very much aware that in ignoring the six-year age difference between them Elizabeth was paying her a great compliment.

Elizabeth went on to chat to her about York-shire, saying she was unfamiliar with the area around Outhwaite, but that she had heard it was very beautiful. By the time their conversation came to a close, Hal was nowhere to be seen.

It was now after three o'clock in the morning and, with the end of the ball almost in sight, the orchestra was letting rip with non-stop ragtime. As it was her ball, Thea knew she should have been dancing the Shimmy, the Jog Trot and the Twinkle with the same abandon as her guests, but she wasn't interested in dancing; she was only inter-ested in spending a few moments of closeness with Hal.

Chaperones, some of whom had spent most of the evening in a bridge room set aside for them, were now filtering back into the ballroom, preparatory to shepherding their charges home. In less than an hour the ball would be over, and Thea couldn't bear the thought of it finishing before she and Hal had spent at least a few minutes together.

Her search of the ballroom was fruitless and she went back down to the garden and the marquee. There was no sign of Hal there – and no sign of Barty Luddesdon, either.

She bit her lip. Had Hal already called it a night and gone to bed? The blood drummed in her ears at the possibility of making a second trip beyond the green baize door and up into the attics. She thought of the risks and knew that at this time in the morning they would be overwhelming.

Fighting temptation, she went back into the house and stood in the grand entrance hall, torn by indecision. Some people were already leaving, and mechanically she accepted their goodbyes. Everyone, it seemed, agreed that the ball had been 'ripping fun' and 'absolutely blissy'.

Suddenly Barty Luddesdon hove into view. He was wearing an evening cape and carrying his top hat and was quite obviously about to take his leave.

She waylaid him, saying urgently, 'Roz said you were talking with Mr Crosby earlier. Do you know where he is now, Barty? I very much need to see him.'

He gave her an attractive lopsided smile. 'As I've promised to give him a lift, I'm hopeful he's outside, waiting for me.'

'A lift? Where to? It's the middle of the night!'

'It's nearer to four o'clock than to three.' His voice was thick with amusement. 'And Mr Crosby wishes to catch the first milk-train north from King's Cross.'

'But he can't!' Thea was both bewildered and appalled. Until now she had taken it for granted that the two of them would be meeting up somewhere, such as a park or a cafe, before he returned to Richmond. Never in her wildest dreams had she imagined he would be returning to Yorkshire without taking the opportunity to spend some time alone with her.

'You'll need a wrap,' Barty said, accompanying her across the hall and towards the front door.

Thea ignored him, just as she then ignored Broadbent, who was speaking to the footman on duty at the door, and whose eyes widened in concern as he saw her intention of leaving the house before the ball had officially ended, with no evening wrap or shawl and in the company of the Marquess of Colesby's eldest son.

Broadbent's concern was of no interest to Thea, for as the door opened she saw a long line of chauffeured motor cars waiting in the gas-lit street – and Hal, leaning against the bonnet of an open-topped Sunbeam sports car.

Leaving Barty settling his top hat comfortably on his head, she ran down the shallow flight of steps and across the pavement.

Hal stood up straight, but didn't stride forward to meet her and didn't open his arms for her to run into them.

With deepening bewilderment Thea came to a sudden halt in front of him. 'What's going on, Hal?' He was no longer wearing evening clothes. The jacket he was wearing was the well-worn one she had seen on the bed. 'Why are you leaving now, when Papa has set aside a room for you and we can spend all of this morning, and perhaps most of the afternoon, together? I'd planned a walk in Hyde Park and then lunch at the Marble Arch Lyons Corner House.'

She was being her usual bossy self, but Hal didn't feel irritated. He felt unspeakable pain that not only would he not be falling in with the plans she had made for them in a few hours' time, but he would never be falling in with any of her plans ever again.

He spoke tautly, knowing there was no easy way of doing what needed to be done. 'There's going to be no Hyde Park and no Lyons Corner House, Thea. Whatever there has been between us has come to an end.'

She stared at him in incredulity. 'I'm sorry, Hal. I don't think I heard you properly. For one silly moment I thought you said everything between us has come to an end. Come back into the house, darling. Taking the milk-train is silly. We can both get a few hours' sleep and then go into the park, and perhaps take a boat out on the lake.'

He shook his head. 'You didn't mishear me, Thea, and I'm not teasing. Tonight has shown me I've been a fool thinking that, for us, class doesn't matter. It does.'

'Of course it doesn't!' At the realization that Hal was only fretting about something that didn't bother her in the slightest, she felt wild with relief. 'If I looked to be smiling and happy tonight, it was only for Papa's sake.' She hugged his arm. 'I couldn't care less about balls like tonight's, and

151

being a debutante and wearing a tiara. None of it matters to me.'

He shook his head. 'Some things matter to you, Thea love. I know, because you told me they did only a few hours ago.'

There was something odd in his voice; something she had never heard before. She let go of his arm, terrified by his lack of physical response, suddenly feeling as if she was standing on the edge of a precipice.

'What did I tell you?'

She tried to think of their last conversation, but couldn't get her mind into gear. It was too frozen with fear.

Fighting the temptation to take her in his arms, Hal dug his fists deep into his trouser pockets, certain that for both their sakes the decision he had come to was the right one.

'You told me not to go down into the ballroom because I hadn't – you thought – the correct clothes, and because I didn't know the correct etiquette. You said it would make me feel uncomfortable, but what you really meant was that it would make *you* uncomfortable, because although you say those things aren't important to you Thea, they are. I'm never going to be able to fit into your world – because I sure as heck don't want to – and you're never going to fit into mine, no matter how hard you try.'

He looked beyond her, to where Barty was standing a few discreet yards away. 'Does the offer of a lift still stand?' he asked, a rasp in his voice, as if he was about to come down with a cold.

As Barty nodded and walked up to the car,

Thea felt as if she was in a horrendous nightmare. How could what was happening be real? How could a few carelessly spoken words have had such a catastrophic effect? Hal *had* to stay in love with her. He was all she had ever wanted. All she ever would want.

Barty began cranking the Sunbeam's starting handle, and Thea said with hysteria in her throat, 'You can't mean what you've said, Hal! It's too monstrous! We're supposed to be battling against class and snobbery, not allowing them to ruin our lives!'

The Sunbeam spluttered into life. Barty opened the low-slung driver's door and got behind the wheel. Hal walked round to the other side of the car, a pulse throbbing at the corner of his implacably set jaw.

Thea knew what that pounding pulse signified. She had seen it before, but never in relation to herself. It meant that his mind was made up about something and that no power on Earth was going to make him change it. As a child he'd vowed that he was never going to follow in his father's footsteps as a tenant farmer. Later he'd vowed that, against all the odds, he would get himself an education. Later still he had set himself the goal of becoming a journalist on the *Richmond Times*. Once his mind had been made up he had never deviated from the decision he'd taken and, feeling despair so deep it threatened to choke her, she knew he wasn't going to deviate from his decision now.

It had started to rain. Hal opened the passenger-seat door and slid into the seat beside Barty, his

153

dark curls tightening into damp corkscrews. Noisily Barty put the Sunbeam into gear.

'Hal!' she shouted as the car began pulling away. *'Hal!'*

He didn't turn his head and the Sunbeam didn't come to a halt. Instead it rounded a rain-slicked corner into Park Lane and vanished into the darkness.

Thea swayed slightly. It was over. In telling Hal not to go down into the ballroom, believing she would be saving him from embarrassment and humiliation, she had destroyed her happiness with her own stupid, careless hands. And it had all been for nothing. Hal had been neither embarrassed nor humiliated, and she had been the world's biggest fool ever to have imagined he could be.

Tears of anger and loss spilled down her cheeks. The anger was with herself, for being so thoughtlessly foolish; and with Hal, for having reacted as he had. The pain she felt was unspeakable. How could she live with it? How could she possible survive it?

'Come along, honey.' The deeply concerned voice was Rozalind's. 'People are watching.' She tilted an umbrella so that it sheltered them both. 'Whatever your quarrel with Hal, it sure looked like a humdinger.'

They turned to face the house, and Thea drew in a deep, shuddering breath.

'We love each other, Roz.' It was the first time she had admitted it to anyone, and the circumstances under which she was doing so hurt like a knife wound. 'We love each other, and he won't fight to make things possible for us. He thinks that now he's broken things off, I'll forget about having a social conscience, and that by the end of the Season I'll be engaged to someone who, if he hasn't already inherited a stately home and thousands of acres, will one day.'

The belief that Hal thought her so shallow made her feel sick with rage.

Fiercely she brushed her tears away. 'And he's wrong, Roz.' There was steel in her voice. 'He's wrong about everything. I've gone along with to-night for Papa's sake, but here it ends. I'm not going to live a life that revolves brainlessly around the social Season. It would bore me to tears.'

Rozalind quirked a sleek eyebrow, genuinely interested. 'Then what are you going to do?'

As the departing guests streamed past them on the porticoed steps, Thea came to an abrupt halt. 'I don't know, Roz. Not yet.'

She stood quite still amid a sea of jostling umbrellas. She was intelligent and articulate; there were surely a hundred and one things she could do that would make a difference to the world.

Gritty determination flooded through every vein in her body. With absolute certainty she knew that she was going to do something exceptional with her life; something absolutely extraordinary. She knew something else as well.

One day she would get Hal back – and, when she did, he would be hers forever.

Chapter Ten

SEPTEMBER 1924

It was a blissfully warm afternoon and Carrie and Olivia were seated in deep grass close to the vole place on the river-bank. Although Olivia had been at Gorton Hall with her father and Violet for the last fortnight, it was the first time within those two weeks that Carrie had had a full day off and had been able to meet up with her, and it was the first time they had met since before Thea's coming-out ball.

Hungry for gossip, Carrie said impatiently, 'I want to hear absolutely *everything*, Olivia.'

Olivia took off her lavishly flower-decorated straw hat and sent it spinning into the grass. 'What do you want to know first?'

'I want to know who Thea danced with. Who you danced with. Who the Prince of Wales danced with. What the Duchess of York wore. If Hal was able to dance with anyone. If—'

'All right. All right. I get the picture.' Deciding to keep her most momentous news until last, Olivia said, hugging her knees, 'Let's start with Thea. She danced with everyone. Or, rather, she should have danced with everyone, but she seemed to get bored with dancing once supper had started. After that I only caught a couple of fleeting glimpses of her, and neither time was she dancing. As for whom I danced with...'Try as she might she couldn't hide the excitement she was feeling. 'I'll tell you all about my knight on a white charger in a minute, but before you ask, he wasn't the Prince of Wales. He was much, much taller. And no, the Prince of Wales didn't dance with me.'

'But he did dance with Thea, didn't he?' There was anxiety in Carrie's voice, for she knew that if Prince Edward hadn't danced with her, Thea would have been devastated.

'He did. They foxtrotted, and Thea seemed to simply float around the ballroom, but that's because Prince Edward is such a superb dancer it would have been impossible for her not to have looked as if she were floating. She didn't scoop all the royal honours, though. The Duke of York danced with me, and with Papa's permission he danced with Violet.'

'With Violet?' Carrie was enraptured at the thought of Violet, who wasn't sixteen until September, dancing around a London ballroom in the arms of a royal duke. 'What about Rozalind? Who did she dance with?'

'Goodness, Carrie, I don't know! I was too busy dancing myself to notice.'

Carrie's face fell and Olivia said contritely, 'I did see her dance a quickstep with Barty Luddesdon.' And then, because Carrie couldn't be expected to know who he was, she added, 'He's the Marquess of Colesby's eldest son.'

Carrie sucked in her breath. 'So he's an earl? Oh, wouldn't it be wonderful if Roz was to fall in love with him? What is his title, Olivia? What is he the earl of?'

'He's the Earl of Bicester. It's a courtesy title.'

'But if they fell in love and married, Roz would be a countess?'

At the thought of her American cousin becoming a countess and one day a marchioness, Olivia giggled. 'Yes, she would. But it's not likely to happen, Carrie. They only danced together, for goodness' sake. One dance doesn't mean an engagement.'

'Maybe not, but all engagements have to begin somewhere.'

Olivia shrugged, too engrossed in her own fast-burgeoning love life to be interested in Rozalind's. 'Roz will marry an American billionaire, not an impoverished English earl.'

'Is Barty Luddesdon poor?' Carrie was all concern.

'In comparison to an American billionaire he is, but not in any other way.' She tilted her head a little to one side, regarding Carrie with amusement and deep affection. 'Why on earth are you still wearing your boater, Carrie? And why is it so drab? Give it to me and I'll liven it up for you.'

With her mind still on Thea's coming-out ball, Carrie handed over a boater trimmed only with a narrow band of serviceable burgundy braid. 'What about Hal?' she asked. 'I've only seen him once since June, and I couldn't get him to tell me anything. Is that because it was all very horrid for him?'

The tall grass around them was thick with buttercups and Olivia plucked one and began weaving its stem in and out of the burgundy

158

braid. 'It wasn't horrid for him at all. He had a wonderful time. He wore white tie and tails. Can you imagine Hal in white tie and tails? The most amazing thing was that he didn't look at all uncomfortable in them. Looking at him, you would never have known he was a working-class Yorkshireman who had never before set foot in a London town house, let alone a ballroom.'

'And did he dance?' With all her heart Carrie wished she had been able to see Hal in white tie and tails, looking no different from all the great and grand people he must have been surrounded by.

'Goose! Of course he didn't dance. For one thing, how could he? I don't suppose Hal can even waltz. And he wasn't there as a guest. Papa had only arranged the white tie and tails for him so that he wouldn't stand out like a sore thumb.' She held the boater aloft. 'I think the buttercups should go all the way round it, don't you?'

Carrie didn't answer her. She still had her mind on other things. 'Why didn't Thea return to Gorton with you and your father and Violet? The Season is more or less over now, isn't it? Who is chaperoning her?'

Olivia picked another buttercup and began threading it through the braid on the boater. 'The same person who presented her at court, Aunt Hilda, my mother's cousin. I don't think Aunt Hilda is very happy about it. She thought she'd be back in the Welsh Borders by now, but Papa has estate matters to attend to here and, as Thea didn't want to come back to Yorkshire, what else could the poor woman do but stay on in London with her?'

At the thought of Thea not wanting to come back to Yorkshire, a frown puckered Carrie's forehead. She had taken it for granted that, after spending all summer in London, Thea would be eager to return to the Dales and Gorton Hall. If she had been Thea, she knew she would have been.

Reading her thoughts, Olivia said darkly, 'You'd hardly know Thea these days, Carrie. She's become unbearable. She bites people's heads off for the slightest thing. Roz says it's because she's had a row with Hal, though if Roz knows what the row was over, she isn't telling – and Thea isn't, either. I always thought sisters were supposed to confide in each other, but Thea barely speaks to me these days. I can only imagine that, now she's "out" and I'm not, she thinks I don't count.'

'Oh, I'm sure that's not true, Olivia.' Carrie was accustomed to smoothing the stormy waters that often arose between Thea and Olivia and she said placatingly, 'Thea is just being Thea. A first London Season must be so exciting for her, and I don't suppose she's realized that, now she's going to things you aren't invited to, it means she isn't speaking to you very much.'

Olivia didn't look convinced, but neither did she look too unhappy about it. As she handed Carrie the buttercup-bedecked boater, her cheeks were flushed and her eyes glowed. 'I've got something to tell you, Carrie. Thea already knows part of it, but she doesn't know the whole of it. No one does. You will be the first person I've told – and the only person I'm going to tell.'

Carrie put the boater on top of her wheat-gold hair. It was coiled into a bun at the nape of her neck – the only style allowed for servants at Monkswood. Despite the addition of the butter-cups, in comparison to Olivia – who hadn't followed fashion by cropping her hair, and whose mahogany-red mane was worn carelessly loose – Carrie looked very prim and proper.

She looked even more prim and proper as she said in alarm, 'You haven't let someone kiss you, have you?'

'I most certainly have – and it was wonderful, Carrie. Absolutely blissful!' Olivia hugged her knees even tighter to her chest. 'He's German. His name is Dieter von Starhemberg, and he's a count and a junior diplomat in the German Foreign Office. As soon as he saw me at Thea's coming-out ball he asked me to dance, and he would have scored out every other name on my dance card and danced with me the whole night long, if it wasn't that it would have attracted Papa's attention.'

Carrie didn't know whether to be filled with admiration or alarm. Some of the maids at Monkswood, who were no older than Olivia, had followers and thought nothing of being kissed, but that Olivia had behaved as a Monkswood kitchen maid or housemaid had behaved astounded her.

'Does Count von Starhemberg live in London?' she asked apprehensively. 'And is he very old? He sounds old.'

'Of course he's not old!' Olivia was outraged at the very thought. 'He's twenty-one. And he doesn't live in London. He lives in Berlin.'

161

Carrie's relief was vast. 'Then how come he was one of Thea's guests?'

'Strictly speaking, he wasn't. Thea doesn't know him from Adam. Dieter's father and Papa went to Eton together, and when Dieter's father told Papa that Dieter was in London in June, it was Papa who invited him.'

Carrie was wondering what Viscount Fenton would say and do if he was ever to find out the liberties that his friend's son had taken with Olivia, when Olivia said, 'And that's not the part of things that Thea knows. What Thea knows is that I'm going to finishing school.'

Grateful that Olivia had apparently changed the subject, and not unduly surprised by the news – the majority of girls of Olivia's class and age spent a year at a finishing school – Carrie said with interest, 'One of Lady Markham's daughters is at a finishing school in Switzerland. Is that where you are going?'

Olivia unclasped her hands from around her knees and stretched her arms rapturously high above her head. 'No!' she said gleefully. 'I'm going to Berlin, Carrie! And when I'm there I'll be able to see Dieter all the time!'

Later, when a very unhappy Carrie had set off back to Richmond by bus, Olivia was still just as euphoric. Carrie hadn't thought the Berlin finishing school a good idea at all, but as Olivia took the shortcut across the fields to Gorton, she shrugged away Carrie's concerns. Carrie was a village girl and couldn't be expected to understand the kind of sophisticated London world

162

that she and Thea now spent so much time in. That Carrie had actually asked if Hal had danced with anyone at Thea's coming-out ball showed how innocent she was.

Not for the first time over the last few weeks, Olivia thanked her lucky stars that her father had decided against a shared coming-out ball for herself and Thea. As her seventeenth birthday had been in August, it had been a distinct possibility, but it hadn't been something either she or Thea had wanted. Olivia having now asked if she could go to finishing school to fill in the time until next year when she, too, would be presented at court seemed highly sensible, whereas if she had already been presented it would have seemed very odd indeed.

'Hey up!' a familiar voice shouted to her from the nearby lane. 'Do you want a ride?'

'Yes please, Jim,' she shouted, beginning to run across the field to the spot where he had brought his horse and cart to a stop.

'Gracious!' She climbed up beside him, out of breath. 'This isn't as comfortable as the pony-trap – and even pony-traps are old-fashioned these days.'

'They mebbe old-fashioned in London, but they'll never be old-fashioned in Yorkshire.' He pushed a battered flat cap to the back of hair that was still as thick, dark and unruly as his nephew's, saying as he clicked the reins and the horse moved off at a steady pace, 'Have you seen much of our Hal lately?'

'Not for ages, Jim. This is my first time back in Yorkshire since Easter.'

'Aye, I know that. I meant when Hal was jaunting down in London at Thea's big do.'

'I saw him, but every time I did I was dancing with someone, so I didn't get a chance to speak with him.'

She didn't like to add that from the moment Dieter had asked her to dance she'd had no thoughts for anyone else.

Jim thought over what she had said and decided there was no point in pursuing it. 'And are you at Gorton now until Christmas?'

'Good heavens, no!' Excitement bubbled up in her throat as she thought of where she was going to be – not only until Christmas, but, if she had her way, for a long time afterwards. Perhaps forever after. 'In two weeks' time I'm going to a finishing school in Germany.'

'Germany?' She now had Jim's complete attention. 'That's a bit of a rum choice, Olivia lass.'

'No, it isn't.' She was immediately defensive. 'English girls have been going to German finishing schools ever since Queen Victoria's day.'

'Mebbe they have, but I don't reckon they've been going there since 1914. The war has only bin over six years – and I still think it's a rum choice.'

'Papa doesn't. He speaks very good German and he's pleased I want to be able to speak it. He thinks it very important that Britain and Germany are on good terms with each other, so that something as appalling as the Great War never happens again.'

Jim cracked with mirthless laughter. 'I doubt that little fella, 'itler, is too worried about being on good terms wi' Britain. Seems to me 'e's a bloke who doesn't want to be on good terms wi' anyone. You just be careful of yourself in Kraut-land. They're 'aving a bad time of it over there. Food shortages. Unemployment. Inflation. It isn't anywhere I'd care to be.'

Olivia tried to think of a crushing reply, but couldn't. All she knew of Hitler was that he was an Austrian corporal recently imprisoned for having led a failed uprising against the German government – and she only remembered that much because he and his followers had occupied a beer hall in Munich, and she found the connection between a beer hall and an uprising droll.

As for food shortages and unemployment... Berlin was a capital city and surely too sophisti-cated and glamorous to be troubled by anything as horrid as that. The word 'inflation' was a little more troubling as she wasn't sure what it meant – and she was furious that someone as un-educated as Jim did. Perhaps it was a word he'd picked up from Hal. It sounded like a word Hal might use when he was on his socialist hobby-horse.

'Charlie's perked up since Miss C's bin back,' Jim said, knowing he'd put her in a huff and offer-ing her a way out of it by changing the subject. 'I saw 'im in t' veg garden this morning, 'arvesting maincrop spuds and whistling like a young lad.'

'And?' Olivia didn't see the point of the remark.

'And I just wonder 'ow long it's going to be afore 'e plucks up courage and pops t' question.'

'What question?' Olivia was too mystified to re-member that she was cross with him. 'Why would Miss Cumberbatch be interested in potatoes?'

Jim cracked with laughter again, this time with genuine mirth. 'I doubt she is much interested in 'em, but she's interested in Charlie – and 'e's allus bin smitten wi' 'er. The two of 'em just need to get their acts together.'

Olivia stared at him. 'You're not making any sense, Jim. You surely can't mean that Charlie and Miss Cumberbatch are ... are...'

'Sweethearts?' Jim finished obligingly. 'Mebbe not yet, but both of 'em want to be each other's sweetheart. If you 'ad eyes in your 'ead, you'd 'ave seen it ages ago.' He let the reins fall loose and lit a Woodbine. Blowing a plume of acrid-smelling smoke into the air, he said, 'I think they make a right grand couple. When Charlie finally pops t' question, I'm going to ask 'im if I can be 'is best man.'

Olivia's jaw dropped. 'But ... but Hermione Cumberbatch is a governess!' she said, when she'd recovered her power of speech. 'How can she marry a gardener? Especially when ... when...'

Once again words failed her, and again Jim obligingly finished her sentence for her. 'When despite all t' miracles done to 'is face, Charlie's still far from being an oil-painting? His face has never bothered Miss C. Besides, she thinks 'e's an 'ero – and 'e is. It only came out a while back, when a bloke 'e'd served wi' paid 'im a visit and chatted in t' Pig and Whistle, but Charlie received 'is injuries carrying a wounded pal to safety.'

'Oh, Jim! How wonderfully brave of him!'

'Aye, and 'ow typical of 'im never to 'ave said a word.'

Olivia wondered if her father knew – and if Carrie knew. Hal would most certainly know, because Jim would have made sure he did. She said musingly, 'If Miss Cumberbatch was to marry Charlie, I wonder who she would have as her bridesmaids? I've never heard her mention any nieces or god-daughters.'

They had reached Gorton and Jim reined the horse in. 'Daft question that, Olivia lass. She'd 'ave you, Thea and Violet.' Then, at the horrified expression on Olivia's face, he laughed so hard he nearly fell off the cart.

Two weeks later, on a train rattling across northern Germany towards Berlin, Olivia said to her father, 'Why is it, Papa, that when Charlie risked his life in order to save someone else's, he didn't get a medal?'

'Probably because, in the heat of battle, only he and the pal he saved knew about it; or, if other people knew of it, they didn't report it. Even if such an act had been reported, it doesn't follow as night follows day that Charlie would have been recommended for a medal. In the nightmare of a full-scale battle such acts of heroism are un-believably commonplace, especially in a Pals Battalion, which is the kind of battalion Charlie was serving in. It's a pity, though. I can only say that if I'd been his commanding officer, I would have recommended him for a medal.'

She looked out of the train window towards the blue haze of distant mountains and Gilbert said, 'Those are the Harz: the highest mountain range in northern Germany. They are the setting for the fairy tales your mother used to tell you when you were little.'

Her father frequently spoke about her mother, and she loved it when he did so. 'Fairy tales such as "Red Riding Hood" and "Hansel and Gretel"?' she asked, remembering the delicious feeling of being on her mother's knee, the delicate fragrance of her rose perfume and the soft, gentle sound of her voice.

'And "Cinderella", "Sleeping Beauty" and "Tom Thumb".'

Olivia glimpsed a small village half-hidden among a sweeping forest of fir and pine and said, 'I can see why such stories came from this part of Germany. It looks as if it's the home of wicked witches and dwarves digging in caverns under the earth, and poor woodcutters living in lonely cottages. I think it's magical, Papa, and I'm going to love living in Germany. I just know I am.'

A frown furrowed Gilbert's forehead. 'Germany isn't much of a magical place any longer – and you must be prepared for that, Olivia. The financial reparations the country has been paying under the peace treaty have been crippling it, and Germans have been having a very bad time since the end of the war. It's all about to change for the better, though. If it hadn't been about to do so, I wouldn't have allowed you to have your way in coming here.'

'How do you know things are about to change, Papa?'

They were in a private first-class carriage and Gilbert stretched his long legs out in front of him. 'Because of something called the Dawes Plan. A little while ago ten expert financial advisers – two each from the USA, the UK, Italy, Belgium and France – met in committee to find a way of helping Germany restructure its economy to end the hyper-inflation caused by reparation payments. To bring this about, the present scale of payments is being temporarily reduced, American banks are loaning Germany a massive amount of capital and the Reichsbank is being reorganized under Allied supervision. So although things may appear far grimmer in Berlin than you had anticipated, there is no cause for alarm, Olivia. Thanks to the Dawes Plan, they are not going to remain that way.'

Even with Hal, Olivia had never been interested in politics – and she wasn't interested now. It was nice to know, though, that despite Germany's massive problems, the future was bright and there was no real cause for concern.

The train was passing a small town and she looked out of the window at a sea of cobbled streets and pretty half-timbered houses. On a nearby crag a turreted castle was perched, looking as if it had just stepped from the pages of a Grimms' fairy tale. Like so much else she had seen on their journey across Germany, it captured Olivia's imagination, and she was grateful to the men who had sat on the Dawes Plan committee and had put in place plans to stabilize the country's economy. With a passion she was quite unused to feeling, she wanted Germany to be a country in which she could happily live indefinitely; a country in which, if her daydreams about Dieter came true, she could quite possibly find herself living for the rest of her life.

Chapter Eleven

MAY 1925

Rozalind strode up the gangplank of the *Aquitania* with a spring in her step and a large hand-stitched leather camera-case slung over one shoulder. She passionately loved the city that she was yet again leaving behind her, but she also loved crossing the Atlantic to stay in London or Yorkshire – and this time she had something extra to look forward to, for as well as England she was also going to Germany, where, in Berlin, she would be shown around by Olivia.

Though the first-class gangplank was crowded, at five foot eight and wearing lizard-skin shoes with teeteringly high heels, Rozalind was effortlessly turning heads. Her bobbed night-black hair was crowned by a brilliant orange cloche hat, and the light tweed of her Poiret tailored suit – bought nearly a year ago when she had been in Europe for Thea's coming-out ball – was a vivid chartreuse. She exuded youthful vitality and *joie de vivre* and something else as well, for her luxuriant eyelashes were darkly mascaraed and her generously curved, voluptuous mouth was painted a glossy garnet-red.

As she neared the point where a uniformed officer stood at the top of the gangplank, welcoming the wealthy aboard, she was jostled on her left-hand side by a heavily built woman wearing a foxtail cape. As a consequence, Rozalind was thrown off-balance and her camera-case bumped the hip of the gentleman on her right-hand side.

'Sorry,' she said automatically, flashing him an apologetic smile.

'No problem,' he said, smiling in return. He looked down at the offending camera-case and, on seeing the name embossed in the leather, quirked an eyebrow. 'A Leica I? Would you mind my asking how you got hold of one of those so fast? I was at the Leipzig Spring Fair when it was shown for the first time. I didn't know they were on sale yet in the States.'

His accent was that of a cultured Bostonian and, side by side, they moved a few steps nearer the welcoming officer.

'My father read about the Leica I in the *New York Times* and asked my cousin, who lives in Berlin, if she would send me one.'

She looked at him properly for the first time and liked what she saw. Wearing heels, she generally towered over most men, but he was well over six foot tall, which meant she didn't have a bird's-eye view of the top of his head. He was wearing a camel-hair coat with a beaver collar and a homburg. Lightly moustached and broad-shouldered, he looked to be in his late thirties or early forties – which to Rozalind was middle-aged – and, despite deep, humorous lines around an attractively straight mouth, seemed a man accustomed to authority and the use of it.

She was proved right in her assumption a few moments later, for as she stepped away after being courteously and admiringly welcomed aboard, she overheard the officer say, 'It's a pleasure to have you sailing with us again, Congressman Bradley.'

Idly wondering why a US Congressman was making regular trips across the Atlantic and whether he was a Democrat or a Republican, Rozalind made her way to her cabin in the happy certainty that her trunks would already be there, waiting to be unpacked.

The Atlantic crossing was one she had been making regularly ever since she was a child, but she never tired of it, especially now, travelling unaccompanied by any kind of minder or chaperone. Because her father took little interest in her, soothing his conscience by ensuring that she had easy access to his vast wealth, and because her stepfather didn't regard her welfare as being any of his concern, she enjoyed a startling amount of freedom for a girl of nineteen and, travelling by choice without a maid, it was freedom she was accustomed to making the most of.

After checking that everything was as it should be in her cabin, she set off for the boat deck, eager to take photographs of the New York skyline. Until the arrival of her new Leica, doing so would have been a near-impossibility because all previous cameras had not only been too bulky to be easily carried, but had required the use of a heavy tripod. The Leica I was the first camera to be easily portable, and that she was now able to take outdoor photographs with true spontaneity filled Rozalind with a dizzying euphoria.

From the vantage point of the *Aquitania,* New

York's skyline was a vista of soaring, needle-thin spires etched against the piercing blue of a late-afternoon sky. All the buildings she knew so well – the crystalline-white Singer Building, once the tallest in the city, the Gothic-inspired Woolworth Building, one of the earliest, and the gold-trimmed American Radiator Building, one of the newest – looked dramatically different when seen from the Hudson and through her camera lens. Instead of the reality of towering gigantic solidity, what she was capturing was image after image of buildings that were ethereal in their shining beauty.

From a yard or so away a voice she instantly recognized said, 'Do you mind my asking if you do your own developing?'

She was screwing a different lens into the Leica and, without looking up, said fervently, 'You bet your life I do.'

He didn't move away, and she didn't mind his not doing so. With the new lens safely in position, she turned towards him.

He said affably, 'As there is no one to introduce us, perhaps we should take the task upon ourselves? My name is Bradley. Maxwell Bradley.'

'And mine is Rozalind Duveen.' She liked it that he hadn't prefaced his name with the title of 'Congresssman' and that he wasn't using his self-introduction as an excuse to stand closer to her. If it was a pick-up, it didn't feel like one, and if all he wanted was to talk photography, then she was quite happy to oblige him.

He watched her as she returned her attention to her camera, saying, 'Most amateur photographers

173

take photographs of people, Miss Duveen. You seem to be concentrating on buildings.'

'I'm not an amateur, Mr Bradley,' she said, looking into her viewfinder. 'I've sold quite a few of my photographs to provincial magazines.'

'And were they photographs of buildings?'

For the next few minutes she was concentrating too hard to reply. It was nearly five o'clock and the light wasn't good for the kind of photographic effect she was aiming for. When she'd finally taken the shot, she put the Leica back in its case and said, 'Most of them, but not all. One was of the Bethesda Fountain in Central Park.'

'The Bethesda is one of my favourite New York landmarks.' It seemed quite natural that they should begin strolling down the busy deck together. 'Was it the stupendous bronze angel that attracted you?'

'That and the fact that the angel is the city's first public artwork by a woman.'

'Emma Stebbins,' he said, as it became obvious from the excitement of people now crowding the deck rails and by the frenzied activity on the dockside that the *Aquitania* was about to get under way. 'Have you seen her statue of Horace Mann? It overlooks the lawn at the Old State House in Boston.'

The *Aquitania*'s great engines were throbbing. Ropes were being cast off. The people standing at the deck rails were shouting goodbyes to the friends and relatives waving to them.

Raising her voice in order to be heard over the din, Rozalind shouted, 'I don't know as much as I ought about Horace Mann!'

174

The *Aquitania*'s whistle blew – and blew again. Over the cacophony, Maxwell Bradley shouted back, 'Mann is a hero of mine! Why don't we have a coffee and I'll tell you whatever it is about him you still don't know?'

It was a tempting proposition, but Rozalind wanted to be taking photographs as they steamed down the Hudson and into the Bay, not drinking coffee.

'Another time!' she shouted, patting her camera-case to indicate what it was she would be doing instead. He gave a slight nod of his head to show he had understood and then, as he came to a halt, quite obviously about to take his leave of her, she said impulsively, 'Perhaps you could tell me more about Horace Mann over dinner, Mr Bradley?'

It was an outrageously forward suggestion for a respectable young woman to make to a man she had not been properly introduced to, and about whom she knew next to nothing, but Rozalind didn't care. Shipboard life was removed from the normal run of things; and besides, it was 1925, not 1905, and she was a modern young woman and he was a cultured, intelligent, personable man. Dining with him – even though he was probably old enough to be her father – would be far more interesting than dining alone.

'Of course, Mann is remembered primarily as being the father of American public education,' Maxwell Bradley said a few hours later as they were served pan-fried foie gras in the *Aquitania*'s chateau-esque Louis XVI dining room. 'But he

175

was also much more. When John Quincy Adams died of a stroke on the floor of the US House of Representatives in 1848, Mann was picked to fill his seat. He then crusaded against slavery with the same zeal he had exhibited in his fight for public schools.'

Rozalind took a sip of her wine and decided it was time to find out if he and Horace Mann had something in common. 'And do you also sit in the House of Representatives, Mr Bradley?'

'As a matter of fact, I do.' The tough, straight mouth twitched in amusement. 'How did you guess?'

'When we were boarding I overheard the welcoming officer address you as Congressman Bradley.' She tilted her head a little to one side and an amethyst drop-earring danced against the side of her neck. 'And do you occupy a seat to the left in the House of Representatives or to the right?'

'Will my answer determine whether our dinner together will, or will not, be repeated during our crossing to Europe?'

She flashed him her wide, easy smile. 'I'm not rabidly political, so you're on safe ground. Now which are you, Congressman Bradley? An out-and-out Democrat or a dyed-in-the-wool Republican?'

'I'm a dyed-in-the-wool, Miss Duveen.'

'Unlike your hero.'

He quirked an eyebrow. 'It would seem you know far more about Horace Mann than you led me to believe.'

'I never said I knew *nothing* about him.'

Rozalind was unfazed at having been caught

out so easily. What did it matter now that he knew she had deliberately angled to pursue their acquaintance? The bottom line was that if they hadn't been seated together as they were, she would have been dining on her own – and that would have led to half a dozen well-intentioned matrons protectively insisting that for the rest of the voyage she dine with them. She wouldn't have accepted such invitations, but they would have been an annoyance.

'Are you disembarking at Southampton or going on to Cherbourg?' he asked as hors d'oeuvre plates were removed and a first course was served.

'Southampton. Then I will be visiting family in London.' She speared a button mushroom with her fork. 'I have three English cousins, and though I'm very fond of all of them, I'm particularly close to Thea and Olivia, who are closer to me in age than Violet, their younger sister.' She laid her fork down. 'Olivia is living in Berlin at the moment and so I'll be joining her there for a week or two. And then, when I return to London, I'm hoping there'll be an opportunity to visit Yorkshire.'

'Yorkshire? Is that somewhere near Scotland?'

Laughter fizzed in her throat. 'Give or take a couple of hundred miles. It's Britain's biggest county, and I adore it. My cousins' family home is on the outskirts of Outhwaite, a small village in the Dales and – apart from the war years – I've been visiting it every summer for as long as I can remember.'

'I envy you. The kinds of visits I make to England are never long enough for me to visit anywhere but London – and I rarely get to meet anyone who is not a politician or a civil servant.'

She didn't ask why. She wanted him to think her sophisticated, not schoolgirlishly predictable. The realization that what he thought of her desperately mattered came with a slam of shock.

When had Maxwell Bradley metamorphosed from a personable middle-aged man who took an intelligent interest in photography and who was pleasant company into a man she found so devastatingly attractive that, even though she was seated, her knees were now weak?

That he was wearing white tie and tails helped, of course. Most men looked devastating in white tie and tails, but there was far more to it than merely what he was wearing. It wasn't anything obvious. He didn't, for instance, look any younger than she had first thought him; if anything he looked a little older. His dark-brown hair, hidden at their first meeting by his homburg, was lightly flecked with silver at his temples. There were creases at the corners of his unusually dark grey eyes. It didn't matter. What mattered was the effect he had on her. No one else she had ever met had caused her heart to beat in short, slamming little strokes that she could feel even in her fingertips.

She also realized that she absolutely couldn't allow him to disappear from her life when they docked at Southampton. Somehow, some way, she had to make the kind of impression on him that he was making on her.

She was accustomed to dazzling men. Until now, though, all the men in question had been a good decade – and in some cases a couple of decades –

178

younger than Maxwell Bradley, and nothing so far in his manner indicated that he was in the process of being dazzled by her. That he found her agreeable company was obvious – otherwise he wouldn't have accepted her suggestion that they have dinner together. It hadn't, though, turned into a romantic dinner *à deux*. His attitude towards her was no different than her Uncle Gilbert's would have been, if he had been dining alone with her.

It was something Rozalind was determined to rectify.

She picked up her wine glass, excitement at the prospect of success singing through her veins. There were six more days before England hove into view – and a girl of her allure could achieve a lot in six days.

She'd hoped to kick off her seduction technique later that evening over coffee in the Adams-style drawing room, but the opportunity didn't arise. He ordered coffee for them at the table and a little later, when other diners began strolling out of the ornate dining room and heading towards the drawing room, smoking room or the ballroom, where a big band was playing Dixieland jazz, he courteously brought their evening together to an end.

With her hopes of a romantic moonlit stroll on deck dashed, Rozalind went for a moonlit stroll by herself, confident that he would seek out her company the next day.

He didn't do so.

By four o'clock in the afternoon, though she

hadn't purposely looked for him, she hadn't seen him anywhere. When she was invited to dine that evening at the captain's table, she accepted, cross that the first day of her six-day seduction campaign had been so unproductive. That evening, knowing that as a single young woman at the captain's table she would be the focus of a great number of eyes, – not least, hopefully, Maxwell Bradley's – she dressed flamboyantly.

Her drop-waisted scarlet silk and satin gown was decorated with panels of jet beading that complemented the glossy helmet of her raven-dark hair. The neckline plunged front and back, and the mid-calf hemline was deeply fringed, fluttering about her legs as she walked. She was wearing flesh-coloured stockings, T-strap shoes and a long pearl necklace tied in a knot and worn so that it dangled down her bare back, emphasizing her flawless skin. The *pièce de résistance* was an exotically beaded headband, worn low over her brow, and a jet slave-bracelet clamped above one elbow.

Taking a last look in the mirror before leaving her cabin she was satisfied that when Maxwell Bradley saw her, albeit from a distance, he would be knocked for six.

She was one of a number of first-class passengers dining with Captain Charles that evening and was introduced as Miss Rozalind Elizabeth Duveen, daughter of Guthrie Clarke Duveen, president of one of the country's most prestigious investment banks.

America's ambassador to Great Britain, Ambassador Alanson B. Houghton, was one of Captain Charles's guests, as was his wife. Other guests were a famous movie actress and her rather less famous husband; a steel magnate; an elderly, wizened French marquise; a British Member of Parliament and his daughter; an athlete who had won a gold medal at the last Olympic Games; a silver-haired Washington newspaper proprietor and his very young, very beautiful wife. Last, and seated on her left at dinner, was a young man whom Captain Charles had judged to be the most eligible bachelor that voyage, Bobbie Hunt, the twenty-eight-year-old heir to a rubber-tyre fortune.

It was an attempt at matchmaking that was doomed to failure because, aping Rudolph Valentino, Bobbie wore his poker-straight hair slicked back with Vaseline. It was not a look Rozalind favoured.

Ambassador Houghton was seated on her right and, when Rozalind told him she would be interrupting her trip to England in order to visit Germany, he was immediately all interest.

'I was head of the US Legation at Berlin from 1922 until February this year, when I was transferred to London,' he said, giving her his whole attention. 'Germany needs a lot of financial help at the moment, but I won't bore you with that. You've probably heard quite enough about war reparations from your father.'

Rozalind hadn't had a meeting with her father for more than a year, and when they had last met it was her own financial requirements that had been under discussion, not Germany's.

Seeing no reason to make Ambassador Houghton privy to her bleak parental relationship, she
said, affecting knowledge of the subject that she
did not have, 'Are all major investment banks
loaning to Germany?'

'Oh, yes. It isn't only Duveen's. The money will
enable Germany to expand industrially and give
it a basis from which it will be able to pay its
reparation debts – especially its debts to Belgium
and France.'

'Which are how much?' Rozalind asked,
politely keeping the conversation going, as she
scanned the chandeliered dining room for sight
of a broad-shouldered Bostonian with stunning
grey eyes.

'Pre the Dawes Plan, the reparation was fixed at
an annual fee of one hundred and thirty-two
billion gold marks.'

The amount was so stupendously colossal that
it did what Rozalind would have thought
impossible. It engaged her full attention.

'*How* much?' she asked disbelievingly. 'One
hundred and thirty-two *billion* gold marks?'

Ambassador Houghton chuckled. 'Astronomical, I agree – and quite beyond Germany's
ability to pay. And we all know what happened
when she defaulted. Though Great Britain's solution was to lower the amount of the annual payments, France and Belgium's solution was to
occupy the Ruhr and take in kind what Germany
couldn't afford to give. Such a volatile situation
couldn't be allowed to continue, hence coordinated action by Great Britain and America,
resulting in the present, very satisfactory solution.'

Interesting though it was, Rozalind had no desire to talk about it further. Once again she scanned the room and this time, by adjusting the angle of her chair, did so with success.

Bradley was seated at a table with five other people, two men and three women.

Her throat constricted so tightly that, even if she'd wanted to continue the conversation with Ambassador Houghton, she wouldn't have been able to do so. Numbers like that meant he was quite obviously paired with one of the women. But which?

'...and did you see *Rose Marie* at the Imperial?' Bobbie Hunt was asking. 'What a swell show!' He began humming the show's title song.

Rozalind was unappreciative, for her thoughts were elsewhere.

One of the women at Bradley's table had her back to her and, judging from her dowager's hump and snow-white hair, was elderly. The other two women were much younger, possibly in their late thirties or early forties – which made them approximately the age she judged Maxwell Bradley, to be.

The constriction in her throat intensified. What if one of the two women was his wife? Why had she never thought to wonder whether or not he was married? Hard on the heels of that thought came the impossibility of it. How could he have a wife, when the previous evening he had dined alone with her so publicly, and when he was well known to the officers on board ship? Congressmen had to maintain spotless reputations. He wouldn't have risked his reputation in order to chat pleasantly about Horace Mann.

'What say we move on to the ballroom and shimmy, when dinner is over?' Bobbie's voice was low in her ear. 'It isn't the Cotton Club, but the band play great ragtime.'

Rozalind didn't reply. Her eyes were still on Maxwell Bradley. One of the women laid an evening-gloved hand proprietorially on his arm, laughing as she leaned intimately towards him. He laughed back at her.

He hadn't laughed once the previous evening over dinner. He had smiled occasionally, but that was all.

She decided that he was boring and that she didn't give a jot if he preferred the company of a woman more his own age to hers. Finding him nerve-tinglingly exciting had been an aberration, nothing else. She remembered their wine. It had been the first time she had drunk Château d'Yquem and although it had been delicious, she made a resolution never to drink it again. It had obviously addled her brain.

'I'd love to shimmy,' she said. 'And I've never been to the Cotton Club. It sounds huge fun.'

'Maybe I'll get the chance to take you there some day.' Bobbie gave her a conspiratorial wink. 'Let's quit the table the first chance we get.'

Forty minutes later, with a cold, hard feeling in the pit of her stomach, Rozalind accompanied him into the ballroom. Bobbie was a good dancer and, as they Charlestoned, she almost forgave him his Vaselined hairstyle. The music changed to a foxtrot to enable people to get their breath back, and she saw Maxwell Bradley lead onto the dance floor the woman he had been laughing with at dinner.

As they danced they were deep in animated conversation, and Rozalind said tautly, 'Is the woman wearing emerald-green with scarlet beading one of the Rothschilds?'

Bobbie followed her line of sight. 'Nope. She's the recently widowed Mrs Clancy, an Astor.'

They executed a smooth rise and fall and then went into a swing and sway. When they were again doing a chassis, Rozalind said, fishing for more information, 'And is her dance partner about to become husband number two?'

'I shouldn't think so. He's a Congressman. Rich, but not Astor-standard rich, and you can bet your life Mrs C is on the lookout for a title, second time round.' He led her into another swing and sway, saying as he did so, 'No doubt she's hoping to bag a prince or a count while she's in Europe.'

Out of the corner of her eye Rozalind saw Maxwell Bradley foxtrot his partner a little closer to them. When their eyes met unavoidably, she gave him the kind of faint smile she would have given to someone she vaguely recognized, but couldn't quite place. Though she was going to great lengths to ensure there was no expression in her eyes, she was thrillingly aware that, as one of his eyebrows lifted ever so slightly, there was a great deal of expression in his.

Outwardly all ice-maiden *froideur*, inside she felt gleeful. He was interested, and not merely in order to talk about Horace Mann, or photography.

185

If she knew anything at all about men – and for a girl of nineteen she already knew a lot – then the game wasn't over. Where Maxwell Bradley was concerned, she knew with exciting certainty that all was still to play for.

'And so the next day I acknowledged him with a little bit more warmth, but declined to have coffee with him in the ship's garden room,' she said to Thea as, in Hyde Park's Rotten Row, they slowed their horses to a walking pace in order to be able to talk and catch up on each other's news.

'Was he put out?' Beneath the shade of her navy-blue riding bowler Thea's eyes were avidly interested. She'd been pushing boundaries of her own of late, but not with anyone a couple of decades her senior.

'If he was, he didn't let it show. An hour later he was strolling the deck with the happy widow.'

'And?'

'And as there were only another three days before we docked in Southampton I decided I couldn't continue playing it ice-cool.' Rozalind's horse skittishly tried to break into a trot. She reined it back to a walk and said, 'The next day we had coffee together in the morning, and dinner in the evening. By the time we said goodnight we were on first-name terms.'

'Rozalind and Maxwell?'

'Rozalind and Max.'

'Did he kiss you goodnight?'

'Not then, and I couldn't understand it. There was enough of a sexual charge between us to light up London.'

186

They had reached a point on the tree-verged bridleway that gave a view of the Serpentine and they brought their horses to a halt. Looking through the trees to the limpid green surface of the lake, Rozalind said, 'The next night – the night before we docked – he told me the reason.'

'He's married?' It was a suspicion Thea had had almost from the moment Rozalind had mentioned how much older than her he was.

'No, he isn't married, but he does have someone waiting for him in New York.'

'So that's it then.' There was a disappointed finality in Thea's voice. 'Your romance is at an end.'

'No, Thea. It's very far from being at an end. I'm going to see him again while he's in London, and I'm certain that he'll write to whoever is waiting for him in New York and end the relationship.'

Thea shrugged. 'And then, Roz? What if he ends up asking you to marry him and you have to turn him down? Think how ghastly that would be.'

'But I wouldn't turn him down.'

'Of course you would. He's miles older than you are! When you are thirty, he'll be fifty!'

'Fifty-two, to be exact.'

'And you don't care?'

At the stunned disbelief on Thea's face, Rozalind laughed. 'No, Thea. I don't care. I've never before met anyone I'm so crazy about, and although Max keeps his cards close to his chest, I know he feels the same about me. This is it, Thea! The big one. The walk-down-the-aisle, happy-ever-after one.'

Thea swiftly averted her head before Rozalind could see the pain in her eyes. The big one – the walk-down-the-aisle happy-ever-after one – was how it should have been between her and Hal. That it wasn't caused her an agony so deep there were days when she didn't know how she was surviving it.

She hadn't seen Hal since the night of her coming-out ball more than a year ago, but she knew, via letters from Carrie, that he was courting a Richmond barmaid. 'Courting' was the word Carrie had used, but Thea was certain he was sowing his wild oats and that, when he had tired of doing so, he would propose to Carrie.

'Let's get back to the stables,' she said abruptly, unshed tears making her eyes overly bright. 'Papa says he has something to tell us. Some kind of a happy announcement.'

'Perhaps he's about to be made Foreign Secretary.' Rozalind turned her horse around. 'Or perhaps he's going to announce Olivia's engagement to Dieter von Starhemberg.'

'Perhaps.' That Olivia was in love with a man who wanted to marry her wasn't something Thea wanted to talk about, when she was beginning to doubt that she would ever achieve a similar happiness. 'The Row is practically deserted,' she said, her face set and pale. 'Let's gallop back.'

She dug her heels into her horse's flanks and, without waiting for a reply, set off headlong for the stables, her heart and mind full of Hal, and hot, tortured tears streaming down her face.

Chapter Twelve

'Now that Rozalind is with us again,' Gilbert said, his obvious happiness touched with a trace of nervousness, 'I have a very special announcement to make.'

Rozalind wondered if his nervousness was because of Dieter's nationality. If so, he was worrying about nothing. The war was in the past. Young people – people like herself, Thea and Violet, who had been children at the time – barely gave it a thought. During the war King George had changed his family name from Saxe-Coburg-Gotha to Windsor, but German blood still ran strong in the royal family's veins. Thea had told her that Prince Edward spoke high German faultlessly.

'...this may seem a little sudden,' Gilbert was now saying.

Rozalind wasn't sure it was sudden at all. As far as she was concerned, it was no coincidence that within weeks of meeting Dieter at Thea's coming-out ball Olivia was at a finishing school in Berlin. This outcome – an engagement between her and Dieter – was what Olivia had been working towards from day one.

She glanced towards Thea, who she knew was of the same opinion. The announcement was taking place in the drawing room, and Thea was looking fixedly not at her father, but at a splendid

George Stubbs painting of a horse and foal that hung above the mantelpiece. Rozalind wondered if Thea minded Olivia being the first of them to become engaged, especially as the engagement was taking place before Olivia had even been presented at court. It wasn't a reaction she would have suspected of Thea, but Thea was more than capable of keeping her feelings to herself, and their long separations – this was the first time Rozalind had been back to England since Thea's coming-out – meant that she didn't always know what was going on in Thea's life and in her mind.

Violet was perched on the arm of one of the deep sofas, hanging on to her father's every word, in happy anticipation of soon being the centre of attention as a bridesmaid.

'I hope you are all going to be as happy as I am,' Gilbert continued, 'when I tell you that my engagement to Lady Zephiniah Pyke will be announced in tomorrow's *Times*. Zephiniah is the widow of–'

He got no further.

Violet gasped and burst into tears.

Thea said crossly, 'Please don't play jokes, Papa.'

'It isn't a joke, sweetheart. I know this has come as something of a surprise, but I was introduced to Zephiniah at a dinner party some months ago and we have been seeing each other constantly ever since. She is an absolutely wonderful person and I consider myself truly fortunate that she has consented to be my wife.'

It was the first time Rozalind had ever seen Thea lost for words. With a face drained of colour, she floundered, 'But ... but if you have been seeing Lady Pyke for months, why haven't we met her, Papa?'

'There have been circumstances – nothing that is of any importance now.' He beamed at them reassuringly. 'Please be happy for me, my darlings. Zephiniah has no children of her own and is so looking forward to having three stepdaughters.'

'Will I have to call her Mama?' Violet asked fearfully, too avidly curious to continue crying.

'Perhaps not at first, but it would be nice if you felt able to do so, when we have all settled down together as a family.'

At the prospect of settling down as a family with a stepmother she had never expected to have and hadn't yet met, Thea winced.

Trying to make amends for Thea's reaction, Rozalind said swiftly, 'I do hope, Uncle Gilbert, there'll be an opportunity for me to meet Lady Pyke before I sail home to New York.'

With relief Gilbert turned his attention away from his daughters and towards her. 'So do I, Rozalind. I can't promise, though, as at the moment Zephiniah is in Argentina, and I am not quite certain of her date of return.'

'Argentina!' Thea looked at him with incredulity. 'But why on earth are you announcing your engagement to Lady Pyke when she isn't even in the country?'

'And why is she in Argentina, Papa?' Violet's eyes were as round as saucers. 'Is she Argentinian? Will she wear a national costume? Can she speak English?'

'Of course Zephiniah isn't Argentinian, Violet.'

Irritation had crept into Gilbert's voice. 'She has, though, lived for many years in Argentina, and now that her homes will be in London and Yorkshire she has returned to settle her affairs there. And now I think it's time to celebrate my announcement with champagne.'

He rang the bell for the butler. Rozalind, realizing they had all been too stunned to offer any kind of congratulations, sucked air into her lungs and, making good the deficiency, said, 'Congratulations, Uncle Gilbert I hope you and Lady Pyke will be very happy together.'

'Zephiniah,' Gilbert said, shooting her a grateful smile. 'Please refer to my future wife as Zephiniah, Rozalind. It is what she would ask of you herself.'

Half an hour later, in the privacy of Thea's bedroom, Thea, Rozalind and Violet sat cross-legged on her bed.

'The champagne was the last straw.' Thea's face was still bloodless. 'What we needed were stiff gins.' Her eyes held Rozalind's. 'I hate even suggesting this, but do you think my father's lost his marbles? Why have an engagement announced publicly tomorrow when we, his children and his niece, have yet to meet her? And do you suppose he's already telephoned Olivia, or is she still in the dark?'

'The Lord only knows. I think it must mean, though, that Dieter hasn't popped the question to Olivia. If that engagement was about to be announced, your father wouldn't be so insensitive as to announce his own engagement first. It would be stealing their thunder, and he wouldn't do that.'

Violet said glumly. 'He might, if he's lost his marbles. And what if Olivia then calls off her wedding? I can hardly be a bridesmaid to Papa and Lady Pyke. It would be just too mortifying. And I want to be a bridesmaid. I've been looking forward to it for ages.'

It was the first time Rozalind could remember Thea including Violet in the way she was including her in the present conversation. Generally she simply shooed Violet away and closed the door on her. That she hadn't done so this time Rozalind found interesting, and she put the change down to the fact that Violet's sixteenth birthday was only a few weeks away and that continuing to treat her as a child was, even for Thea, getting a little difficult. It didn't mean, though, that Violet no longer exasperated her.

'Stop being so utterly self-absorbed,' Thea said now, crosser than ever. 'Why does being a bridesmaid matter so much? What matters is that this Zephiniah person is going to become part of our lives and we have no idea what she's like, or even how old she is.'

'If she's a widow, she must be very old – at least as old as Papa.'

'Papa is forty.' Thea looked across at Rozalind. 'I suppose the Zephiniah person could be forty as well, but she could also be much, much younger. Papa's friend, Lord Brassington, remarried last year and his wife is young enough to be his daughter.'

At the thought of such a scenario they stared at

each other in growing horror.

Violet said with fierce passion, 'If she's only old enough to be my sister, then I'm not going to call her Mama.'

Thea ignored her. 'Is that why she wants us to call her by her Christian name?' she said to Rozalind, her horror growing. 'Is it because she's close to us in age?'

'I don't know.' All Rozalind could think of was that Max Bradley was Gilbert's age; that she certainly wouldn't think marrying him was an odd thing for her to do; and that if her circumstances were similar to Lady Pyke's, then she too would ask any adult stepchildren to call her by her Christian name. Which wouldn't be much comfort for Thea and Violet.

Two weeks later she was having almost exactly the same conversation with Olivia in the Cafe Kranzler on Berlin's Unter den Linden.

'But when does this Zephiniah person come back from Argentina?' Olivia asked in bewilderment.

She was wearing a cherry-red polka-dot silk dress, a white cloche hat and white high-heeled sandals. Fourteen months ago, when Rozalind had last seen her, Olivia had been a typically gauche English rose. Now she looked every inch a sophisticated Berliner.

'She hasn't yet left Buenos Aires, so your guess is as good as mine.' Rozalind wondered if the startling change in Olivia was due to finishing school or whether Count von Starhemberg was responsible. Either way Thea was going to have to look to her laurels if she didn't want to find herself in Olivia's shade, when Olivia returned to London.

'I was hoping to see her when I came home for Hermione's wedding, but that's only six weeks away, so it looks a little problematical.'

'Hermione?' Rozalind stared at her blankly. 'Hermione who?'

'Our Hermione, of course! Hermione Cumberbatch. Good gracious, hasn't anyone told you?'

That they hadn't was obvious by the stunned expression on Rozalind's face.

Olivia flipped open a grosgrain envelope bag and withdrew a cigarette-case and a lighter. Both were silver. Both were monogrammed.

'Hermione,' she said, fitting a Sobranie into an ebony cigarette-holder, 'is to become Mrs Charlie Hardwick on the tenth of August. The wedding is to take place in Outhwaite's Methodist chapel. It's going to be quite an event. Papa is giving her away. Jim is to be best man. All of Outhwaite is bound to be there. How it can have slipped anyone's mind to tell you, I can't imagine.'

'I'll have to alter the date of my return to New York.'

Rozalind felt so dazed it was almost disorientating, though whether that was because of news of the wedding or because it was Olivia who was transfixing her, she wasn't sure. She wondered when Thea had last seen Olivia; when, in fact, her father had last seen her. One thing was certain, when Olivia arrived back in Outhwaite, the eyes of the entire village would be out on stalks.

'How about another two coffees?' she asked,

feeling in the need of one. 'And bring me up to date on you and Dieter. When your father said he had a happy announcement to make, we were all certain it was about your engagement, not his.'

'If Papa had been reasonable,' Olivia said bitterly, tapping ash off her cigarette with a red-lacquered nail, 'it would have been. As it is, he says I'm too young. He says that if I had come out as a debutante this summer it would be different, but that under the circumstances it would raise eyebrows. After much wrangling we've come to an agreement. If I still wish to become engaged to Dieter at Christmas – which of course I will do – then he'll give his consent, but only on the under-standing that the wedding won't take place until my eighteenth birthday next August.'

She paused, ordered two more coffees from a smartly uniformed waitress and then said, 'The downside of all this is that once my engagement to Dieter is announced, I can't stay on in Berlin without having a family member here as a chaperone. Until now it hasn't really been an issue. At finishing school the authorities served as chaperones – and a huge nuisance they were. Then when I left finishing school and stayed on by going to language school, I moved into a house with other English girls studying German, and we are collectively chaperoned – supposedly – by Frau Würtz, who runs the house. Having a family friend such as Count von Starhemberg calling for me, and squiring me around, has caused no problems whatsoever. One thing I've learned is that Germans are just as snobby as anyone else.'

'But if it's known that your relationship with Dieter is a romantic one, not just a family friendship, the situation will be different?'

The answer was so obvious that Olivia didn't even bother to put it into words. Crushing her barely smoked cigarette out in an ashtray and pushing it to the far side of the table, she said, 'Papa wants me home now. Either that or he's sending Aunt Hilda out as a chaperone. Hideous as that thought is, I was going to opt for it, but there's no need now. Dieter put in for a posting to London as early as last Christmas, and it's just come through.'

She shot Rozalind a smile of mischievous triumph. 'From the first of September Dieter is going to be at the German Embassy in Belgrave Square – and Belgrave Square is so near Mount Street that I'll be able to see the German flag from the attics!'

Minutes later, as they left the cafe and began strolling arm-in-arm down the tree-lined boulevard, Olivia said, 'What about your love life, Roz? Are you and Barty Luddesdon a couple yet?'

'Barty?' Roz's sleek eyebrows rose nearly into her hairline. 'Great Scott, no! I haven't seen him since Thea's coming-out ball.'

'But there is someone?'

'Oh, yes. There's certainly someone. Someone very, very special.'

As they continued walking in the direction of the Brandenburg Gate, attracting admiring male glances all the way, Rozalind began telling Olivia of her meeting with Max aboard the *Aquitania*. Her thoughts, though, were not of their initial awareness of each other on the ship's gangplank, or of their self-introduction to each other as she was taking photographs before they sailed, but of what had happened the night before they had steamed into Southampton. To Thea, she had said that Max had admitted there was someone waiting for him in Boston. What she hadn't told Thea was the circumstances in which that admission had been made – or what had happened after Max had made it. And what she hadn't told Thea, she certainly couldn't tell Olivia.

'Do you really think he'll break it off with whoever it is he's been seeing in Boston?' Olivia asked.

Rozalind nodded, heat surging through her body as she remembered the sexual tension there had been between her and Max on the last night of the crossing.

The final night of any voyage was always special and she had dressed for it by wearing aquamarine jewellery with a halter-necked pale-blue beaded dress. Waistless, it fell straight from her creamily bare shoulders to deep fringing around her knees.

The ship's ballroom had been en fête. Balloons and coloured streamers had rained down as they danced. Champagne corks had popped. It had been as hectic and as fun-filled as a New Year's Eve party. But it hadn't been fun for her – and though Max had been as inscrutable as ever, she'd been sure he shared her feelings. How could he not, when tomorrow they were destined not only to go their separate ways, but to do so with no acknowledgement of the overwhelming physical attraction sizzling between them?

By now she'd only been able to think of one reason for his not having made a romantic move on her. Despite her intuition to the contrary, it had to be that he was married – and though she'd vowed she was never going to ask, that vow had been taken days ago, when it had seemed impossible that Max wouldn't volunteer such information, or show by his actions that he was free and available.

And so she'd made up her mind to ask the question she had so far been avoiding.

She'd known, though, that the ballroom would not be the right place – not when she was determined that, whatever the answer, she was going to ensure his straight, tough mouth came down hot and hard on hers.

'I need to change into another pair of dance shoes – the ones I'm wearing are killing me,' she'd said as they made their way to their table after an exhilaratingly fast quickstep. 'Would you keep me company while I go and change them? Everyone is as high as a kite tonight, and I don't want to run into unwelcome attention en route.'

With the amount of champagne everyone was drinking it had been a reasonable request and, with an assenting nod, Max had walked her out of the crowded ballroom and in the direction of the first-class passenger accommodation. As always when they were, walking side by side he'd kept a couple of inches of space between them, so that their hands didn't accidentally brush against each other. The contrast to the close hold they had been enjoying only moments earlier, as they danced, had been so stark that Rozalind had felt completely disorientated by it.

As they had neared the door of her cabin and she had wondered what his answer to her question was going to be, her inner tension had become almost uncontainable. Was he married or wasn't he? The question had roared through her brain until she'd been dizzy with it. If he wasn't married, why was he behaving towards her with such stiff propriety when she knew – absolutely *knew* – that he was as mad for her as she was for him? And if he was married...?

As they'd come to a halt outside her cabin her mouth had been dry, her heart racing. One thing she'd known for certain. If he was married, then the sooner she knew about it, the better.

'I'll wait here,' he'd said, leaning nonchalantly against the far wall of the narrow corridor, one foot crossing the other at the ankle, his arms folded.

She'd opened her cabin door and had then taken a deep breath and turned to face him, the ice-blue of her dress shimmering in the corridor's muted light. 'There's something I have to know,' she'd said, holding his eyes steadily.

He'd waited. Not moving. Not speaking.

Now, days later as she neared the Brandenburg Gate with Olivia, Rozalind remembered how furious she'd been with him for not making it easier on her. She hadn't hesitated, though. She'd said starkly, 'Are you married, Max?'

'Why?' he'd asked, the expression in his dark-grey eyes unreadable.

'Because ... because I'd much prefer it if you

weren't,' she'd said.

All nonchalance gone, he'd straightened up and unfolded his arms. 'No,' he'd said. 'I'm not married.'

Her immediate reaction was a relief so vast that her knees felt weak, and then she'd said in utter incomprehension, 'Then why...?' Unable to complete the sentence, she'd made an expressive gesture with her hands.

'Why no shipboard romance?'

She'd nodded, and beneath his dinner jacket she'd been aware of his muscles bunching with a tension almost equal to her own.

'Because there's someone in Boston waiting for me.'

'You're engaged?' A new, but not impossible anxiety followed hard on the heels of her relief.

'Not officially,' he'd said.

'Then I don't understand.' Her bewilderment had been total. 'You're still free – and you've wanted a shipboard romance with me just as much as I've wanted one with you. I know you have.'

His eyebrow had quirked. 'A shipboard romance? Is that all you wanted? Then perhaps it's best that my head ruled my heart.'

'By "shipboard romance" I didn't mean a romance that would have ended when we sailed into Southampton.' Her mouth had been dry. 'Brief, meaningless flings aren't my style.'

'Or mine.'

'They why have you kept your distance?' she'd asked, her voice thick with emotion.

'Because I'm twenty-two years older than you,' he'd said. 'Because I've long outgrown the hand-holding, chaste-kiss romances of girls of your age. And last, but by no means least, because I never seduce virgins.'

Nothing could have been blunter or more explicit, and she'd known that she had two choices. She could say that she quite understood. She could change her shoes and return to the ballroom with their relationship the same as when they had left it. Or she could take another, far different course. It would mean, of course, telling the most monumental lie.

The only doubt she'd had about telling it was what would happen when she was found out. That was *if* she was found out. Blood on a sheet didn't, surely, follow the loss of virginity as night followed day. Even if it did, the deed would have been done and their relationship would have been changed in a way that could never be altered. Whoever was waiting for him in Boston would wait in vain.

'I'm not a virgin,' she'd said, and then, as she'd seen that he didn't believe her, she had said vehemently. 'It's 1925. Queen Victoria has been dead for a quarter of a century. I'm a modern young woman. A flapper. I smoke. I drink. I have a career. I'm financially independent. I travel unaccompanied. I've read Marie Stopes. There is absolutely no need to treat me as if I'm a pre-war virginal shrinking violet.'

'Then I won't,' he'd said, 'but I'm not in the habit of ravishing young women just because they've given me permission to do so. Change your shoes. I'll wait for you here.'

With burning cheeks she had entered her cabin,

certain she'd made an absolute fool of herself. As she'd changed her shoes her hands had been shaking. Ever since he'd first spoken to her she'd wanted him to think well of her and she'd been convinced, as she'd walked back out into the corridor, that even if he'd thought well of her when they'd left the ballroom, he did so no longer.

It was a fear he'd immediately vanquished.

Putting a finger beneath her chin, he'd tilted her head to his so that their eyes met. 'You didn't misjudge my feelings,' he'd said thickly, and the next moment his mouth had come down hot and sweet on hers. It had been a long, passionate, expert kiss – a kiss totally unlike any she had previously experienced. When he had finally raised his head from hers, her senses had been reeling.

This time, as their eyes held, the expression in his hadn't been unreadable. It had told her all she'd needed to know and as they'd walked back down the corridor towards the ballroom, thigh-to-thigh and with hands tightly clasped and fingers intertwined, Rozalind's heart had been singing like a lark's.

It was singing like a lark's now too, as she and Olivia came to a halt outside the hotel she was staying in.

'Do you really think he'll break it off with whoever it is he's been seeing in Boston, Roz?' Olivia asked again, impatient for an answer to her question.

'I'm absolutely positive. He's as crazy about me as I am about him. I'm so crazy I was tempted to cut short my time in England by returning to

New York with him in two weeks' time. The only reason I'm not doing so is because he'll then be in Washington and I'd be in New York, twiddling my thumbs. Plus he's due back here towards the end of July, so I'm continuing with my original plans and then we'll return to America together.'

'And Hermione and Charlie's wedding?'

'Oh, I'll be in Yorkshire for that.' She gave Olivia's arm a loving squeeze. 'And, if I have my way, so will Max.'

Chapter Thirteen

'Oh, Hal! A motor car! How wonderful!' Carrie clapped her hands in delight.

They were standing in Richmond's cobbled town square. It was the morning of Charlie and Hermione's wedding, and in order to attend it they had arranged to travel to Outhwaite together. Normally this would have meant an hour's journey by bus on narrow, winding country roads, but to Carrie's wonderment Hal had roared up the steep street into the square in an open-topped motor car.

Hal grinned, pushing his driving goggles up into his dark curls. 'It is pretty wonderful, isn't it?' he said, with the engine still running. 'Hop in and I'll tell you how I got it.'

Carrie didn't need to be asked twice. She'd been enraptured by motor cars ever since her chauffeur-driven ride with Blanche in the Fenton

Rolls-Royce. Mindful of how blowy a ride that had been, she took off the flower-decorated hat she'd bought especially for the wedding and hopped in.

'How on earth have you managed to afford it?' she asked as Hal, looking strangely formal in a navy-blue suit, put the car into gear.

'It's a Clyno,' he said, circling the obelisk in the middle of the square and heading off in the direction of Frenchgate. 'They've been making motorcycles for years, but now they've moved into car manufacturing and, to get a foot in the market, they're undercutting every other motor-ca[r] manufacturer. It's a beauty, isn't it? It's got wh[eel] brakes, balloon tyres, a four-cylinder water-coo[led] engine, electric starting, a spare wheel and tyre[.]'

Carrie giggled. He was rhapsodizing about [the] car in the same way he used to rhapsodize ab[out] the baby voles. 'However cheap it was compa[red] to other cars, it must still have cost a lot of mo[ney.]'

'Oh aye. It cost enough.' As they buck[led] down Frenchgate he shot her an amused gla[nce.] 'But I'm not without a penny or two these d[ays,] Carrie. I write all the political stuff for the pa[per] now, as well as what my editor likes to call "Yor[k]shire high-society coverage". It won't be long[g] afore I'll be heading down to London to work on a national paper – and, when I do, I'll be driving myself down, not going by train.'

At what to Carrie was a giddying speed they roared through the cobbled streets and swooped over the bridge.

Carrie didn't like to think of Hal leaving Yorkshire for London. It was bad enough Thea being there almost permanently, without Hal being there as well. It had been months since she had seen Thea and Violet, and months and months since she had last seen Olivia or Roz. Almost as much as she missed her friends, she missed Gorton Hall. That she was going to be there in little over an hour's time filled her with elation.

It was Gorton, not the tied cottage she had been brought up in and which her granny still lived in, that she thought of as home – and she didn't do so because she had illusions of grandeur; she did so because it was where she had always been happiest, and because it was the family home of the people who were the dearest to her in all the world.

She said now, tentatively, 'Do you think your editor will want you to write about Lord Fenton's wedding to Lady Pyke?'

With Richmond behind them, Hal had increased speed and they were now spinning along the country roads at an exhilarating rate. As stone walls flashed past he said, 'He's already made it clear he wants me to use all my contacts with the Fentons to write an exclusive on the wedding. Have you heard yet where it's to be held? As it's a second marriage for both of them and they've both been widowed, I imagine it will be a low-key affair. They may even end up marrying here, in Yorkshire.'

Carrie was silent, trying to imagine Gilbert Fenton marrying again. No image of it would come. When she thought of him loving anyone, then she thought of Blanche.

'She was so lovely, wasn't she?' she said, tears

suddenly, pricking the backs of her eyes.

He didn't need to ask who she was thinking about.

'Lady Fenton?' he said, his voice gentling. 'Yes, she was a lovely lady.'

Carrie's clasped hands tightened in her lap. 'I think of her often, Hal. And though it's a long time since I've been at Gorton, I know the instant I step over the threshold it will be as if she's still there. She was always so kind to me. I'll never be able to forget her. Never.'

He slowed down a little and there was gruff concern in his voice as he said, 'You never have to forget. Memories are precious – and if remembering her is a comfort to you, keep on remembering her. She wouldn't want remembering her to make you sad, though, Carrie. She'd want you to be happy. And she'd have wanted Lord Fenton to be happy, too. How long has he been a widower? Five years? Six? It's long enough for him to remarry without his being disloyal to her memory.'

The River Swale came into view again, its banks edged with glorious clumps of purple-headed knapweed and button-like yellow tansy.

'You still haven't said if anyone has written to you saying where the wedding is to be,' Hal prompted as she remained quiet.

'I don't think anyone knows yet.' Though she'd taken comfort from what he had said about memories, Carrie's eyes were still overly bright. 'Both Thea and Olivia are unhappy at the thought of their father marrying again – especially to someone they haven't yet met. I haven't had a

207

letter from Violet, but Thea says Violet is too curious about Lady Pyke to be deeply distressed.'

'And Roz?'

'Roz thinks like you. That her uncle remarrying was bound to happen.'

'That's what I like about Roz.' Hal swerved to avoid a straying sheep. 'She's always so clear-eyed about things.'

Though Carrie's mane of wheat-gold hair was anchored in a plaited bun, the air rushing past them had tugged tendrils free around her face. Pushing them away from her eyes, she said with concern in her voice, 'I just hope she's being clear-eyed about this man that she says she's head-over-heels about.'

Hal gave a dismissive shrug. 'Stop worrying. Lord Fenton wouldn't be allowing their friendship unless he'd vetted him thoroughly.'

They were nearly at Gorton now and Carrie's tummy muscles tightened with anticipation. 'Which he has,' she said, leaning forward as if, by doing so, she would see the view of the house a fraction earlier. 'They're both on something called the Dawes Plan committee, which is something to do with helping Germany pay its war debts.'

'War reparations,' Hal corrected automatically. 'A debt would be just a debt. A reparation payment is a payment compensating for an injustice done.'

He changed gear as they approached the bend in the road that gave the first sighting of Gorton. 'And stop worrying about Roz's love life. If Lord Fenton and Congressman Bradley know of each other because of the Dawes Plan, then Congressman Bradley's intentions are honourable. If they weren't, he'd have dropped Roz like a hot brick the minute she mentioned her uncle's name – so put your mind at rest, Carrie.'

Carrie did so, sucking in her breath as they rounded the bend and Gorton came into view. Backed by trees and then by rising moorland, the house shimmered in the August heat, its mellow Yorkshire stone glowing like dull gold.

She let out her breath on a long, ecstatic sigh. 'It's so good to be back, Hal,' she said, a lump in her throat as they began skirting the river in the direction of the bridge.

'Even though it's only for a day?'

'A day is better than nothing. And it was so thoughtful of Lord Fenton to suggest that I come here first and then leave for the church with Olivia, Thea and Violet.'

'And with him as well?'

'Oh, no. Miss Cumberbatch's father is dead and, as she doesn't have a brother, Lord Fenton is going to give her away. He'll be leaving for the church with her.'

Hal raised an eyebrow. 'From Gorton Hall?'

'Of course from Gorton Hall. Miss Cumberbatch doesn't have a private home in Outhwaite. As Violet's governess, her home is wherever the family is.'

As he sped over the bridge and turned into the long drive that wound through Gorton's parkland, Hal wondered if, because Carrie's father was also dead and because, like Miss Cumberbatch, she had no brothers, Gilbert Fenton would take it upon himself to give Carrie away, when the day came for her to be married. Knowing how red she would blush if he said such a thing, he kept his thoughts to himself. To the best of his knowledge, Carrie hadn't done any courting as yet and though he knew it was none of his business, the thought of her doing so always disturbed him.

'There's nearly two hours to go before the wedding,' he said. 'So after I've dropped you off, I'm going to the Pig and Whistle for a pre-wedding celebratory pint, which is where I'll likely find the groom and best man.' He brought the car to a squealing halt before the house and flashed her a broad grin. 'Don't forget your hat – and I'll see you in church at two o'clock.'

Using the side-entrance to Gorton – the entrance she had used ever since she had been a child, and the one Thea and Olivia regularly used in preference to the front entrance – Carrie stepped inside and, as the door closed behind her, took a deep steadying breath.

For a long moment she stood quite still, remembering how overcome with awe she had been on her first day there, and how Blanche Fenton had calmed all her anxieties and had chatted to her about the people in the portraits hanging on the wall of the grand staircase. In her memory she could smell the delicate fragrance of Blanche's rose perfume and hear again the low, soft tones of her voice. She remembered, too, how Blanche had taken her with her when she had sought out Charlie Hardwick and, in order to offer him sanctuary from the thoughtless cruelty he was meeting in the village, had offered him the position of head gardener at Gorton.

It was a long time now since Charlie had met with thoughtless cruelty. Thanks to the genius of Harold Gillies – the surgeon now famed throughout the world for his reconstruction of hideous facial disfigurements suffered by soldiers and sailors in the war – Charlie now had a face that, though not the handsomest Carrie had ever seen, was no longer mind-numbingly horrific.

It was a miracle and, where once he had been ostracized, now, with the piratical black eye-patch he still wore, he was something of a celebrity, and Carrie knew that the whole of Outhwaite would be turning out to see him get married.

'*Carrie!*' Violet shouted, breaking into her thoughts and running up to her. 'I've been waiting *ages* for you. Hermione wasn't going to have any bridesmaids – she said when middle-aged spinsters married they didn't have bridesmaids – but I've talked her into it, and I'm to wear my yellow satin party dress and carry a posy of white roses.'

She hugged Carrie's arm. 'Hermione is getting ready in her own room, and Miss Calvert is here, helping her. Thea and Olivia are in Olivia's bedroom, and Roz hasn't arrived yet. For some reason, I don't know why, she's been in Paris for three days and she's travelling up to Yorkshire straight from the boat-train. Papa's new chauffeur has gone to Richmond station to meet her. Papa is in the drawing room and is looking forward to giving Hermione away. He says it will be a practice run for when he has to do the same for Thea and Olivia and me – though he'll never have to do it for me, because I shall elope.'

Ignoring the threat of elopement, Carrie said, a

little shocked, 'You don't call Hermione "Her-mione" to her face, do you, Violet? She is still your governess.'

Violet's exuberance vanished, to be replaced by a deep glumness. 'She won't be, when this Pyke person marries Papa. Papa says that once I have a stepmother I won't need a governess. Even if I did, my governess wouldn't be Hermione, be-cause she has explained to me that she doesn't want to live for large parts of the year in London. She wants to be in Outhwaite, with Charlie.'

As they talked they began walking up the grand staircase, the portraits looking down on them as familiar to Carrie as if they were her own ances-tors.

'If Lady Pyke has had no children of her own,' she said, 'she'll probably be so pleased to have daughters that she'll spoil and indulge you. It could be quite nice for you, Violet.'

'It would only be quite nice for me if she per-suaded Papa to let me go on the stage.'

'The stage?' Carrie came to a sudden halt. 'You can't go on the stage. You're a viscount's daughter. Your mother's father was an earl. You will be sixteen next year and a debutante. Whoever heard of a debutante who was an actress?'

'That's probably only because none of them have ever wanted to *be* actresses.' Violet, too, stopped walking. 'If you were born to go on the stage – and I was – then that is what you do. Only Papa doesn't agree with me – and I'm very dis-appointed in you, Carrie. I thought you at least would back me up. Olivia doesn't. She says Dieter's family will be horrified if they think

Dieter is marrying someone who has a sister on the stage – as if anyone cares what they think. And Thea says the only girls who become actresses are those who have been born into a theatrical family.'

As they began walking up the stairs again she said crossly, 'Thea also said that Papa wouldn't like it if I became an actress, and that my being one would distress him. Well, Papa doesn't like her being a socialist, and I'm sure her being one distresses him, but she still is one, isn't she?'

Privately Carrie doubted if Lord Fenton was distressed by Thea's socialism, but she didn't say so, because she knew it would only send Violet off on another argumentative tack. Instead, as they reached the first landing, she said, 'Are you going to change into your bridesmaid's dress in Thea's room?'

'No. Hermione says it's tradition for the bride and bridesmaid to get ready together, and my dress is in her room, which is where I'm going now.'

She walked to the foot of the right-hand run of stairs leading to the second floor and paused, one hand on the balustrade. Then, looking back over her shoulder, her face framed by her deeply waving blazing-red hair, she said fiercely, 'I *am* going to go on the stage, Carrie. Acting is my destiny.'

Carrie believed her, but as she made her way to Thea's bedroom, she didn't see how, for Violet, it could be an achievable ambition.

The minute she stepped into the room Thea

rushed up to her, hugging her hard. 'You're lovely and early, Carrie! I didn't think the Richmond bus to Outhwaite got in until twelve o'clock.'

'It doesn't. I came in a motor car.'

'Whose motor car?' It was Olivia who was hugging her now, an Olivia looking breathtakingly sophisticated in a knee-skimming turquoise silk dress and a long rope of pearls.

'Hal's.'

Olivia's reaction didn't disappoint her. 'Hal has a motor car? How spiffing! He must be the first person in Outhwaite village to have one, apart from the vicar and the doctor.'

Seating herself at her dressing table so that they wouldn't see the expression that had flooded her eyes on hearing Hal's name, Thea said much less effusively, 'A couple of local farmers have trucks.'

'Maybe they do.' Olivia hooked her arm through Carrie's. 'But they're not nineteen years old. For someone of Hal's background, owning a motor car is pretty exceptional. I can't wait for him to take me for a spin in it.' Another thought struck her. 'D'you think he would take all three of us for a spin in it later this afternoon, after the wedding?'

Before Carrie could say that she thought he would love to, Thea said swiftly, 'And leave Violet behind, throwing a tantrum to end all tantrums? I don't think so. The best plan would be if he took you, Carrie and Violet for a spin. I get queasy in cars.'

Thea's wedding outfit was a mustard-coloured tunic dress that, in comparison to Olivia's turquoise silk dress, was almost masculine in its

214

severity. It didn't make Thea look masculine, though. The colour brought out the red undertones in her chestnut hair – hair not merely bobbed, but shingled – and the startling greenness of her eyes.

She turned around to face them, determined that her reactions where Hal was concerned were not going to show again. Roz might guess at them, but as she didn't know everything about her and Hal, she wouldn't guess too much.

Putting out her hand, she took hold of Carrie's and pulled her down onto the dressing-table stool beside her. 'I miss you, Carrie. I do wish we could get our plan for you to be my lady's maid off the ground. Papa said he spoke to Lady Markham and that she wasn't happy about the idea of her lady's maid training you up.'

'That's because she doesn't want to lose me.'

'Well, she's going to have to lose you. It doesn't matter that you aren't trained – I only suggested you being trained so that Papa could have no objections. When you get back to Monkswood you must give in your notice.'

Olivia, who had been watching Carrie's face, said, 'You're being impossibly bossy, Thea. Perhaps Carrie doesn't want to leave Monkswood.'

'Of course she does! When she's my lady's maid she'll be with me all the time – and that's something we both want.'

Gently Carrie said, 'But not if you are living mainly in London, Thea.'

Thea stared at her disbelievingly and Carrie gave her hand a loving squeeze. 'This is the first

215

time you've been back at Gorton in nearly a year and, when the wedding is over, you'll be leaving it for London again. If I was your lady's maid I would be going with you, and I can't face the thought of ever having to leave Yorkshire for long periods in London. I'm sorry, Thea. I wasn't going to tell you until after the wedding. I didn't want to spoil the short time we all have together.'

Thea sucked in her breath and, aware of how deep her disappointment was, Carrie said, 'Being apart for such long periods doesn't alter our being best friends, Thea. Think how long we're often separated from Roz.'

Thea swallowed hard. If Carrie didn't want to leave Yorkshire for Mount Street, then there was nothing she could do about it. She certainly couldn't promise Carrie that she'd begin spending the greater part of her time at Gorton. London was where all her socialist friends were, and where all the excitement of socialist meetings was. It was also where other, very different friends – friends such as the Duke and Duchess of York and the Prince of Wales – were. Though her London life was loveless, it was full of interest and it had another advantage over Gorton, one that was overwhelming. It was 250 miles away from Richmond and Hal.

She gave Carrie's hand an answering squeeze. 'I do understand, Carrie, but I can't pretend I'm not hoping that one day you'll change your mind.'

Carrie was saved from having to say she was sure that was never going to happen by a maid knocking on the door.

'His lordship says to remind you of the time,

216

Miss Thea, Miss Olivia,' she said as she entered the room, her face shining with excitement at the fairytale prospect of Miss Violet's governess leaving Gorton for her wedding, just as if she were a daughter of the house. 'And his lordship says when you are ready, would you and Carrie please join him in the drawing room.'

'Countdown time.' Olivia darted across the bedroom and retrieved a shiny straw cloche dyed the exact colour of her dress from a hat-box with the words *Hohe Modenhüte Berlin* emblazoned on the side of it. 'I was hoping I'd have time to show lots of photographs of Dieter before we left for the church,' she said, pulling the cloche snugly over her orange-tawny hair, 'but now that will have to wait until later.'

Without bothering with a mirror, Thea placed a wide-brimmed, shallow-crowned hat on her head and picked up a slim envelope-bag. 'Where on earth is Roz?' she said to Olivia as they all headed out of the room. 'She's cutting it very fine.'

'If she's coming from Paris, perhaps the boat-train was late.'

Fervently hoping that Olivia was wrong, Carrie hurried with them down the grand staircase, her heart beating fast and light. In another few moments she would be being greeted by Lord Fenton, and for her such occasions were always momentous.

'I'd hoped we'd have a glimpse of Hermione in her wedding gown before we left the house,' Olivia said as they crossed the hall towards the drawing room. 'Do you think she'll be wearing white? I can't imagine Hermione in a white bridal gown and veil.'

'I can't imagine her without her pince-nez,' Thea said, wondering how she was going to maintain her composure when she saw Hal in church; wondering what his attitude towards her was going to be; wondering how, if he ignored her, she was going to be able to ignore him.

As they walked into the drawing room, her father strode to greet them, immaculately handsome in a grey morning suit and sporting a white rose *boutonnière*.

'How delightful to see you at Gorton again, Carrie,' he said, shaking her hand. 'Are you still happy at Monkswood? Lady Markham tells me you've forsaken parlourmaid duties and that you are now a chambermaid. Does that mean you are earning a little more money each month?'

'Yes, sir.' Carrie blushed rosily. 'And I'm very happy at Monkswood – though I do still miss Outhwaite.'

'Ah,' he said understandingly, and she knew he knew she really meant Gorton, and that although she did miss Outhwaite, it was Gorton she missed the most.

'All three of you are looking very fetching,' he said, resisting the temptation to say that Olivia looked so different from the girl who had left for Berlin a little less than a year ago, and that he doubted anyone in Outhwaite was going to recognize her. He didn't like the fashion for mascaraed eyes and oxblood-red lips on unmarried young women, but as it was a fashion Zephiniah also followed – with results that made his heart beat like a hammer – he didn't feel comfortable criticizing it.

Glancing towards the ormolu clock on the marble mantelshelf he said, 'Although you may feel it's a little early, I think it's time you were leaving for the church. It's always better to be seated in good time at a wedding.'

'But what about Roz?' Thea's eyes darkened in concern. 'Shouldn't we wait for her a little bit longer?'

'Because of how late she's running, Braithwaite will take her straight to the church. She may be there already.'

'I hope she has her camera with her,' Olivia said, not turning to leave the room as he had suggested. 'Violet will never forgive Roz if her moment as a bridesmaid goes unrecorded.'

Carrie was aware of Thea asking a question about the church and photographs and of Lord Fenton replying to her, but she was no longer standing with them and no longer listening. When Lord Fenton had made his remark about how fetching the three of them looked, her blush had deepened to the point where she'd been desperate to hide it and she had stepped back and turned away, fixing her unseeing gaze on the grand piano and the gold-framed watercolours hanging on the wall behind it.

Always sensible, she told herself that the remark had simply been a pleasant, throwaway remark to his daughters and that she had been included in it simply because she had entered the room with them. She dared not imagine anything else; to do so would be foolish to the point of imbecility.

'Rozalind rarely goes anywhere without her camera,' Lord Fenton was saying, as common sense took over and the scarlet banners in her cheeks ebbed, 'and so I think you are worrying unnecessarily, Thea.'

Carrie dropped her gaze from the watercolours, about to turn and rejoin Thea and Olivia. As she did so her glance fell on the silver-framed photograph of Blanche that, ever since her death, had held pride of place on the piano, always with a slender vase of fresh-cut flowers next to it.

The flowers were there now, a delicate arrangement of sweet-smelling freesias. Something else was also next to it. Another photograph. One she had never seen before.

It wasn't of Blanche, with her cloud of smoke-dark hair, warm loving smile and pearls at her ears and throat.

It was of a woman in an off-the-shoulder, daringly décolleté black taffeta ballgown. Night-black hair was swept high in a gleaming, complicated chignon, and there were diamonds at her ears and throat and around her slender wrists. Lady Pyke – for Carrie knew the photograph could be of no one else – wasn't smiling, but then in formal photographs (and the photograph was very formal) people seldom smiled.

Carrie tried to look away from Lady Pyke's glittering, elegant image, but couldn't.

She'd known Lord Fenton was engaged and would soon be remarrying, but until now such an event had seemed unreal. If she had given any thought as to what the new Lady Fenton would be like, she had imagined a paler version of Blanche.

As shockwave after shockwave washed over her, she knew, without a shadow of a doubt, that the woman in the photograph was nothing like Blanche.

Dimly she heard Lord Fenton say, 'Time is ticking away, girls. Any minute now Hermione will be coming downstairs, and I don't want you here when she does so. She doesn't want you seeing her in her wedding gown until she arrives at the church.'

Carrie knew she should turn and begin walking to the door, but her legs felt too weak to be trusted. What if the new Lady Fenton didn't approve of her friendship with Thea and Olivia and Violet? What if she thought Carrie visiting Gorton Hall as a family friend was déclassé?

There was movement behind her and as Lord Fenton, with a hand on his daughters' shoulders, began propelling them firmly towards the door, Carrie finally found the strength to turn around and follow them.

She did so ashamed of the selfishness of her feelings. The most important thing about Lord Fenton's second marriage wasn't whether his new wife would approve of her, and of her friendship with Thea, Olivia and Violet. The most important thing was that she should make Lord Fenton happy; as happy as he had been with Blanche.

As he led them across the neatly raked gravel to the first of three ribbon-bedecked motor cars, she knew one thing for certain: Lord Fenton's happiness was far more important to her than her own.

It was, and had been for as long as she could remember, the most important thing in the world to her.

Chapter Fourteen

The drive from Gorton Hall to the tiny Methodist chapel in Outhwaite's High Street church took barely ten minutes, but during those ten minutes Thea's tension increased until it was nearly unendurable. What was going to happen when she and Hal were again face-to-face? Would he realize that he still loved her? That he had behaved idiotically in believing the class difference between them was unbridgeable? Was today going to be the day when everything would finally be made right? She closed her eyes, imagining his arms around her once again. His hands hard upon her body, his mouth dry as her tongue slipped past his.

'Golly!' Olivia said. 'Look at the number of people outside the chapel waiting for Papa and Hermione's arrival.'

Thea opened her eyes. The chapel faced directly onto the High Street and both sides of the steps leading to its open double doors were crowded with people eager for a glimpse of the bride. Inside it would, she knew, be packed to the rafters, with the only available seating the seating reserved for them. Charlie would probably already be there, and Jim would be with him.

222

The car drew to a halt and she wondered feverishly if Hal had already arrived. If he had, he was bound to be sitting in the first or second row of right-hand pews, along with Charlie's family. As Hermione had no family, when she, Olivia and Carrie entered the chapel they would be led to the front left-hand pews, which meant there would only be a matter of yards between her and Hal. Would he immediately try and make eye contact with her? There was still ten minutes before Hermione was due to arrive. Would he take advantage of that time and walk across and speak to her? He wouldn't be able to say the kind of things she ached for him to say, in front of Olivia and Carrie, but she would know by his eyes if he had missed her as much as she had missed him.

'It's a shame Methodists don't go in for candles and incense,' Olivia said as they entered the chapel. 'It's a much nicer smell than lavender polish.'

'I like the smell,' she heard Carrie say. 'Look how wonderfully shiny all the mahogany is, and there's something calming about plain white walls and polished brasswork.'

Thea couldn't have cared less about the chapel's interior, which didn't have one main aisle, but a right-hand aisle and a left-hand aisle, with pews at the sides of both aisles and central pews between them.

Hal was seated in a front left-hand pew and, as they walked down the right-hand aisle to take the places reserved for them, she had a clear view of the back of his head. No one else in Outhwaite had such a head of unruly dark curls. She knew he often tried to subdue them with brilliantine, but he rarely did so successfully and, if he had tried to do so today, he had failed miserably.

Carrie parted company with them in order to sit next to her granny, and Olivia said, as she too spotted Hal, 'I can't wait for us to be a circle of five again. D'you think there's time for me to go over and have a quick word with Hal, before Papa and Hermione arrive?'

'No,' Thea said tersely, stepping into the front central pew. 'I don't.'

A buzz of interested comments on their wedding outfits had followed them down the aisle and she knew that although Hal hadn't turned his head, he was aware of her arrival. It was impossible for him not to be.

She seated herself on the unforgivingly hard wood and looked determinedly straight ahead to where, in front of the communion table, Charlie and Jim were deep in conversation with the pastor.

Had Hal not looked towards her for the same reason that she, now, was not looking towards him? Because he was afraid of what her response might be? Or was it because a hot, urgent glance passed between them would be endlessly gossiped about and conjectured on? Or, worst thought of all, had he not turned his head towards her because he no longer had the slightest interest in her? If that was the case, how was he going to explain no longer even being friends with her to Olivia, Carrie and Roz?

And where was Roz?

'She's only got another five minutes, if she

wants to be here before the bride,' Olivia said, reading her thoughts and turning round to make sure Roz hadn't come in after them and taken a seat at the back of the chapel.

'I can't see her anywhere,' she said, 'but the Hardwicks are out in full strength. I'd no idea Charlie had such a lot of relatives – and they must be relatives, because none of them are from Outhwaite. Mr and Mrs Lumsden are here – and Mrs Lumsden is wearing a very splendid purple hat with a feather! Mrs Mellor is sitting on Charlie's side of the chapel. It's odd to think that if it wasn't for the ghastly scene in her post office, Mama would never have offered Charlie a position as a gardener at Gorton, and Papa would never have referred him to Mr Gillies, and Charlie wouldn't have the face he has now.'

Thea was just about to say that if all that hadn't happened, it was highly unlikely Charlie and Hermione would have met and be now getting married, when the pastor terminated his conversation with Charlie and Jim and faced the congregation.

An expectant hush fell.

Charlie stood as erect as a guardsman on parade.

Jim nervously slicked back his hair.

Olivia said in a whisper to Thea, 'Roz is not going to be happy at missing this.'

The organist began to play and, to Handel's 'The Arrival of the Queen of Sheba', Hermione stepped into the chapel on Gilbert Fenton's arm.

Tall and gaunt-framed, she wasn't wearing white. Her narrow-skirted ankle-length silk gown was pewter-blue. With it she was wearing a matching straw hat with an upturned brim and matching silk gloves. Her wedding bouquet was a posy of white Yorkshire roses bred by Charlie and named 'Hermione' in her honour.

Walking behind her was Violet, so ecstatic at being a bridesmaid that her smile was as broad as the Cheshire cat's.

The service began with the Methodist hymn 'Love Divine, All Loves Excelling'.

Halfway through it, instinct made Thea turn her head just as Roz stepped into the chapel. With the service in progress, Roz made no attempt to find a seat, but instead stood unobtrusively to one side of the open doorway, her camera-case slung over her shoulder.

'Roz is here,' Thea whispered to Olivia. 'And she has her camera with her.'

Now there was no longer Roz to worry about, Thea's thoughts immediately returned to Hal. Because their distant pews were level with each other, she could only get a glimpse of him if, before looking in his direction, she leaned forward – but to do that would make her interest in him titillatingly obvious to those seated behind her.

She wondered what Hal was thinking as Charlie and Hermione made their vows. She wondered if the beauty and solemnity of the simple service were making him think differently about marriage – but she only wanted him thinking differently about marriage if *she* was the girl he was thinking of marrying.

The register was signed, with Miss Calvert and Jim acting as witnesses. Another hymn was sung.

A final prayer was said. The organist began playing Mendelssohn's 'Wedding March', and Hermione and Charlie began their joyous walk out of the chapel as man and wife.

The congregation filed into the aisles to follow them, and Hal's head finally turned in her direction, his eyes meeting hers, hot and hard.

She stumbled and Olivia said with a giggle. 'Steady, Thea. You don't want Hermione's Methodist friends thinking you're squiffy!'

As she walked out of the chapel down the right-hand aisle she was parallel to Hal, now walking down the left-hand aisle. When they got outside he would speak to her – he had to – and one way or the other the suspense she felt would be over.

Outside there was much happy jostling as people crowded onto the pavement to watch Rozalind taking photographs. Thea's attention was elsewhere – on Hal, who was pushing a way through the throng towards her. She dug her nails into her palms, her heart racing so fast she felt giddy.

Coming to a halt in front of her, he shot her the old familiar grin, but the hot, hard look she had surprised in his eyes was there no longer. It could have been Olivia he was speaking to. Or Rozalind.

'You're looking well, Thea,' he said, as casually as he would have done in the old days; the days before he had first kissed her and had changed her world for what she'd been certain was for-ever. 'The wedding breakfast is being held in the village hall, though I expect you know that.'

It was so obvious he wasn't going to make right

what had gone wrong between them that it took every ounce of her self-control to feign equal nonchalance.

'Yes,' she said in a voice unrecognizable even to herself. 'Hopefully everyone will be able to get in. I've never seen so many people at a local wedding.'

There were limits to how long she could keep up the pretence that being just jolly good friends again was as acceptable to her as it evidently was for Hal, and where for hours she'd been counting the minutes until she was face-to-face with him, now she was desperate to get away before he should see how deep her heartbreak was.

Confetti was being thrown, and beneath a shower of it Carrie threaded her way towards them. Hal threw an arm round her shoulders, and a local farmer standing cheek-by-jowl with them said, 'So when are you and Carrie goin' to name t' day, Hal lad?'

Hal roared with laughter. 'When Carrie stops eyeing up t' footmen at Monkswood.'

His arm was still round Carrie's shoulder and, looking at the two of them, Thea could understand why the remark had been made. Not only had Carrie and Hal been seen constantly in each other's company since they were children, but they looked right together. There was a sense of unity between the two of them that was palpable. She wondered if anyone had ever thought the same thing about her and Hal, and doubted it. The only teasing remarks about Hal and anyone else had been Charlie's and Jim's sly references to his having a crush on Olivia – something they

228

had been laughably wrong about.

'I need to speak with Roz,' she said, with a composure so false it occurred to her that she, and not Violet, was the born actress in the family.

Sobs were rising in her throat and, keeping them in check with difficulty, she pushed a way through the crowd to where Roz was putting her camera back in its case.

'Job done!' Roz flashed her a wide smile. 'Sorry about being so late – and, before you ask, Max isn't with me. He's had to hare off to a conference. Have we to walk to the hall, and have a catch-up of news over lemonade – or whatever else it is Methodists serve at wedding breakfasts?'

'I'm not going to the reception.' Thea's voice cracked and broke. 'It's the first time I've seen Hal since our falling-out and it hasn't gone well.'

Swiftly Roz tucked her arm in hers. 'In that case I'll give the reception a miss too. Where have we to go for a chat where we'll be undisturbed? The vole place?'

Thea nodded. The vole place would be perfect. No one else would be within a mile of it.

Wedding guests were now streaming down the High Street in the wake of Hermione and Charlie, who were travelling the fifty yards to the village hall in a flower-decorated pony-trap.

'Is the problem the same one it was a year ago?' Roz asked as they fell into step at the rear of the procession.

'I imagine so, but as we didn't talk about it then, I don't know.'

'But if you didn't talk about things, how can you know things aren't going well?'

229

'His attitude towards me.' Thea's voice was taut with the effort of maintaining her reputation for never crying. 'He simply treated me as if all the long months of our being passionately in love had never happened – I could have been anyone. "You're looking well," he said, just as he might have said it to Mrs Lumsden or Mrs Mellor if he hadn't seen them for more than a year. Then he said, "The wedding breakfast is being held in the village hall, though I expect you know that." *That's* what I mean about it not going well! It was so obvious he hadn't been suffering over our break-up – as I've been suffering that it was insulting.'

In front of them people were disappearing through the doors of the village hall. Hal and Carrie were clearly visible, walking together as if they were a couple.

'They're not holding hands,' Thea said, not needing to say who she was referring to. 'But they might as well be.'

'I thought Hal was sowing his wild oats with the Richmond barmaids?'

'He probably is. It would be hard to sow them with Carrie, when she's at Monkswood. You know what the rules are for household staff. No followers, no matter what the circumstances. A day like this is probably the most freedom Carrie has had in ages.'

'Yes, well. I don't think you have anything to worry about there. I think they're simply just the very best of friends.'

Thea took her hat off and ran her fingers through her short-cropped springy waves. 'I just don't understand why he's letting the class difference ruin our lives,' she said, bewildered and despairing. 'Hal's a socialist. He wants to see an end to class divisions. You would think our taking no notice of class divisions would be a statement he'd be eager to make.'

'I don't have an answer for you, Thea. Hal is Hal. He makes up his mind about something and then, if the past is anything to go by, never changes it.'

'You think he won't change it now?'

'If he did,' Rozalind said as the river came into sight, 'it would be a first.'

Thea drew in a deep, shuddering breath.

Disturbed that Thea was taking her altered relationship with Hal so much to heart, Rozalind said, 'What will you do?'

'I'll go out with other men: lots of other men. But none of them will be another Hal. How could they be? I'm never going to get over Hal, Roz. Never, never, never.'

They didn't speak again for a long time and, when they did, sitting in deep grass by the vole place, they deliberately talked of other things: of Max, of Charlie and Hermione's wedding, of Olivia having finally returned for good from Berlin.

'Though she's bound to go back sometime in the future if she marries Dieter,' Roz said. 'Even taking into account Berlin's hectic nightlife, I wouldn't want to live there. Germany is too chaotic and unsettling.'

'But inflation has stopped, hasn't it?'

'Yes, but political extremism hasn't.' Rozalind, who had been lying on her back, rolled over onto

231

her tummy, with her weight on her elbows. 'I wonder what political colour Dieter is? Olivia never gives politics a thought, so I don't suppose she's ever asked.'

Thea hugged her knees, her eyes on the familiar spot where the voles might appear at any moment. 'He'll be a monarchist who wants the Kaiser back,' she said, knowing that in talking about politics Roz was trying to give her something other than Hal to think about. 'Anyone whose family is listed in the *Almanach de Gotha* is bound to be a monarchist.'

Two bright eyes and a quivering nose and whiskers appeared at the entrance of the vole hole, and for a long time all talk ended as they vole-watched as raptly as they had when they were children.

Later, walking along the river-bank towards the bridge and Gorton, Rozalind returned to the subject of Dieter von Starhemberg and his probable politics. 'The way Germany is at the moment, Dieter could well be anything – even an admirer of Hitler, the man who tried to overthrow the German government last year. It could be quite interesting. Just think how politically varied we already are as a family. Your father is a Conservative who sits in the House of Lords and is a government minister. You are a socialist. Max is a Republican. Kyle, who is due to take up his post at the American Embassy any day now, is a Democrat. Olivia is apolitical. Goodness only knows what Violet is going to be, and we've no idea of Lady Pyke's political persuasion.'

'Having seen her photograph, I imagine she'll be a little to the right of Attila the Hun.'

Thea came to a sudden halt, knee-deep in buttercups. 'Before we get back to Gorton I have to talk to you some more about Hal, Roz. I have to tell you something you don't know. It's something that happened the night of my coming-out ball – something that, if I'd behaved differently, might have made all the difference.'

Rozalind waited, and Thea said very fast, 'When I left the dinner table before the ball, it was to go and find him so that I could tell him he needn't attend the ball in order to write about it – not if being there would make him uncomfortable. He'd been given one of the valets' rooms to change in. When I walked in on him he was naked to the waist and there were water droplets on his chest, and when he kissed me I wanted him so much, Roz – so much that I didn't care about losing my virginity or what would happen if I became pregnant – and the bed was so near and he swept me up in his arms to carry me across to it and then ... and then...'

Tears she'd held at bay for so long scalded the backs of her eyes.

'There was hardly any time left before my guests arrived, and I had to be at the head of the grand staircase with Papa in order to greet them. If I wasn't beside him, I knew how mortified Papa would be and I just couldn't do that to him, Roz. I just couldn't. And so we didn't make love. I made Hal drop me to my feet, hurled at him the stupid reason I was there and ran. I ran all the way along the corridor and down the stairs and back through a baize door and down other stairs, until I reached Papa's side – and I was only just in time, for moments later Prince Edward arrived. But oh, Roz! I can't help wondering how different things might be now, if we'd gone to bed together that night – and I wish and wish and wish that we had!'

Tears poured down her face and Rozalind closed the space between them, giving her a fierce, comforting hug. 'Things might now be different, Thea. Or they might not be. But think how much worse you'd feel if the two of you had made love and he'd still said the things to you that he said later that night.'

'Would I feel any worse? I don't think I could, Roz. And at least it would have been something to remember.' Thea wiped her face with her hands, saying in a flat, bleak voice, 'I'm sorry if I've shocked you.'

'Shocked me? No, you haven't shocked me. But I may be just about to shock you.' They began walking again in the direction of the bridge and Roz said, 'Just as there are things you hadn't previously told me about you and Hal, so there are things I haven't told you about Max and me.'

'You're lovers?'

'We are indeed. But what will shock you is the lie I told in order for us to become lovers.'

'A lie? But why on earth did you have to lie?' Thea was so intrigued that for the first time in hours Hal was no longer in her thoughts. 'I'm sorry, Roz. I don't understand.'

'He'd made it quite clear to me that, as a point of honour, he never seduces virgins – and he quite correctly assumed that was what I was. And so I told him I wasn't.'

They had reached the bridge now, and Thea was so shell-shocked she once again stopped walking. 'You did *what?*'

'I told him I wasn't. And he believed me.'

'But what about ... I mean, when you did go to bed together, surely he must have realized?'

'Oh, he realized all right, but by the time he did, it was too late to change anything. The deed was done. I was well and truly deflowered.'

'Dear Heaven!' Thea began giggling. 'You're right, Roz. You've shocked me. And you've no regrets?'

'Do I look as if I have regrets?' They began walking again, arm-in-arm. 'There was a time, though, when I thought I might have some, because when he realized how I'd lied, he was *furious* with me.'

'And now?'

'And now I'm just back after spending three idyllic days with him in Paris.'

'Don't let Olivia know, because I'm sure she can't wait to lose her virginity as well, and I believe German aristocracy is even hotter about virginity before marriage than we are – which is saying something. I don't want her queering her pitch. Not if Dieter von Starhemberg really is "the one".'

Grateful for the miracle of having been made to giggle even when she was heartbroken, Thea entered Gorton with Roz fifteen minutes later to be met by her father, still in his morning suit and with a telegram in his hand.

'Wonderful news,' he said ebulliently, striding

235

towards them. 'Zephiniah has sent a cable from the *Laconia*. She will be in England in just under two weeks!'

Chapter Fifteen

JANUARY 1926

It was the second week of a freezing-cold New Year, and Olivia, a large diamond encircled by sapphires sparkling on the ring finger of her left hand, was cosily ensconced in the drawing room of Curzon House in Curzon Street, enjoying a long-overdue gossip with the Duchess of York.

'It's been such ages and ages since I've seen you that I really don't know where we should start,' Elizabeth said, pouring tea for them both from a silver teapot. 'The last time we had this kind of meeting together, you weren't engaged, Bertie and I hadn't left for our East Africa tour and I wasn't even pregnant – now look at me!' She gave a delicious giggle. 'I've still three months to go and Bertie thinks I'll be as round as a ball by then.'

She put the teapot down.

'Milk or lemon? You will have to forgive me, but I can't remember. Apparently it's what happens when you are *enceinte*. The most ordinary every-day things simply fly out of your head.'

'Lemon, please.' Because so many months had gone by since their last meeting, Olivia had been nervous that the first few minutes of their reunion would be a little awkward, but she had forgotten Elizabeth's natural warmth and un-affected nature.

'I want to know all about Count von Starhem-berg,' Elizabeth said now, dropping a slice of lemon into Olivia's teacup with a lemon-fork. 'Thea tells me he is very *Berlinerisch*.'

Her voice was full of happy interest and, rem-embering how many of Bertie's German relatives could be similarly described, Olivia knew the remark carried no criticism. 'He is,' she said as Elizabeth handed her a cup and saucer. 'He does all those old-fashioned *Berlinerisch* things, such as clicking his heels and bowing when being introduced to a lady. He's very blond and very tall and utterly, utterly wonderful. The very best thing about him is that he is now Third Secretary at the German Embassy, and so we still see each other just as often as we did when I was in Berlin.'

'And are you going to have a long engagement or a short one?'

'A short one. Though Papa did say we would have to wait until my nineteenth birthday – which isn't until August – he's now agreed we can marry at Easter.'

'Wonderful! I think short engagements are so much more romantic. Bertie and I were engaged from January to the end of April, which is nearly exactly the same length of time. And oh my goodness, what a rush and a whirl everything was.'

Olivia giggled. 'Mine isn't a royal wedding, Elizabeth.'

'For which you can thank your lucky stars. You have no idea the number of family members that a royal family can drum up, when it comes to a wedding. I read in the *Morning Post* afterwards that there were one thousand seven hundred and eighty people squeezed into the Abbey, including,' Elizabeth – always a good mimic – adopted mock-stentorian tones, *'many leading personages of the nation and Empire*. But d'you know my mother had to haggle like a fishwife to ensure that all my Bowes-Lyon cousins were included on the guest list?'

Olivia helped herself to a petit four. 'I wish my mother was alive to be haggling on my behalf. All I have is the former Lady Pyke.'

Elizabeth settled herself even more comfortably on the sofa they were sharing in front of a cosy coal fire. 'Ah,' she said in deep satisfaction. 'I so want to hear all about your new stepmother. I've asked around, of course – just as everyone else has been asking around – but no one seems to know much about her, except that her previous married life was spent almost entirely in Argentina. Is she scrumptiously lovely?'

Olivia grimaced. 'My father obviously thinks so – and for his sake we are all doing our very best to get on with her, but she's such an unlikely sort of person for him to have married that it isn't easy. She's hardly spent any time at all at Gorton, and yet she's ordered such sweeping changes there that it no longer feels like home. The housekeeper we've had for years and years has gone, and housemaids with a broad Yorkshire accent – which is just about all of them – have been replaced by maids recruited from a London staffing agency. It caused the most terrible row between Thea and Papa, but Papa said he most certainly was not going to over-rule any decisions Zephiniah had made, and that Thea had to realize that although there had been no weekend house-parties at Gorton since before Mama died, all that was now going to change – and that changes in staffing had to be made accordingly.'

'Goodness. I'm riveted! Are changes taking place in Mount Street as well?'

'Mount Street is apparently far too informally furnished. Out are going all the comfy chintz-covered sofas and in – when a team of decorators has finished preparing the way for them – are coming French Empire antiques, and you know how uncomfortable French Empire sofas are to sit on.'

Next morning, trudging with Thea in a light fall of snow around the southern edge of the Round Pond in Kensington Gardens, Olivia said, 'Elizabeth was just as easy to chat to as always. I really do think she's one of the nicest people in the world.'

'She is. Everyone adores her. According to David, even his father can find no fault with her.'

Olivia's friendship with the Duke and Duchess of York hadn't yet led to friendship with Prince Edward, though she was hoping for Dieter's sake that it would soon do so and that it wouldn't be long before they, too, would be able to refer to the Prince as David. For a young German diplo-mat to become part of the Prince of Wales's circle would be viewed by his superiors in Berlin as a great coup and would be a huge step up the promotional ladder towards his goal of one day becoming an ambassador.

Thea was saying that the Prince of Wales's long affair with his mistress, Freda Dudley Ward, had become 'relatively detached', but Olivia was too busy wondering where Dieter would be posted when ambassador to pay much attention.

London was always Dieter's first choice whenever they spoke of the golden future lying in wait for them. It was never her first choice. London was home ground and therefore not glamorous enough. 'Paris,' she would say dreamily, 'or Washington.'

'This is too cold to be fun.' Thea's voice brought Olivia sharply back into the present. 'I know I said I'd act as chaperone for you while you had lunch with Dieter, but Zephiniah demanding that I do so is ridiculous. It's not as if I'm married, and I'm only a year older than you. Why she thinks my being with you will make your lunch respectable, I don't know.'

'It's because she's hostessing a luncheon of her own today and because we haven't – thank God – an army of aunts and married cousins living near at hand that she can call on. Nor has she women friends in London who can chaperone for her.'

Of all the aggravations that had come with Gilbert's marriage, the chaperone issue had been the one they had found most tedious.

'We haven't been chaperoned since Aunt Hilda was in London for my coming-out ball,' Thea had said to Gilbert in a voice of sweet reason when the subject had first arisen. 'It's nonsensical that we should start being chaperoned now. How ridiculous would it look, my attending Labour Party meetings with a chaperone in tow? Please thank Zephiniah for her concern, but the only person needing a chaperone in this family is Violet.'

She'd hoped that would be the end of the matter, but it hadn't been. Her father had said how guilty he felt about his previous neglectful attitude where chaperoning was concerned, and how grateful they should all be that Zephiniah was being so caring and diligent in her duties as a stepmother.

'I'm not at all convinced about the caring bit,' Thea had said to Olivia. 'It's her own reputation she's concerned about, not ours. She doesn't want any gossip about the new Viscountess Fenton not being quite up to snuff.'

Remembering Thea's comment, Olivia said now, 'I suppose we shouldn't give the gossips any ammunition, Thea.' As they left the park she dug her gloved hands deep into a beaver muff that matched her hat. 'It will only cause a row – and I hate rows. They make Papa so unhappy.'

'Then he shouldn't have married the Pyke. If there's one thing I've realized these last few months, it's that although Papa is very much a man of the world where politics are concerned, he's pathetically unworldly about women. It comes of him having fallen in love with Mama when he was so young, and of his being faithful to her memory for so long. Where is it we are

241

meeting Dieter for lunch? The Savoy?'

'Claridge's. Dieter likes it there.'

'Then I'm going to flag down a cab – which is something else that will give Zephiniah the vapours if she gets to hear of it.'

On the cab ride from Kensington to Mayfair, she asked, curious, 'What does Dieter think of Zephiniah?'

'He thinks she's jaw-droppingly beautiful and extremely exotic. So exotic he finds it hard to believe she has no Latin blood in her veins.'

'She does look very Latin, but according to *Burke's Peerage* she's English all the way through and Dieter is probably using "Latin" as a euphemism for "Jewish".'

'Why on earth should he?' Olivia stared at her, mystified. 'Sometimes, Thea, you do talk the most awful rot. If Dieter thought Zephiniah had Jewish blood in her veins, he would say so. Why would you think he wouldn't?'

'Because Roz told me that when she visited you in Berlin last year she heard the word "Jew" used quite often on the streets and in cafes – and not always about people who were obviously Jewish. She said it seemed to be a catchall phrase used disparagingly for anyone not obviously fitting in – people such as Eastern Europeans and gypsies. So Dieter would be careful, don't you think, about using that word in connection with Zephiniah?'

'I think you're cracked and you go to too many socialist meetings and that, when she's with you, Roz falls too quickly and easily into your cracked way of thinking. That's what I think. Now are you coming with me into Claridge's, or aren't you?'

Just as had happened so often when they were children, they were on the verge of falling out with each other for no real reason. Aware of it – and aware that their falling out was senseless when in order to cope with Zephiniah they needed to maintain a united front – Thea said, 'I'm coming in. And just remember that I'm here as a chaperone, so no holding hands.'

As the head waiter led them across the dining room to Dieter's table, Thea appreciated for the first time just how distinctive-looking her future brother-in-law was. Until now she had only seen Dieter at Mount Street and – once – at a German Embassy function she had attended with Olivia and their father, at her father's request. Her attitude then had been churlish. True, the war had long been over, but she'd still found Olivia's choice of a German for a fiancé – and the ready way she had adapted to life in Berlin – crass.

Now, as he rose from the table to greet them, she suddenly saw why Olivia was so smitten. Tall and athletic, with a lean face and high cheek-bones, piercing blue eyes and straight blond hair swept away from his forehead, he had the look of a Viking god. It wasn't a look that did anything for her, but combined with his aristocratic lineage and what her father predicted was going to be a dizzyingly successful diplomatic career, she could quite see that it was a package few women would be able to resist.

He clicked his heels, kissed the back of her hand and said how pleased he was that she was joining them for lunch.

Over glasses of Pol Roger champagne and

sautéed scallops he told her why Claridge's was his favourite place for lunch.

'The Prince of Wales and his brother, Prince George, dine here together. It is a good recommendation, I think.'

'If you start patronizing everywhere the Prince of Wales patronizes, you're going to be kept very busy,' she said drily. 'He can fit in more social engagements in a day than most people manage in a year. As for Prince George...'

It occurred to her that Dieter probably didn't yet know about Prince George's bisexuality and, as the kind of clubs Prince George favoured were not the kind that would enhance Dieter's reputation if he were to be seen in them, she decided not to get involved in talking about him.

He didn't seem to notice.

'It is good you and Olivia are such friends of Prince Albert and Princess Elizabeth. Albert is much different from his brothers, yes? More ... what is the word in English? More the introvert?'

'He's certainly quieter,' Thea said, 'but so would we all be, if we had his stammer. And a word of advice, Dieter. In society Albert and Elizabeth are almost always referred to simply as the Duke and Duchess of York – and Bertie is never referred to as Albert. Speak of Prince Albert and people will think you are referring to the Prince Albert who married Queen Victoria.'

He shot her a smile so charming she found herself definitely warming towards him. 'Thank you for that tip. We Germans always err on an excess of formality, and it is good to be checked when we do so inappropriately.'

The sommelier hovered at his elbow.

Dieter looked from her to Olivia and said, 'Would you like a different wine order now, or would you rather stay with champagne?'

'Champagne,' Olivia said instantly.

Thea, now enjoying herself, nodded agreement.

Their conversation returned to the Yorks, with Dieter saying that Bertie and Elizabeth's home life sounded very *gemütlicht*.

'Which means cosy and unpretentious,' Olivia said for Thea's benefit. 'And the word *Hausfrau* is used for Elizabeth's way of dressing – but that is because to be fashionable in Berlin means being a flapper and sporting short, cropped hair and mannish clothes.'

'A look that Elizabeth is wise not even to flirt with.' There was thick amusement in Thea's voice. 'Good Lord, can you imagine Elizabeth as a flapper? She's far too softly rounded and pudgy and, between ourselves, I like her floaty pastel dresses and the three-string pearl necklace she wears with nearly everything...'

'...and her shoulder-hugging fur collars and long skirts,' Olivia finished for her. 'It may be a style unique to her, but it is instantly recognizable, and men do seem to like it. Perhaps we should all be dressing in pink and cornflower-blue and dove-grey and wearing our hair parted in the middle and prettily curled.'

There was no malice in her voice, only deep affection.

Dieter covered her hand with his. 'I think, *Liebchen*, that I prefer you just as you are.'

Olivia flushed with happiness and, as they looked deep into each other's eyes, it was so obvious that he loved her just as much as she loved him that Thea was overwhelmed with heartache. Why couldn't Hal love her as Dieter loved Olivia? Why couldn't he love her so much that he wanted to marry her, have children with her and grow old with her?

It was a question she had no answer to and it was still gnawing at her heart when, an hour later, they went their separate ways – Dieter by cab to the German Embassy, Olivia by cab to a hairdressing appointment in Bond Street, and Thea on foot to nearby Mount Street.

The light fall of snow had long since stopped and only the merest dusting still lay on the ground. As she approached the house, wondering how, when she entered it, she could best avoid Zephiniah, the front door opened and a man she had never seen before stepped out. As the door closed behind him he paused on the top of the shallow flight of wide stone steps, as if wondering where he should go next.

She quickened her footsteps, intrigued. Just as her eyes were on him, so his eyes were now on her.

She came to a halt at the foot of the steps and he began walking slowly down them. She judged him to be in his mid-twenties. He was wearing a black double-breasted overcoat and a grey fedora. Though his clothes shouldn't have given his nationality away, he couldn't have been mistaken for anything other than an American – and an American who was a New Yorker.

He had a very neat, very dark, very attractive moustache above a well-shaped mouth, a pleasingly straight nose, satanically winged eyebrows – and beneath them eyes as distinctively slate-blue as Rozalind's.

'Hello, Kyle,' she said as he came to a halt in front of her. 'Roz forewarned us you'd soon be turning up here.'

'I don't think she forewarned Lady Fenton,' he said in dry amusement. 'I seemed to have taken her completely by surprise and I'm still not sure she understands my connection to the family.'

'Don't worry. She will. But as she wouldn't give us any privacy in which to chat and get to know each other, I'd prefer not to make things clear to her right now. Shall we pick up a cab and go to the National Gallery? We can stroll there in the warm to our heart's content and when we're tired of looking at great art and deciding if we have mutual tastes in it, we can have tea and cakes in the cafe.'

'Done deal, Thea.' He flashed her a broad smile and crooked his arm.

She slid her gloved hand through it. 'How do you know I'm not Olivia?'

'Because Roz described you as being bossy and decisive.'

Companionably, as if they had known each other forever, they began walking in the direction of Park Lane, keeping an eye out for an empty taxicab as they did so.

By the time one stopped for them, Thea was giving him an update on Olivia's recent engagement to Dieter. By the time they reached Trafalgar

Square and the National Gallery she was telling him about Violet's obsession with becoming an actress.

'Does she get any encouragement?' he asked with interest after he'd paid off the cab.

'Not one iota. My father has said he's happy to send her to finishing school now she's sixteen, but all she says is that she doesn't want to go to a finishing school; that she wants to go to the Royal Academy of Dramatic Art.'

As they strolled through the galleries devoted to paintings dating from 1200 to 1500, which Thea said was her favourite period and Kyle said left him totally cold, he gave her an update on Rozalind's affair with Max. 'She'd thought she would have been sporting an engagement ring by now,' he said as they stood in front of Giorgione's *The Adoration of the Kings*, 'but Max seems content to let things stay as they are.'

Thea wondered if Kyle knew exactly what letting things 'stay as they are' meant. Would Roz have told her stepbrother that she and Max had been lovers within days of meeting – and of the lie she had told to ensure that they were? She doubted it – and if he didn't know, then it wasn't for her to tell him.

As they moved from the Florentine art of the fifteenth century to the Venetian art of the sixteenth century, Kyle said, 'Roz tells me you're finding it difficult adjusting to having a stepmother.'

'I would probably have adjusted to someone else quite well. It's Zephiniah I'm finding it difficult to adjust to. She's such a snob – and I find

248

that so odd, when my father has always been so egalitarian.'

There was a padded leather seat in the centre of the room and they sat down on it, facing the blazing reds and blues of Titian's *Bacchus and Ariadne*.

'At our family home in Yorkshire we never stood on ceremony – Mama would simply never have allowed it.'

At the thought of her mother, and of how perfect life had been when Blanche was alive, tears stung her eyes.

She blinked hard, focusing fiercely on the band of revellers following Bacchus's cheetah-drawn chariot. 'Some of our closest friends when we were children were people who worked for us; people like Charlie Hardwick – and I know Roz will have told you all about Charlie. We've also been best friends with Gorton's odd-job man, Jim Crosby, since the time we were able to walk – and we still are best friends with him. In a time of trouble both Charlie and Jim are the first people Olivia and I – and Violet – would turn to.'

'If Zephiniah is the snob you say she is,' Kyle said sagely, 'she's not going to like that.'

'No, she isn't. But she's jolly well going to have to put up with it.'

Kyle frowned. From the little he'd seen of Zephiniah he didn't think she was the kind of woman who would put up with anything she didn't want to put up with. Rather than endure the embarrassment of having stepdaughters who fraternized with the estate staff, she would ensure that the staff in question were no longer at Gorton to be fraternized with.

249

He looked at Thea's profile as she stared straight ahead at the painting in front of them. Her jawline was strong and determined, and though her mouth was full and generous, it was also the mouth of someone who could be as obstinate as a mule if she chose to be. When it came to laying down the law as to who Thea could, and could not, be friends with, Zephiniah was going to have a battle royal on her hands – and the main issue wouldn't be about Charlie and Jim. It would be about Hal Crosby and Carrie Thornton.

'Though far more Carrie than Hal,' Roz had said to Kyle, when they had dined together in New York the evening before he had sailed. 'Things are a little sticky between Thea and Hal at the moment. They had a falling-out a year ago and it still hasn't been resolved. Carrie is a different matter. Both Thea and Olivia think of Carrie as family. They are as close to her as they are to me, and Carrie has been in and out of Gorton just as if she was their sister, or a cousin, ever since she was eight years old. From what Thea and Olivia have written to me about the former Lady Pyke, it isn't an arrangement she is going to find acceptable.'

Kyle said now, wanting to prepare Thea for a situation she clearly hadn't yet envisaged, 'How do think your father's marriage is going to alter things where your friendship with Carrie is concerned?'

Startled – and with the threat of tears finally vanquished – Thea turned to face him. 'Why should it alter things?'

250

He hesitated, hating the thought of giving her more distress than she was already coping with, where her father's marriage was concerned.

'You've just said yourself that Zephiniah is a snob. Carrie may be the granddaughter of your father's old nanny, but she's still a village girl. And if Zephiniah isn't going to like you being friends with Charlie and Jim, then sure as God made little green apples she's not going to like you being friends with Carrie.'

Thea's thick-lashed eyes widened. Her mouth opened on a gasp. No power on Earth – and certainly not Zephiniah – could prevent her from being friends with Carrie, and it wasn't that fear that was flooding her with unspeakable horror.

The horror was because of what Zephiniah could – and most certainly would – do. She would put an end to Carrie's happy certainty that she was always welcome at Gorton. And for Carrie, a life without visits to Gorton would be no life at all.

'Oh God!' she whispered, uncaring that they were in a very public place. Uncaring of the kind of language she was using. Uncaring that she could be overheard. 'Oh Christ, Kyle! Oh shit! Oh hell!'

Chapter Sixteen

On a blowy bright day in mid-March Hal strolled out of the offices of the *Richmond Times* for the last time, good wishes mixed with envy ringing in his ears. At twenty years old he had achieved the ambition he had set for himself years and years ago when, after long days labouring on the farm, he'd run across the fields to Miss Calvert's house to receive an education. His goal had been to become a journalist on a national newspaper or on one of the leading London newspapers, either the *Evening Standard* or the *Evening News.*

Today, in his inside jacket pocket, was a copy of a signed contract with the *Evening News*, a newspaper with a circulation of more than 900,000.

900,000!

It was a figure he still couldn't quite believe, and the numbers sang in his head as he left his parked car in the market place and headed towards Finkle Street and the Black Horse pub. He wasn't going to the Black Horse for a celebratory pint – though he would, of course, be having a pint. He was going there to tell Rosie, the pub's most popular barmaid, that he was leaving that evening for London – and that he wouldn't be returning.

Unlike his former co-workers on the *Richmond Times*, Rosie was not likely to wish him good luck and certainly wouldn't be envious. What she was most certainly going to be was very, very upset – and then very, very angry.

The Black Horse had originally been an old Georgian coaching inn, and Hal liked the low beamed ceilings, the uneven dark wooden floors and the atmosphere it gave of being a little bit of old Yorkshire.

There was nothing even vaguely old Yorkshire about Rosie Beck. Rosie was nineteen and as fresh as paint. In many ways she reminded him of Carrie. There was always a smile on her face and a giggle in her throat. But in other ways Rosie was far different from Carrie, for Rosie was 'fast' – and she wasn't too fussed who knew. It was her frank openness that had appealed to him the first time he had chatted her up, nearly a year ago – that and the mesmerizing way she looked to be permanently on the verge of escaping from her clothes.

She looked to be escaping from them now as he walked into the public bar at what was, for him, an abnormally early time in the day.

Astonishment showed on her face, and then delight. 'Blimey, sweetheart! To what do we do owe this pleasure? I wasn't expecting to see you till this evening.'

He slid onto a bar stool, glad to see that the other occupants of the bar were all seated at tables. With no one at his elbow, it meant he would have relative privacy when he broke his news to her. He hadn't wanted too much privacy. Too much privacy and she was likely to do him serious harm.

'A pint of Tetley's,' he said, knowing he was going to be in need of one.

With a happy grin Rosie began pulling his pint. Her dress was made of cheap, shiny red material. The seams were strained around generously curvaceous hips – no way did Rosie fit into the fashionable ideal of a flat-chested flapper – and the neckline was a deep V, revealing a cleavage so luscious that Hal knew he was going to have his work cut out, if he was to remember just why he was there.

'So why are you here before midday?' she asked, managing to imbue the mundane query with all kinds of erotic possibilities.

Hal felt a rising in his crotch. He was going to miss Rosie. There were countless men in Richmond who would crawl over broken glass to enjoy what he had been enjoying these last twelve months.

She pushed his frothing pint across to him.

He closed his hands around it, grateful for its familiar feel. 'I have news, Rosie.'

'Oh, aye?' She grinned at him, her eyes sparkling at the thought of a possible treat.

He took a deep drink of his ale, too fond of her not to care that he was about to hurt her. What else, though, could he do? He couldn't take her with him to London and he couldn't promise her that he'd be back, because it would be a lie, and though he was every kind of a heel, he wasn't a liar.

In his inside jacket pocket the contract rustled. It was all the encouragement he needed. In the spirit of soonest said, soonest mended, he said bluntly, 'I've got a new job, Rosie. In London. I'm leaving today.'

She sucked in her breath, speechless with shock. She wasn't speechless for long.

'And just how long have you bloody well known about this job?' she demanded, her eyes blazing. 'A few days? A week? A month? For just how long, Hal Crosby, have you been behaving as if you're going to put a ring on my finger, when all the time you've been planning to leave me in the lurch? And that is what you're doing, isn't it? It's not a case of "I've got a new job in London and I'm taking you with me, Rosie", is it? No; it soddin' well isn't!'

'Be fair, Rosie!' He was genuinely aggrieved. 'I've never said I was going to put a ring on your finger. I'm never going to put a ring on anyone's finger. And I didn't see the sense in telling you the job was in the offing, because why would I want a scene like this, if it proved to be all for nowt?'

'All for nowt? That's what this bloody relationship's been!' Her eyes blazed with frustrated fury. 'I thought you and me were goin' somewhere, Hal Crosby. I thought you were a cut above what passes for men in this neck o' the woods. But you're no bleedin' different. You're a manky, minging, clarty...' Running out of adjectives, she wildly looked around for something to throw at him. All that was at hand were bottles and glasses.

Reading her mind, and having no intention of being a sitting target, Hal relinquished his pint of Tetley's and slid smartly off the bar stool.

There were guffaws of laughter from a group of farm labourers hunched around a nearby table.

'That's right, Rosie lass!' one of the labourers

255

called out. 'You tell 'im what's what. You give him 'ell and come out wi' me tonight!'

'You sling your hook,' she shot back at him. 'I wouldn't go out wi' you if you were the last man on Earth!'

She returned her attention to Hal, but this time her eyes were bright with tears, not rage. She said deflatedly, 'Are you really going to London, Hal?'

He nodded. 'It was always the plan, Rosie.'

'It wasn't my plan.'

There was such bleak disappointment in her voice that when another of the labourers sniggered, his mate sitting next to him gave him a silencing shove in the ribs.

Aware that all the occupants of the Public Bar were now avidly waiting for what he was about to say next, Hal decided his best plan was to ignore his audience and plough on as if it wasn't there.

'We'd have run out of steam in another few months, Rosie,' he said gently. 'It's best this way. Look after yourself, love. Be happy.'

It was as good an exit line as any and, leaving her standing at the pumps, a picture of dejection, he walked out of the bar, letting the ancient oak door of the Black Horse slam shut behind him for the last time.

Once out in the narrow cobbled street, he pulled the collar of his jacket up as protection against the stiff, chill breeze. Hal wasn't easily fazed, and he hadn't been so in the pub. He hadn't enjoyed his ten minutes in there, though, and he wasn't looking forward to the next goodbye he was about to make. Carrie's feelings wouldn't be hurt in the same manner as Rosie's

256

had been, but his moving down to London would affect her far more deeply than it was going to affect Rosie. Rosie's love life would be up and running again as fast as light, but the gap his going would make in Carrie's life wouldn't be filled so easily – if at all.

Of their childhood circle of five, he was the only one living within easy reach of Monkswood. Every time she had a day off Carrie would cycle from Monkswood into Richmond and meet Hal in the cafe in the market place for tea and cakes. Sometimes, if one of his days off coincided with hers, he would drive her to Outhwaite so that she could visit her granny, and they would meet up with Charlie and Hermione, and Jim. His move to London wouldn't mean an end to her trips to Outhwaite. She would, he knew, still go, catching the bus in Richmond's market place and getting off it an hour later opposite the Pig and Whistle in Outhwaite's High Street. She would, though, feel isolated and lonely – how could she not, when he would be 200 miles away in London, as, for most of the year, were Thea, Olivia and Violet, and when Roz was thousands of miles further away, in America?

She was seated at their usual corner table, dressed in a serviceable navy coat and navy Mary-Jane shoes, her dark-red, modestly plain hat a perfect foil to the heavy wheat-coloured knot of hair coiled low at the nape of her neck. In serviceable clothes that didn't even give a nod towards fashion and without a hint of powder and lipstick, she should have looked plain and dowdy. She didn't. She looked as pretty as a picture and as

257

wholesome as a sunny May morning.

'I haven't ordered tea yet,' she said as Hal joined her at the table. 'I didn't want it to have cooled before you got here. Why was it so important we met up today, and with so little notice? I had to promise I'd do without a day off for two weeks to make up for taking today off.'

'Sorry, Carrie. It couldn't be helped.' A waitress approached and he said, 'A pot of tea for two, and two toasted teacakes and a stand of fancies, please.'

'At least I haven't had docked the time I've arranged to have off at Easter, but that's because Lady Markham will be on the Riviera and so my taking two days of my annual week's holiday doesn't matter too much.'

'Which is important because...?'

'Because Thea, Olivia and Violet are all at Gorton over Easter and because they want me to spend as much time with them as possible.' Her eyes glowed in happy anticipation. 'There's to be a weekend house-party and a ball. Thea said in her last letter that there hasn't been a ball at Gorton since 1912 when she was six years old.'

'And all this so that the new Lady Fenton can be introduced to the other idle rich of the county?'

Carrie was too used to Hal's derogatory remarks about the upper classes to begin a squabble with him.

'All this so that she can meet people in Yorkshire who are her social equals,' she said tranquilly. 'It's no different from you having a cousin from Cornwall move to Outhwaite. What is the first thing you would do? You'd take him to the Pig and Whistle so that he could meet everyone and make friends.'

He grinned, knowing that when it came to the class divide he and Carrie were never going to sing from the same hymn sheet.

The waitress arrived with the tea, toasted tea-cakes and cake-stand. As they were put on the gingham-clothed table, Carrie said, 'Roz is coming over for the ball. She hasn't met Lady Zephiniah yet, either.'

'As you won't be a guest at the ball, are you sure you'll be meeting her?'

Carrie stared at him, startled. 'But of course I shall meet her! How could I not, when I'll be at Gorton with Thea and Olivia before the ball begins?' Recovering her equilibrium, she began pouring the tea. 'I've never seen the ballroom without dust-sheets. It's going to be so marvellous to see all the mirrors and chandeliers gleaming, and all the flowers. Even though it's so early in the year there are going to be lots of flowers. Her-mione says Charlie and his gardeners have been nurturing lilies and peonies for weeks in the hothouses.'

Hal knew all about the hive of activity that had been taking place at Gorton in preparation for the family's arrival at Easter because on his jour-ney back from London, after his interview for the job on the *Evening News,* he'd stopped off at Outhwaite to tell his uncle about his exciting new job prospect.

Jim had been sanguine about it. 'London, is it?' he'd said. 'I wouldn't fancy it myself. I reckon it'd be too much like Bradford – noisy and dirty, only an 'ell of a lot bigger. Still, if that's what you want, lad.'

'It is what I want,' he'd said. 'Anyway, I've always liked Bradford. If it had ever come to a toss-up between my working on the *Richmond Times* or the *Bradford Telegraph & Argus*, I'd have chosen the *Telegraph & Argus* every time.'

It occurred to Hal now, as he watched Carrie pour milk into the teacups, that he was going to miss Bradford far more than he was going to miss Richmond. Bradford had one of the finest Mechanics' Institutes in the country and he regularly attended the lectures given by visiting speakers there. It was also the city where, in January 1893, the Independent Labour Party had been born and its programme laid out.

The aims of that programme were carved in Hal's heart. Medical treatment and school feeding programmes for impoverished children. The establishment of public measures to reduce unemployment and provide aid to the unemployed. Welfare programmes for orphans, widows, the elderly, the disabled and the sick. The abolition of child labour. The abolition of piecework and the establishment of an eight-hour working day. Free education up to university level. Housing reform.

When he thought of how much on that magnificent programme was still to be achieved, impatience roared through his veins. A better day was coming, but it was far from being here yet.

'...and so why was it important for us to meet up today?' Carrie asked, breaking into his thoughts.

'Because I've been given a job on a London paper and I'm leaving for London directly we leave the cafe.'

It was a brutal way of breaking the news, but, as with Rosie, he couldn't see how breaking it gently would make the end result any easier.

She stared across the table at him for a long moment, assimilating the news and what would it mean for him, and what it would mean for her. Then she said, not wanting her sense of loss to spoil things for him, 'I'm so pleased for you, Hal. It's what you've always wanted, and you so deserve it. You must be over the moon – and so must Miss Calvert. You have told her about it, haven't you?'

'I told her even before I told Jim.'

Aware that she was dangerously close to revealing how desperately she was going to miss him, she forced a giggle into her voice as she said, 'And just how did a twenty-year-old Yorkshire tyke get himself a job on a London newspaper?'

'Connections,' he said teasingly.

'You don't have any connections,' Carrie replied, amused despite her pain at the thought of their regular meetings in the cafe coming to such an abrupt end.

'That's where you're wrong – and when I dropped a hint of them to the sub-editor who interviewed me, he had a word with the paper's editor, Frank Fitzhugh, and he then interviewed me. First thing he asked was where my interests lay and I said politics.' Hal grinned. 'He told me I was a cheeky bugger and that his political editor would have ten fits if he was assigned a junior reporter straight down from the outer darkness of North Yorkshire.'

'And what did you say? Did you tell him you were a Labour Party member and went to meetings and rallies?'

'No, because that wouldn't have impressed him and would probably have counted against me.'

Seeing her bewilderment, he said, 'It helps if a political reporter is objective – unless, of course, he's working on a paper devoted entirely to one particular party, such as the Independent Labour Party's *Clarion*.' He spooned sugar into his tea. 'What I told him was that I was on personal terms with a government minister – Lord Fenton. Which is the truth,' he added, as Carrie's eyes widened in alarm at his taking such a liberty. 'If Fenton was ever asked, he wouldn't let me down. He's not a snob, I'll give him that. I then told Fitzhugh I was on personal terms with the Third Secretary at the German Embassy. Which was stretching the truth a bit, because I haven't met Olivia's fiancé yet, but I will be doing. Olivia will see to that. By this time I could see the cogs in Fitzhugh's brain whirring away at the thought of having a staff reporter who had inside contacts both in Parliament and at the German Embassy. Then, to put the icing on the cake, I told him I had a family connection, Kyle Anderson, who had recently been appointed attaché at the American Embassy and that I had an "in" with Maxwell Bradley, a Republican member of the US House of Representatives, presently serving on the Dawes Committee. From then on it was plain sailing. How could he *not* have hired me?'

Carrie's eyes were still wide with alarm. 'But not only have you not even met Dieter von Starhemberg – though I do agree that you will, because Olivia has said repeatedly in her letters that she can't wait for both of us to meet him – but you haven't met Kyle Anderson or Max Bradley, either.' Anxiety for him filled her voice. 'And what if you never get to meet them? Or if, even if you do, they are so close-mouthed you learn nothing whatsoever from them?'

'Don't be so negative, Carrie. I will get to meet them – and they'll all be massively useful to me. As today is our last regular day here, have we to finish off with a fresh pot of tea and some vanilla slices?'

She nodded and smiled, and hoped he wouldn't see how very much she was going to miss him.

He did see, though. Not for the first time he wondered if Carrie had secret hopes that one day he would propose to her. It was, he knew, what the villagers of Outhwaite expected him to do. Sometimes he almost expected it was something he would do, but although she was an integral part of his life and he loved her dearly and knew he'd be capable of killing anyone who harmed Carrie, he didn't love her in the sexual, all-consuming, gut-wrenching, soul-destroying way he loved Thea.

Thea.

Trying not to think about her was an impossibility. He thought about her all the time. Even Rosie, at her glorious, sexiest best, hadn't obliterated Thea from his thoughts; and moving to

263

London – where he would be nearer to her – certainly wasn't going to do so. Somehow, though, he was going to have to maintain the stand he had taken up the night of her coming-out ball – which was that the class divide between them was too deep to be overcome. It was something common sense had told him, even before passion had sprung up between them like a forest fire, but until the night of her coming-out ball it had been something he'd preferred not to face.

He pushed his cup and saucer away. If he wanted to reach London in time to sleep at the Fleet Street pub that was to be his address until he found a more permanent one, he had to set off now.

'I have to be off, Carrie.' He dug a piece of paper out of his pocket with the name and address of the pub on it. 'I'll write, and you can write to me here.'

She took the piece of paper and put it in her handbag.

'Any problem you have, love – anything, at any time – let me know and I'll be back in Yorkshire as fast as light to deal with it. Understand?'

She nodded, not trusting herself to speak, knowing that if she did her voice would be unsteady.

He didn't wait for the waitress to come with the bill. Pushing his chair away from the table, he simply put more than enough money down on the table and rose to his feet.

Carrie followed him out of the cafe and into the market place. Hal's little car was parked where he always parked it and, as they approached it, she could see a shabby suitcase on the rear seat. It had been secured by a leather strap and the initials HG had been painted in white near the handle.

Her heart felt as if it was being squeezed very tightly.

'Is that all you are taking with you?' she asked, trying to sound jolly and teasing, and not let her true feelings show.

'It's all I have and all I need.'

He opened the car door. This was it. He was finally leaving Yorkshire behind him. Though Hal knew he shouldn't be, when his leaving would make such a large hole in Carrie's life, he was exultant. He was going to wring the last drop of political gossip out of the contacts he had, and he was going to use those contacts to make even more influential contacts. One day he wouldn't be pussyfooting around the *Evening News*'s political editor. One day he would be the political editor. He was going to make a name for himself. Most of all, when it came to socialist politics, he was going to make a difference to the world. Come hell or high water, he was going to do his best to make it a place where equality counted.

Before getting into the car he gave Carrie an almighty bear-hug. 'I'm only a day's drive away, Carrie love. In a few days' time Thea, Olivia and Violet will be at Gorton Hall and Roz will have joined them.'

He didn't say goodbye. He couldn't bring himself to say the words.

Neither could Carrie.

He slid behind the wheel and switched on the ignition.

With a bright, strained smile she stepped away

from the car. 'Look after yourself, Hal. Don't be too naughty with the Fleet Street barmaids.'

He cracked with laughter, put the car into gear, gave her a goodbye wave and drove off. In the seconds before he turned out of the market place he looked in his driving mirror for a last glimpse of her.

She was standing in front of the market cross, holding a handbag that had once been her granny's. Now that she thought he could no longer see her, her smile had died and, though he couldn't be sure, he was almost certain there were tears in her eyes.

Chapter Seventeen

Zephiniah was sitting at her kidney-shaped dressing table in the master bedroom at Mount Street. In forty minutes' time she and Gilbert would travel the short distance in the Fenton Rolls-Royce to 10 Downing Street, where they were to dine with the prime minister and his wife. It would be her first visit to Number 10 and her sense of satisfaction was dizzying. Among the other guests at dinner would be the Chancellor of the Exchequer, Winston Churchill, and his wife, Clementine; Lord and Lady Dalwhinnie, whom she had already met; Viscount Hubholme; the Dowager Duchess of Merion, a relation of Mrs Baldwin's; and an American, Mr Maxwell Bradley, a member of the House of Representatives.

When Gilbert had told her an American would be one of the guests she'd quirked a sleek, interested eyebrow.

'Max is aide to one of America's two representatives on the Dawes Reparation Commission's Committee,' he'd said. 'It's something both Hubholme and I have a deep interest in.'

He had kissed the nape of her neck and then said, 'Max is also acquainted with Rozalind. I rather think wedding bells will be ringing before the end of the year.'

Zephiniah's scarlet-painted fingernails clicked like castanets as she tapped the glass-topped surface of her dressing table. She hadn't yet met Rozalind, who would be arriving in London in a few days' time, but she was fervently hoping that, when she did, she would find her to be far more like Olivia than like Thea and Violet, both of whom she found incomprehensible. Violet, being only sixteen, she could handle. Though Violet didn't know it yet, she was about to be sent to a finishing school in Switzerland. No such easy solution was available where Thea was concerned.

Zephiniah continued drumming her fingernails on the glass surface. She wasn't a woman who was easily shocked, but when Thea had announced baldly that she was a socialist who believed that all hereditary titles, such as her father's, should be abolished, Zephiniah had been astounded. How on earth could she subscribe to such preposterousness, when her father was both a viscount and a minister in Mr Baldwin's Conservative government? And why hadn't Gilbert thought to tell her of his daughter's radically eccentric political views?

'Surely it must be damaging to your career to have a daughter who is a member of the Independent Labour Party and goes to meetings and sings the Internationale?' she had said, unable to understand why Gilbert hadn't put a halt to Thea's idiocy when it had still been in its early stages. 'It's the kind of thing that could put an instant stop to you being talked of as a future prime minister.'

'There are quite a few men ahead of me in that race,' he'd said, both amused and pleased that she thought such a thing a genuine possibility. 'And I respect Thea's passion for what she believes in. Tolerance in all things is one of my watchwords.'

It wasn't one of Zephiniah's watchwords, but she'd had more sense than to say so.

Her mouth, painted the same searing scarlet as her nails, tightened. The problem with allowing her true feelings to show, where Thea was concerned, was that the Prince of Wales counted her a personal friend – and Zephiniah had no desire to fall out with a stepdaughter who was on such close terms with Prince Edward.

Olivia, too, of course, had an 'in' where royalty was concerned, but her friendship was with the less glamorous Duke and Duchess of York. As a stepdaughter, Olivia had so far presented her with no unwelcome surprises. She was gratifyingly presentable and stylish, her only concern her forthcoming wedding to Dieter von Starhemberg. Olivia wanted it to be as lavish as possible, and as

Zephiniah – mindful that society's eyes would be on her as well – wanted exactly the same thing, the two of them were getting along remarkably well.

Thinking about her stepdaughters brought another thought to mind, and she stopped drumming her nails. The indisputably good thing about Thea, Olivia and Violet was that they didn't have a brother. Gilbert had no male heir. When they had a son – and she was determined that she and Gilbert would have a son – their son would inherit both Gorton Hall and the title.

There was a perfunctory tap on the door and Gilbert, dressed for the evening in white tie and tails, entered the room. She didn't turn her head, and he smiled at her through the looking glass.

'I've never known any woman look so ravishing in black,' he said with stark truthfulness.

'Thank you, darling. I dismissed Angelique without asking her to fasten my necklace. Would you mind?'

She wore a rich black satin gown, very décolleté and lavishly trimmed with black lace. Her hair was the same gleaming black and framed her face in fashionably rigid waves. Her skin was, thanks to rice-powder, breathtakingly white, her eyes night-dark. The effect was purposely dramatic. Zephiniah liked there to be a concerted intake of breath when she entered a room, and knew exactly how to ensure there was one.

Still seated and with her back to him, she handed him the diamond necklace that had been his wedding gift to her.

Carefully he slid it around her neck and

fastened it. Then, with quickening heartbeats, he rested his hands gently on her shoulders, holding her gaze through the looking glass. The diamonds glowed like live things against her flawless skin, drawing his eyes down to snowy breasts lapped by tantalizing froths of black lace.

He wasn't a lascivious man. He had been nineteen when he had married Blanche and his sexual experience before marriage had been limited. It was almost obligatory for a young man of his class to be initiated into the mysteries of sex by a prostitute, and his initiation had taken place in Paris, when he was eighteen. He had been grateful for the experience, but by then he had already met Blanche and, wanting to keep his body clean for her, had made no return visits.

Never once, not even during the war when he had been in Flanders and any diversion from the hell of the trenches would have been welcome, had he been unfaithful to her, and for a long time after her death he had been faithful to her memory.

The spasmodic affairs that had then followed had been discreet and never earth-moving. No one had replaced his beloved Blanche, and he'd believed that no one ever could. Then, on a brief visit she had made to Britain after her husband's death, he had met Zephiniah.

For the first time in his life he'd understood what the phrase *coup de foudre* truly meant. It had been like stepping off a cliff edge. Though no one could have been more different in personality from Blanche, Zephiniah's hourglass figure, exoticism, vitality and sheer sexual allure had mesmerized him. Even before their formal introduction was over, he had been her willing prisoner, totally in thrall to her. It had been like nothing he had ever previously experienced – and he'd been determined not to let her slip through his fingers.

His intimate life with Blanche had been perfect and passionate – but it hadn't been charged with Zephiniah's effortless eroticism. Every married woman he knew had a black lace-trimmed evening gown in her wardrobe – and never before had he regarded the lace as being erotic. Now, though, he couldn't tear his eyes away from it.

Zephiniah knew very well what he was feeling and thinking. Slowly, knowing how it would shock and arouse him, she slipped her hand inside the neckline of her low-cut gown and lifted the heavy, full lushness of her right breast free.

Her nipple was large and dark and silky.

He sucked in his breath, desire flooding his eyes, as she had known it would.

There was no time to take advantage of his arousal. She wasn't going to arrive at Number 10 with mussed hair and surrounded by the scent of recent sex.

'We haven't time,' she said firmly, adjusting her clothing as his fingers dug deep into her shoulders.

Always a gentleman, Gilbert gave a heavy sigh of acceptance.

Aware that his being so easy to handle could easily become boring, and wondering what she would do when it did, Zephiniah rose to her feet.

'I think we've just time for a very quick cocktail before we leave, darling. What would you like? A

271

whiskey sour or a gin-and-French?'

Later that evening the talk across Number 10's dinner table ricocheted from the faults and failings of the former prime minister, Ramsay MacDonald, to the present state of Russia and the danger posed by the Bolsheviks; from the Prince of Wales and speculation as to whether his relationship with Mrs Freda Dudley Ward had finally petered into nothing more than friendship, to the identity of her possible successor.

'An American?' Viscount Hubholme suggested as a footman refilled his glass of hock. 'The Prince of Wales likes Americans.'

'But then so do we all,' Ottoline Dalwhinnie said, with a naughty look towards Maxwell Bradley.

A ripple of laughter ran around the table.

Mr Baldwin, whom Zephiniah found to be less imposing than she had expected, said drily, 'He's certainly always trying to go to America. And Americans love him. Isn't that so, Max?'

Max gave a wry smile. 'It certainly is, Prime Minister. New York is still recovering from its euphoria over his last visit, two years ago.'

Zephiniah hoped the euphoria she was experiencing would last just as long. For the first time in her life everything was going just as she wanted it to. She was married to a man who was not only of her own class, but was a leading political figure; a man spoken of as being a future prime minister. Her past mistakes were behind her, buried deep in Austria and Argentina.

The conversation around the table had moved

from the Prince of Wales to Italy and Mussolini.

'Of course, the woman who attempted to assassinate him is being deported back to Britain,' Mr Baldwin was saying, in a voice that indicated how much his patience had been tried by the recent events in Rome. 'Why a fifty-year-old Irish woman would want to shoot him in the head, I can't imagine.'

'Mad, I expect,' Lord Dalwhinnie said. 'I understand Il Duce was most put out when he discovered it was a woman who had tried to kill him. Felt it insulting, I shouldn't wonder.'

There was more laughter.

Zephiniah's thoughts were on neither Mussolini nor mad Irish women. They were on a registration-of-births vault in Vienna. Over the last fifteen years she'd often thought of how the notification of her illegitimate daughter's birth – and her daughter's subsequent adoption certificate – might be removed from Austrian public records. No method had ever occurred to her and, until now, she had never perceived it as being a pressing problem.

Only two people had ever known of the disaster that had ruined her life when she'd been a debutante – and that had been her mother, and the aunt who had taken her to Vienna and lived with her there throughout seven months of her pregnancy and for two weeks after her daughter's birth. Both her mother and her aunt were now dead and, although the father of her child wasn't dead, he had simply been relieved at the outcome and didn't count. Her secret was safe – unless someone should trawl through the registration of

273

births in Vienna in 1911, looking for a certificate bearing her name as the mother of the registered child. And who would do that? The answer was that nobody would. What was past was past and would never resurface.

'Someone should shoot that upstart ruffian Hitler,' Viscount Hubholme was saying. 'He may still be virtually unknown outside Bavaria, but mark my words, I've heard the man address a public meeting and he's Trouble with a capital T.'

'He's not so much trouble that he can't be contained,' Winston said phlegmatically. 'His party can only come to power if he gets enough votes – and the German people aren't going to vote for an Austrian you so well describe as being an upstart and a ruffian. He's tried a putsch once, and it failed. A second attempt at an armed overthrow of the rightful government will get him nowhere. From now on, if he's ever going to come to power, he's going to have to rely on votes, and outside Bavaria no votes will be forthcoming.'

It occurred to Zephiniah that if she was ever going to be able to take part in the kind of conversations now taking place, she was going to have to become much more knowledgeable about the current political situations in France, Italy and Germany.

As the present conversation was one she couldn't yet take an intelligent part in, her thoughts slipped back to the ghastly hideousness of the summer of 1911.

When she had returned to England with her aunt, leaving behind her a baby girl who had been adopted by a childless Viennese couple, she had done so believing she would be able to pick up the threads of her life as if they had never been broken.

Her mother had instantly put an end to that daydream. 'You're damaged goods,' she had said harshly. 'Don't think that just because no one knows about the child, the child's father hasn't boasted about how easy a conquest you were. Every deb's delight of the Season will know by now, and there will be no marriage proposals coming your way. Not one.'

To her incredulity, her mother had been proved right. No debutante of that year's Season was more popular with the opposite sex, and no debutante was more obviously destined to remain very firmly on the shelf.

Then she'd met Reggie. Reggie Pyke was the middle-aged youngest son of the Earl of Warham. The family was from the Scottish Borders and, when Zephiniah met him, Reggie, who had sailed financially too close to the wind just once too often, was about to emigrate to Argentina, where he intended breeding polo ponies.

'I intend mixing thoroughbreds with Criollas, the local horses,' he'd said enthusiastically. 'They have the best endurance of any horse breed in the world. I'm on to a sure-fire winner. I can feel it in my blood and in my bones.'

When, within a week of knowing her, he'd asked her if she would marry him, Zephiniah hadn't had to think about it. Just like Reggie, she needed a new start, in a new country. A month later, as man and wife, they had sailed for Buenos Aires.

It hadn't been a marriage made in heaven. He drank too much and soon, out of sheer boredom, she got in the habit of drinking too much too. He had affairs, and she had affairs. There had never been any children and, although Reggie accused her of being the one who was at fault, she had known, because of the secret she had never shared with him, that the fault lay with him. Out of the blue, aged fifty-eight, he had dropped dead of a heart attack while watching a tournament at the Campo Argentino de Polo de Palermo.

At thirty-two, and at the height of her beauty, she was a widow. She hadn't been a merry widow, though, because the financial position Reggie had left her in was dire. What she had needed was another husband – one with money, and fast.

Reggie's brother, who had now inherited the title and who, like herself, was widowed – had written and asked if she would consider bringing Reggie's ashes home to England so that they could be interred in the Warham family vault. Aware that agreeing to do so could well bring advantages in its wake, she had left for England carrying Reggie's ashes in a tasteful silver-plated urn.

Reggie's brother had received the ashes with great courtesy and had shown more romantic interest in a male companion than he had in her. With hopes of becoming the next Countess of Warham swiftly extinguished, Zephiniah had shaken the Scottish Borders dust from her feet and headed speedily for London, where she intended devoting the summer to serious husband-hunting.

At the first dinner party she had been invited to she had been introduced to Gilbert.

'He's very eligible, and I've seated you next to him,' her hostess, a distant cousin, had whispered to her as they had made their way into the dining room. 'He's a government minister and a widower with three daughters, the eldest two well out of the school room. He's owner of a divine country estate in Yorkshire, and his Mount Street house has one of the prettiest ballrooms in London. Add to that whispers that he could well be the next Tory prime minister, and you can well understand why he is so in demand socially.'

Even before he had seated himself next to her, Zephiniah had been determined to end his days of widowhood.

Doing so had been as easy as shooting fish in a barrel. That had been months ago now, and Zephiniah hadn't looked back.

Mrs Baldwin interrupted her thoughts by rising to her feet and saying, 'I think it's time we left the gentlemen to their port, ladies.'

As Zephiniah, Clementine Churchill, Lady Dalwhinnie and the Dowager Duchess of Merion followed their hostess out of the dining room, Zephiniah gave a last interested glance in Max Bradley's direction.

He really was a most attractive man and possibly eight or nine years her senior, which meant he had to be at least twenty years older than Rozalind. Though he had said very little at the dining table, he had effortlessly made his presence felt. There was an exciting toughness about him; an overt sexuality. She had no doubt at all that if Max had been in Gilbert's shoes a few hours earlier, he would have taken no notice when she said there was no time for lovemaking and her hair would now be disgracefully mussed. The thought sent a rush of heat through her body. She was looking forward to Max Bradley and her stepniece marrying. He would be a very welcome addition at family events.

Unbeknown to her, the moment the dining-room door had closed behind her, Gilbert was discussing with Max exactly the kind of family events she had in mind.

'You will be joining us at Gorton for Easter, won't you?' he was saying genially. 'Rozalind arrives in London in a few days' time and has written to say that you will still be this side of the Atlantic and able to join us all.'

At the far end of the table the prime minister, Winston, Lord Dalwhinnie and Viscount Hubholme were occupied in lighting up Romeo y Julieta cigars. As they began puffing on them and discussing the difficulty the government was having with disaffected miners, Max said, 'I appreciate the invitation, Gilbert. However, it's one I'm unable to accept.'

'That's a shame.' Gilbert was sincerely regretful. 'I hadn't realized you were heading back to Washington immediately.'

'I'm not. It's simply that my friendship with Rozalind is at an end – or will be very shortly.'

Gilbert stared at him, bewildered. 'I'm sorry, old chap. I don't quite follow...'

Max chewed the corner of his lip. He'd known this hellish conversation with Gilbert Fenton was

going to have to take place sometime before Rozalind's arrival, but he hadn't envisaged it taking
place this evening, at Number 10.

'I've delayed getting married for long enough,'
he said, wishing he had a bottle of Jack Daniels in
front of him instead of a bottle of port. 'And in
Washington there are limits to how high a man
can rise politically without a suitable wife at his
side.'

'I understand that.' Gilbert was more bewildered than ever. 'But surely that means you and
Rozalind should be announcing your forthcoming marriage – or is it that you've asked her to
marry you and she's turned you down? Is she
finding the age difference too great? Is that the
problem? Is–'

Max lifted a hand, forestalling him. 'You don't
realize it, but you're making this even more
difficult for me. What you have to understand –
and what I have to make stone-cold clear – is that
I've never led Rozalind to believe I was one day
going to marry her. She's known from the outset
that there's been someone waiting for me.
Someone I've known since childhood. Someone
with whom I've long had an understanding and,
most importantly of all, someone who is far more
suitable to be the wife of a politician than a
dangerously headstrong girl who has only just
celebrated her twentieth birthday.'

Aware now where the conversation was heading, Gilbert was no longer bewildered. He was
appalled.

Under cover of loud laughter from the far end of
the table, he said in a low, urgent voice, 'Now look

279

here, Max, let me put you straight before you say anything further. You've been Rozalind's escort for nearly a year. Her father's understanding – and mine – was that your intentions were honourable. If we'd thought otherwise we wouldn't have been so tolerant. If, unknown to us, Rozalind has condoned your continuing friendship with an old flame, then I can only imagine she has done so out of youthful innocence as to the true nature of that friendship. Your action now, as an honourable man, is to end your former liaison once and for all – and, on your return to New York, to ask my brother-in-law for my niece's hand in marriage.'

A pulse throbbed at the corner of Max's jawline. 'That's not possible, I'm afraid.'

'Of course it's damned well possible!'

Winston and Viscount Hubholme, finally realizing that a heated exchange of words was taking place, shot them swift, curious glances. The prime minister and Lord Dalwhinnie, chuckling over a risqué joke, were oblivious to it.

Max, wishing himself a million miles away, drew in a deep, steadying breath. 'The reason it isn't possible is a watertight one. My second cousin, Myrtle Benson-Davidson, is ideal in every respect as the wife of a man as politically ambitious as I am. She is mature, sophisticated – and as ambitious for me as I am myself. There are times in life when rational decisions have to be taken.' He paused, unable to bring himself to continue.

'And?' Gilbert prompted, taut with tension.

'And I took one.' Looking like a man who already knew of the mistake he had made, Max said, 'Three days before I sailed, I married Myrtle.'

Chapter Eighteen

JUNE 1928

'So much has changed over the last couple of years,' Thea said to Roz as they sprawled amidst deep grass at the vole place, 'and yet where my love life and your love life are concerned, nothing has changed at all, has it? You are still unhappily in love with Max, and I'm still unhappily in love with Hal.'

Roz rolled over onto her back and shielded her eyes from the hot sun. Where Max was concerned, there was a lot she wanted to share with Thea, but not knowing what her reaction was going to be when she did so, she put the moment off, saying instead, 'When we were all last at Gorton at this time of the year, it was Zephiniah's first visit. Where is she this year? Vichy again?'

Thea pushed herself up one elbow. 'No. This time she's taking the waters at Aix-les-Bains. Papa misses her, but no one else does.'

'Not even Olivia?'

Thea shook her head. 'Not even Olivia. They were in cahoots over Olivia's wedding arrangements, because both of them wanted the same thing: to have *Tatler* trumpet it as the wedding of the year–'

'Which it did.'

'But once the wedding was over, their initial

281

enthusiasm for each other cooled.'

'D'you think that none of you much liking Zephiniah is the reason she isn't here? In London, not spending time in each other's company is easy, isn't it? At Gorton it's pretty impossible to avoid one another.'

'I rather think Zephiniah is indifferent as to whether we like her or not.' Thea pushed herself up into a sitting position and hugged her knees. 'She'd hoped to be pregnant by now. If she had been, I think she would be trying to focus all Papa's attention on the newborn – especially if it was a boy – and trying to distance him from us. She doesn't like the fact that he always has so much time for us, even when he doesn't always approve of the causes we have taken up or the things we do.'

'Those causes being your socialism, and Olivia following Dieter like a sheep in believing that the way ahead in Germany is Hitler's National Socialist German Workers' Party?'

Thea gave a mirthless laugh. 'Right. And let me tell you that the word "socialist" in the National Socialist German Workers' Party has nothing to do with real socialism. Hitler has simply redefined the word by putting "national" in front of it, in order to appeal to the greatest number of people.'

Tired of squinting against the sun in order to look at Thea, Rozalind too sat up, planting her hands flat on the grass behind her to give herself some support. 'I don't understand what attraction there is for Dieter in such a tinhorn political party. I thought its appeal was to the uneducated – and then only in Bavaria.'

282

Thea ran a hand through short, turbulently curly hair. 'Not according to Kyle. He says lots of educated Germans want to see their country as a force in the world again and not, as it is, a country humiliated by the terms of the Versailles Peace Treaty.'

'And they think an Austrian corporal can bring that about?'

'Apparently so.'

They giggled at the silliness of it and then fell silent, enjoying the blissful heat of the sun on their backs and the soothing sound of the slow-moving river.

After a little while Rozalind said, 'And what about Violet? Is she still in disgrace?' Her hair fell dramatically forward at cheekbone level on either side of her face, accentuating a fringe that came down to her eyebrows.

Wishing that her own hair could be worn in such a straight and sleek fashionable style, Thea said with amusement in her voice, 'She is, where Zephiniah is concerned. It was Zephiniah, after all, who selected the finishing school. Papa was shell-shocked – and most likely still is. An illicit romance between a pupil and a boy of about the same age from nearby Le Rosey would, after all, be understandable – or at least understandable where Violet is concerned. And as nearly all Le Rosey boys are the sons or grandsons of crowned heads, even Zephiniah would have forgiven Violet, in the hope of a happy outcome. But an illicit romance with the father of a fellow pupil? And a fellow pupil who is also the head girl?'

They looked at each other and burst into help-

283

less laughter.

When she was able to speak again, Thea said, 'Violet did it on purpose of course, in order that Papa would be asked to remove her. It was her way of showing Zephiniah – whom she refers to as the "wicked witch" – that she was never going to get the better of her.'

Rozalind rose to her feet and walked the few steps to the edge of the river-bank. There was no sign of the voles, which wasn't a surprise to her, after all the talking and laughing they had been doing.

Laughing no longer, she stared down into clear grey-green water. 'It's a shame there couldn't have been such a good outcome where Carrie was concerned,' she said sombrely. 'She wrote me about the uproar when Zephiniah discovered she was the granddaughter of your father's old nanny, and of how outraged Zephiniah was that Carrie was treated at Gorton as if she were family.'

Thea's hands tightened around her knees. 'That was when, with the exception of Papa, we all stopped feeling guilty about not liking Zephiniah. When she said that in future Carrie would not be welcome at Gorton, there were the most blistering rows. Though he tried hard to hide it, Papa was just as appalled as we were.'

'Then why didn't he overrule her?' Rozalind turned to face her. 'That was the part of things I didn't understand. And though Carrie never said so in her letter, I know that was the part of it that hurt her the most.'

Thea rose to her feet as if all her limbs ached. 'Zephiniah conveniently announced she was *enceinte*. She wasn't, but Papa didn't know that and he wasn't going to take the risk of her having a miscarriage. He met Carrie in Richmond, and Carrie said he explained to her how impossible it was for Zephiniah to cross class barriers, and that he owed it to Zephiniah to respect her wishes. He told her he hoped the situation would soon change, and that nothing would ever diminish the affection he held her in.'

Rozalind said nothing, because there was nothing she could say. They both felt Gilbert should have behaved differently, and because they both thought the world of him, neither of them wanted to put their disappointment in him into words.

She walked towards Thea, slipping her arm through hers. 'Let's get back to the house. The voles aren't coming out to play, and we're just depressing ourselves talking about the wicked witch. I suppose all that really matters is that your father is happy with her.'

Thea made a moue of doubt. 'He gives the impression he is, but between you and me, I think he's beginning to find it a bit of a struggle.'

As they began walking through buttercup-deep grass towards the bridge, Rozalind was very aware that although they had chatted about lots of things, they hadn't chatted about what was going on in their personal lives. Thea had made one brief mention of Hal, as she had of Max, and then their names hadn't been mentioned again – and Kyle's name had only been mentioned in passing.

Tentatively Rozalind asked, 'How are things

between you and Kyle? I know he's pretty keen, because he's told me so. Are the two of you on, or off?'

'Oh God, Roz! I don't know! Thea ran a hand distractedly through her hair. 'I like him an awful lot. He's a million miles more intelligent than most of the men I meet. He's attractive, fun, and it's nice having someone genuinely in love with me.'

'But?'

Beneath a V-necked, low-waisted silk dress the colour of burnt umber, Thea lifted slim shoulders and then dropped them eloquently. 'But he isn't Hal.'

'You can't go carrying a torch for Hal forever.'

'Why not? You may be seen out and about with Barty whenever you're in London, but you'd drop him in a flash if Max was single and crooked his little finger.'

'That's different.'

'No, it isn't.' Thea's eyes flashed fire. 'When you love someone – *really* love someone – you don't just stop loving them because they no longer love you. You keep on hoping that one day they'll come to their senses and come back to you. Because, if you didn't hope that, it would be so unbearable you would go mad.'

Tears glittered on her eyelashes.

'I love Hal so much, Roz, I simply can't get my head around loving anyone else – not even when that someone else is as dishy as your stepbrother. What makes it worse is that I know Hal wants me as much as I want him. He won't acknowledge it, though. Where the class war is concerned, he sees

286

loving me as being a sign of weakness and giving in to it would, in his eyes, be a betrayal of all his left-wing principles.'

'Do you think he'll marry Carrie?'

'I think he'll think about it – and he may well one day even ask her. But can you see Carrie living in London? It's impossible, isn't it? And what is even more impossible is the thought of Hal moving back to Outhwaite or Richmond.'

Twenty minutes later they stepped inside Gorton and Rozalind was immediately encircled by its mellow charm. It wasn't quite the same charm as in the past, though. There were flowers every-where, as always, but the effect wasn't the same as it had been when Blanche was alive. Then the flowers had nearly always been in gentle, subtle tones: milk-white roses massed in Chinese por-celain bowls; pink clove-scented carnations, ruffled and fringed; lilac anemones with indigo hearts; fragrant, pale-lemon freesias. Now the colour of the flowers was strident. Vivid reds, searing blues, blistering oranges, and whereas previously the flowers had always been arranged with great simplicity, now the arrangements were stiffly formal and overpoweringly ornate. There were lots of other changes, too.

Blanche's taste had been for cool, delicate colours. For as long as Rozalind could remember, the dining-room walls had been a translucent duck-egg blue and the walls in the main drawing room a pale yellow, offset by touches of white. Though Gorton itself was a stately Georgian gem, the overall feel of its interior was that of informality. No one stepping inside it could ever have been in any doubt that it was first and foremost a family home.

Because Zephiniah was absent and Thea, Olivia and Violet were all present, that sensation wasn't completely lost, but it was certainly diminished. The drawing room was a sea of crimson and gold. Sofas that were deep-cushioned and covered in chintz, so that it didn't matter if a Fenton dog made itself comfy on them, had been replaced with brocaded, spindly-legged, French Empire sofas and chairs. Everywhere the rich wooden panelling had been ornately gilded.

There had, been a time at Gorton when, if she stood very still and closed her eyes, Rozalind had been able to evoke Blanche's presence and hear, in memory, her low sweet voice. On this visit, for the first time, she failed to tap into any such comforting experience. Blanche's spirit was no longer in the home she had made so happy. Unintentionally or intentionally, Zephiniah had banished her.

'Miss Violet and Count and Countess von Starhemberg are taking tea on the lawn,' a butler who was new to Rozalind said to them as they began making their way to the drawing room.

'Thank you, Miller.' Thea didn't break stride. 'We're going to join them, so will you ask for a fresh pot of tea to be sent out?'

In the drawing room double French windows stood open, looking out over the vast lawn. In the centre of the lawn Violet, Olivia and Dieter were gathered around a low table spread with a snowy-white tablecloth.

288

As they drew nearer, Rozalind was glad to see that afternoon tea at Gorton was reassuringly the same as it had always been. A magnificent silver teapot held centre-stage. On doily-decorated plates were three different kinds of delicately cut sandwiches: egg and cress, ham and cucumber, smoked salmon and mayonnaise. On other plates were iced fancies, fresh scones and Yorkshire parkin. There were four different kinds of cake and, as a final touch, a big bowl of strawberries and a jug of cream.

'*Wilkommen!*' Dieter called out cheerily to her as they approached and then, indicating the deckchair next to his own, 'As they say in English: take a pew. You will not be depriving Thea. She always prefers the grass to a chair.'

Violet and Olivia had also opted for grass, Violet sitting with her legs crossed as if she was eight, not eighteen, and Olivia lying on her back near Dieter's deckchair, her head resting comfortably on a small cushion.

'I don't know who is being mother,' Roz said as she sank down next to Thea, 'but don't bother pouring tea. A fresh pot is on its way out.'

'Have a slice of *Schokoladenkuchen*,' Dieter said. 'It isn't, of course, as wonderful as German chocolate cake, but it is still very good.'

'You really can't continue with this ridiculous notion that everything German is superior to its opposite number in England.' Thea helped herself to a slice of cake. 'It's just too pathetically tedious, Dieter.'

There was amused affection in her voice and Dieter took not the slightest offence. 'It may be tedious, sister-in-law *Liebe*, but where chocolate cake is concerned, it is, alas, true.'

He was wearing white flannel trousers and an open-necked white shirt and his blond hair fell attractively forward across his eyes. Though Nordic-looking men held no special appeal for Rozalind, she could well understand why Olivia had fallen for him so hard, and so fast.

He said now, as a parlourmaid in a black dress and lacy apron and cap delivered a fresh pot of tea, 'Germany is where everything is happening, Thea. How can I help that?'

'You can help by not being deliberately provocative, darling.' Olivia dispensed with her cushion and sat up, resting her back against his long legs.

He stroked her hair lovingly. 'But I like being provocative, *meine Liebe*. It's fun.'

He dropped his hand to her shoulder and Olivia covered his hand with hers.

Rozalind felt her heart tighten. They were so obviously in love, and love for them was so uncomplicated. There had been a time when she had thought it would be like that for her and Max. Now, however, she knew differently. She wondered when she would have the nerve to tell Thea of the decision she had made. It would have to be before they returned to London, and it would have to be before someone else told her first.

'I'll be mother.' Thea poured a cup of tea and, knowing how Rozalind liked hers, dropped a slice of lemon into it. 'Anyone else?' she asked as she handed the cup and saucer to Roz.

'Me, please.' Dieter stopped stroking Olivia's

hair and picked up the cup and saucer by the side of his deckchair. Passing it across to Thea, he said, 'I wasn't making a joke when I said that Germany is where everything is happening. It's true. Hitler may not be a name well known in England yet, but in Germany he is filling people with hope.'

'Not here he isn't,' Thea retorted tartly, adding milk to his tea. 'Here he's seen as a ruffian and a troublemaker.'

Unperturbed, Dieter smiled across at her. 'That is because you have not yet met him. To be able to judge his formidable magnetism – all of which is dedicated to the nation's welfare – you have to meet him.'

'And I have yet to meet the Prince of Wales,' Rozalind said, deciding it was high time the subject was changed to something less controversial. 'What chance do I have on this visit, Thea?'

Thea handed Dieter his cup of tea. 'Plenty, if you'll settle for being introduced to him in a night-club setting, the Embassy Club or Quaglino's. After that – if you're still hankering to photograph him – you're on your own. It will depend on what impression you make on him.'

'Rozalind is dark-haired, and the Prince likes dark-haired young women, does he not?' Dieter always enjoyed talking about British royalty. They were, as he never ceased telling his wife and sisters-in-law, all as German as he was.

'She's too tall.' Violet tilted her head back and dropped a small strawberry into her mouth. There was a beaded headband around her hair, which, unbobbed and unshingled, tumbled waist-length down her back. 'I've been telling her that for years

291

now, but being an American she never gives up hope.'

'And you,' Dieter said teasingly. 'Do you never give up hope also, Violet?'

With her face still raised to the sun Violet closed her eyes. 'I don't have hopes,' she said in her husky, languid voice. 'I have certainties.'

Thea rolled her eyes. Olivia laughed. Rozalind wished she had her Leica with her. A photograph of Violet, languorously dropping strawberries into her mouth, her hectic red hair rippling and shimmering, would have been pure Pre-Raphaelite.

The parlourmaid who had brought out the fresh pot of tea crossed the lawn to them again.

'There's a telephone call for Miss Duveen,' she said to Thea.

Thea looked enquiringly towards Rozalind.

'Who from?' Roz asked.

'Lord Luddesdon, Miss Duveen.'

Rozalind gave a heavy sigh. 'Barty,' she said wearily. 'Do me a favour, Thea. Tell Barty I'm in Richmond, or the Hebrides, or anywhere. I just don't want to have to bother with him right now.'

Thea helped herself to a scone and rose to her feet. 'No more gossip about the Prince of Wales until I get back. Understood?'

'How can there be?' Olivia said reasonably. 'You're the only one who knows any gossip worth having, where Edward is concerned.'

Not denying it, Thea took a bite of her scone and, with long, almost masculine strides, headed back to the house.

'Barty?' she said minutes later. 'It's me. Thea. Rozalind isn't around at the moment. Can I take a message?'

'Yes, you bloody can!' he thundered down the phone. 'You can tell her I ran into Max Bradley at the Cafe de Paris an hour ago. And you can tell Roz he told me the two of them were seeing each other again, and that he didn't want me hanging around her. If it's true – and if she's been so reckless as to involve herself with a married man old enough to be her father – then you can tell her that Bradley need have no fears about me hanging around her, because I sure as dammit won't be!'

Chapter Nineteen

When Thea hung up the phone, her hand was trembling. Though she didn't want to, she believed every word of what Barty had said to her. Roz might seem full of common sense, but she hadn't shown any when she'd fibbed her way into Max's bed within days of meeting him, and she quite clearly wasn't showing any common sense now. With rising alarm, Thea accepted what she had once thought unbelievable. Violet wasn't the only person in the family who was dangerously reckless and heedless. In her own way and where Max was concerned – Rozalind was just as bad.

When she walked back out onto the lawn all she said in answer to Rozalind's raised eyebrow was, 'Barty just wanted to make sure you'd

293

arrived here safely.'

What she said when, at the first opportunity, she got Rozalind on her own was far different.

'Max has told Barty the two of you are an item again!' she said explosively, rounding on her. 'And it's true, isn't it? I can see by the expression on your face that it's true!'

They were in the bedroom Rozalind always stayed in when visiting Gorton. Olivia and Dieter were in their own room at the far end of the corridor. Where Violet was, Thea neither knew nor cared. All that mattered was that she wasn't within earshot – and that neither was her father, who was in another part of Gorton entirely, playing host to his weekend guests.

'Yes, it's true. I've been waiting for the right moment to tell you.'

She was so completely unperturbed that Thea gaped in disbelief. 'He married another woman little more than a year ago,' she said finally, as if speaking to someone mentally retarded. 'He could have married you, and he didn't. He married someone else.'

'I know.' Rozalind sat down on the edge of the bed and slipped her feet out of her shoes. 'He's explained why.'

'Dear Lord, Roz! What possible explanation could there be? He may have had a longtime understanding with the woman he married in preference to you, but according to you they weren't formally engaged. And what explanation is there for his being unfaithful almost before his honeymoon was over? If he was already bored with his wife, why didn't he follow time-honoured fashion and embark on an affair with a married woman? Society understands that. A married woman's reputation is protected simply by the fact that she *is* married. Your reputation will be shot to pieces – is probably *already* shot to pieces!'

Rozalind reached for her cigarette-case and lighter, saying, 'For heaven's sake Thea, stop pacing the carpet like a lion in a cage and shooting questions at me without waiting for answers.' She took out a cigarette and lit it. 'First of all,' she said, 'Max has known Myrtle all his life. She's a second cousin. She comes from a political family, as he does. The two of them had an on-off affair throughout most of the years of Myrtle's marriage. When she was widowed two years ago, it was expected – but unspoken – that after a suitable period of mourning they would marry. Myrtle's husband was in government. They lived in Washington. She understands all the stresses, strains and complexities that go with being the wife of a politician. Socially, and in every other way, she was a huge asset to Oscar.'

'Her late husband?'

Rozalind blew smoke into the air and nodded.

Thea prayed for strength. 'Let me get this right, Roz. What you are saying is that when it came to making a choice as to which of the two of you he should marry, Max chose Myrtle purely because he thought she would be the most help to him in his career?'

'That's right.'

'And, knowing this, you find his action *acceptable?*'

'I never said I found it acceptable, but I do find it understandable.'

'Then it's more than I do!' Thea, who rarely smoked, snatched Roz's cigarette-case and lighter from her.

Rozalind, anticipating what would be coming next, remained silent.

Thea lit a cigarette, inhaled deeply and, with her left arm pressed hard against her body, her hand cupping her right elbow, said, 'And do you also find it acceptable that, after a brief year of marriage, he should be renewing his affair with you?'

'Actually yes, I do. They both married for reasons other than being crazily in love with each other. I've told you Max's reasons. Myrtle's weren't so different. She'd enjoyed being the wife of a respected politician and she wanted to be one again. It's what she's good at.'

'And you're the one who is good at sex? Is that where this is going?'

Rozalind jumped to her feet and crossed the room. Angrily stubbing her cigarette out, she said with barely controlled patience, 'Why are you being so nasty about this, Thea? Myrtle is a natural-born Washington queen bee. I have no desire to be one – and, even if I had, I wouldn't make a very good one. How could I, when my photography is so important to me? I thought you, of all people, would understand.'

'All I understand is that I think you're being taken advantage of! Even worse is that Max doesn't seem to have any regard at all for your reputation. Why would he tell Barty that the two of you had got together again? Why would he tell anyone?'

'I don't know. I imagine it was Barty who made the approach, not Max. He's been badgering me to marry him for months, and it would be typical of him to gloat to Max that we were on the verge of announcing our engagement. Max was simply putting him straight. And though Barty told you, he only did so out of rage and frustration and he probably also hoped you'd react exactly as you have done, and that you'd try and get me to break things off with Max.'

'Which you are not going to do?'

'Which I am not going to do.'

They stared at each other, at an impasse.

'He's what I want, Thea.' Rozalind took both of Thea's hands in hers. 'I love him. Any way I can get him, I want him in my life.'

'And Myrtle?'

'Myrtle has got what she wants. There won't be a divorce – and neither will I be sitting at home waiting for Max to spend a few stolen hours with me. I've got a contract with Pullman's, a New York press agency. I've been a semi-professional photo-grapher for years. Now, thanks to Pullman's, I'm a fully professional one. I have family wealth behind me. I can go where I want, when I want. Best of all, when it comes to having love in my life, the man I love with all my heart loves me in exactly the same way. You may doubt this, Thea, but I don't. Not for a second.'

Thea took a deep, steadying breath, finally accepting what she so clearly couldn't change.

At last she said: 'Will you tell Olivia?'

'I'll tell Olivia, and I'll tell Violet. Where my family are concerned, I've no intention of keeping Max in a cupboard. My life is going to be permanently intertwined with his. It may not be a situation anybody wants, but it is a situation I want accepted by the people I love.'

'And Carrie?'

'Of course Carrie!' Rozalind was indignant. 'I said family – and, for me, that includes Carrie. We're seeing her tonight, aren't we? At Charlie and Hermione's?'

'Yes. It's going to be a nice little party. You. Me. Olivia and Dieter. Violet. Jim. Miss Calvert. Hermione and Charlie.'

'But no Kyle, and no Hal?'

'Kyle would have travelled up for the weekend if I'd invited him.'

'And you didn't invite him because...?'

Thea flushed. 'Because Carrie wrote to Hal about the get-together. His driving up for it is a long shot, but still...'

'But still you were hoping?'

Thea nodded, not trusting herself to put her hopes, where Hal was concerned, into words.

On marrying Charlie, Hermione had never moved into the tied cottage that had been Charlie's home since the day Blanche had first met him and offered him work. Instead, with legacies left her by her parents, she had bought an attractive double-fronted terraced house that faced Outhwaite's village green and war memorial. Compared to other local houses it was comfortably spacious. Carrie thought it positively grand. Thea, Olivia and Violet, all of whom had grown up regularly visiting much smaller houses – houses such as Miss Calvert's pin-neat terraced home and Carrie's granny's tied cottage – piled into it without giving it another thought. Dieter, who had never socialized in any private home smaller than, in Germany, a little palace and, in England, Gorton Hall, looked and felt dazedly bemused.

'So nice to meet you, Count von Starhemberg,' Hermione said, her long nose twitching, her pince-nez hanging from a mulberry-coloured ribbon the exact same shade as her silk dress. *'Möchten Sie lieber sprechen Englisch oder Deutsch?'*

'Thank you for your courtesy in asking, Mrs Hardwick. In England, and out of deference to my English family, I prefer to speak in English.' Dieter clicked his heels, bowed formally and kissed the back of her hand.

Hermione flushed with pleasure.

Olivia's eyes sparkled. She knew her Hermione, and she knew Hermione had only asked the question in order to be able to show off her German.

'So that is why your German is so good,' Dieter whispered to her as Violet enveloped Hermione in a giant bear-hug. 'I always thought you began learning it in Berlin, at finishing school. I didn't know you had been taught it as a child.'

'Actually, I wasn't. When I was of an age to begin a language, it was the Great War – and the aftermath went on a long time. Hermione might have been capable of teaching German, but even Papa wouldn't have thought it a patriotic choice. She taught us French instead.'

299

'Lieber Gott!'

For a second Olivia thought Dieter was giving vent to an unnecessarily harsh reaction to French having being the preferred choice, and then she saw that Jim had entered the room. Scrubbed up, his curly hair brilliantined halfway into submission and in his Sunday best – a shiny suit and a collarless shirt worn with a remarkably clean red-spotted neckerchief – he couldn't have been mistaken for anything other than a common workman, albeit a rather good-looking one.

Aghast, Dieter said weakly, 'Please tell me I am not expected to rub shoulders with this person also?'

His shock and horror were so deep that Olivia giggled. 'Yes, you are, darling. Jim is one of the best friends Thea and I have.' She frowned, suddenly serious. 'And think how difficult it is for him, stepping into the same room as you – a German.'

'He fought in the war?'

'No. Jim was born lame and the army wouldn't accept him. He and Charlie are as close as brothers, though – and you've seen what German shell-fire did to Charlie.'

Dieter had. One of the first things Gilbert Fenton had done after their arrival at Gorton had been to introduce him to Charlie. 'Best to get it out of the way,' Gilbert had said to him. 'Though, knowing Charlie, there won't be a problem.'

Incredibly to Dieter, on Charlie's part there hadn't been – and Dieter had envied him. Though he'd hid it with the ease of a professional diplomat, he had been the one who'd had a problem – and

300

his problem had been threefold.

Though Dieter had been too young at the time of the Great War to have fought in it, he knew that if he had, and if he'd suffered injuries as grievous as the ones Charlie had suffered, he would never have forgiven any member of the nation responsible, let alone seemed genuinely pleased to meet one of them.

He'd also found looking at Charlie's destroyed face far more difficult than he'd anticipated. When he'd admitted this later to Olivia, she'd said it was a good job he hadn't seen Charlie prior to all the years of structural surgeries he had undergone at St Mary's, and that compared to how he'd looked then, he was a living miracle now.

Lastly, he found the way the Fentons socialized without thought with people who had worked for them, such as Hermione, with people who still worked for them, such as Jim and Charlie, and with other people not of their class, such as Miss Calvert and Carrie – whom he had yet to meet – mind-bogglingly difficult to comprehend. Even more difficult for him was that they expected him to act in the same way.

The head-on collision between English eccentricity and Prussian formality was one he had so far survived, but being asked to socialize with Gorton estate's odd-job man was, he felt, extreme to the point of insanity.

'Dieter, I'd like to introduce Jim to you,' Olivia was saying as a fair-haired girl with the look of a Sunday-school teacher stepped into the room to cries of delighted welcome.

Carrie's arrival saved Dieter from having to engage other than very briefly with Jim. He did, though, sense that the distaste he felt at their introduction was fully reciprocated.

Carrie he liked instantly. Almost from his first meeting with Olivia he had heard of how her best friend was the granddaughter of her father's old nanny, of how they had been friends ever since they had been eight years old, and of how Carrie was in service at Monkswood, the home of Lady Markham some thirty miles from Gorton.

'I'm so pleased to meet you,' she said with an engaging smile and in a manner that was polite and friendly, and not, as he had anticipated, embarrassingly deferential. 'Do you like North Yorkshire, Count von Starhemberg? Is it much different from the countryside around Berlin?'

'The countryside around Berlin is more wooded – and we have more lakes. We don't have your wonderful moors, though, and we don't see sheep everywhere, as you do here.'

She gave a little laugh and he said, 'Olivia tells me Prussian-style formality doesn't exist at Outhwaite and that we should be on first-name terms. I would like that very much, if it doesn't displease you?'

Carrie blushed rosily. 'Of course it doesn't displease me. First-name terms are much friendlier. Olivia tells me you've already met Hal. Did you like him? Did you think him wonderfully clever?'

'I thought him very interesting,' Dieter said truthfully, both amused and charmed by her simple directness and unsophistication. 'He is greatly interested in Germany and German

302

politics, and far more knowledgeable than the majority of people I speak with in London.'

Her blush deepened and he knew it was with pleasure at hearing Hal complimented. Olivia had told him that Thea was in love with Hal, that Hal was no longer responsive to her and that everyone – including Thea herself – thought Hal would one day marry Carrie.

Even though he had spent less than five minutes in Carrie's company, Dieter was certain Hal would do no such thing. Carrie was too gentle-mannered and uncomplicated, and Hal too politically passionate and fiercely driven for him ever to imagine them as compatible life partners.

As the evening progressed he found that, contrary to all his expectations, he was enjoying himself. Hester Calvert and Hermione Hardwick, both severely and elegantly dressed, reminded him of his many very intelligent, very proper middle-aged aunts. The oddness of sitting down at table to something called high tea, a meal that was neither afternoon tea nor dinner, didn't faze him. He liked cold, thickly sliced Yorkshire ham served with home-made chutney. He even enjoyed his introduction to English trifle, all its various layers and colours shining jewel-like in a large cut-glass bowl.

What floored him was the lack of alcohol. 'You could have warned me,' he whispered to Olivia when it became apparent that the choice of liquid refreshment was ginger beer, sarsaparilla or tea.

'It would have spoiled my fun,' she whispered back. 'I wanted to see your face when you realized.

303

Hermione is a strict Methodist. She doesn't allow any swearing either – or card-playing. It makes things a bit difficult for Charlie, but he idolizes her all the same.'

Dieter was just about to say that Charlie was a hero in more ways than one, when, from the other side of the table, Carrie said with shy pride, 'I have some news to share with you. Mrs Appleby, Monkswood's housekeeper, is suffering from rheumatism in her legs and although there has never been an under-housekeeper at Monkswood, Lady Markham has asked me to take on that position in order to ease Mrs Appleby's workload.'

'Under-housekeeper?' Hermione clapped her hands together in delight. 'And at twenty-one? You have done very well for yourself, Carrie dear. Your late granny would be proud of you.'

'Will you have to wear a black dress and carry a huge bunch of keys at your waist, like Mrs Fairfax in *Jane Eyre?*' Violet asked, enraptured at the thought of how dramatic Carrie would then look.

'Don't be so daft!' Jim helped himself to a large slab of Wensleydale cheese. 'She weighs nobbut more than a feather. How could she walk around all day wi' keys weighing a ton and a 'alf at 'er waist?'

'It means that when you've gained enough experience, you'll be able to look for a position as a housekeeper,' Hester Calvert said, as pleased as Hermione at the way Carrie had worked her way from being an insignificant tweeny to being a step away from the most prestigious domestic position a great house could offer.

When sincere congratulations from everyone were over, Olivia regaled them with an example of the Duke and Duchess of York's idyllic family life. 'Elizabeth invited me for afternoon tea two weeks ago,' she said, knowing how Hester, Hermione and Carrie loved hearing royal gossip, 'and we spent a hilarious half-hour playing hide-and-seek with little Elizabeth.'

Charlie shot her a grin; proud, for Hermione's sake, that such intimate chat about royalty was taking place around their dinner table.

Rozalind saw an opportunity and seized on it. 'I'd love to be given the opportunity to photograph the Duke and Duchess of York with Princess Elizabeth. Would you put in a good word for me, Olivia, the next time you are with the Yorks?'

Olivia promised that she would, and Dieter said, 'Why don't you do some portraiture work in Berlin, Rozalind? Both the British and the American press are growing increasingly curious about Hitler and the growing strength of the NSDAP. They are a perfect subject for a press photographer, and I could arrange some introductions.'

A week later, Thea and Roz were sharing a first-class compartment on a train speeding towards London. 'Dieter's offer could really kick-start my career, Thea,' Rozalind said, breaking through Thea's thoughts. 'I've wanted to go back to Berlin ever since I visited Olivia there. It's a very photogenic city.'

Thea gave a rude snort. 'It's a very politically

troubled city. There are more different political parties in it than I can count – and the NSDAP is the one least likely to gain any prominence. Don't let Dieter influence you into looking at it with any admiration, Roz. A left-wing friend of mine who visited recently says brawls between communists and Nazi Brownshirts are nightly events.'

'Is your friend a communist?'

'Yes.'

'And are you?'

'Not quite. Not yet. But I feel the day approaching.'

For the rest of the train journey, as Rozalind read F. Scott Fitzgerald's *The Great Gatsby*, Thea was sunk deep in thought. Her disappointment that Hal hadn't walked into the room when they were all gathered at Hermione and Charlie's was crucifyingly deep. Time wasn't helping her get over him. What, then, would?

As she watched Rozalind read, Thea pondered her life and her future. Compared to what was happening in the lives of Olivia, Violet, Carrie and Roz, her life was bleak. Olivia was deliriously happy in her marriage to Dieter. Violet had at last persuaded their father to allow her to study drama at the Royal Academy of Dramatic Art and was quite obviously going to go through life always getting exactly what she wanted. In becoming under-housekeeper at Monkswood, Carrie had achieved far more than she had modestly hoped ever to achieve. Roz had both her photography and Max.

And she, if she wanted to, had Kyle.

The train stopped at Nottingham. Roz, who was now asleep, never stirred.

Thea wondered if, for her own survival, she should give up all hope of Hal returning to her and instead accept Kyle's proposal of marriage. The more she thought about it, the more it seemed to her the best course of action she could take. There was no logical reason she could think of why the two of them shouldn't be happy together. Kyle was handsome in the same dark, sleek way that Roz was beautiful. He was intelligent. He was ambitious. He made her laugh. Perhaps most importantly, as a Democrat he was tolerant of her socialism. If she couldn't be with Hal, then there was no one else she would rather be with than Kyle. Marrying him made absolute sense. It would be a brand-new start: a completely new way of life.

By the time the train pulled into King's Cross she had even decided on where they would marry – St George's, Hanover Square – and which designer she would go to for her wedding dress: Paul Poiret.

As she stepped down from the train and began walking with Roz towards the barrier she was filled with such relief at having come to a decision about her future that she felt almost light-headed.

Then, within shattering seconds, everything changed.

Roz let out a deep-throated cry and, with one hand holding onto her summer hat, broke into a headlong run towards the barrier.

A crowd of people was standing there, but Thea – like Roz – saw only one of them. He was tall

307

and broad-shouldered, a man with a strong-boned face and hair attractively touched with silver at the temples. As Rozalind raced towards him, he pushed the barrier aside and sprinted to meet her.

Thea came to a halt, unable to move, barely able to breathe as, uncaring of the spectators at the barrier, Rozalind hurtled into his open arms like an arrow entering the gold.

It was then that she knew there would be no wedding at St George's. No Poiret-designed wedding dress.

To marry Kyle, when she knew it wasn't within her ever to greet him in public – or anywhere else for that matter – with the blazing joy and naked fervour with which Roz had just greeted Max, would be to short-change him. And she liked and respected Kyle far too much to do that to him.

Slowly she began walking down the platform, knowing that unless Hal returned to her one day, the happiness that Roz had found in her relationship with Max was a happiness she would never know.

'Hello, Mr Bradley,' she said, moments later. 'I've been hearing a lot about you for a long time now.' She held out her hand, saying with a warmth towards him she had never thought she would feel, 'It's very nice finally to meet you. I do hope that we'll be friends.'

Chapter Twenty

SEPTEMBER 1930

'Okay. Let's wrap this up in one last take. Back on your marks, everyone – and this time, Violet, when I say swoon, you *swoon!*'

Violet nodded indifferently. Sárközy always treated everyone on-set with high-handed contempt, believing that such behaviour went with his job description of director. He knew, and she knew, that there had been nothing wrong with her swoon in the previous takes. It had been Basil Curtis, an actor with years of film experience under his belt, who on the first six takes had fluffed his lines and, on the last six, had swept her up from her swoon as if she was a sack of potatoes, not the most beautiful, desirable woman in all of ancient Israel.

Violet, her turbulent hair streaming waist-length, and wearing an ankle-length gown of emerald silk girdled low on her hips, walked back onto the set and hit her marks, every inch Delilah standing before a Philistine ruler who wanted Samson, scourge of the Philistines, dead.

'Ready?' Sárközy barked as Curtis fidgeted nervously. 'Let's try again. This is a talkie, remember? A groundbreaking movie. And make it good this time, Curtis. You're supposed to be a ruling despot, not a frightened mouse. Quiet on the set, everybody. Hold it down. Roll 'em.'

The focus boy checked the focus. The clapper boy stepped forward in front of Violet and Curtis and held the clapboard up before the camera.

'Scene forty-six,' Sárközy said through gritted teeth. 'Take thirteen.'

Violet slid silently and effortlessly into the part. The lead actor who was playing the part of Samson, and who was seated in a canvas chair next to Sárközy's director's chair, watched in disdain as, yet again, Curtis launched into a thundering rendition of his 'I am ordering you to lure Samson into showing you the secrets of his great strength so that we can overpower him and slaughter him!' speech.

Violet gasped, clutched at her heart and slid into a graceful faint.

This time Curtis scooped her up in his arms without fumbling and, as Sárközy rasped, 'That's it. Print it!' there were sighs of relief from both cast and crew.

Violet walked swiftly in Sárközy's direction. Dieter had asked if he could visit the Beaconsfield Film Studios and be shown around them, and when she had told Sárközy that he was a German diplomat familiar with the Babelsberg film studios in Berlin, Sárközy had given permission with alacrity. All during the last take she had been aware that Dieter was standing only yards away from where Sárközy was sitting.

Now, already, the two men were in conversation.

'It's a great privilege to be allowed on-set,' Dieter was saying to Sárközy as she joined them.

'Beaconsfield Film Studios are even bigger than Studio Babelsberg.'

'How many sound stages does Babelsberg have?' Sárközy rose to his feet, deeply interested. The sound stage on which he was shooting was Beaconsfield's first sound stage, and the movie he was now filming the first talkie he had ever shot.

'Just the one, I believe.' Dieter replied smoothly. Though he had no intention of admitting it, he had no first-hand experience of Babelsberg, but via a friend whose mistress was one of Germany's most popular actresses he knew enough Babelsberg gossip to sound as if he had. 'The first feature-length talkie shot on it was *Melody of the Heart* starring Willy Fritsch.'

'And directed by Hanns Schwarz, a Dane,' Sárközy said with a rare glimmer of a smile. 'Do you know Schwarz, Count von Starhemberg?'

'Sadly, no. I am, however, familiar with Josef von Sternberg.'

That at least was true. He'd met von Sternberg at a party the last time he'd had diplomatic leave and spent it in Berlin with Olivia.

'And von Sternberg is an Austrian,' Sárközy said, beginning to lead the way off the set and towards the VIP lounge, where the conversation could be continued comfortably over ice-cold vodka. 'I – as Violet will have told you – am Hungarian.'

Violet didn't excuse herself in order to change out of her costume and remove her stage make-up. Instead, discreetly silent for once, she walked at Dieter's side, wondering what his reaction

311

would be if she were to tell him truthfully that she and Sárközy were lovers – and that it wasn't only her extraordinary acting skills that had got her the plum part of Delilah.

'What is the latest news from Babelsberg?' Sárközy asked as they settled themselves around a small table in the lounge. 'What is von Sternberg directing now?'

'His latest film, *The Blue Angel*, is just about to be premiered. Gossip is that the unknown actress, in the lead part is sensational.'

Sárközy gave a wolfish grin. 'Whoever she is, she will not be as sensational as Violet. Violet's portrayal of Delilah is going to be a ... what is the French expression the English use? A *tour de force*.'

Dieter didn't doubt it. The part of beautiful seductress was one tailor-made for Violet.

He shot her a burning glance. She met it with a naughty glint in her eye, well aware of his thoughts where she was concerned. They didn't disturb her. She had very similar, reciprocal thoughts of her own.

'Everyone is directing talkies now,' Sárközy was saying to Dieter. 'The subjects chosen are interesting, don't you think? In Germany, Hanns Schwarz makes *Melody of the Heart*, based on an operetta. In America, the first talkie is also a musical, *The Jazz Singer*. In Britain, Alfred Hitchcock makes *Blackmail*, a thriller. No one has done what I, Sárközy, am doing. No one has taken a great biblical epic, like Samson and Delilah – the kind of epic that talkies were made for.'

Knowing the conversation was likely to continue in the same vein for quite some time, Violet allowed her thoughts to drift. After only a year at RADA, she had attracted the eye of a talent scout and had been cast in small parts in several silent films. The films had been made at Beaconsfield in Buckinghamshire, and it was when she was at Beaconsfield that she had first seen Sárközy. He, of course, thought that *he* had initiated their first meeting and done the chasing. Violet knew differently.

As Sárközy and Dieter's conversation moved on to a discussion of Alexander Korda's first talkie, *The Squall*, which had been made in Hollywood, Violet wondered who had made the running in Rozalind and Max's relationship and in Olivia and Dieter's relationship. She rather thought that although Roz liked to think she called a lot of the shots where she and Max were concerned, in reality it was Max who had made the running and Rozalind who had been caught.

She was aware, of course, that most people who knew of Roz and Max's adulterous affair thought it a tragedy – or certainly did so where Roz was concerned. Because of the way Roz ran her life, Violet didn't see it as a tragedy at all. Roz was an independent young woman who travelled the world as a press photographer. Every few months she and Max would meet up in New York, or in London. Once or twice they had met in Berlin – a city Roz had made very much her own, since Dieter had introduced her to the up-and-coming leaders of the National Socialist German Workers' Party and she had become their favoured and accepted foreign-press photographer.

313

'The Nazis make rich pickings,' Violet had heard Roz say to Thea, when Thea had queried why she was, yet again, en route to Berlin. 'Of all the countless political parties fighting and arguing themselves to a standstill in Germany, the Nazis are the only party growing at a rate of knots – and their meetings are always accompanied by high drama. Pullman's can't get enough of the photographs I'm able to take.'

She took other kinds of photographs when in Berlin – photographs that weren't for her press agency. She loved the grandeur of the buildings. The neo-Romantic splendour of the Kaiser Wilhelm Church on Breitscheidplatz. The Italian Renaissance majesty of the Reichstag. The grandeur of the Brandenburg Gate surmounted by its statue of the Roman goddess of victory driving a four-horse chariot.

She took photographs in the pearly light of early dawn and in the hazy dusk of twilight. As well as buildings, she took photographs of Berliners going about their daily life in the leafy acres of the Tiergarten, the great tree-studded park that lay at Berlin's heart. In October 1929 there had been a small exhibition of these photographs in a prestigious Manhattan Lower East Side gallery. If anyone had been in any doubt about Roz's professionalism, after the exhibition they had been so no longer.

'Apart from Sternberg's *The Blue Angel*, most films being shot at Babelsberg are of individuals battling against nature in the mountains,' Dieter was saying wryly and in a way that, if Violet hadn't known better, would have convinced even

her that he was speaking from first-hand information.

Whatever was going on at Babelsberg, her present ambitions lay in another geographic direction. For a film actress, Hollywood was the place
to be, and it was Hollywood she had in her sights.
It was, she knew, where Sárközy wanted to be, and
it was why she had every intention of clinging to
him like a limpet.

She wondered what it would be like to be so far
away from family and friends. She would miss Hal
– whom she met up with in Fleet Street pubs quite
often – far more than she would miss Carrie, for
being at Outhwaite so rarely, she only saw Carrie
two or three times a year. She would also miss
Olivia far more than she would miss Thea.

Ever since they had been children she and Thea
had been incompatible. When she had been small
she hadn't understood why she irritated Thea so
intensely. Now, however, she understood very
well. It was because she was frivolous, and Thea
didn't have a frivolous bone in her body.

Why Kyle Anderson – who was handsome
enough to commit suicide for, and who could certainly have had a career in films if he had wanted
to – was so besotted with a serious-minded blue-
stocking like Thea she couldn't imagine. The only
interesting aspect of Thea's life was her long-
standing friendship with the Prince of Wales, and
even that friendship was built on the boring
interest that the two of them had in social and
economic wrongs. To listen to Thea, unemployment and hellish housing conditions were the only
things the two of them ever talked about.

Violet couldn't imagine how both of them could be bothered with something so dreary, but when she had once said so to Hal, he had astounded her by saying in a hard, fierce voice, 'Unlike you, Violet, Thea has a code of principles that she lives by. You can chatter idiotically to me about anyone else, but never about Thea. Understand?'

She had been completely taken aback – but she had understood. What she had also understood was that there was never going to be any delicious naughtiness between her and Hal, which was, she still thought, a pity. Dieter, however, was another matter entirely.

For nearly a year now Violet had sensed that Dieter *was* quite capable of being naughty – and probably was naughty – just as long as his beloved Olivia didn't find out about it. By her own lights Violet had behaved very well about this. She had been flirtatious (it would have been impossible for her not to be), but had never given him blatant encouragement – a romantic romp with a brother-in-law seeming, even to her, a little excessive.

However, as Olivia quite obviously knew nothing about Dieter's spats of unfaithfulness, and they consequently never upset the tenor of his own and Olivia's marriage, she had decided she was being overly well-behaved. It had been Dieter's suggestion that he drive out of London to visit her at Beaconsfield, ostensibly out of curiosity to be shown around a film studio. Violet hadn't been fooled. He just wanted her on her own, away from the family. It was a situation she

316

was entirely happy about. A girl could only be good for so long, and with Dieter no harm would be done.

When Sárközy brought his tête-à-tête with Dieter to an end, she took Dieter on the tour they were both pretending was the reason for his visit.

'We'll go to the sound stages first,' she said, still in her Delilah costume. 'And then out to the back lot, where workmen are building a Dickensian asylum.'

'Sounds grim. What film is it for?'

The Woman in White. It's some kind of ghost thriller.'

'If it's from the book of the same name, it is. It seems Sárközy is right in that, where talkies are concerned, no one else is yet doing biblical epics. He's a man with the market cornered.' Dieter was enjoying himself. The sun was hot on his back. He had Violet all to himself, and striding around the studios with her he felt like a king – or, at the very least, like a film director.

On the sound stages she introduced him to sound men, prop men, gaffers and focus boys. On the back lot she introduced him to a wizened little man, 'Ginger' Martin, who boasted that his 'boys' could build anything that was asked for – and that they could do so overnight, if need be. Dieter was duly impressed and even more impressed when, in the canteen, as well as introducing him to Basil Curtis and to the American actor who was playing the part of Samson opposite her Delilah, Violet also introduced him to Sybil Thorndike, an acclaimed actress he had seen in many West End stage productions.

317

Miss Thorndike's friendliness and lack of pretentiousness was, Dieter thought, extraordinary.

'I saw her on-stage four or five years ago in a Bernard Shaw play,' he said as he and Violet walked down a covered walkway towards her dressing room. 'The play was *Saint Joan*, and Shaw wrote the part of St Joan specifically for her.'

'Then perhaps you'd have a word with him and ask if he'd write a part specifically for me,' Violet said as they came to a halt in front of a door bearing her name.

She was only half-joking. To appear on the West End stage in a play written for her by Bernard Shaw would send her stock as an actress soaring into the stratosphere.

She opened the door and Dieter followed her into a small, untidy room dominated by a large dressing table and an even larger, bulb-surrounded mirror.

It was taken as a given by both of them that he should follow after her.

She went straight to her dressing table and seated herself in front of it. He perched on the arm of a small sofa that was cluttered with clothes. 'Sybil has an advantage you don't have, where Shaw is concerned,' he said, fighting to keep his desire for her under control for a little while longer, as Violet set about removing her Delilah make-up with cold cream. 'She's as passionately left-wing as he is.'

Violet, who hadn't the least interest in politics, rolled her eyes. 'So she is. I'd forgotten. Do you know that during the first run of *Saint Joan*,

318

when the General Strike was on and the strikers closed the theatre down, she gave them her support?'

'No, I didn't,' he said, knowing that when she had finished removing her make-up she would then remove her Philistine princess costume – and that, being Violet, she would do so in front of him.

He shifted uncomfortably on the arm of the sofa, his erection so hard it was making his eyes water. Would she do so because she wanted the outcome that he already yearned for so badly? Or would she do so simply because she was naturally shameless – as shameless as the cabaret artistes in Berlin's raunchy nightclubs?

He missed his city's nightlife. London nightlife was sophisticated, of course, but prudishly tame compared to Berlin's sexually uninhibited night-life. He remembered a night when he'd been with friends in the El Dorado, on the Ku'damm. A sensationally beautiful woman had walked into the club who was quite obviously naked beneath her white mink coat, a gold bracelet around her ankle and with a pet monkey sitting on her shoul-der. In the El Dorado her arrival had caused barely a stir. In Bond Street's Embassy Club she would have caused a riot.

The only woman he had met in London whom he could imagine effortlessly dressing and be-having in such a way was Violet. Violet was fun – and having fun with her would, he knew, come with no strings. She would never expect, or want, a serious commitment from him. She would never be clinging. She would never tell Olivia and, best of all, she would be very, very naughty in bed.

Naughtiness had been lacking in his life since his marriage.

Olivia was passionate – she was, after all, as deeply in love with him as he was with her – but she wasn't naughty, and nor did he want her to be. Naughty women did not, in his book, make good, faithful wives. Violet, he was quite sure, would one day make some man an appalling wife.

For romps in the hay – which is all she would ever want from him she would, though, be mesmerizing.

She removed the last of the cream from her face and he walked across to her, saying thickly, 'I'll help with your zip.'

Through the mirror she shot him a bright, wicked smile and rose to her feet.

He stood behind her, his mouth dry with sexual tension. Still holding her eyes through the glass, his fingers closed on the zipper tab and then, slowly, he ran it down to the base of her spine.

With no help from either of them, the emerald silk gown slithered from her shoulders, falling into a pool around her feet.

Beneath it she was stark naked.

He sucked in his breath. Her tousle of pubic hair curled even more tightly than the hair that streamed waist-length down her back, but it was the same spicy fox-red. Until now he'd always considered himself married to a redhead, but Olivia's bush was a dark, burnished mahogany and his excitement spiralled to unbearable proportions as he realized he was about to have his

320

first experience of sex with a true redhead.

Violet forestalled him.

'Not here,' she said throatily, stepping swiftly away from him in the direction of the sofa and unearthing a yellow polka-dot dress from the mayhem of tumbled clothes. 'There's a darling small hotel this side of Gerrards Cross on the way back to London, and if you're thinking of problems at home, booking in for the night doesn't mean we have to stay for the night.'

She stepped into the dress and then, still minus lingerie, into a pair of high-heeled shoes. Impishly she looked across at him. 'I'm ready, if you are,' she said, picking up a pair of white gloves and not feeling a twinge of guilt. 'Let's go and have some fun!'

Chapter Twenty-One

Two months after Violet had embarked on her casual, reckless affair with Dieter, Carrie was on a train bound for London. It was a dull misty day in mid-November, but as the train steamed out of Yorkshire and into Derbyshire her spirits were high. All domestic staff at Monkswood were allowed an annual week's holiday so that they could spend time with their families. Family, to Carrie, meant Hal, Thea, Olivia, Violet, Roz and Lord Fenton.

After finishing a British film in which she had a leading role, Violet was in Hollywood and Roz was in Kenya, photographing the wildlife and native inhabitants. Hal, Thea, Olivia and Lord Fenton were all in London, and although November was an unseasonal time of year for a precious few days' holiday, Carrie was unconcerned about this. All that mattered was that she would be spending time with three – and possibly four – of the most important people in the world to her.

Hal's landlady, Mrs Dabner, was happy to put her up for seven nights, on the strict understanding that they would keep to their separate rooms and that, in her words, there would be no 'funny business' going on between them. Hal had written to her:

She can't believe we're friends, not sweethearts, but she's a kind old stick and she'll make you very welcome.

When she had written to Thea about her plans, Carrie had received quite a cross letter back:

Why are you staying with Hal's landlady when you could be at Mount Street? The wicked witch isn't in residence and, even if she were, it was Gorton she barred you from, not Mount Street. Do change your mind, Carrie.

Carrie hadn't changed her mind. Zephiniah Fenton hadn't wanted someone who was in service as a guest in her home, and just as Carrie would never have taken advantage of Zephiniah's absence to step inside Gorton, so she had no intention of stepping inside her London home.

322

She had far too much pride and, even if she hadn't, deceit of any kind was alien to her.

Olivia, of course, had been adamant that she should stay with her and Dieter in their Belgravia Square home, but although Dieter had been faultlessly courteous to her when he had met her at Charlie and Hermione's, she had known that he thought bizarre his wife's friendship with someone who was under-housekeeper to one of her father's friends. Not only that, but Olivia led a super-sophisticated life, mixing with royals such as the Duke and Duchess of York as easily and regularly as Carrie mixed with her Outhwaite friends. She couldn't be certain, of course, but she rather thought staying with Olivia and Dieter could be a little too nerve-racking for comfort.

The train drew into Newark. A scattering of passengers got off the train. A much larger number boarded.

Watching them, Carrie pondered why Thea being good friends with the Prince of Wales didn't unnerve her in the same way that Olivia's friendship with the Yorks did. And then she realized that it was because Thea was friends with lots and lots of ordinary working-class people as well – people that she, Carrie, would be instantly comfortable with.

She opened the magazine she had bought while waiting for the train and turned to the classified section, where scores of domestic positions were advertised. As always, she read the columns advertising vacant positions for maids and footmen with interest, curious to see how the pay and conditions being offered compared with those of the staff at Monkswood.

There was a separate section for housekeeper vacancies, but she didn't bother to read them. What was the point, when she wasn't interested in looking for a new position? Monkswood was the nearest house of its size to Gorton, and even though she could no longer visit Gorton itself, she didn't want to be even a mile further away from it than she presently was.

Gorton... The rhythmic movement of the train had made her sleepy and, as her eyelids closed, she remembered the first time she had entered it. She remembered the feeling of safety and warmth she had felt as Blanche had taken hold of her hand and led her down blue-carpeted corridors lined with marble busts, and then up the grand balustraded main staircase, just as if she was a very special guest – a princess guest. She remembered again the light rose fragrance of Blanche's perfume and the gentle tones of her voice. From that moment on, until Lord Fenton's second marriage, Gorton had been a second home to her and, because the people who lived in it were people she loved, she had loved it. Forbidden to enter it now, she loved it still and, as she dreamed herself back there, her mouth curved in a deep smile.

Hal was waiting for her at the barrier when the train steamed into King's Cross station. It was a damply chill day. His coat collar was turned up and he was wearing a shabby flat cap, as if to advertise to everyone that he was a northerner and proud of it.

She hurried towards him, her suitcase in one hand, a wide sunny smile on her face.

'I'm so glad you're here, Hal! I've never seen so many people crowded on a station platform before, and I kept thinking of what to do if you'd been delayed by work.'

He hugged her, kissed her on the cheek, took her case from her and said, 'You'd have done the sensible thing, just as you always do, love. You'd have waited for twenty minutes and, if I still hadn't turned up, you'd have made your own way to Deptford and Mrs Dabner's.'

She giggled. 'I would certainly have waited for twenty minutes, but though I could have found my own way to Mrs Dabner's – I made a note of the tram numbers you sent – I wouldn't have wanted to find my own way there, not going for the first time.'

'It's a simple enough journey, once you know the tram stops.'

They were out of the station now and on the pavement of a road so heavy with traffic it made Carrie's head spin.

'First off, we get a tram from here to Trafalgar Square, and then in Trafalgar Square we catch the 392 tram to Deptford.' He shot her a broad smile. 'I'm going to settle you in at the digs, and then we're going to a cafe for some fish and chips. London fish and chips aren't a patch on Yorkshire fish and chips, but they're better than nowt.'

'What's with the "nowt"?' she asked teasingly. 'I thought you spoke the Queen's English, now you were a journalist on a posh national newspaper?'

'I do.' He flashed her another smile, happy as a proverbial pig in muck at spending time with her again. 'I was just trying to make you feel at home.'

She gave him an indignant dig in the ribs, and they were both still laughing as they boarded the tram.

As the tram clanked and trundled on its rails, unimpeded by the rest of the busy traffic, he said, 'I'll be working through the day – and maybe some evenings as well – so you'll likely see more of Olivia and Thea than you will of me, but that can't be helped, Carrie love.'

'I know. There's no need to explain.'

He squeezed hold of her hand. Ever since he could remember there had never been a need for explanations between them, not about anything.

'As you've put your foot down about not visiting Thea at Mount Street, she'll be meeting up with you at Olivia's. I'm going to drop you off there tomorrow morning before going in to work. You'll soon get the hang of getting around London, though I don't think Thea or Olivia will give you much opportunity for doing so on your own. Both of them want to spend every available minute with you.'

She hesitated and then said, 'Are you and Thea still pretending nothing's gone dreadfully wrong between the two of you?'

The laughter left his eyes and voice.

'That's a very sensitive way of putting things, Carrie lass.' He pushed his cap back on his unruly hair, as if doing so would help him with his answer. After a pause he said, 'Yes. I suppose we are. There doesn't seem to be any other way for us to behave. We can't be friends in the way we used to be, because it's impossible for us to go back to that kind of friendship, and we can't be anything else, because the class difference between us is too great to be overcome – and don't go trying to tell me it isn't, Carrie, or this will end in a row.'

She didn't want a row, but she did want to know how he felt about Kyle Anderson.

'Do you think Thea will marry Roz's step-brother?' she asked, determined that not every subject should be a no-go area.

A muscle pulsed at the corner of his jaw. 'She will, if she's any sense. Olivia thinks there will be an engagement announcement at Christmas. English blue blood and American blue blood. *Tatler* will love it.'

His voice was hard and tight, and Carrie knew that although *Tatler* might love such an announce-ment, Hal would hate it – and would hate the groom-to-be, whoever he was. However far the romance between Hal and Thea had progressed, it was shatteringly clear to her that Hal still wasn't over it.

When Carrie entered Olivia and Dieter's Belgravia home the next morning, it was to find it just as grand as she had expected, but with the same distinctive touches with which Blanche had always made Gorton so comfortable. Instead of hothouse flower arrangements, exquisite vases held sprays of berries and burnished red and gold autumn leaves. In the large circular hall a large Japanese vase held a single, statuesque branch of sweet-smelling, yellow-flowering mahonia. Everywhere in the drawing room there were bowls filled with snow-white, late-flowering anemones.

The simplicity of them was so artless and perfect, and so like Blanche's style of doing things, that for a moment Carrie's throat closed with emotion. And then Olivia rushed towards her, hugging Carrie so enthusiastically she nearly knocked her off her feet, and from where she was perched on the arm of a deep-cushioned sofa, Thea said with a catch in her throat, 'Welcome to London, Carrie. We've missed you like crazy.'

When Olivia finally allowed her to break free, Carrie and Thea hugged, and Thea said as they mutually plumped down together on the sofa, 'So what are conditions like in darkest Deptford? Are you quite sure you want to remain there and not at Mount Street, or here with Olivia?'

'Hal's landlady runs a very clean lodging house. I'm going to be perfectly all right staying there. I now know the number of the trams I need to get from there to here and back again – and I have a map of London in my handbag, in case I should ever get lost.'

'In which case,' Thea said, 'you'll have to put our minds at rest on another matter. Someone in Outhwaite is having a baby and has asked Papa to stand as the baby's godfather. He simply won't part with who it is, though. He says he wants you to have the pleasure of telling us.'

'We're thinking Jim must have got married without letting anyone know.' Seated in a nearby armchair, Olivia curled her legs beneath her. 'Has he finally married one of the Pig and Whistle's barmaids?'

'No. Jim's still heart-whole and fancy-free.'

Thea lit a cigarette and blew a plume of blue smoke into the air. 'Then who is it? Papa's adamant it's someone in Outhwaite, but who else there is on the kind of terms with him that they could ask him to stand as godfather to one of their children? Even more to the point, who is there in Outhwaite whose child he would *agree* to be godfather to? The only people in that category are Hester Calvert and Charlie and Hermione.'

'And Hester isn't married,' Olivia said helpfully, 'and Charlie and Hermione...'

She saw the expression on Carrie's face and came to a halt. 'No!' she said. 'It can't be true. It can't be.'

'It is,' Carrie said with immense satisfaction. 'Charlie and Hermione are expecting a baby in March. Isn't it wonderful? Hal is so thrilled he says he's going to be at the christening.' With the hand holding her cigarette stationary with shock in mid-air, Thea said in a stunned voice, 'It's unbelievable. Hermione's forty-two!'

Unsure as to whether Thea was referring to news of the baby or the thought of Hal at a christening, Carrie said, 'Unbelievable or not, it's happened, and gossip in the village is that your father is to give them a baby carriage from Harrods.'

'Well, that I *can* believe,' Olivia said, 'and I think your news is so magnificent it should be celebrated with champagne.'

'It's a little early in the day. It's only just gone ten o'clock.'

'We can have it with orange juice. We have to wet the baby's head. It's traditional.'

Thea said caustically, 'You can only wet the baby's head *after* it's been born, Olivia.'

Olivia, who had already jumped to her feet and pressed the bell to summon a maid, said crossly, 'Do you have to be so pedantic? We're celebrating something, and champagne is what you drink when you're celebrating. You'd like champagne, wouldn't you, Carrie?'

Carrie, aware that Thea and Olivia were on the verge of having one of their regular disagreements, said, with her fingers crossed because it was a fib, 'I'd love to celebrate news of the baby with champagne.'

For the next two hours they exchanged news and gossip as avidly as they had once done in Gorton's playroom.

'I want to know everything about Violet,' Carrie said. 'There was a piece in the *Richmond Times* about her having gone to Hollywood, and the whole of Outhwaite is agog as to what she's doing there and what film stars she's mixing with.'

Thea gave a rude snort.

Olivia said, 'She's making a film for a director called Alexander Korda. He used to make films in England and he's a friend of Zsigmund Sárközy, who directed her last picture, *Samson and Delilah*. When Korda was last in London, Sárközy showed him some uncut footage of *Samson and Delilah* – which will be shown in cinemas all over the country in the spring – and

330

he was so impressed that he invited her to Hollywood to star in a film he's making about the Queen of Sheba.'

'And is Violet to be the Queen of Sheba?'

Before Olivia could answer, Thea said, 'Apparently. Knowing Violet, she wouldn't have left Sárközy unless it was for something bigger and better than he could provide for her.'

Her voice was so disparaging that Carrie sprang to Violet's defence. 'But surely it was a sensible thing for her to do?'

'Not when she has a contract with Sárközy and he's suing her.'

Carrie looked stricken, and Olivia said, 'Violet has no sense of right and wrong, Carrie. She never has had.'

'It isn't that she's no sense of right or wrong – it's that she's got no sense at all.' There was barely controlled anger in Thea's voice. 'The hat-shop photograph business was the last straw, as far as I'm concerned. She doesn't give a damn if people are upset by what she does. If she wants to do something, then she goes ahead and does it, no matter how outrageous it is and how much pain she causes. In this case it was Papa she distressed the most, and for that I'll never forgive her.'

Carrie struggled to understand. 'How could a photograph taken in a hat shop cause him distress? It sounds very tasteful.'

Thea breathed in so hard that her nostrils were white. 'Apart from a hat, she was stark naked.'

Carrie gaped at her, stupefied.

Olivia said, 'She had the photograph taken in order to be noticed by Zsigmund Sárközy. We

331

only found out about it by accident. I don't think there are many copies.'

'Though what copies there are, are probably changing hands for astronomical amounts.' Thea's fury was deep, and for once Carrie understood it.

Olivia said in a strained voice, 'She's behaving very badly, Carrie. Especially with men. Dieter keeps all of his married men friends well away from her.'

Not wanting to talk about Violet for a second longer, Thea jumped to her feet. 'Let's go for lunch at the Ritz. While we're on our way there I want you to tell us all about life at Monkswood. Have you got a gentleman friend, or aren't there any opportunities?'

'And what are your duties as under-house-keeper?' Olivia said, forestalling Carrie from saying that she couldn't possibly go to the Ritz for lunch; that her serviceable hat and coat weren't smart enough. 'Do you get to hire and fire people, and do you carry a huge bunch of keys around all day? Do tell.'

Ten minutes later, as the three of them made the short journey to Piccadilly and the Ritz in the back of a chauffeured motor car, Carrie said, 'I'm far too busy to have any gentleman friends, and no, I don't hire and fire staff. Mrs Appleby still discharges that duty. I do carry a bunch of keys, though. I have to, because I oversee the store-rooms, still room, linen cupboard and china closet, and I keep the household account book. Mrs Appleby said it was a job that made her head hurt, and I'm good at figures.'

'And you oversee all the female staff?'

'In theory Mrs Appleby still does that, but in practice, yes, I oversee all female staff other than the cook.'

Thea took her gloved hand in hers. 'And you're happy, Carrie? You would tell me if you weren't?'

'I'm happy because I know how fortunate I am to be under-housekeeper at twenty-four at a house like Monkswood.' She didn't answer Thea's second question because she'd schooled herself to keep to herself the loneliness that often made her very unhappy. Instead she said, 'I do miss you and Olivia, though. And Hal.'

At the mention of Hal – and because Thea was still holding her hand – Carrie felt Thea wince. She'd known from the way Hal had reacted to the prospect of Thea becoming engaged that his feelings for her were still strong and deep, but because of Thea's long-standing romance with Kyle, she'd believed Thea wasn't suffering in the same way. Now, knowing differently, she was appalled. How could Thea become engaged to anyone if she still had such strong feelings for Hal? The answer was that she couldn't, and Carrie knew that she was going to have to tell her so.

The opportunity didn't come that day, or the next, because just as they had done as children, they remained a firm threesome, and when Carrie spoke to Thea about Hal, she wanted to do so when it was just the two of them together.

By now when she left Deptford on a morning for Belgravia Square, she did so unaccompanied by Hal, whose working hours as a journalist were, she'd soon realized, chaotic. She had wanted to sightsee while in London, and Thea and Olivia were happily taking her wherever it was she wanted to go. By her third morning she had seen the Houses of Parliament and been to the Tower of London, St Paul's Cathedral and Madame Tussaud's. Now, this morning, she was hoping to feed the pigeons in Trafalgar Square and go to the National Gallery.

Seconds after the butler opened the door to her and she entered the house, all thoughts of Trafalgar Square and the National Gallery vanished from her mind.

'How wonderful – if a little strange – it is to see you in London and not in Outhwaite,' Gilbert Fenton said as he strode from the drawing room to greet her, a beaming smile on his face.

Carrie didn't blush now as much as she had when younger, but heat flooded her cheeks and, as she shook hands with him, her legs felt wobbly with surprise and pleasure.

He was wearing a grey suit and his spicy red hair was neatly parted on one side and slicked back as straight as the natural kinks in it would allow. His moustache was a little narrower than when she had last seen him, but the effect he had on her was exactly the same. She thought him the handsomest man she had ever seen, and the kindest man she had ever known.

'Olivia told me last night that she and Thea were going to take you to Trafalgar Square and the National Gallery today,' he said as they walked into the drawing room together, 'but as today is the only time I have a few hours free this week – and as I wanted to see you – I do hope

334

you won't mind that I've scuppered their plans with plans of my own?'

'Oh no, of course I don't mind!' Carrie was overcome at his having set aside precious free time to see her. Her one fear, though she hadn't expressed it to Thea and Olivia, was that in staying at Hal's digs, instead of Mount Street, she perhaps wouldn't see him at all.

Still standing, and not suggesting that she sit or allow someone to take her coat, he said, 'I understand you've seen the Houses of Parliament, but haven't been inside them?'

'Yes.' At the thought that he was perhaps going to offer to take her there, her mouth was dry.

'Then I'd like to show you around them. Would you mind very much if we left for the House now? We can have coffee when we get there.'

'Yes,' she said again, wondering where Thea and Olivia were and then realizing that it didn't matter; one or other of them had probably asked their father if he would take her to the Palace of Westminster, and they had probably known days ago what it was she would be doing today.

Together they walked back out into the hall. A maid handed him a homburg and minutes later, to her absolute incredulity, Carrie found herself seated beside him in the back of a big black car as it sped down Victoria Street, heading for the river.

'It was amazing, incredible,' she said late that night to Hal as they sat in the kitchen at Mrs Dabner's, eating fish and chips out of newspaper. 'Lord Fenton offered me his arm as we went into

335

the House of Lords, and I felt like a queen. We sat in the gallery of the debating chamber and he explained to me everything that was taking place. Afterwards we had lunch in the peers' dining room and he introduced me to the Speaker and to the government chief whip as Miss Carrie Thornton, a close family friend, visiting from Yorkshire.'

'Well, of course he did,' Hal said, amused. 'That's who you are.'

'I didn't feel like me – or rather I did, but a different me. I felt...' Ignoring her fish and chips, she struggled for words that would sum up her feelings.

They came, and her cheeks grew hot.

She'd felt loved and cherished – and the sensation had awoken other feelings, feelings she'd never experienced before. Knowing she couldn't possibly say this to Hal, she said instead, 'I felt proud and happy.'

But proud and happy didn't come close to describing how Lord Fenton had made her feel.

It didn't come close by a long way.

Chapter Twenty-Two

JUNE 1931

'Come *on*, Olivia!' Dieter shouted impatiently up the main staircase of their Belgravia Square home. 'We don't want to be the last to arrive! You know how impatient Edward can be.'

'Coming, darling!' Olivia ran out of their bedroom and, still clipping on her earrings, ran down the broad sweep of stairs. 'There,' she said a little breathlessly as she reached the foot of them. 'Will I do?'

'*Ja, meine Liebling,*' he said in fond exasperation. 'You'll always do.' She was wearing an ivory silk, halter-necked summer dress that would, he knew, be perfect for the kind of afternoon they would be spending at the Fort, where informality was the name of the game.

Taking her by the arm, Dieter ushered her swiftly out of the house and across the pavement to where his two-seater sports car was parked, saying, 'You and the rest of the girls will be able to lounge in the sun, while we chaps work like navvies clearing laurels and planting rhododendrons.'

As she seated herself in the car, Olivia giggled. Fort Belvedere was situated on Crown land in Windsor Great Park near Sunningdale, and Prince Edward's acquisition of it a little over a year ago had resulted in him taking up gardening with a passion. An eighteenth-century pseudo-Gothic castellated folly complete with tower, battlements, cannon and cannonballs, the Fort had gardens that had been left untended for years and were a wilderness of dense under-growth and impenetrable laurel. Edward had set about clearing the land himself, and male guests, much to their startled astonishment, were expected to strip to the waist – as he did – and work alongside him, armed with billhooks or scythes.

Dieter sped out of the square, heading west towards the busy King's Road, and Olivia glanced across at him with a loving smile. A superb athlete, he was in peak physical condition and, despite his grumble about navvying, she knew he secretly enjoyed showing off his well-toned body and putting his muscles to good use.

Becoming part of Prince Edward's close circle of friends was something that was relatively recent and was important to him. Dieter's governmental superiors in Berlin had been delighted at his royal friendship with the Duke of York, but friendship with the heir to Britain's throne was in a different bracket entirely, and the Reich's foreign minister's delight was sky-high.

'It means I'll be in the running for the post of deputy chief of mission in London when von Neurath is moved on,' he'd said to her. 'With personal contacts such as I now have in Britain, how could I not be?'

The prospect of such an appointment when Dieter would be only in his thirties was dizzying

– but, like Dieter, Olivia couldn't see why it shouldn't happen.

She put on a pair of sunglasses and, wondering who the other guests at the Fort would be, settled back to enjoy the fifty-minute journey out of the London suburbs and into Surrey. There was always a possibility that Elizabeth and Bertie would be there, for as well as their home in London, they had a country retreat at nearby Royal Lodge. But it was more likely that another of Edward's brothers, Prince George, would be there. Unknown to the British public, George's life was scandalously bohemian, and Edward far preferred his company to that of Bertie, whose life was – in Edward's eyes – one of dull propriety. Thelma Furness, Edward's mistress, would certainly be there. Like Edward's previous long-standing mistress, Freda Dudley Ward, Thelma was married and sparky and full of fun.

People who knew Freda well – which Olivia didn't – said Thelma wasn't as good for the Prince as Freda had been, in that Freda had always encouraged him to be conscientious about his royal duties, something Thelma had no interest in. Olivia, who had long ago tired of hearing from Thea of Edward's visits to impoverished industrial cities in northern England, or coal-mining communities in Wales, had no interest in that side of his life either, and it gave them something in common.

'Penny for them,' Dieter said as they began heading south-west on the A30.

'I was just wondering who else will be at the

Fort this weekend.'

'With luck, Georgie Milford-Haven and Nada.'

George Mountbatten, 2nd Marquess of Milford Haven, was a first cousin of Prince Edward, and he and his exotic Russian-born wife were regular guests at the Fort.

Olivia didn't say anything in return. Nada was famously promiscuous – with both sexes – and she knew that Nada's lesbianism fascinated Dieter, as it did most men.

Anxiety flickered in her heart. She was too fiercely in love with Dieter to want him to be fascinated with anyone other than herself. Over the last couple of years she had discovered that the downside of being married to a man of such startlingly blond good looks was that other women constantly showed improper interest in him. She had never seen him respond in like manner – and never wanted to. Though marital unfaithfulness was rampant in aristocratic circles, she had no desire to be unfaithful herself – and she knew that if Dieter was unfaithful it would utterly destroy her happiness.

She put a hand out and rested it on his thigh. He made a small noise of appreciation and her smile deepened. She was lucky, lucky, lucky, and all that was now needed was that her luck held and she finally fell pregnant.

Until this last year she had never realized how difficult conceiving a baby could be: month after month brought disappointment. Her heart began to race as she thought of how wonderful it would be if she conceived over the weekend, while they were at the Fort. If she did, and the baby was a boy, perhaps Dieter would agree to naming him Edward? Whatever the sex of the baby, perhaps, under the circumstances, he or she would have a royal godfather?

Her daydreams of the family they would one day have occupied her for the rest of the journey. Dieter had told her he wanted them to have the same kind of family as the exiled Kaiser – six sons and a daughter. They had even, in bed and tipsy on champagne cocktails, given their hoped-for children-to-be names.

Their firstborn was to be named Dieter Heinrich, after Dieter and his father, though she was sure that would change, if the baby was conceived while they were Edward's guests. Their second son was to be named Gilbert Günther, after her father and Dieter's favourite uncle. As the name Gilbert was German in origin it caused Dieter no problems, but erotically running his forefinger slowly down the length of her naked back, he had told her that he would like more obvious German first names for their next four sons. Together they had agreed on Bruno, Karl, Lukas and Christian, names that although popular in Germany were only a smidgen away from being traditional English names as well.

Their only brief moment of disagreement had been over what they would name their hoped-for future daughter. 'Blanche,' Olivia had said, her voice husky with desire as he began caressingly paying attention to a more intimate part of her body. 'I couldn't possibly have a daughter and not name her after my mother.'

To her disappointment, his hand stopped

341

moving. 'Blanche is neither English nor German,' he had protested. 'It's French.'

'It's beautiful,' she had said. 'You can have any German name you like for a second name, no matter how ghastly. Walburga or Edeltraud, I don't care. Only our daughter has to go through life with a pretty first name – and a name that has deep meaning for me.'

'*In Ordnung, Liebling*,' he had said, giving in. 'Okay. Blanche it is.'

And then he had begun making love to her, just the way she liked it.

Her happy reverie ended as the car swung into the approach to the Fort. A gravel drive wound through woodland and then, on the last turn, the Fort came into sight, looking so much like a toy that one guest in Olivia's hearing had said with vast amusement that all it lacked were tin soldiers on its battlements.

From its tower flew not the Prince of Wales's standard, as might have been expected, but the flag of the Duchy of Cornwall.

'To David, the Fort is a private house, not a royal residence,' Thea had said to her when she had mentioned this anomaly. 'When he's here he likes to forget his royal position.'

Even before the car ground to a halt in front of the main entrance a skinny, tousle-headed figure, wearing nothing but a pair of baggy shorts and sandals and carrying a billhook, hurried to greet them from the direction of the gardens, a small dog at his heels.

'Jolly good, you two!' Prince Edward called out cheerily and then, to Dieter, 'You're just in time to help with digging out a damnable fir that blocks the light and spoils the view. Dickie and Georgie are down there now, struggling like the very devil with it. I've come up to the house to grab a couple of extra hatchets.'

To Olivia he said, 'You're looking stunning as usual, Olivia. Thelma, Edwina and Nada are by the pool, sunbathing. Elizabeth and Bertie will be here any minute. Only ten of us this weekend. Very nice and intimate.' Then, to Dieter in fluent German, *'Bist du bereit für ein wenig harte Arbeit, meine Freund?'*

'Ich kann es kaum erwarten loszulegen,' Dieter responded with a grin.

Olivia knew enough German to know that Edward had asked Dieter if he was ready for some heavy work, and that Dieter had said he was more than ready. It fascinated her that Edward so enjoyed lapsing into German whenever Dieter was with him.

'Why shouldn't he?' Dieter had said when she had remarked on it. 'He's almost as German as I am.'

Staff came out, removing their suitcase from the car's boot and taking it into the Fort and up to their room. Dieter disappeared with Edward in search of extra hatchets and Olivia made her way to the swimming pool to join Thelma, Edwina and Nada, feeling euphoric at the realization that – other than Thelma – she and Dieter were the only non-royals Edward had invited.

'Dahlink! How splendid to see you again.' Nada was on a sun-lounger and was wearing a wine-red bathing-suit. 'Where is your delicious husband?

343

Already wielding a machete with David?'

'Probably. Though when I left Dieter and David, they'd gone off in search of hatchets.'

Referring to Prince Edward as David still felt strange to her. Thea, of course, had been invited to do so years ago, but to Olivia the privilege was still a novelty. Thea rarely accepted weekend invitations to the Fort.

'And I'm not about to change the habit,' she'd said, when Olivia had asked her why this was. 'An entire weekend chatting with Thelma and her friends about nothing more stimulating than fashion and who is sleeping with whom and, if Nada is present, avoiding her sexual overtures is more than I can stand. If you enjoy the mindlessness of it all, good luck to you!'

Olivia, who did enjoy the mindlessness of it all, seated herself in a deckchair next to a table laden with drinks and cigarettes. Her bathing suit was still in her suitcase and she was relieved to see that although Edwina, as well as Nada, was wearing one, Thelma was, like her, wearing a sundress.

Edwina rose to her feet and walked over to the pool's springboard, saying as she put on a white swimming helmet, 'I saw your stepmother in Deauville's casino last weekend, Olivia. Not to speak to. She was far too busy playing blackjack.'

Barely causing a ripple, she dived into the pool, lithe, streamlined and athletic.

Olivia tried to keep her face expressionless, but it was difficult. Zephiniah's frequent absences from Gorton Hall and Mount Street were always accounted for by what she said was a need to visit spas regularly for her health. Gilbert only ever spoke with stoical resignation about the loneliness her absences caused him, but that his second marriage hadn't turned out to be the kind of marriage he had hoped for was clear to everyone who knew him. Whether he was aware that Zephiniah didn't always arrive at the destination she said she was leaving for, or that when there she visited places far racier than health spas, was impossible to tell, but that she was so obviously making her father unhappy was something Olivia found impossible to forgive.

'Edwina and I are planning a trip,' Nada said, as Thelma closed her eyes and raised her face to the sun.

Unsurprised, Olivia poured herself a glass of lemonade from an iced thermos. Edwina was always either planning a trip or away on one. She moved around Europe faster than anyone else she knew, her travelling companion always another woman – never Dickie.

'Where to this time?' she asked idly as, with the speed and grace of a seal, Edwina did a flip-turn at the end of the pool.

'Arabia. Why don't you come with us?' Nada regarded her with slumberous, speculative eyes. 'Sometimes, as guests of a king, a sheik or a sultan, we'll sleep in a palace. Sometimes we'll camp in the desert, beneath the stars. We're going to visit Jerusalem and Damascus and drive six hundred miles across the desert from Damascus to Baghdad and then on to Teheran.'

'From Mesopotamia to Persia? *By car?*'

'But of course. What could be more delightful?'

345

Olivia could think of a lot of things more delightful.

Edwina climbed up the steps out of the pool and, aware of Olivia's reaction, said in her distinctively staccato voice, 'Where is your spirit of adventure, Olivia?'

She took off her swimming helmet, shaking her gleaming dark hair back into shape. 'Don't you ever yearn for a little danger and discomfort?'

'No,' Olivia said with utter truthfulness. 'Never.'

Still with her eyes closed, Thelma giggled.

Edwina made herself comfortable on a sunlounger and lit a cigarette. 'Last year I went to the wilds of Mexico, Guatemala and Honduras with a cousin. We trekked through jungles, climbed mountains and ate whatever the natives ate.'

Olivia shuddered.

'And Arabia will be even more extreme,' Nada said languidly. 'There will be warring tribes, the danger of dying of sunstroke, the risk of death from a scorpion bite.'

At this, Thelma opened her eyes, paling a little. 'Doesn't Dickie mind you taking off into the blue to places you may never come back from?'

Edwina gave a careless shrug of gleaming wet shoulders. 'Dickie and I understand each other. His life is the Royal Navy. Mine isn't. It's as simple as that.'

As she watched footmen begin to set a table for lunch at the far end of the pool, it occurred to Olivia that Edwina, Thelma and Nada were not only alike in looks – Edwina's Jewish ancestry, Thelma's Chilean ancestry and a dash of Abyssinian in Nada's Russian ancestry meant they were all dark-haired and dark-eyed – but that all three of them arranged their lives so that they spent the greater part of it with people other than their husbands.

Thelma and her husband, Lord Furness, were rarely seen together, the general opinion being that he bored her and she exasperated him. Certainly he never seemed to give a damn that she was the Prince of Wales's mistress.

Nada, too, was only seen with her husband at events such as Wimbledon or Ascot. As promiscuous as Edwina, she was also – like Edwina – restless in a way that Olivia couldn't understand.

It was a relief to hear the sound of heeled sandals approaching the pool from behind her and to hear Elizabeth's clipped, light voice say, 'So sorry to be late. Bertie couldn't tear himself away from baby.'

The baby in question, Princess Margaret, had been born the previous year, and Olivia knew that for a while at least the conversation would revolve around the kind of subjects she was happiest with: babies and domesticity.

A little later, over lunch, with Edward wearing a shirt and a sprucely pressed clean pair of shorts, the conversation turned to Hollywood and Violet.

'Is it t-true she's being romanced by Ch-Charlie Chaplin?' Bertie asked, his stammer just as much in evidence with friends as when – as rarely as he could manage – he spoke in public.

Olivia laughed. She'd always had more time for Violet than Thea, and she enjoyed it that *Samson*

347

and Delilah had made her little sister a household name.

'According to the gossip columns she is, but then, every time I see a photograph of Violet she's with a different Hollywood star. Last month she was draped in white fox and on John Gilbert's arm. There's no telling whose arm she'll be on by next month.'

'Or what she will be draped in,' Dieter said to general amusement, wondering what excuse he could make for a trip to Hollywood in order to give Violet something else to think about other than Chaplin.

Dickie Mountbatten speared a tomato with his fork. 'Edwina and I had a marvellous time in Hollywood with Charlie when we were on our honeymoon, didn't we, darling?'

'Marvellous,' Edwina said, in the voice of a wife who knows she is about to hear, yet again, the retelling of one of her husband's favourite anecdotes.

'Charlie shot a short movie for us,' Dickie said. 'We starred in it. The storyline is that Edwina has a pearl necklace that a gang of crooks wants to steal. Charlie – in his tramp costume – is called in to hunt down the crooks, armed with a wooden hammer. There are lots of chases until, at the end, all the crooks are laid out flat by Charlie and lined up on the lawn next to his great friend Jackie Coogan, who for some reason that I can never remember is lying there hidden under a blanket.'

'Charlie gave the movie to us as a wedding present,' Edwina said to Olivia. 'And he made a pass at me.'

'Of course he did, darling.' Dickie beamed across the table at her. 'And now he's made a more successful pass at Violet!'

Edwina gave Olivia a wink to indicate that Charlie's pass at her had also been successful and said, changing the subject, 'Does anyone fancy a stroll down the hill to Virginia Water after lunch? We could take row-boats out and have a race: chaps against girls.'

In the end the race was between Edward and Dickie in one boat, and Edwina and Nada in the other. Everyone else lounged on the banks, alternately cheering and booing, depending on whose boat was ahead.

In the evening Edward appeared for dinner in full Highland rig: bonnet, jacket, kilt, sporran, silver-buckled shoes and with a small dirk tucked into the hose of his right leg. After dinner the evening became even more Scottish as, with two pipers in attendance, he marched around the table enthusiastically playing the bagpipes.

Later there was dancing to gramophone records, and then there were some not very strenuous paper games, with one, suggested by Edward, reducing them to hoots of laughter.

'Every time the King has a rant about my continuing bachelorhood he says there is a score of European princesses I could be choosing a bride from. I can only think of three, so what say you all have a go and see who comes up with the longest list?'

The winner by a long way, with a list of seventeen names, was Dickie.

'And that,' Dieter said as he began undressing

for bed in the second-floor bedroom they were always allotted at the Fort, 'is because he's linked ancestrally some way or other with nearly every royal house in Europe, and because genealogy is his passion.'

Pink-shaded lamps gave the room a sensuous glow, and Olivia, in a nightdress that was a mere wisp of oyster silk, lace and satin, was already in bed. 'It seems to me the difficulty isn't the number of eligible princesses,' she said, impatient for him to join her, 'the real problem is their ages. David is thirty-seven, and any princess still single is either a nun or years and years younger than him. Elizabeth said the princess Bertie suggested, Princess Thyra of Mecklenburg-Schwerin, was a mere child.'

Dieter chuckled at the thought of Edward, who never showed interest in any woman not already married and vastly experienced, becoming betrothed to a princess who, even in a couple of years' time, would still be a virginal seventeen. However much King George wanted such an outcome, it was Dieter's opinion that it was never going to happen.

Edward's problems about a future heir were, however, not his problems. As his eyes held Olivia's, darkening with heat, he knew she was hoping what he was hoping – that tonight, at the Fort, she would conceive the child they both so desperately wanted.

As he moved towards the bed, the glow of the lamps gave his firmly muscled suntanned flesh a honeyed sheen. His stomach was as flat as a board, his sex firm and big and in a state of erection.

A valet had laid black silk pyjamas out for him. Dieter ignored them.

Dizzy with desire, Olivia opened her arms to him and pulled him down towards her. Kissing her with deep passion, he removed the nonsense of a nightdress with expert ease and slid her body beneath his. She lifted her legs high, linking her arms and ankles behind him, her silent prayer, as he entered her and they began moving together towards an explosive, cataclysmic climax: 'Please let there be a baby this time, God! Please! *Please!*'

Chapter Twenty-Three

AUGUST 1932

With one arm pressed hard across her waist in a fierce *noli me tángere* kind of way, the other holding a long jade cigarette-holder and lighted cigarette, Zephiniah stared flinty-eyed through a French window streaked with heavy rain.

On the terrace late-summer roses in antique pedestal urns shed sodden petals. The copper beech in the centre of the lawn was so wet that its leaves had a metallic sheen. The lawn was saturated. Beyond the river, where the ground rose up and merged into moorland, sheep huddled grimly together, seeking what protection they could.

Zephiniah didn't envy them, and nor did she envy herself.

Why was it that things never turned out as she'd thought they were going to? When she'd been seventeen – in what seemed a lifetime ago – she had been certain she was on the threshold of a glorious year as a debutante and that, at the end of it, she would be engaged to a member of the peerage – or at least to the son of a member of the peerage.

Instead, one little slip and what had followed had been the nightmare banishment to Vienna in the company of an unsympathetic aunt.

When she'd returned and found herself, in her mother's words, 'damaged goods', she'd thought she'd found salvation when Reggie proposed marriage and whisked her off to Argentina.

Argentina!

She blew a plume of blue smoke through her nose. Argentina hadn't turned out as she had thought it would, but at least – unlike Yorkshire – there had been sun and heat and the excitement of racetracks and casinos. She tapped the end of her cigarette, letting the ash fall carelessly to the Aubusson carpet.

Of all the disappointments, of all the times when she'd thought things were going to turn out well and they hadn't, the biggest disappointment was the one she was now enduring. Nothing in her marriage to Gilbert had turned out as she had thought it was going to. She had believed her marriage would bring a dizzying social life in its wake; that her long-held dream of being part of the small and elite circle of people who were personal friends of the royals would, at last, be realized.

It had been a shattering blow to discover that Gilbert actively disliked socializing unless it was with fellow members of the government, all of whom had wives who were, in Zephiniah's by now vast experience, frumpy and tediously boring.

What made the lack of her own and Gilbert's social life even harder to bear was Thea and Olivia's close friendship with the Prince of Wales and with his brother and his sister-in-law, the Duke and Duchess of York.

She removed the cigarette from the jade holder and crushed it out in a nearby ashtray and then, folding her arms and hugging them tight against her chest, continued to mull over the things that were so different from the way she'd thought they would be.

She had been looking forward to having three stepdaughters, not because she was maternal, but because where Thea and Olivia were concerned, she had imagined photographs of herself with them in the *Tatler*, carrying captions such as: *The scintillating and beautiful Lady Fenton seen at the opening of this year's Royal Academy Exhibition with her stepdaughters, the Honourable Thea Fenton and the Honourable Olivia Fenton.*

Reality had ensured there'd been fat chance of any such photographs or mentions. She chewed the corner of her lip until she tasted blood. If Thea and Olivia had wanted, they could have engineered situations and invitations where she would have become as familiar with Prince Edward and the Yorks as they were. They hadn't done so and, to her fury, Gilbert had been equally obstructive, refusing to patronize the nightclubs Edward patronized – where, if Edward had seen them, he might have invited them to join his table.

'The Embassy Club and the Kit-Kat Club are far too noisy to be relaxing,' he said in a voice of sweet reason every time she suggested they go. 'It's not only non-stop dancing these days, it's non-stop jazz as well.'

Gilbert's reluctance to draw attention to his disabled arm meant that dancing of any kind played little part in their social life. He was, she'd discovered within weeks of their marriage, a quiet man who preferred the company of a few tried and tested friends to raucous partying. The bottom line was that his idea of a good time was not hers.

Not only their social life, but their sex life too, was nothing like she had thought it would be. Gilbert was a tender, considerate lover. But after nineteen years of extra-marital Latin lovers in Argentina, tender consideration didn't fire Zephiniah. Stormy, passionate, jealousy-fuelled relationships were what thrilled her; fighting and shouting and then falling into bed for glorious, uninhibited reconciliations. She hadn't known it at the time, but she realized now how much she needed the heightened emotions of excitement and drama.

There was precious little excitement and drama at Gorton.

She stared with loathing at the view of sodden lawn, sodden moorland and sodden sheep. On the evening she had met Gilbert, her cousin had told her that, as well as being spoken of as a future prime minister, he owned a divine country estate in Yorkshire. The vision those words had conjured up hadn't proved to be the reality. Though other people – Winston Churchill and the prime minister, for instance – rhapsodized about Gorton, she thought it mediocre. Its ballroom was small compared to what she had expected. It wasn't – as she felt she'd been wrongly led to believe – a stately home on a par with Chatsworth or Knole, both of which had more than a hundred rooms. It wasn't even an historical jewel, such as Hever. It was simply an unpretentious Georgian mansion in what most people – though not her – deemed to be an idyllic setting.

It was the tedium of her marriage, and the tedium of every parliamentary recess being spent at Gorton, that had driven her into taking trips abroad. She said these were for the good of her health – which in a way they were, for if she hadn't taken them she was convinced she would have lost her reason. Fortunately most spa towns boasted casinos, and in the racy, adrenalin-fuelled atmosphere of a casino she no longer felt half-alive. A lucky and a habitual gambler, she felt like her old self.

She put another of her favourite Camel cigarettes in her holder and lit it. Until the beginning of summer her system of maintaining her sanity had worked wonderfully well. Then, in June, in the Casino Grand Cercle, in Aix-les-Bains, she had run into Roberto Di Stéfano, a lover from her Buenos Aires days, and her trips had taken on a new, dangerous dimension.

Extramarital affairs in British aristocratic

circles were just as common as they were in Argentina. The rules were, though, that a woman didn't indulge in one until she had given her husband a son and heir. Then, duty done, she could look elsewhere for entertainment, as her husband was no doubt already doing. The rule wasn't, of course, universal. Winston and Clementine Churchill were renowned for their faithfulness to each other, and Gilbert had the same reputation as Winston for fidelity. Which meant that even if she had already given Gilbert a son and heir, the usual modus operandi would not have been acceptable to him and, knowing Gilbert as she did, she knew it never would be. All of which ensured that her revived affair with Roberto was a secret that was going to have to be very carefully kept.

She blew a jet of smoke towards the ceiling irritably. She was good at keeping secrets. It was something at which she'd had an awful lot of experience. As a child the big secret had been her mother's Jewishness. She had grown up knowing it was never to be referred to. Not until she was in her twenties had she realized that, as Jewishness was passed down in the female line, she was also Jewish.

It wasn't something that had ever troubled her. Her father's family had seen to it that she had been christened an Anglican, and though she only ever stepped inside a church at society weddings and funerals, that was most definitely how she thought of herself. Only in Vienna, when it had been cautiously mentioned to her that perhaps the arranged adoptive parents weren't so suitable after all, being Jewish, had she been reminded of it.

'The Zimmermann family are a respectable family, aren't they?' she'd said waspishly to her aunt, wanting to have the matter done and dealt with, so that she could return hot-foot to London. 'What the devil does it matter whether they are Jewish or not?'

'Then the Zimmermanns would like the baby given a suitably Jewish name,' her aunt had said, thin-lipped at the distastefulness of it all. 'Something on the lines of Sarah or Miriam.'

'Judith,' she had said. It had been her mother's second name and, as far as Zephiniah was concerned, was as good a name as any.

Ever since then she had barely given Vienna – or the daughter she had given birth to there – a thought. It was in the past, and simply another secret that had to be kept.

Only when she had acquired three stepdaughters had she sometimes wondered about Judith. She would be twenty-one now, three years younger than Violet, though Zephiniah rather thought a Jewish upbringing would have resulted in Judith being far different from Violet in both personality and behaviour.

The rain had begun to ease and, as a glimmer of sun touched the tops of the hills, three shooting brakes could be seen in the distance, coming down from the moor and heading towards the bridge.

She knew who was in them. It was mid-August and three days earlier the grouse-shooting season had opened. Gilbert and a group of male friends

357

were returning from a shoot – and were no doubt just as sodden as the sheep.

She turned away from the window, knowing that all the evening ahead held was conversation about who had performed best with a shotgun that day and, when that palled, that it would be politics, politics, politics.

'This recent election victory of Hitler's means his National Socialist Party is now the biggest in the Reichstag.'

They were in their bedroom and Gilbert was tying his bow-tie. There was concern in his voice, and Zephiniah, mindful of how she needed Gilbert to be in a good mood for when she told him she was leaving again soon for Aix-les-Bains, said, 'And is that so very bad, darling? I was always under the impression you thought the National Socialists could be a good thing for Germany.'

'I did. They're fervently anti-communist and, with the German economy in mind, that has to be a good thing. Herr Hitler has also said – and I have to agree with him – that if Germany fell to the communists, we in Britain would have to look to our laurels.'

Zephiniah was on the verge of asking tartly how he felt about that, considering that he had a daughter who was as near to being a communist as made no difference. But, remembering how desperately she wanted to be in Aix-les-Bains before the month was out, she bit back the words.

'And now?' she asked, as her maid finished zipping her into an emerald chiffon, ankle-swirling dress.

'And now it's not only the communists and the Versailles Peace Treaty that he's blaming for Germany's ills, it's German Jews – and that sort of thing will increase instability in Germany, not ease it.'

Zephiniah took a satisfying look at herself in her cheval-glass and dismissed her maid. Gilbert's interest in Germany arose, she knew, because of his onetime involvement on a committee that had sought to ease Germany's war debt liabilities. To Zephiniah, committees and Germany were subjects just as boring as grouse-shooting and sheep, and the effort of feigning interest was more than she could be bothered with.

Gilbert's bow-tie was fastened now and, before he reached for his dinner jacket, she stepped towards him, sliding her arms up and around his neck.

'The lack of sunshine this summer is affecting my health, Gillie. I'm sure it's one of the reasons I'm having such difficulty in conceiving. Would you mind awfully, darling, if I left next week for a week or two's rest at Aix-les-Bains? It's a bore for both of us, I know, but I do so want to conceive, and the doctors all suggest rest.'

She kissed the end of his nose and managed a smile that was both winning and regretful.

His shoulders slumped in bitter disappointment. 'You've only been back less than a month, Zephiniah. Couldn't you stay on here, at Gorton, when Parliament reconvenes? At least then the two of us would be in the same country.'

She gave a light, dismissive laugh. 'It's a rest in sunshine I need, and I think I've little chance of finding sunshine in Yorkshire. So far the summer has been ghastly and it looks as if it's going to continue being so.'

After his soaking earlier in the day, it was a statement Gilbert couldn't argue with.

He said sadly, but with wry humour, 'Perhaps the doctors could take into account that you're very unlikely to conceive if we're constantly on opposite sides of the English Channel.'

She lowered her arms and put them around his waist, hugging him tight, her cheek pressed close against his chest so that he was no longer looking into her eyes.

In Argentina a cervical cap had ensured that she'd never had to face a second, unwanted pregnancy. On her marriage to Gilbert she had jettisoned it as being obsolete. Now she realized she was going to have to get herself fitted with a new one, for if she became pregnant by Roberto, she would never be able to pass the baby off as Gilbert's. Like all redheads, Gilbert's skin was almost unnaturally pale, and Roberto, as well as having raven-black hair, was olive-complexioned.

When she was quite sure that none of her thoughts were showing in her eyes, she eased herself away from him. 'Then, although it will break my heart to do so, I'll leave Gorton for Aix-les-Bains at the weekend – and every minute that I'm away I'll be thinking of you.'

Without calling his valet back into the room, Gilbert eased himself into his dinner jacket.

As they were about to leave the room he paused at the door. Turning her towards him, he said gravely, 'You do love me, don't you, Zephiniah?

You're not unhappy with me, are you? Because if you are–'

'Of course I'm happy with you!' The lie was off her lips as fast as light. The last thing she wanted to hear was any suggestion of what he might do if she wasn't happy. Divorce, once such a no-no, was becoming increasingly common, and she didn't want to be divorced. Unless a better offer came along, she wanted to continue being Viscountess Fenton.

She slid her evening-gloved hand into the crook of his arm. 'I'm deliriously, *passionately*, happy with you.' And with her thoughts once again on Roberto and Aix-les-Bains, she accompanied him along the corridor and down the grand curving staircase to where their weekend guests were waiting for them in the drawing room.

Chapter Twenty-Four

In a Kensington mansion flat Thea and Kyle lay entwined in a tangle of sheets, their skin warm and flushed, their hearts racing, pulses pounding. Thea lifted a hand to the nape of Kyle's neck and slid her fingers caressingly into his dark, silkily straight hair.

'Wonderful,' she said dreamily, every atom of her body in a state of heavenly sexual satisfaction. Then, in amusement, 'Thank God for Marie Stopes and Whitfield Street.'

Instead of grunting agreement, Kyle rolled off

her and onto his side. Resting his weight on his elbow he said, looking down at her, 'Why does the Whitfield Street clinic make such a difference?'

'Because, without the clinic, I wouldn't be in bed with you. Or,' she added teasingly, 'with anyone else.'

Kyle let the 'anyone else' tease pass. Thea wasn't promiscuous. He knew that unless Hal Crosby was taken into account, there wasn't anyone else. And he also knew, without a shadow of a doubt, that she wasn't sleeping with Hal, rarely saw him and, when she did, it was only in passing.

He said reasonably, 'If we were married you wouldn't have to take precautions against becoming pregnant.'

She untangled her legs from the twisted sheet and pushed herself up against the pillows. 'We've had this conversation before, Kyle. Why are we having it yet again?'

It was the middle of the day. His Hornton Street flat was a penthouse and neither of them had bothered to lower the blinds. Though the October sun wasn't strong, as he got out of bed it cast a gleam on the well-toned muscles of his arms and legs.

'Because we might be having it for the last time,' he said, yanking on a pair of trousers. 'I'm thirty. You're twenty-six. We've been in love for five years, maybe six. We're both single and I've been asking you to marry me for the last four years. What's going to happen when I'm recalled to Washington, or when I'm posted elsewhere? Is it going to be a case of "Thanks a lot, Kyle. It's been nice. Look me up next time you have an

362

odd couple of days in London?"'

'You're being childish!' Crossly she swung her legs from the bed and reached for silk cami-knickers. Once she was wearing them she didn't feel at quite such a disadvantage in what was obviously going to be a serious argument. 'I simply don't see being a diplomat's wife as part of my future,' she said, as he began buttoning up a shirt. 'And just think what a hindrance I'd be to your career if we were married.' She stepped into her skirt. 'Can you imagine ever being offered an ambassadorship if you had a British wife with a track record of left-wing political activism?'

'You've never been arrested. You're not a card-carrying communist.'

She put on her bra. 'That's not to say I might not be one in the future.'

He fastened his tie and slicked back his hair. Hot electric-blue eyes held hers. 'Let's not reduce this to a point-scoring slanging match, Thea. I sincerely want to know where the two of us are going.' The anger had gone from his voice. It was simply a flat, unhappy statement.

She pulled on a tawny-coloured jumper that emphasized the red lights in her hair.

With the fire now gone from her own voice she said, 'Why can't we just continue as we are? We're happy together, aren't we? We're good together in bed. Being married wouldn't make it any better. It couldn't. It would be impossible.'

His eyes continued to hold hers. 'If we were married, we'd have children. And I want children, Thea. I want to be a reasonably young father, not an old one. I want to share in what they do. I want to be able to play baseball and football with them.'

She was about to ask if he only intended fathering boys, and then knew the moment didn't call for such a glib comment. The problem was she didn't know what response to give him. Did she want children now? The answer was that she didn't. Would she want them in the future? How could she tell? Unlike Olivia, she simply couldn't imagine having children; couldn't imagine being a mother.

Neither, though, could she imagine Kyle not being in her life. She needed him in order to endure her searing sense of loss where Hal was concerned. Common sense – and Roz – had told her that she would, given time, get over him. She hadn't. In the eight years since her coming-out ball she hadn't got over him by as much as one jot.

Though she rarely saw Hal, she was aware of him all the time. She could tell at a glance what pieces in the *Evening News* had been written by him. Though she never asked directly for news of him, Carrie, Olivia and Roz always updated her on their contacts with him.

It wasn't only Carrie, Olivia and Roz that he kept in contact with. He kept in touch with her father and, via Olivia and Roz, he'd forged friendly contacts with Dieter and Max. Sharing the occasional drink with them gave him a feel for what was going on behind the scenes in Westminster, Berlin and Washington. He was even on easy terms with Kyle, proof to Thea of his uncanny ability to get on with everyone he came into contact with – if, of course, he wished to do so.

She dragged her thoughts back to the present tricky conversation.

'I don't want to lose you.' Her eyes pleaded with him to accept their present relationship and not to spoil it by demanding more. 'But I'm not ready for marriage and children yet.'

'You're twenty-six,' he repeated again, this time through gritted teeth. He ran a hand exasperatedly through his hair. 'Land's sakes, Thea. If you're not ready now, when are you going to be?'

Helplessly she said, 'I don't know, Kyle. I'm sorry.'

'So am I.' There was no sarcasm in his voice, only a deep weariness. He began putting on his socks. 'Let's leave it for now, shall we? I have to get back to the embassy. I'm on a two-till-eight. What say we meet up for dinner at eight-thirty at the Savoy?'

She nodded and, as he slid his feet into his shoes, made no effort to put on her own shoes, or pick up her jacket or handbag. She didn't want to leave the flat with him. She wanted a few minutes on her own, to gather her thoughts.

'I'll tidy up here and let myself out.'

He nodded, put on his jacket and closed the distance between them. Gently putting his hands on her shoulders, he said thickly, 'I love you, Thea. Let's stop this nonsense. In your heart of hearts, you know our getting married makes sense. It's not too late for a Christmas wedding – or, at the very least, a Christmas engagement.'

She remained mute, not able to say what he wanted to hear.

He kissed her on the mouth and then, his

black-lashed blue eyes looking bleakly unhappy, turned and left the room.

She waited until she heard first the entrance door to the apartment close behind him and then, seconds later, the hum of the cage-lift as it carried him down to the ground floor.

When she faintly heard the lift gates open and then close again, she forced herself into movement. She put on her shoes. Made the bed. Washed up their wine glasses, dried them and put them away. Then she walked to the windows, looking out over a view of sky and rooftops and of nearby Kensington Palace.

The nearness of the palace emphasized to her the way Kyle would always live. Like Roz, he was rich on a grand scale, the heir to two generations of railroad and steel wealth. If he had wanted to live in a house in Belgrave Square, as Olivia and Dieter did, then he could have done. He could live wherever he chose and, like tonight, dine wherever he chose. As a Democrat he was sufficiently left-wing not to find her political views offensive, but appalled as he was by the unemployment destroying the lives of millions of Americans and causing unimaginable hardship in Britain, he would never, as she did, march and protest on the streets – and not only because it would be the end of his career if he were to do so, but because it was simply beyond him to identify so personally with abject poverty.

She picked up her suit jacket and slid her arms into the sleeves. Today workless men from all over the country were gathering in Trafalgar Square at a massive rally organized by the National Unemployed Workers' Movement. The rally was in protest at cuts to dole money and at the means test that had to be undergone when unemployment lasted for longer than six months. There had been other national rallies, but this was going to be the biggest yet, and she had every intention of giving it her support.

The mansion block in Hornton Street sat corner-ways on to Kensington High Street and she had only yards to walk in order to catch a number nine bus heading for Trafalgar Square.

'Though I doubt we'll reach it,' the conductor said cheerfully as he took her money and cranked out a ticket. 'Not with the Hunger Marchers' rally taking place there. All roads around the square are jam-packed. Shouldn't wonder if the nearest we get is the Haymarket.'

He was being overly optimistic. The nearest they got was Piccadilly Circus.

She got off the bus into a packed crowd, clapping and cheering a column of exhausted men trudging beneath a banner emblazoned with the words: LANCASHIRE CONTINGENT MARCH TO LONDON.

'They've tramped a long way!' a woman nearby in the crush said admiringly. 'Are they taking a collection as they march? I'd like to give them something.'

Leaving her to fumble with her purse, Thea continued to push her way forward, anxious to be at least on the periphery of the square by the time the speeches were being made.

She knew there would be lots of people that she counted as friends on whatever makeshift platform had been erected. As well as speakers from the National Unemployed Workers' Movement, there would be speakers from the Trades Union Congress and the Communist Party of Great Britain. Hal was too aware of his position as a journalist ever to mount a platform, but if his situation was different, she could well imagine him on one. What the badge in his lapel would then be – a Communist Party of Great Britain badge or a Labour Party one – was, though, anyone's guess.

'You're going in the wrong direction!' a policeman yelled at her. 'There's going to be trouble before too long. Best get clear while you can.'

Thea ignored him, and a gaunt-faced man pushing through the crowd shoulder-to-shoulder with her said with the flat vowels of a northerner, 'That's all starving men and their families are, to the likes of 'im. Trouble. I'd give 'im trouble if I could, 'im and all the other smug buggers who don't know what it's like to go 'ungry.'

'Where are you from?' she asked, as over a sea of heads the corner at the bottom of the Haymarket came into view.

'Doncaster – and I've walked every step o' the way. It's taken me three weeks and, apart from a couple o' nights in what had once been workhouses, me and the rest o' the blokes in my contingent 'ave slept rough ever since we set out.' He shot her a good hard look. 'Don't mind me saying so, but are you sure the bobby weren't right about you going in t' wrong direction? You don't look like someone who's ever been on dole or 'ad the means test leave you wi' next to nowt.'

'I'm not, but I'm a socialist, and my blood boils

368

at the miserable amount of relief being given – and at the way it's given.'

'Aye, I know all about the way it's given,' he said grimly. 'Round 'e comes to my 'ouse, the means-test man. "Nah then, Ted Finch," he says to me, "it's thirty bob a week for you, your wife and five children, but only after everything you 'ave – save for two beds, a table and four chairs – is carted off and sold." Round 'e went with a stick o' chalk, marking up everything to be taken. My wife pleaded wi' 'im to leave 'er the brass fire tongs which 'ad been 'er mother's, but they got a chalk mark just like everything else. All we were left with at the end o' it was what 'e'd said we'd be left wi'. Two beds, a table and four chairs that I'd made missen.'

It was a story Thea was long familiar with, and every time she heard it rage roared through her veins.

A man who had overheard Ted shouted across to him, 'What we need is a ruddy revolution like the one they had in Russia!'

From all around came similar opinions and then, as they finally edged around the corner and caught a glimpse of the square, the shout went up: 'Watch yourselves! They're bringing in horses! Now we'll never get any nearer.'

From past experience Thea knew how difficult – and dangerous – it was to be in a crowd being driven back by mounted policemen.

'Lock arms wi' me,' Ted Finch said, 'keep your 'ead down and keep 'eading for t' square. I 'aven't walked a 'undred and sixty miles to be stopped by bobbies on 'orses.'

369

Thea did as he said. Tucking themselves behind a giant of a man carrying a poster on which was written in bright-red paint NO MORE STARVING IN SILENCE, she and Ted continued forging a way forward. They were among the last of those in the Haymarket able to do so.

'They're sealing the street off,' Ted said as mayhem broke out behind them. 'Don't waste time turning round to look, lass. Just keep going.'

They kept going and, as they did, Ted said, 'Why would they do a thing like that? Seal a street off, when all folk want to do is exercise rights as old as Magna Carta? Because that's what me and my mates are 'ere to do today. At the end of t' rally a deputation including representatives from every contingent will march from t' square down Whitehall with a petition calling for the abolition o' the means test and the restoration of benefit cuts. It's been signed by more than a million names and they're going to present it at the Bar of the House of Commons, just as anciently all petitions were presented. Then summat'll 'ave to be done, won't it? The government won't be able to ignore us then, will they?'

Not wanting to dent his optimism, Thea said, 'I hope not, Ted.'

Privately she doubted if the police would allow any deputation within a hundred yards of the House of Commons. The Bar – a line marking the boundary between the House of Commons and the House of Lords – may have been where public petitions were anciently presented, but she couldn't see the practice being honoured where the Hunger Marchers were concerned.

They reached the square just as the stocky figure of Wal Hannington, head of the National Unemployed Workers' Movement, bounded onto the platform in front of Nelson's Column, a megaphone in his hand.

'There are thirty million workless people in the world today!' Hannington thundered, not wasting time on preliminaries. *'And three million workless people in our own country!'*

The din that erupted was deafening.

'For over fifty years, before the war, the average amount of unemployment in this country, year in and year out, was four per cent. Now it's over twenty-two per cent!'

The square was a sea of waving banners. From where she was standing Thea could see the Worcester contingent's banner, the Scottish contingent's banner, a banner declaring NO TO THE MEANS TEST and one demanding WORK OR FULL MAINTENANCE AT TRADE-UNION RATES OF PAY.

The size of the banners made scanning faces in the crowd difficult, and ever since she had entered the square Thea had been scanning the crowd for just one face: Hal's.

She knew he'd be there, reporting on the rally for the *Evening News*, and that he'd be somewhere with a bird's-eye view of things, which meant he'd be on the steps leading down from the National Gallery on the square's north side, or on the back of one of the square's four monumental bronze lions.

Her problem was that, from where she was standing, she only had a clear view of three of the

371

four lions, and Hal most definitely wasn't among the dozens of people who had climbed their plinths and clambered onto their backs.

'One worker out of every five is unemployed,' Wal Hannington bellowed. 'Two out of every five miners. One out of every two iron and steel workers. One out of every three workers in the engineering trades. Three out of every five shipbuilding workers. These men and their families are being reduced to destitution because of cuts to dole money that, even before the cuts, was too paltry to live on. Today, Friends and Comrades, we are going to petition Parliament for change. Britain has the greatest empire the world has ever known – the least its government can do is create jobs for the unemployed and pay an amount in relief money that will give men their dignity back!'

A deafening roar of approval went up from the crowd.

Ted cupped his hand to the side of his mouth and leaned towards her. 'Can you see over to the roads left and right o' the square?' he shouted in her ear. 'That's a fearsome amount o' bobbies, don't you think?'

Thea stopped trying to get a glimpse of Hal in the crowd and looked to her far left and far right. To the left, in Charing Cross Road and on the steps of St Martin-in-the-Fields church, where she would have expected people who hadn't been able to squeeze into the square to be standing, there was an unbroken line of helmeted, blue-uniformed police officers.

It was the same in the street running down the right-hand side of the square. There were no members of the public: only policemen.

'They've blocked off all t' roads around t' square, not just the one.' There was puzzlement in Ted's voice. 'D'you think they've done it so that all eighteen contingents can march out in grand order when t' rally's over?'

To Thea, an old hand at protest rallies, the idea was so unlikely as to be derisory.

'No,' she shouted back as the roars of approval for Hannington went on and on. 'I don't. When that policeman told me I was going in the wrong direction and that there was going to be trouble before too long, he wasn't speaking of a probability. He *knew* there was going to be trouble – police-provoked trouble.'

Ted Finch, in London for the first time in his life, looked disbelieving.

Thea's stomach muscles tightened. What trigger would give the police the excuse they needed to storm the square, break up the rally and make hundreds of arrests? So far the men who had trudged to London on foot from all corners of the country – often taking weeks to do so – had done so without causing a civil disturbance. Not only that, and despite passions running high, their march through London's streets and their assembly in their thousands in Trafalgar Square had been orderly. No laws had been broken. Processions within a mile of the Houses of Parliament were illegal, but deputations weren't – and the planned walk with the petition would be a deputation. Whether the petition was accepted or whether it wasn't, the act of presenting it would be legal.

'*This is our purpose!*' Thanks to the megaphone,

373

every corner of the square resounded with Wal Hannington's closing words. *'To reverse the cut in the dole and see the degrading and humiliating means test abolished! That is what we are fighting for! And it is a fight we are going to win!'*

It was a gauntlet thrown down, and was all the excuse for action that the police needed. Batons in their hands, they closed in on the square from all four sides.

Thea and Ted Finch were near the speakers' platform. All around them shouts went up: 'Don't let them arrest Wal!', 'Don't let the bastards scupper the deputation!', 'Form a wall and hit 'em where it hurts!'

In a matter of minutes what had been a peaceful rally descended into a bloody, brawling battlefield. Hitting the police where it hurt was no easy task for men who, apart from protest banners and the occasional walking stick, were weaponless, but what they lacked in weapons they made up for in outrage and fury.

Thea was knocked to her knees as, only yards in front of her, the police finally laid hands on Hannington. She struggled to her feet, just in time to see Ted Finch go down under a rain of blows.

Nothing she had ever experienced matched the sheer scale of what was taking place. All around her Hunger Marchers were being dragged, fighting and kicking, into Black Marias. Mounted police had ridden in from Charing Cross Road and Whitehall. Wal Hannington was in the centre of a furious melee as police tried to manhandle him out of the square and into a Black Maria, and Hunger Marchers tried to prevent them from doing so.

No one, neither police nor Hunger Marchers, was making any attempt to help Ted; not the police, because all their attention was on hauling Hannington away, and not the marchers, because all their attention was on ensuring the police didn't achieve their objective.

How Ted, lying sinisterly inert, hadn't yet had the life trampled out of him, Thea didn't know. A brick came whizzing past her head, not aimed at her, but at one of the score of policemen fighting with marchers on the speakers' platform. Sirens were going off. Police helmets were flying through the air. Women were screaming abuse and sometimes screaming because they'd been hurt. Thea knew there was only one course of action she should be taking – and it wasn't remaining where she was, in the thick of the fighting.

That was what she did, though, because Ted Finch wasn't moving. His eyes were closed and his skin was grey. She hurled herself towards him, kneeling beside him on knees scraped bloody from her fall.

As she heaved his shoulders from the ground, trying to shield him from the booted feet kicking and flailing all around them, a baton, aimed at a Hunger Marcher hanging grimly onto a board on which was written WE WANT BREAD NOT CRUMBS, came down hard on her head.

With a scream of agony she keeled over Ted, blood flooding down her face. A helmet thudded into the middle of her back, rolling away into a sea of rampaging feet.

Only half-conscious, sick and giddy with pain, Thea knew she had to somehow get out of the square – and that she had to haul Ted with her. She tried to move and couldn't and then, in a moment so wonderful she thought for a moment she was hallucinating, she heard Hal shouting above the din, 'Sweet Christ! Are you conscious, Thea love? Can you hear me?'

As he spoke he was tearing off his jacket, wrenching his shirt over his head.

She nodded, and as he pressed his shirt to the side of her head to soak up the blood, she took hold of the bunched-up linen herself, holding it in place.

'Let's get you out of here!' He yanked his jacket back on over his singlet, his face contorted with rage and fear: rage at what had been done to her, and fear at how bad her head wound might prove to be.

As he took hold of her, about to lift her into his arms so that he could carry her, she said thickly, 'Not me, Hal. Ted's unconscious. We have to get him out of here before he's trampled to death.'

Hal took one look at the man on the ground – at his closed eyes and deathly skin colour – and knew it wasn't a time for argument.

With Thea unsteadily on her feet, her face a mask of blood, he hauled Ted Finch upright. Then, as the battle between policemen and Hunger Marchers continued all around them, Hal heaved Ted over his shoulder so that Ted's head, arms and upper body were hanging down his back. Gripping a tight hold of Ted's legs, he put his free arm around Thea's waist and, taking nearly all of her weight and overcoming all obstacles, proceeded to make a beeline towards the top north-west corner of the square.

The outer edges of the square were coming under the control of the police, but with a senseless man slung over his shoulder and a bloodied girl leaning heavily against him, the police left Hal alone. As they reached the top of the steps near the National Gallery, Ted Finch made a noise deep in his throat and stirred.

'He's coming round!' Thea's relief was vast. Then, in sudden alarm she said, 'And when he does, he'll think you're a policeman carrying him off to a Black Maria and he'll start struggling.'

'Don't worry. I'll reassure him.' There were beads of perspiration on Hal's forehead. 'I don't want to put him down till we're clear of the police, otherwise the next thing he'll know, he'll be in a cell and then up before a magistrate. How's the bleeding? Is it easing off, or can't you tell?'

'I can't tell.' Her voice was weak, but not as faint and dazed as it had been.

'My flat's in Orange Street, at the back of the Gallery. Once there I'll be able to take a proper look at what's been done to you – and we'll be able to see how badly your friend's been hurt. Heading straight for a hospital is useless. Every hospital within reach will be overrun with casualties. There must be hundreds of people injured – policemen as well as marchers.'

Thea didn't reply. Despite the strength of his arm around her waist and the weight he was taking as she leaned hard against him, just remaining on her feet was taking all her strength.

Even once they had left the square and were in Whitcomb Street there were still mounted policemen milling around.

'What the bugger...?' Ted mumbled, his eyes opening.

'You've been hurt, pal,' Hal said swiftly, 'but there are still bobbies everywhere and, if I put you down now, it's likely you'll be arrested. Another couple of minutes and we'll be free of 'em.'

Recognizing Hal's accent as being that of a northerner, Ted did as he was told.

After only another few yards they turned a corner out of Whitcomb Street into Orange Street. Apart from a couple of placards lying on the ground and a policeman's helmet in the gutter, the street was blessedly empty.

'Thank God!' Hal said devoutly, stopping at a doorway and sliding Ted off his shoulder and onto the pavement.

Ted slumped down against the wall, his legs splayed out in front of him.

'I feel as if I've been 'it by a tank,' he said as Hal, still with one arm supporting Thea, slid a key into the door's Yale lock.

'Aye, well. It's same difference, if you get set on by baton-wielding bobbies with their blood up.' He pushed the door open. 'Can you get inside by yourself or do you need help?'

'I'll be fine in a minute or two and, if it's all the same to you, now I can feel the use of my legs returning I'll be off; I want to find the mates I walked down from Doncaster with. We got separated in Piccadilly Circus and I need to find 'em again.'

Hal swung Thea up into his arms. 'You took quite a hammering, to be unconscious for so long,' he said, looking down at Ted in concern. 'I reckon you should come in and have a pint of strong tea before you go anywhere.'

Ted struggled to his feet. 'Nah. I'll be fine. You just look after this young lady. She's a right grand lass and she needs that bleeding stopped. I'm very grateful to you, mate, but I'm going to be on my way.' And without more ado he turned his back on them and began walking unsteadily back down the street.

'Shouldn't you go after him?' Thea asked, alarmed.

'Nope. He's a Yorkshireman. Arguing with him would be like arguing with a brick wall. Besides, it's not him I'm concerned about. It's you.'

He carried her into a narrow hallway, up a steep flight of stairs and then into a small room modestly but adequately furnished.

'I thought you lived in Deptford?' she said as he lowered her gently onto a moquette-covered sofa.

'I did, but I needed to be nearer to Fleet Street.'

Their intimate closeness, after eight years of agonizingly avoiding any such situation, was almost more than he could handle. Hal gritted his teeth, fighting down the overpowering emotion that only she ever aroused in him.

'Stay still.' His voice was raw. 'Keep holding the shirt to your head till I've run a bowl of warm water.'

Seconds later she could hear the sound of a tap

379

opening in what was presumably his kitchen, and of water being run into a bowl. Then there was the sound of cupboard doors being opened and slammed shut.

'I've found some hydrogen peroxide,' he said, coming back into the room carrying the bowl, a towel, a facecloth, the bottle of peroxide and a newspaper.

Kneeling beside her, he put everything within reach, saying gently, 'Lie still, Thea love, while I get rid of this sodden shirt.'

Fearful of what the blood-soaked shirt was going to reveal, he carefully lifted it away from her head and dropped it on the newspaper. Her hair was matted with blood, but it was blood that was beginning to congeal.

Still unable to see just how deep and wide the wound was, he plunged the facecloth into the water to which he'd added the hydrogen peroxide.

'This is going to sting like the very devil,' he warned.

She knew it would, and she didn't care. They were together again in a way she'd almost given up hope of ever happening. The love he felt for her was in his eyes, his voice and – as with infinite tenderness he cleaned the wound in her scalp – in his hands.

If she'd known who the policeman was who had wielded the baton that had injured her, she would have thanked him from the bottom of her heart. After this, Hal couldn't possibly deny his feelings for her. After this, everything was going to be all right. His face was barely inches from hers and she feasted her eyes on it, loving the way his unruly hair fell low over his brow; loving the gold flecks in his dark-brown eyes; the strong line of his jaw and the slight cleft in his chin.

'How does it look?' she asked huskily as he squeezed out the flannel and reopened the bottle of peroxide.

'It looks better than I'd hoped it would. I'm going to swab it with neat peroxide, so take a deep breath.'

She did so, her eyes watering as the peroxide fizzed and foamed into the cut.

'It needs stitching,' he said tautly. 'The hospitals will still be run off their feet, but the minute you get home, call your doctor. He'll stitch it for you.' He leaned back on his heels, his eyes holding hers. 'It's the best I can do, love. How do you feel?'

Her head was pounding so hard she thought it was going to leave her shoulders. The peroxide was stinging like a million tiny knives. She said with a heart bursting with joy at his nearness, 'I feel wonderful!'

He didn't attempt to misunderstand her. His eyes dark with emotion that he could no longer control, he knelt forward again, taking hold of her hands, gripping them tightly. 'I'd already seen you before you were hit, and I was on my way to get you out of the thick of things when the baton came down on your head.' His voice broke. 'Dear God, Thea. When I saw you keel over, I thought you were dead!'

'I probably soon would have been, if you hadn't got me out of there.'

He was still shirtless and the powerful muscles in his arms and shoulders bulged with tension. In singlet and trousers he looked more like a professional boxer than he did a journalist. Knowing how much she and Ted Finch owed to his physical strength, she said, 'I don't know how you did it, Hal. I don't know how you managed to carry Ted Finch, and half-carry me, all the way from the square to here.'

Despite the overwhelming temptation he was fighting, a grin tugged at the corner of his mouth. 'It was nothing compared to the weight of the injured calves I had to carry when I was a lad.'

She giggled and suddenly it was just as it had always been between them.

From the moment his arm had encircled her waist and, with Ted Finch on his back, he'd begun battling a way out of the chaos of the square, he'd sworn that whatever the outcome he wasn't going to kiss her; that he was not going to break the vow he'd kept for eight agonizingly long years.

Now, with her giggle, the vow he'd taken for both their sakes went whistling down the wind. One minute he was kneeling on the floor beside her, and the next he was on the sofa with her, pulling her hard against him, as her arms slid with the speed of quicksilver up and around his neck.

His mouth crushed hers, his hand cupping her breast over the silk of her blouse. She moved a hand from around his neck, feverishly undoing mother-of-pearl buttons, and as she did so he pushed her skirt high, sliding her with hungry impatience beneath him.

It was a movement that ended everything. Blood began streaming from her head again, trickling down her face and dripping onto her breasts and the backs of his hands. The sight of it brought Hal to his senses in a way nothing else could have.

Instantly he released his hold of her, horrified that he'd been about to make love to her when she was so injured, his only concern being to stop the bleeding.

'Don't move,' he said urgently, springing to his feet and wringing the flannel out in water that was now cold. He pressed it to the side of her head. 'Hold it in place while I get some clean warm water.'

Sitting upright, her feet on the floor, she did as he told her.

When he came back in the room, she said wryly, 'I've never hated the sight of blood more. Next time we start to make love there won't be any such hiccup.'

He put the bowl of water down, a pulse pounding at the corner of his jawline.

Oblivious of the change in his manner and his extreme tension, she said with happy confidence, 'I'll never forget today, because it's shown us we still love each other – that we've always loved each other.'

'Aye, we love each other, but loving each other isn't always enough.'

Her eyes widened as she realized something was wrong.

Squatting down in front of her, he took hold of her free hand. 'I shouldn't have behaved as I did,

Thea. I shouldn't have confused you.'

'Confused me?' There was no confidence in her voice now, only apprehension. 'How could you have confused me, Hal?'

'I've confused you because nothing's changed between us. I'm still never going to marry into a class I despise – and before you start trying to change my mind again on that, there's another, even sounder reason for nothing having changed. I know in my gut that, try as I might, I wouldn't make you happy, and that the man who will make you happy is Kyle.'

'Kyle?' She stared at him, saying the name as if she'd never heard it before.

'Kyle,' he said again. 'So there's an end to it, Thea love. Things are just as they've been for eight years. Nothing's changed.'

She tried to speak and couldn't. The plunge from joy to despair was so total, so cataclysmic, that she could hardly breathe. Sobs rose in her throat and she fought them down, determined she'd burn in hell for a hundred years before giving way to them in front of him.

'Okay.' As she fought to keep her dignity, her voice was so brittle she barely recognized it. 'Nothing's changed. Stupid of me to have thought it had. If you aren't going to marry me, then who are you going to marry? Carrie?'

It was said without thinking – a jibe to get her through a nightmare moment. The last thing she expected was his serious, measured response.

'Yes,' Hal said, his eyes just as full of pain as hers were. 'I think so. I've been thinking so for a long time.'

Chapter Twenty-Five

SEPTEMBER 1933

Rozalind stepped out of her agent's office and onto a crowded Manhattan sidewalk, her Leica slung over her shoulder, a small-brimmed white hat worn at an angle on jet-black, glossily straight, jaw-length hair. For the last couple of years she had spent almost as much time in London and Berlin as she had in New York, but New York was special, not because it was where she had been born and brought up, but because it was the place where – every couple of months or so, and for as much as a few days at a time – she and Max were able to enjoy the kind of domesticity that married couples enjoyed.

The apartment Max had leased near Washington Square wasn't glaringly fashionable, which meant that so far they had never run into anyone they knew when going in and out of it. That, because of Max's position as a Congressman, such care had to be taken was an inconvenience that often infuriated her, but she wasn't letting it infuriate her today. Today was a good day. Max had been in town for two days and would be in town until tomorrow morning, when he would leave for Washington and she would move into her apartment on the Upper East Side until, on Saturday, she left for England aboard the liner they had met on, the SS *Aquitania*.

She flagged a cab down, already thinking of what she hoped to achieve in London. So far, despite many near-misses, she had never achieved her ambition of taking private photographs of the Prince of Wales, or of the Duke and Duchess of York and their two little princesses. It was an ambition she was determined to achieve this trip.

A cab screeched to a halt and she darted into it. 'West Ninth Street,' she said, her thoughts still on the kind of photographs she wanted to take of Edward and the Yorks. She didn't want to take shots that were stilted and formal. She wanted shots that would reveal her sitters' personalities; shots that other photographers wouldn't think of taking, or have the opportunity of taking.

As they approached Fifth Avenue's intersection with 49th Street the traffic was so heavy the cab was reduced to a near-standstill. Curbing her frustration, Rozalind pondered on the best locations for the shots she wanted to take. She knew from both Thea and Olivia that Fort Belvedere was where Edward was at his most relaxed. She also knew that at the Fort he would have his two cairn terriers, Cora and Jaggs, with him.

Traffic had begun moving again, but Roz, whose thoughts had flicked to Edward's father, was oblivious to it. King George was sixty-eight years old. It wasn't a vast age, but his health was poor and people in the know, such as her Uncle Gilbert, were convinced he was likely to die at any time. When he did, Edward would not only be King of the United Kingdom and Ireland and of the British Dominions Beyond the Seas, but Emperor of India as well.

The burdens he carried now would be nothing compared to the burdens he would carry then, and she liked the idea of capturing Edward playing with his dogs at the Fort in the days just before his life changed forever.

She grinned to herself, knowing it was highly unlikely King George was going to die just as doing so would add resonance to the photographs she hoped to take. As well as being imaginative, though, she was also pragmatic, and one of her favourite mottos was her old Girl Scout motto: 'Be Prepared'.

Rozalind liked to think she always was.

The cab drew up outside her apartment block and she paid off the driver, having made up her mind that when it came to photographing the Duke and Duchess of York and their children she would ask to do so at Royal Lodge, their country retreat in Windsor Great Park.

With her decisions made, and determined that on her upcoming trip to England she would achieve the aim that had so long eluded her, she ran into the entrance hall and then, not wanting to spend a second longer out of Max's company than was absolutely necessary, didn't wait for the lift, but ran with ease up the stairs to their second-floor apartment.

He was out on the balcony, sitting at a wrought-iron table drinking coffee and reading the *Chicago Tribune*. She dropped her Leica on the nearest available surface and ran across to him, standing behind him and sliding her arms around his neck.

'What's the latest with Chicago's new mayor?' she asked, reading the headlines over his shoulder. 'Is he still firing on all cylinders?'

'Unfortunately.' Ed Kelly, the new mayor, was a Democrat and Max wasn't a fan. He put the newspaper down and covered her hand with his. 'Have you noticed that ever since Roosevelt replaced Hoover in the White House, Republicans have dropped out of sight – and even those who have been left behind seem to have changed political colour from red to blue.'

Rozalind laughed, 'But not you, sweetheart.'

'No,' he said with feeling. 'Not me.'

Wishing she hadn't brought up the subject of American politics, she withdrew her arms from around his neck and pulled up a chair at the other side of the small table on which, next to his newspaper, a coffee pot stood.

Changing the subject to Germany, she said, 'What fresh outrage is Hitler up to?'

His face hardened. 'What fresh outrage isn't he up to? The latest is official confirmation of the way he's rounding up large numbers of Jews and sending them to makeshift prisons. The *Chicago Tribune* quotes Germany's outlawed Socialist Party as saying forty-five thousand prisoners are being held at scores of different locations.'

'And is that information right?' Rozalind put a hand against the coffee pot on the table to see if it was still hot.

'Yes. It accords with the information we have on the Hill.'

'On the Hill' was the way he always referred to the Capitol Building in Washington. Quite what

388

Max's responsibilities were in Congress, over and above those of every Congressman, she didn't know, but whatever they were, she strongly suspected they were to do with foreign affairs – and with Germany in particular.

She rose to her feet. 'The coffee is still hot. I'm just going to fetch a cup.'

Once in the kitchen, she stood for a moment, thinking. Whenever she crossed the Atlantic, Berlin was always her next stop after London. Thanks to Dieter, who had been posted back to Berlin more than a year ago, her contacts there were as good as they had always been and she knew at first hand about the abuses of freedom that had been taking place since Germany had become a one-party state.

Until now, though, the photographs she had taken from privileged viewpoints had been of Nazi parades, conventions and rallies, or occasions such as Hitler arriving at a meeting to explain why he was taking no further part in the Geneva Disarmament Convention and was withdrawing from the League of Nations.

There was a big difference between photographs like those appearing in British and American newspapers, and photographs of prison camps where people were being imprisoned for crimes as trivial as reading a banned book, writing anti-Nazi graffiti or simply being a Jew, a homosexual, a prostitute, a Jehovah's Witness or a gypsy.

Once those kinds of damaging photographs began appearing, her unique contacts with the Nazi hierarchy would be over and she would be lucky even to be allowed back in the country.

She walked out onto the balcony, reflecting that it was a difficulty almost as great as that of maintaining a good relationship with Dieter – without which she would be just another freelance news photographer without special access to anything.

'He just doesn't see what horrors Hitler is plunging Germany into,' she said to Max, pouring coffee and not bothering to preface what she'd said with the name of the person she was talking about. Like an old married couple, the two of them picked up on each other's half-begun or half-finished sentences instantly.

He pulled her down onto his knee. 'He will – eventually.' He slid a hand up her leg until he reached the smooth, firm flesh above her stocking top. Pleasurably he let it linger there, saying, 'At the moment all Dieter sees is the way Hitler has brought unemployment under control and suppressed the communists.'

'And as he and Olivia are happy to see the communists being suppressed, Thea is no longer on speaking terms with either of them. She and Olivia have always had frequent spats, but this is the first time they've ever not been on speaking terms with each other.'

'I think,' he said, his voice thickening as his hand moved a fraction higher, 'that it's time we stopped talking about Germany and went indoors for a little while.'

Her eyes darkened with heat. 'I think so, too. In fact, I rather think the bedroom for preference.'

'My thoughts entirely.'

She slid from his knee and, as he rose to his

feet, the telephone in the living room rang.

The only people who had the apartment's phone number, other than themselves, were Rob Dawkins, Max's chief of staff, and Doris Tyndall, his personal secretary – and neither Rob nor Doris ever used it except in matters of emergency.

With his mood instantly altered, Max strode towards the phone.

'Yes?' he said peremptorily as, certain their already too-short time together was about to be cut even shorter, Rozalind sat on the arm of a sofa and waited. 'Yes,' he said again, his jaw tightening. 'I understand. Thank you, Doris.'

One look at his face as he hung up and Roz knew without being told that their precious time together was at an end.

'I'll pack your bag,' she said, knowing there was going to be no languorous goodbye lovemaking, only a fierce hug and a hurried passionate kiss.

The packing of what was only a weekend bag took no more than three minutes. She did it while he rapidly changed out of his casual clothes and into Congressman mode: a dark suit, white shirt, subdued tie and well-polished black leather shoes.

He held her against him tight and hard, kissing her as if he was doing so for the last time ever and then, ten minutes after he had answered the telephone, he was striding away in the direction of the lift and all she had left of him was a lingering tang of lemon cologne and the feel of his hands on her body and the taste of his mouth on her lips.

She walked slowly back out onto the balcony, picked up the newspapers and took them into the kitchen ready to be dropped into the rubbish bin. Then she went back outside to clear the coffee pot and coffee cups away.

She was just wondering whether to take a shower before heading off to her apartment on the Upper East Side when the doorbell rang.

The sound knocked the breath from her body. No one, not even Rob Dawkins and Doris Tyndall, had the address of the apartment, and nothing was ever delivered to them there. Max wouldn't have left without his key, so it couldn't be him coming back after having forgotten something. Yet if it wasn't Max, who could it be?

The bell rang again.

Aware there was only one way of finding out, she moved quickly across to the door.

When she opened it, the world seemed to rock on its axis and, even as Rozalind struggled with her disbelief, she knew the world – her world – was never going to be the same again.

'Good afternoon, Miss Duveen,' Max's wife said. 'I'd like a few words. May I come in?'

Speechlessly Rozalind opened the door wider.

Perfectly composed, Myrtle Bradley walked past her. She was a tall woman, verging on plumpness. The plumpness didn't matter, though, for she was supremely elegant. Her beige midcalf-length suit was worn with a fox-fur flung carelessly over one shoulder. There were pearls at her throat. Her fair hair was streaked with silver and was worn in a chignon beneath a coffee-coloured pillbox hat decorated with a wisp of net veiling.

Elegance personified, she seated herself on the sofa, took a cigarette-case and lighter from her clutch-bag and said without preamble, 'You and I have to talk.'

Rozalind struggled to gather her wits, and her composure. 'Before we do,' she said tartly, 'I'd like to know how you got hold of this address, because no one has it. Absolutely no one.'

There was a suffocating tightness in her throat. Myrtle at a distance, unintroduced and never spoken to, was one thing. Myrtle, cool and insultingly composed and seated opposite her in the apartment that was her own and Max's sacred space, was quite another.

'I've always had it. Max gave it to me the day he signed the lease.'

The floor tilted beneath Rozalind's feet. The room swam.

'Sit down,' Myrtle said with almost disinterested practicality. 'We can't talk about serious matters if you're going to behave like an old-fashioned Victorian maiden in need of smelling salts. Would you like a brandy?'

She made a movement as if about to rise to her feet and get her some.

Indignation cleared Rozalind's head in a flash. 'I don't need a brandy, and if I did I'd get one for myself!'

Myrtle pursed her lips. 'I accept that my coming here this afternoon has been a surprise to you, Miss Duveen, but there's no need for rudeness.'

Her effrontery and self-possession were on such a scale that although Rozalind didn't want to sit down – didn't want to do anything to indicate the two of them were settling in for a cosy chat – she had no choice. Not to sit down would be to risk her legs giving way.

She sat down on the stiffest-backed chair the room possessed, hoping it would somehow give her an advantage.

Myrtle adjusted her fur.

'Before you think my finding you here alone was a coincidence, Doris's telephone call was prompted by me: which may indicate to you, Miss Duveen, just how serious my meeting with you is.'

Rozalind felt sick with giddiness. First had come the utter shock of finding herself face-to-face with Myrtle. Then had come the devastating revelation that Myrtle knew the address of the Greenwich Village apartment – and that she knew it because Max had told her. Now Myrtle had come to a matter that was obviously of great importance to her – which could only mean she'd become afraid Max wanted a divorce.

She said dismissively, 'There's no need for anxiety, Mrs Bradley. Max has no intention of divorcing you, and I have no intention of asking him to divorce you.'

Myrtle arched a finely plucked eyebrow. 'I'm well aware Max has no intention of divorcing me, so whether you would or wouldn't like it if he did so is immaterial to me, Miss Duveen. What I have come about is something completely different.'

Until now, happily certain that it was her own relationship with Max that mattered to him, and not his relationship with Myrtle, Rozalind had scarcely given a thought to his wife. She was doing so now, though, because Myrtle was giving her no option not to. After all, Myrtle *should* have been concerned that Max might one day ask for a divorce. Her complacency as to the stability of her marriage wasn't just infuriating. It was insulting.

Tight-lipped, Roz waited to hear what the different matter was.

Myrtle lit a cigarette and said starkly, 'Max has been asked to run for office.'

Rozalind stared at her, understanding now why Myrtle was so confident that Max wouldn't ask for a divorce. No divorced man could ever hope to run for the highest elective office in the land.

She said slowly, wanting to be sure she hadn't misheard, 'Max has been asked to be a nominee in the primaries?'

Myrtle nodded. 'And he would stand a good chance of winning.' She paused, and added with steel in her voice, 'He would stand a good chance of winning all the way.'

Rozalind thought of Max as a presidential candidate. Of course he would stand a good chance of winning all the way.

'The difficulty, Miss Duveen, is that the nomination process will entail rigorous scrutiny into his private life – and at the moment his private life won't stand up to such scrutiny. You can imagine Max's dilemma. Does he end his affair with you and seize the chance he is being given to embark on a four-year battle for the White House? Or does he continue with your affair and never know whether he could, or could not, have won for his party the greatest position any American can hold?'

The room was very quiet.

Somewhere Rozalind could hear a clock ticking faintly.

As if from a vast distance she heard Myrtle say, 'My reason for being here, Miss Duveen, is because of the decision Max has made.'

Rozalind remained perfectly still, not daring to move. Not daring to speak.

Myrtle reached over the arm of the sofa to crush out the cigarette she'd just lit in the ashtray on the small adjacent table. After a pause that seemed to last an eternity, she said, 'Max has decided to decline the invitation he has been given, his reason being that he loves you too much ever to end his affair with you.'

As relief surged through every vein and nerve-ending in Rozalind's body, Myrtle rose to her feet. 'That decision needn't be the end of the matter, Miss Duveen. Max could still achieve his life's ambition of becoming a presidential candidate, but only if – just as he loves you enough not to end your affair – you love him enough to end it for him.' She tilted her head a little to one side, her eyes as glacial as a winter sea. 'I wonder what choice you will make, Miss Duveen? I wonder how deep your love for Max really is?'

And, without waiting for a response, without another word, she walked from the room. Seconds later Rozalind heard from the hallway the click of the door as it opened and then closed.

She remained where she was, her legs still too

weak to bear her weight, question after question, and realization after realization, thundering through her brain.

That Max had told Myrtle the address of the apartment was something so shattering that she didn't know how she was going to come to terms with it. And when Myrtle had arranged with Doris for Max's recall to Washington, just how had she done so? It indicated a closeness and a trust between Myrtle and Doris that Roz had never remotely suspected. Did Max know of it? Did he sometimes discuss her with Myrtle? It was a crushing thought, but it paled into insignificance compared to his having been invited to stand for office.

She knew, just as much as Myrtle did, what a chance at the presidential candidacy would mean to Max – and yet, rather than end their affair, he was going to turn his back on it.

Faced with such evidence of how much she meant to him, tears burned in her eyes. Unsteadily she rose to her feet and went in search of the brandy she had previously scorned and now so desperately needed. With a glass in one hand and the bottle in the other, she went out onto the balcony, sitting where, such a short time ago, she had sat with Max and been so thoughtlessly, idyllically happy.

There was no way she could ever be so happy again. If she behaved as if Myrtle's visit had never happened, and as if she had no knowledge of the sacrifice Max was making, how would she live with herself? It would be impossible.

The late-afternoon light smoked into dusk. The

traffic noise changed in character as the evening street scene began to get under way. Not until darkness fell did she know not only what she must do, but how she must go about doing it.

She wouldn't end her affair with him face-to-face. She couldn't; she simply didn't possess that kind of strength. She would treat the next few days as if they were perfectly normal. Max would telephone from Washington, telling her how much he was missing her and how he hoped she'd have a good trip. And, though it would near kill her, she would respond in a similar manner, not letting him know by so much as an inflection in her voice the bombshell she was going to drop once she was thousands of miles away in London.

And, once in London, she wouldn't return to America. Her agency had an office in Knightsbridge. Nearly all her work was in Europe. She had no home of her own in London – even under Zephiniah's reign she always stayed at Mount Street – but finding a flat in Knightsbridge or Kensington wouldn't be a problem.

Her problem would be a quite different one. Her problem would be how to live without Max in her life.

The prospect was unimaginable – seemed inconceivable; and as the stars came out and the moon rode high in the sky, she remained sitting on the balcony that she would never sit on again, her heart breaking with the knowledge that her world had altered and would never be the same again.

Chapter Twenty-Six

JULY 1934

'The situation isn't good, Congressman Bradley. Not for us, and not for the British.'

That the situation in Germany wasn't good for America and Britain – and for the French too, come to that – was something Max was well aware of

Tom Kirby, the man he was seated across a desk from, was a senior officer in the State Department's European intelligence and research section and their meeting was taking place in a small room in the Office of Public Affairs, not far from the White House.

'We have good people undercover in Munich and Berlin, of course, but in the situation we are now facing there can never be enough of them.'

Max nodded agreement and waited, curious as to what might be coming next.

'I understand you have contacts in Berlin?'

Max's face remained inscrutable, but his brain was racing. What contacts were being spoken of? His contacts with Olivia and, via her, with Dieter? Since Rozalind had so abruptly ended their affair nearly a year ago he'd had no contact at all with either of them.

'I was once on social terms with Olivia von Starhemberg and, to a much lesser extent, with her husband, Dieter. I've had no contact with them now for a long time.'

'Ah, yes.' Kirby looked down at a sheet of paper in front of him. 'The von Starhembergs are admirers of Chancellor Hitler, I believe.'

Max nodded, impressed by the scope of his country's intelligence-gathering, but wary of the direction in which the conversation seemed to be heading.

'Because of their sympathies, the von Starhembergs are of little interest, Max. However, Olivia von Starhemberg's younger sister, the movie actress Violet Fenton, is. Are you on social terms with her as well?'

'Yes. I've known the family well ever since serving on the Dawes Committee when their father, Lord Fenton, was my opposite number in London. Look here, Tom, it's quite obvious you know everything there is to know about my friendship with the Fenton family, so let's cut to the chase. Just what the heck is this all about?'

'Violet Fenton is about to leave Hollywood for Berlin, where she's to make a film at the Babelsberg film studios. She's a bit of a catch for them. The Reich's newly appointed Minister for Public Enlightenment and Propaganda, a guy named Goebbels, is eager to trumpet Babelsberg as an international film studio, and she is unwittingly helping him do so.'

'And...?' Max asked, wondering what on earth was going to come next.

'And we want to know if her sympathies are the same as her sister's?'

Max cracked with laughter. 'God, no! Unlike

400

her sisters – the other sister is a paid-up member of the British Socialist Party and virtually a communist – Violet hasn't the remotest interest in politics. I can no more imagine her a Nazi sympathizer than I can imagine her a nun.'

'Then have a word with her, Max. Put her in the picture about the war-mongering side of Hitler and what a European war could mean for us, here in America. Impress on her how important small details of information can be for us – especially if that information is picked up when socializing with men like Goebbels. That she doesn't come with any political baggage will be an advantage to her. An even bigger advantage is her brother-in-law's position in Germany's Foreign Office. With a connection like that, she isn't going to be regarded with suspicion – especially if she makes the right kind of Hitler-admiring noises.'

Max said slowly, 'You want me to recruit Violet Fenton, who is British and whose father is a member of the House of Lords, to be an agent for American intelligence?'

Tom Kirby grinned. 'That's just about the sum of it.' He eased his chair away from his desk and stretched his legs out, crossing them at the ankle. 'You can see what a brilliant position she would be in, as an agent? She's a glamorous movie actress. Every high-ranking Nazi in his right mind is going to be fawning around her. The minute she arrives at Babelsberg, Goebbels will seek her out – and the only person higher in the Nazi hierarchy than Goebbels is Hitler. Add in her von Starhemberg family connection and the people they will introduce her to, couple it with her sounding like

401

a dame who can get any man she wants eating out of her hand, and you've got a bullseye. With luck, probably a whole string of bullseyes. All you have to do, Max, is persuade her to play ball.'

Max realized that for the last few minutes he'd been holding his breath. Slowly he let it out.

There'd been no mention of Roz. He wondered if it was because they knew he no longer had any contact with her, or if it was because they didn't realize that Roz's contacts in Berlin were very similar to the kind of contacts they hoped Violet would make? Whatever the reason, Rozalind's name not being mentioned was a vast relief.

He said, still not knowing how he felt about the suggestion that had been put to him, 'How would Violet pass information on?'

'She'll be given a contact in Berlin's US Embassy.' Tom Kirby shifted position again, this time nudging his chair forward and resting clasped hands on his desk top. 'Both the British and the French believe Germany is secretly re-arming. None of our agents in the field have a hope in hell of mixing in the kind of Nazi circles Violet Fenton will have automatic entrée into. We need to know what the Nazis are up to. Make sure she knows that whatever she does for us, she's doing for Britain also.'

Max quirked an eyebrow. 'When I tell her that will I be speaking the truth?'

'Yes. When it comes to the re-arming question – and others like it – we'll be sharing it with the Brits. They're the ones at the sharp end. What we're concerned about is having enough in-formation to steer well clear. Involvement in one

European-triggered Great War is quite enough for us, don't you think? To hell with the thought of a second one!'

Five days later Max strolled into the lobby of the Beverly Hills Hotel. He'd arranged to meet Violet by the poolside and although he was carrying a briefcase, he was dressed in cream-coloured flannels, an open-necked short-sleeved shirt and loafers.

'Miss Fenton, sir?' a bellboy said. 'This way, sir.'

Max followed him through tropical gardens and down pink-walled steps to an azure pool.

Violet was reclining on a sun-lounger, wearing sunglasses, a silver swimming costume, silver hoop earrings and silver nail varnish, her torrent of Titian hair held away from her face by a silver headband.

She patted the lounger as an invitation that he should seat himself next to her beautifully shaped legs.

He grinned. 'I'll take a deckchair if you don't mind, Violet. I'm in for the long haul of a presidency election. I have to mind my dignity.'

Violet gave a throaty giggle. 'You need to let rip occasionally, Max. And why the briefcase? Have you brought your lunch with you?'

He chuckled. 'No. I'll explain later. What are you drinking? Would you like a Pimm's?'

'I'd love one, but why are you here? Have you had a reconciliation with Roz? And if you have, why isn't she with you?'

'No reconciliation – and I'm here because I've

403

learned you're about to leave for Berlin.'

He raised a hand for a pool-boy. 'A jug of Pimm's Number One,' he said when the pool-boy came running, and then, returning his attention immediately to Violet, 'Why are you off to Germany when you're doing so well here, in Hollywood?'

'My current fiancé – did you know that if you have an affair with anyone in Hollywood they have to be referred to as your fiancé, even if they're married? He's called Gunther Behr. He began his career at Babelsberg, and now they want him back. As I've fallen out with my last director, Alex Korda, and as Zsigmund Sárközy is suing me, I thought a spell in Berlin, with Gunther, would be rather fun. Gunther suggested it to Babelsberg, and they leapt at the idea. It's so nice to be wanted.'

'I'm not surprised Babelsberg leapt at the idea. Have you any idea of the number of actors and directors who have recently fled Babelsberg for Hollywood?'

'Marlene Dietrich? Peter Lorre? I can't think of anyone else. And why shouldn't they come here if they want to?'

'It isn't a case of them wanting to, Violet. It's a case of them having to, either because they're Jewish, like Lorre, or because, like Dietrich, they are no longer willing to live under the current regime. In the last year directors such as Karl Freund, Joe May, Edgar Ulmer and Billy Wilder have all kicked the Nazi dust from their heels. You, on the other hand, are voluntarily heading into it. It doesn't make sense.'

404

Their Pimm's arrived and was poured into ice-filled glasses.

Violet took a long drink of hers through a pink straw. Finally, toying with the straw, she said, 'I thought this meeting – when we haven't met for so long that I can't remember when it was – was going to be fun. Instead it's turning into a lecture. Please don't lecture me, Max darling. It's so unnecessary and I can't bear it.'

Ignoring his drink, Max said grimly, 'You're wrong about it being unnecessary, Violet. It's very necessary and I'm going to continue.'

He leaned towards her, his hands clasped between his knees.

'I know you're criminally uninterested in politics, Violet, but if you're going to make a film in Berlin, you have to know the state of the German film industry. For starters, it's a far cry from anything you've experienced in London, or here. Since earlier this year, everything filmed at Babelsberg comes under the control of the Minister for Public Enlightenment and Propaganda.'

'The film I will be making is a historical romance. It has nothing to do with propaganda.'

'It will have, in some way or another. Trust me. And there won't be a Jewish person on the set, either in front of the cameras or behind them, because the Reich Chamber of Film officially excludes Jews from employment in the film industry. No one in Germany, if they are a Jew, can by law appear on-stage or in a film.'

'But that's outrageous!'

'Glad you think so. In March the German parliament voted Hitler the right to make his own

405

laws – and the ones he is making are all out-rageous. No Jew can work for the Civil Service any more. All trade unions have been abolished and their leaders have been arrested. All political parties have been banned – which means the German people can't get rid of Hitler, even if they want to. In July he passed a law whereby anyone deemed to be an "inferior" citizen is compulsorily sterilized. God only knows what he's got up his sleeve for next year.'

'My God!' Violet's amber eyes flashed fire. 'Something should be done about him.'

'America – and Britain – certainly need to keep a step ahead of Hitler. In defiance of the Versailles Peace Treaty, he's re-arming – building up both the German army and the navy. It indicates he's got war on his mind. The State Department needs all the clues it can get as to what he's going to do, long before he does it. Which is where you come in, Violet.'

'Me?' Violet's eyebrows shot nearly into her hairline. 'What can I do? All I'm going to be doing is making a film. Except that I'm probably not going to be doing so now, because you've put me right off the idea. With what you've told me, I can't understand why Olivia loves living in Berlin. She must be going around with her eyes shut.'

'She is. And I want you to go around Berlin with your eyes – and especially your ears – wide open.'

Violet took off her sunglasses. Her black-lashed, extraordinary-coloured eyes held his. She said flatly, 'You want me to act as a spy.'

He'd forgotten how quick on the uptake she was.

With a flash of amusement he said, 'In a nutshell, Violet. Yes. Because of your movie-star status at Babelsberg, and because Dieter is your brother-in-law, you're going to be socializing with the kind of people few intelligence agents have the opportunity of mixing with and eavesdropping on. You would have to appear either indifferent, or simpatico, to what is taking place in Germany, and you'd have to maintain that stance with Olivia and Dieter. Would that be a problem for you?'

Violet looked at him witheringly. 'Do me a favour, Max. I'm a movie actress. Whatever part you want me to play, I can play it.'

All the time they had been talking there had been activity going on around them. Bellboys delivering drinks; swimmers diving into the pool and climbing out of it; swimsuit-clad figures walking along the side of the pool within feet of them. Until now Violet had resolutely avoided eye contact with anyone, but just then a statuesque brunette strolled past, saying as she did so, 'Hi, Violet. Let's catch up later, okay?'

'Okay, Joanie.'

'Was that Joan Crawford?' Max asked, as the brunette sashayed on her way.

'Yes. She's the one person I'm really going to miss when I go to Babelsberg.'

'You're going to go then? And you're up for what I'm asking you to do?'

'Why not? It's not going to take much mental effort, is it? Besides, I'd like to help put a stop to

all this Nazi Jewish nonsense.' She put her sunglasses back on. 'I don't usually give a rap for
what governments do, but refusing to let Jews
work on-stage or in films is the living end – and
being a spy in real life will be even more fun than
being one in a film.'

It was then that Max very seriously reconsidered
his request. He thought of the consequences if she
was discovered passing information to the American Embassy. Whatever they were, they would
certainly be grim. Her father was, though, a British government minister. The Brits would
intervene. They'd have Violet out of the country in
a twinkling of an eye.

He said sternly, 'Don't go into this thinking it's
a game, Violet. You'll only be passing on gossip,
not military documents, but even so, if anyone
becomes suspicious of what you are up to, there
is no telling what the consequences will be.'

'Thank you for the fatherly advice. And now,
are you going to tell me what you have in your
briefcase?'

'What I have in my briefcase are photographs
and résumés of some of the key people we'd like
you to become on chatting terms with: Joseph
Goebbels, the Reich's minister in control of film-
making and Hitler's right-hand man, being top of
the list. I want you to look through them in the
privacy of your room and commit them to
memory. I'm assuming you'll have no problem
with that, being an actress?'

'None at all.'

'What else would you like to know?'

'I'd like to know what happened between you

and Roz. She's been very close-mouthed about it. Thea doesn't know. Olivia doesn't know. According to Thea, Carrie doesn't know. So why the split?'

Max sucked in his breath. The last thing he wanted to do was talk about the ending of his affair with Roz. Considering the magnitude of what he'd just asked of her, though, Violet did deserve as much of an explanation as he could give.

Another jug of Pimm's later, when he had told her of Roz's phone call to him from London, she said, 'It doesn't make sense. Why would Roz find the difference in your ages a problem now, when she never has before? Why would the two of you only having snatched, irregular meetings matter now? The reason you sometimes didn't see each other for a couple of months at a time was her fault, not yours. She's the one who, by choice, was always on the other side of the Atlantic.'

'I think,' he said slowly, 'that there's someone else. Someone who, to spare my feelings, she doesn't want to tell me about.'

'If there is, no one else knows about him, either. The reason she ended her affair with you is because of your decision to stand as a candidate in the next presidential election. If she hadn't finished it, you would have had to.'

Max shook his head. 'No, it wasn't that. Though I had been asked to stand as a candidate, at the time she broke things off with me, Roz didn't know that; plus I'd turned the invitation down the minute it was offered. I only

409

accepted it weeks later, after I realized there was no way she was coming back to me.'

Violet spread her hands out expressively, palms upwards. 'Then, darling Max, I don't understand it. All affairs have to end, but they don't usually cause long-term heartache. When I arrive in Berlin I'll be finishing my affair with Dieter – not that it's much of an affair, only a catch-as-catch-can one. He'll quite likely blow his top when I tell him that even Olivia would cotton on to it, if it was taking place beneath her own roof, but give it a week or two and he'll be over it.'

He stared at her. Other than Roz's last phone-call to him, he couldn't remember another time when he'd been so shocked that he felt as if he'd been slugged in the guts by a baseball bat. When he could trust himself to speak, he said disbelievingly, 'You've been having an affair with your sister's husband?'

'Only a teensie-little one. Nothing full-blown.'

'Nothing full-blown? Dear God, Violet! He's your *brother-in-law!* Have you no morals at all?'

Violet regarded him in amusement. 'Apparently not. It's one of the reasons I'll make such a wonderful Mata Hari. Do sit down again, Max, and stop making a mountain out of a molehill. I'm not ruining anyone's marriage. Dieter adores Olivia. It's just that Olivia takes things so seriously, and Dieter needs a little fun every now and then, just as I need to be naughty every now and then.'

Max put a hand over his eyes, his doubts growing as to the saneness of what he'd asked of Violet. How could Tom Kirby's section ever be

410

certain of her? How could anyone ever know what she was likely to do next? And why did she have to be so damned *likeable* about being so outrageously amoral?

Seeing how deeply perturbed and exasperated with her he was, Violet rose to her feet, closed the distance between them and hugged his arm. 'Don't let's fall out, Max. I'm going to be the most marvellous intelligence-gatherer for you. Mr Goebbels – and lots of other nasty Nazis – will be putty in my hands.'

He didn't speak. Speech was beyond him.

Laughter bubbled up in her throat. 'Think how aghast Thea is going to be when she thinks I've become a Hitler admirer. Poor Daddy, too – and Roz and Carrie and Hal. It's going to be the greatest tease ever. I'm going to have such a wonderful time in Berlin, I might never come home!'

Chapter Twenty-Seven

OCTOBER 1934

'Home' was a word Carrie still never used about Monkswood, even though she had been living and working there for more than twelve years. Whenever she thought of home she thought of Gorton Hall, and though she tried hard not to, whenever she thought of Gorton she thought of Gilbert.

It was a Friday at Monkswood and the last day

of a three-day shooting party, which meant she was so run off her feet in seeing that the house ran like clockwork that the last thing she should have been doing was letting her thoughts wander. She hadn't been able to help it, though, when Lady Markham's lady's maid had said as they passed each other on the back stairs, 'Thank goodness my weekend off is next weekend. I haven't been home for six months and I can't wait to see my nieces and nephews again.'

Carrie hadn't made a response, because for one thing a response hadn't been necessary, and for another they had both been in such a hurry that by the time she'd made one, there would have been a flight of stairs between them. It had made her think about her own next weekend off, though, and of how, having no home to go to, she would be spending it at Monkswood as she always did.

A stab of bleakness entered her heart, to be firmly banished before it took hold. It was mid-afternoon and the lunch that had been taken out to the shooting party, where it would be eaten in a marquee at tables carried out earlier by footmen and set with glistening white napery and heavy silver, would now be nearly over. This meant that the ladies who had been taken out by shooting brake to join the party for lunch could be expected back at the house at any moment.

'Ah, there you are, Mrs Thornton.' Briggs, Monkswood's butler, hurried towards her, addressing her as a married woman, as all house-keepers – even under-housekeepers – were addressed, whether married or not. 'General

Elphinstone has just been brought back to the house with an injury. Nothing serious,' he added speedily, as he saw by her expression that she was fearful it had been caused by a careless gunshot. 'He's twisted his ankle in a rabbit-hole. He's been helped to his room – not an easy task for the footmen, as he weighs at least eighteen stone.'

'Is his valet with him?'

'Yes, and I don't envy him – or you. According to Jack and Wilf, who half-carried him up the stairs, the general was still swearing like a trooper when he'd been heaved into a chair, and is probably still swearing now.'

'I'll make a mustard foot-bath mixture and take it up to him straight away.'

Not wasting any time, Carrie headed for the kitchen. General Elphinstone was a regular visitor to Monkswood. A red-faced, choleric man, he was a difficult guest even at the best of times. Now, having been cheated of finishing the last day of the shoot, she could well imagine the kind of temper he was in.

The mammoth-sized kitchen was a hive of activity, with Cook overseeing the preparations for dinner that evening. Pans were being slammed on and off giant ranges; two kitchen maids were labouring over hors d'oeuvres while another was pounding cooked chicken and cream in a mortar.

'It's for Cook's *Consommé à la Comtesse*, Mrs Thornton,' Ena Batty, the girl doing the pounding, said, eager to come to Carrie's attention.

'And it's about time you were sieving it,' Cook said to her sharply. And then, to Carrie, 'Jack and Wilf have told us what happened. Do you want a

413

mustard-bath mixture made?'

'You have enough on your hands at the moment, Cook. I'll do it.'

She walked across the kitchen, opened the door of a tall cupboard and took down from the shelves baking soda, mustard powder, peppermint oil, rosemary oil and eucalyptus oil. As she combined all the ingredients she could hear Ena, now sieving energetically, say, 'Can I add the eggs now, Cook? I know it's one whole egg to every three yolks. I won't make a mistake, I promise.'

Carrie smiled to herself, remembering how keen she had been at Ena's age to progress from mundane tasks to more interesting ones, no matter how small the step of progress was.

Swiftly she combined her ingredients and then, covering the bowl with a clean teacloth, she hurried out of the kitchen with it.

'Blasted rabbit!' were the first words she heard as she entered the bedroom that had been allocated to the general. 'Bloody vermin! What the devil is Lady Markham's gamekeeper doing, not keeping the land free of 'em? The man needs to be given his marching orders!'

Carrie, who had a very different opinion of Ted Ramsden, Monkswood's gamekeeper, pursed her lips and then, when she knew her feelings wouldn't show in her voice, said to the general's harassed valet, 'A foot-bath of hot water from the bathroom, please,' and to the General, 'A half-hour mustard-bath will soon ease the pain and reduce the swelling, sir.'

Elphinstone glared at her. 'I'd taken out twenty-six pheasants on the second drive of the afternoon!

If it hadn't been for the blasted rabbit hole, I'd have bettered that on the last drive. Bloody rabbits! Bloody vermin!'

He made no attempt to apologize for swearing in front of her, and Carrie reflected that when it came to good manners, General Elphinstone could have learned a lot from Ted, who would never, in a million years, have sworn in front of any woman, no matter what her class.

The valet came back into the room with the foot-bath of hot water and Carrie ladled into it a generous amount of the mixture she had made.

'The foot and ankle need soaking for at least half an hour,' she said to the valet. 'When this first lot of water begins to cool, replace it with hot, and each time you do so, add a fresh ladle of mustard mixture.'

Still indignant at the high-handed way General Elphinstone had said that Ted needed his marching orders, she made her way down the back stairs to the room that had once been Mrs Appleby's office and, now that Mrs Appleby was an invalid, was accepted as being her office. For the last few months she and Ted had been 'walking out'. To 'walk out' with anyone had not been an easy decision for Carrie. Ever since Gilbert had taken her to the House of Lords four years ago, she had known she was in love with him – and that it was a hopeless love.

Not long after her trip to London, Ted had asked her if she would like to spend one of her days off with him. 'I have a motorbike and side-car,' he'd said. 'We could spend the day at Knaresborough. Visit Old Mother Shipton's Cave.'

She had turned the offer down and, because she liked him, had done so being careful not to hurt his feelings.

When her next day off had been due, he'd made a similar offer, this time suggesting they go to a race meeting at Richmond. Again Carrie had turned the offer down – though this time with more reluctance, as she had never been to a race meeting and was certain it would have been good fun.

Just when she thought he was never going to ask her out again, he had done so, and this time, after a lot of thought, she had said yes. She was, after all, twenty-seven years old. Nothing could come of her feelings for Gilbert. That being the case, if she wanted to marry and have children – and she did – then she had to begin accepting offers such as the ones Ted was making. She already liked and respected him and perhaps, if she was very, very lucky, from liking and respect, love would grow.

Although it had done so on his part, it hadn't done so on hers, but it had grown into deep affection, and she hadn't liked hearing General Elphinstone malign Ted – especially when the remark had been so nonsensically unfair.

There was a knock on her door and Cissie Calthrop, Lady Markham's lady's maid, entered the room. 'Sorry to disturb you, Carrie, but the new tweeny has been found in the scullery in floods of tears. Apparently it's not the first time. No one in the kitchen thought it was serious enough for you to be told about it, but the girl looks more than unhappy to me. She looks ill. I just thought you ought to know.'

'Thanks, Cissie.'

Cissie was nearer to being a friend than anyone else at Monkswood, and Carrie trusted her judgement. As Cissie went briskly on her way, Carrie left the room in search of Tilly Armstrong, Monkswood's fifteen-year-old tweeny.

'I'd like to speak to you in my office, Tilly,' she said, when she found her. 'You're not in trouble, so please don't look so worried.'

'No, Mrs Thornton. Yes, Mrs Thornton,' Tilly said, looking absolutely terrified.

Carrie was accustomed to receiving respect from the staff she oversaw, but she was unused to inspiring terror – and didn't like the sensation of having done so.

Once the two of them were in her office she asked for tea to be sent in and then said gently, 'I understand you've been found crying, Tilly. Are you unhappy at Monkswood?'

'No, Mrs Thornton. Yes, Mrs Thornton. Only I wouldn't be, if it wasn't for ... if it wasn't for...' Tears poured down her cheeks.

'Is it the work? Do you not like being a tweeny?'

Tilly knuckled her tears away and, as fresh tears replaced them, said, 'It isn't the work, Mrs Thornton.'

'Then is everything all right at home, Tilly?'

Tilly nodded vehemently. 'Oh yes, Mrs Thornton. Mam and Dad are proud as Punch at my having a place here.'

'And you're not ill? You're not feeling poorly?'

This time Tilly gave an energetic shake of her head.

Carrie bit her bottom lip, unable to think of what else could possibly be causing Tilly so much distress. In the end she said, 'I was a tweeny here once, Tilly. Although I was often lonely, being away from my granny and from my friends, I was never unhappy in the way you are unhappy, and I would like to make things all right for you if I can. No matter what it is, I can promise you that if you tell me, you won't get in trouble for having done so.'

Tilly stopped crying and stared at her with hope in her eyes. 'Do you really mean that, Mrs Thornton? Because he said ... he said...'

Seized by a sudden dark suspicion, Carrie took Tilly's hands in hers. 'Is someone making you do things you don't want to do, Tilly? Is someone bullying you?'

Tilly's hands tightened on Carrie's. 'Yes,' she whispered. 'It's Wilf Preen, Mrs Thornton. Whenever I have to pass him in a corridor and if no one is there to see, he touches me where he shouldn't. And he said that if I told anyone, he'd tell everyone I'd let him do worse things than that to me, and if my mam and dad thought I'd done those things with him, it would kill them, Mrs Thornton.' She began crying again, tears dripping onto her starched white apron.

It was rare that Carrie was angry, but now anger flooded every vein in her body.

She rose to her feet. 'I want you to stay in my room until I return, Tilly – and I want you to stop crying and to stop being afraid. Wilf is never going to touch you again, and he most certainly isn't going to spread lies about you to anyone.'

Then, with a white, set expression on her small pointed face, she set off to find Mr Briggs.

Fifteen minutes later Mr Briggs, who had charge of the male staff at Monkswood just as she, on behalf of Mrs Appleby, had charge of the female staff, stared at her in great discomfiture.

'I will severely reprimand Wilf, Mrs Thornton. I quite agree that it is reprehensible behaviour on his part and–'

'Far too reprehensible to be dealt with by a mere reprimand, Mr Briggs,' Carrie said, interrupting him. 'Wilf is twenty-four years old, six foot four and as well built as a wrestler. Tilly is fifteen and weighs no more than a feather. He not only forced his attentions on her...'

'Surely just a little horse-play, Mrs Thornton?'

'...he blackmailed her. And if you regard as horse-play his touching her where no girl should be touched against her will, then you are very, very wrong, Mr Briggs. If you are not willing to fire Wilf, then I will have no option but to go over your head and explain the situation, and your reluctance to take action, to Lady Markham.'

Briggs blanched. Lady Markham had a soft spot for Carrie, and he rather thought she would view Wilf's behaviour with Tilly in exactly the same light as Carrie did. If that happened, his reluctance to take instant action would reflect badly on him. All of which meant that he was going to have to fire Wilf, and be a footman short until a replacement was found.

'If that's your judgement on the situation, Mrs Thornton,' he said stiffly, hating having to give way to a housekeeper young enough to be his

419

daughter, 'then of course I will take the action you recommend.'

'Thank you, Mr Briggs.' Carrie gave him a smile that went a long way to soothing his feelings. 'Hopefully this will be a lesson to Wilf, and we won't now have to worry about him treating other members of the female staff in the same offensive, bullying manner that he treated Tilly.'

Later that evening, after the formal dinner was over and Carrie could at last relax, Ted put his head around her office door, as she had known he would.

'Fancy a late-night stroll?' he asked. 'It's a lovely clear night.'

Late-night strolls together, well away from the house, were something they often discreetly indulged in.

Fifteen minutes later they were skirting the wood at the edge of Monkswood's parkland, Ted's black Labrador at their heels.

'Was it a good shoot today?' she asked, her hands deep in her coat pockets for warmth.

'Yes – apart from General Elphinstone's mishap.' Ted grinned. 'The man created as if he'd broken his leg. How he managed at Passchendaele I can't imagine.'

'I don't think generals were ever in the front line.'

Ted, who had been eight when the Great War had broken out and so had missed his chance of fighting in it, grinned. 'That's the gossip, Carrie. And even if they were, I don't think Elphinstone would have been among their number.'

He lifted her gloved, hand out of her pocket, interlocking her fingers with his. 'Lord Rochdale's offered me the job of head-keeper at his estate near Fylingdales. His shooting parties are far bigger than any held here. On a Rochdale shoot it's not unusual to have a hundred beaters out at a time.' He stopped walking, turning her to face him. 'There's a grand house goes with the job and it would be perfect for us, Carrie. All I need to know, before I accept the offer, is that you'll finally consent to marry me and come with me.'

All the welcome relaxation Carrie had been feeling ebbed away. She'd had a long day and gently telling Ted, yet again, that she wasn't ready to marry him, was not the way she had wanted to end it.

'I love you, Carrie,' he said fiercely. 'We'd be grand together, and when it comes to marriage, we're both of us nearing thirty – me being a bit nearer to it than you. If we want to have bairns, we need to be getting a move on.'

She looked up into his attractive, homely face and knew that as she couldn't envisage a time when they could be moving on together, it was time she told him so with utter finality, so that he could begin walking out with some other young woman: one who would love him in the way he deserved to be loved.

'I'm honoured that you want to marry me, Ted,' she said gently, 'but I've always meant it when I've said I'm not ready for marriage – and I never will be.'

'But why, Carrie love?'

He looked so mystified and disappointed that her heart hurt.

'Because for as long as I can remember I've only been ready for marriage with someone else, Ted. Someone who doesn't know I love him and who, even if he did know, couldn't love me back because he's not in a position to.'

Ted stared down at her, thunderstruck. 'Are you telling me you love someone who's married?'

She nodded. It was the first time she had admitted it to anyone and tears sprang to the backs of her eyes as she said, 'Yes, Ted. And I love him far too much ever to be able to love someone else in the same way.'

Chapter Twenty-Eight

In a Morgan sports car Thea drove from London to Fort Belvedere with mixed feelings. Generally the people Prince Edward surrounded himself with on his weekends there were not the kind of people she was much interested in, but he had been insistent that she spend some quality time with the woman around whom his world now revolved. 'Wallis is the most wonderful woman, Thea,' he had said enthusiastically. 'And as you like Americans just as much as I do, I know the two of you will get along famously.'

The 'like Americans just as much as he did' was a direct reference to Roz, and an even more direct reference to Thea's on-off affair with Kyle.

Edward had met Kyle several times and, a little over a year ago, when her affair with him had been going through one of its 'on' periods, they had spent a weekend at the Fort together in the company of Elizabeth and Bertie, Lady Cunard, Mr Esmond Harmsworth and Mr and Mrs Anthony Eden.

Lady Cunard was a society hostess, Esmond Harmsworth was a newspaper magnate, and Anthony Eden was a government minister. That Wallis Simpson and her husband, Ernest, had been absent from the party had only been because Wallis had been visiting family in Baltimore.

The little three-wheeled Morgan went like a rocket and Thea, suitably dressed in warm tweeds, headscarf, goggles and gauntleted leather gloves, liked driving fast.

As she left London behind her and began speeding through countryside full of the autumn tints of red and gold, she wondered who, apart from Wallis and Ernest, her fellow guests would be this time. Edward hadn't mentioned Kyle, but she wouldn't put it past him to have invited Kyle, even though he knew they hadn't been seeing each other for several months and that Kyle was presently squiring a blonde debutante around town.

For a fleeting moment she wondered if Edward might have invited Kyle *and* his blonde. She dismissed the idea as soon as it entered her head. Edward wasn't mischievous and, when he thought of Kyle, she knew he only did so in relation to herself – as did all her friends.

It was her fault, of course. If, when she and Kyle had been going through a period of not seeing each other, she had taken up with someone else, her friends would long ago have stopped thinking of them as a long-term couple.

Her problem was that although she had a lot of male friends, with none of them had she ever wanted to change friendship into romance. If she couldn't have Hal, then she only wanted Kyle. And Kyle wanted marriage, and she simply couldn't make that commitment; not when she still loved Hal so deeply that it was like a stab to her heart whenever she saw him.

She changed gear, wondering if things would have been different if, over the last ten years, Hal had married. Would she then have been able to draw a line under her love for him and move on with her life? Was it because he was still very firmly a bachelor that she still lived in a world of hope?

There were woods on either side of the road and she slowed down, eased the Morgan off the road and came to a halt. Taking off her gloves, she lit a cigarette, aware that if Hal had married Carrie, no line would ever have been drawn; instead, things would have been much worse.

But Hal hadn't married Carrie. He hadn't married anybody.

From a nearby tree a scattering of bronze leaves fell into her lap. Automatically she brushed them away. Was the reason Hal never formed a serious relationship with any of his long line of girlfriends because, deep down, he was still in love with her? Or was it because he wasn't capable of long-term

424

emotional attachment to anyone, including her? It was a conundrum she had no answer for.

She glanced down at her watch. She was only fifteen minutes away from the Fort and, not knowing if Kyle would be waiting for her when she got there and not knowing how she felt about that, she was in no hurry to arrive.

Still with a cigarette in her hand, she stepped out of the Morgan. A short trudge in Gorton's woodland nearly always cleared her head. Hopefully a short trudge in the Surrey woodland would be no different.

She was wearing the sensible brogues she always wore for driving, and leaves crunched thickly beneath her feet as she wondered in all seriousness if, in affairs of the heart, she was suffering from some kind of genetic flaw and, if she was, if Roz suffered from it as well.

It was little over a year ago now since Roz had ended her affair with Max, and although Barty Luddesdon was often Roz's escort when she was in London, there was no hint that wedding bells would ever ring for them.

Just as she couldn't get over Hal and put him firmly in her past, so Roz was clearly incapable of doing the same thing where Max was concerned. In society's eyes, both of them were on the shelf – and needlessly so, for Barty would, she was sure, have happily married Roz, just as Kyle would, given the chance, happily marry her.

Of their childhood circle of five, only Olivia was married, and her marriage was flawed by her unhappiness at still being childless.

She dropped her cigarette to the ground and

crushed it beneath her foot. Plunging her hands deep in the pockets of her coat, she began making her way back to her car, wondering what Blanche would have thought of their lives. Would the relationships between herself, Olivia and Violet have been smoother if Blanche were still alive? Her mother had always kept the peace between them and would, she was sure, have still been doing so. She wondered what her mother's advice would have been where Kyle was concerned. Would she have advised Thea to marry him? And what would Blanche have thought of her beloved husband's marriage to Zephiniah?

Knowing her mother as she had, Thea knew she would have wanted Gilbert to marry again and to be happy. A foreknowledge that his second marriage would bring him deep unhappiness – unhappiness that he so unsuccessfully tried to hide – would have broken her mother's heart.

What had gone wrong within her father's marriage to Zephiniah she didn't know. In the early days Zephiniah had clearly relished her title of Viscountess Fenton and had seemed as eager as Gilbert that they would have a son who would carry on the Fenton family name and title. Then had come her long – and frequent – solo trips to European health spas.

That she, Olivia and Roz suspected Zephiniah of having a lover – or even several lovers – when she was not in London or at Gorton was something they hadn't spoken of to Carrie. Carrie was deeply fond of their father and they had known how the thought of his unhappiness would distress her. Carrie, though, had come to the same

426

suspicion via servant gossip at Monkswood.

'I'm not sure how to say this,' she had said when, on one of Olivia's trips home from Berlin, the three of them had met up on the banks of the river, by the vole place, 'but there's unkind gossip at Monkswood about your stepmother.'

'There's unkind gossip about our very own wicked witch all over the place,' Olivia had said dismissively. 'Unfortunately, I think most of it is true.'

'Is it about men, Carrie?' Thea had asked bluntly.

Carrie had nodded, her eyes deeply troubled. 'The sister of one of Monkswood's footmen is Gorton's parlourmaid. She's told him Lady Fenton often holds house-parties at Gorton when Parliament is sitting and your father is in London.'

Olivia had rolled over onto her back in the deep grass. 'Well, there's nothing too dreadful about that,' she had said fairly.

'Though other guests vary, there is one gentleman who is invited to every house-party,' Carrie had continued unhappily. 'He's a friend of your stepmother's from her days in Argentina. His name is Mr Di Stéfano.'

'If Monkswood's servants are only linking her name to one man, it's probably something to be grateful for.' Thea had known she was being nasty, but had been unable to help it.

Carrie had bitten her lip. 'It's not only the servants who are talking, Thea. Lady Markham likes gossip, and when her lady's maid told her how Lady Fenton's name was being linked to that of Mr Di Stéfano, she said she'd heard similar gossip when she'd last been in Aix-les-Bains. Of course,' she added hastily, 'that doesn't mean the gossip is true. Lady Markham was such a close friend of your mother that, in her eyes, no one could be good enough to fill her place and so she's always been willing to believe the worst about your stepmother.'

'The worst is probably true,' Olivia had said, her eyes filling with sudden tears. 'But whether Zephiniah is being unfaithful to Papa or she isn't, and whether he knows about it or he doesn't, there's nothing we can do about it. Can you imagine his dear, kind face if we told him of what was being said?'

All three of them had been able to imagine all too well.

It had been Carrie who had ended their conversation. With her face set and pale, she had said fiercely, 'I hope you're wrong, Olivia. I hope everyone is wrong, because if anyone deserves to be happy it's your father.' And she had turned away quickly before they should see the expression in her eyes and correctly read the reason for the searing depth of her feelings.

Thea opened the Morgan's low-slung door and slid behind the wheel. Brooding over things she had no control over was of no use whatsoever. Her life was as full as she could possibly make it without Hal being in it, or, at the moment, Kyle.

For the past few months she had been heavily involved in the running of the Feathers Clubs, a project close to Prince Edward's heart. With his sincere and deep concern for his father's un-employed subjects, he had suggested the setting up of clubs that would offer men on the dole some kind of social life. The name of the clubs came from the three feathers on his heraldic badge as heir apparent, and the person who had put his scheme into action was the woman who had been his first long-term mistress, Freda Dudley Ward.

Thea, always looking for active ways to put her socialism into practice, had become Freda's right-hand helper. Her long-term ambition, though, was to stand as a Labour Party parlia-mentary candidate. One thing in her favour was that she was a fiery and fearless public speaker. The things not in her favour were legion. Top of the list – apart from the fact that she was a woman – was that she wasn't, and never had been, a trade-union leader; she had never chaired her local Labour Party; she wasn't a local Labour Party councillor; she didn't come from a work-ing-class background; she didn't have a univer-sity degree. The list of reasons why her standing for Parliament was a pipe-dream was endless. Thea didn't care. In her mindset, obstacles were there to be overcome – and, one by one, she was determined to overcome them.

She put the Morgan into gear and spun back out onto the road. Very soon she was in Windsor Great Park and Fort Belvedere's turrets peeped above the trees. All she had to think about now was Kyle. Would he be there, or would he not? And if he was there, was she going to maintain the standoff of the last few months?

429

Kyle stood back from the bonfire of burning leaves, his eyes smarting. Edward was well known for being able to find things to do in the Fort's gardens at any time of year, but he'd thought that on a late afternoon in October even Edward would have given his gardening passion a rest. Unwisely he had arrived at the Fort a little early, rather than a little late, and Edward had immediately pounced on him.

'Jolly good show. An extra pair of hands is just what I need,' he had said cheerily. 'I'm just about to do a bit of leaf-burning. Change into something suitable and join me. There's a good chap.'

A royal command – even a royal command coming from a boyishly slight figure dressed in well-worn tweeds and with a pitchfork in one hand – was not to be ignored. Kyle had done as he'd been bidden and now the two of them were taking it in turns to fork piled-up dead leaves onto a slow-burning, pungent-smelling fire.

'George and Marina are going to be with us this weekend,' Edward said. 'Dickie and Edwina, Fruity and Baba, Chips. Have you met Chips?'

There was only one Chips in British high society, and that was a fellow American, Chips Channon. Though they had never met before at the Fort, Kyle knew him well. He had also met Edward's younger brother, Prince George, though not George's recently acquired fiancée, Princess Marina of Greece. Neither had he met Fruity Metcalfe and his wife, though he knew of them by reputation, and everything he had heard indicated they would be easy, amusing company. Dickie and

Edwina Mountbatten he had met previously, though never when they had been together. Ernest Simpson's name was conspicuously absent from the guest list, and Wallis was more the Fort's permanent hostess than she was a guest.

The other name missing from the list, and the one that was causing Kyle crushing disappointment, was Thea's. Just as he was wondering why he had been invited, if Thea hadn't, Edward closed a fair-lashed eye in a naughty wink. 'Forgot to mention that Thea should be arriving at any time. Wallis likes her.' He forked more leaves onto the fire. 'She says Thea is the only blunt-talking, non-prevaricating, straight-to-the-point Englishwoman she's yet met.'

Kyle laughed. Where Wallis and Thea were concerned it was, he felt, a question of like being attracted to like. They both possessed the same kind of vitality, forthrightness and frankness of speech.

One of Edward's two small terriers came trotting up to join them and Edward bent down and scratched the back of its head, saying as he did so, 'Like Wallis, you're an American. What d'you think your government would make of it if, when I become King, I make Wallis my queen?'

Kyle was about to laugh at what he thought was a joke, but something in the tone of Edward's voice stopped him.

He said, uncertain as to whether or not he was going to make a fool of himself by having taken the question seriously, 'But that couldn't happen, sir. Could it?'

Edward stared broodingly into the bonfire of

dead leaves. 'I love Wallis,' he said. 'I'm going to marry her – and in English law a wife takes the title of her husband.'

Kyle stared at him. As an American, his knowledge of British constitutional law was sketchy, but he knew enough to know that no divorced woman had ever been Queen of England – or was ever likely to become a Queen of England.

As if reading Kyle's mind, Edward said, 'Nothing can happen – except perhaps Wallis's divorce from Ernest – until my father dies. Under the provisions of the Royal Marriages Act, marriages of Princes of the Blood Royal are under the Sovereign's control and – ultimately – Parliament's. So you see, a veto power over my choice of a wife rests with my father. And because of the divorce thing – and perhaps also because of her being American – my father will never give his consent.'

Kyle wondered if he should point out to Edward that where the 'divorce thing' was concerned, Wallis would – if she and Ernest divorced – have been twice divorced, for in order to marry Ernest, Wallis had had to divorce an American naval pilot, E. Winfield Spencer.

As Edward made no attempt to put further leaves on the smouldering, charred pile in front of them, Kyle thought of another major barrier to Edward's dream of marital bliss with Wallis. When he became King, Edward would also become titular Head of the Church of England. And the Church of England didn't recognize divorce. With such an obstacle in his path, even his father's death wouldn't be enough to enable

Edward to marry Wallis. He was simply never going to be able to marry her. Not ever.

As, with the terrier skittering around their heels, they began making their way back to the house, it occurred to Kyle that he and Prince Edward had something in common. Both of them were deeply in love and, for both of them, a happy outcome to that love was distinctly remote.

Other cars had now arrived. Parked on the gravel beside his own car was a plum-coloured Riley. A few yards further away was a Bentley Silver Goddess and, a little apart from them, Thea's distinctive little green Morgan.

Kyle felt his heart tighten. Whenever he and Thea had been going through an 'off' period, the first few seconds of any meeting were always crucial, because he could instantly tell by her manner if there was any hope of a passionate reconciliation.

'His Royal Highness and Princess Marina are in the drawing room, as is Mrs Simpson, sir,' Edward's butler said to him as they entered an octagonal hall with stark white walls, a floor of black and white marble and with yellow leather upholstered chairs in each of its eight corners. 'Mr and Mrs Metcalfe are with them. Miss Fenton arrived some minutes ago and has been shown to her room. Lord Louis and Lady Edwina are yet to arrive.'

Edward nodded his thanks and, despite having come in straight from the garden and smelling of wood-smoke, bolted straight for the drawing room to greet his brother, Princess Marina and the woman he found it so hard to be apart from,

433

even for a second.

Not being royal, and not being able to be so careless about the smell of wood-smoke clinging to him, Kyle headed straight for his first-floor bedroom. The valet he had been allocated was waiting for him and, aware of what Kyle's occupation had been for the past hour, had already run a deep, hot bath for him.

Swiftly Kyle shed his clothes and sank gratefully into it. Then he leaned back, closed his eyes and thought of Thea.

The second he'd met her, on the doorstep of the Fenton town house when he had first come to London, he had been instantly smitten. Being Roz's stepbrother, and therefore extended family, he had automatically seen a lot of her even before they had begun dating. Everything he had come to know about her – her fierce social conscience, her shining honesty, her refusal to back down from any stand once she had taken it – he had liked and admired.

In the early days of their courtship it had never occurred to him that it was the qualities he admired in her, far more than it was her infatuation with Hal Crosby, that would be the stumbling block to their happiness.

Hal Crosby was someone Kyle was certain that, once they were married, Thea would soon have put firmly in her past. When he had told her so – when he had said that he didn't give a rap for whatever feelings she thought she still entertained for Hal and that he wanted to marry her, those feelings notwithstanding – she had been deeply shocked.

'But that wouldn't be an honest thing to do!' she had said, her green cat-eyes widening. 'I can't stand in front of an altar and make sacred promises to you, when we both know how I feel about Hal!'

'Then we'll get married in a register office,' he had said, struggling for patience.

'You don't take any of this seriously, do you?' She had hurled the words at him. 'You certainly don't take my feelings for Hal seriously.'

'Why should I?' He had barely been able to resist the urge to give her a good shake. 'He was a childhood sweetheart who, for one year, at the most two, was something more when you were a teenager. Whatever that something more was, you've told me yourself it was a typical first love that didn't go far beyond hugs and kisses. You didn't lose your virginity to him in his father's hay loft, or down on the banks of the Swale. And by the time you were eighteen – and on your eighteenth birthday – it was all over.'

She'd been about to shout something hurtful at him, but he hadn't given her the chance.

'It was all over, Thea, because Hal could see what you still can't. He could see that the two of you came from entirely different worlds, and that if you had spent time living with each other for even a couple of weeks you'd probably have fought like wild cats or been bored to death with each other.'

'Never!' she had shouted back at him. 'Never! Never! *Never!*'

It had been a long time before things had got back to normal after that little scene.

435

He was, however, convinced he was right. Because she had spent so much time in Hal's company as a child, Thea thought she knew him. She had never, though, spent any time with him in company other than Olivia, Carrie and Roz, and she had never spent time with him anywhere else but at Gorton – and even at Gorton they hadn't spent time in each other's homes. He doubted if Thea had even seen the inside of the Crosbys' tied farmhouse and, though Kyle knew Thea's father had no objection at all to Thea's friendship with the son of one of his tenant farmers, Hal had never been treated as one of the family at Gorton Hall in the same way that, until Lord Fenton's second marriage, Carrie had.

Being Thea, she had done the typical Thea thing of taking a stand – this particular stand being that Hal was her first love and therefore her only real love – and sticking to the conviction through thick and thin.

Not for the first time he found himself wishing that Hal had deflowered her on the night of her birthday ball. Thea would then have expected far more commitment from Hal than he would have been prepared to give, and she would soon have stopped viewing him through rose-tinted glasses and seen him for the person he really was: a man with a great deal of cheeky charm who was also a natural loner, and always would be.

Kyle heaved himself out of the bath and wrapped a generous-sized towel around his waist. What were the next few hours going to bring, where he and Thea were concerned? Was it time he, too, stopped being hopeful and moved on? In so many ways it would make sense. He had been in London far longer than he could ever have hoped for, and it couldn't be long now before he was posted somewhere else, quite possibly somewhere on the other side of the world. A diplomat was automatically accompanied by his wife, but that wouldn't work with Thea unless she abandoned her intention of becoming a Labour Party parliamentary candidate. No marriage could work if the husband was resident in one country and the wife in another. Then there was her unflinching honesty, which in the tricky social milieu in which a diplomat's wife moved would far often be more of a handicap than a help.

Unlike Olivia, who saw her role in life totally in terms of being everything a diplomat's wife should be, who was charm personified to absolutely everyone – no matter how boring they might be – and who was always a picture of sophisticated elegance, Thea never hid her feelings, and high fashion was unimportant to her.

His clothes had been laid out for him and he began to dress, reflecting that, all in all, Thea had few qualifications for being the wife of an ambitious American diplomat. It made no difference. His wife was what he was determined she would one day become.

What other option was there when, no matter how often the thought of moving on popped into his head, when it came down to taking action he simply couldn't do it?

None of the far more suitable women he dated whenever the two of them were going through an 'off' period amused, exasperated or excited him as Thea did. In comparison to her, they simply paled into insignificance. There was no rhyme or reason where love was concerned – and he loved Thea. It was as straightforward and as simple as that. Though she would be appalled at the thought that she sometimes needed protection, he wanted to protect her. Wherever he was posted in the world, wherever his career led him, he wanted her by his side. He was bound to her with hoops of steel and there was not a darned thing he could do about it.

He gave a last look in the cheval-glass, adjusted his bow-tie and smoothed a hand over blue-black hair that was already glossily sleek. All he had to do was make her see that what the two of them shared was something deep and true that would last lifelong, and what she had experienced with Hal had simply been an extension of her child-hood; that, precious as it had been, it belonged in the past and that even if events on the night of her birthday ball had been different, her romance with Hal would never have survived into the present.

He grinned wryly. Set out like that, it was a simple enough task, and he left the room deter-mined that, with an entire weekend at the Fort in front of him, this time he would achieve success.

When he entered the drawing room it was to find all his fellow guests, apart from Dickie and Edwina, already gathered there. Thea was seated on a sofa deep in animated conversation with Wallis. Both of them had a glass of whiskey and soda in their hands. Fruity Metcalfe and Chips Channon were over by the French windows, chuckling at something Princess Marina was saying to them. Baba Metcalfe and Prince George were seated by the fire with cocktails and a half-finished jigsaw on a low table in front of them. There was no sign of their host, who was presumably still steaming in a hot bath.

'Nice seeing you again, Anderson,' Prince George said, looking up from the jigsaw. 'Baba and I could do with a bit if help here. I swear this damned puzzle has been waiting to be finished for over a month.'

Without pausing in her conversation with Wallis, and without indicating that he was welcome to join them, Thea raised her eyes to Kyle's. He lifted an eyebrow queryingly. She shot him a look that told him they were going to be 'on' again and, with vast relief, he strolled across to join Prince George and Baba.

Half an hour later, when Dickie, Edwina and their host had joined them and they were all making their way from the drawing room to the dining room, he whispered, 'You should always wear shot-silk taffeta, Thea. You look ravishing!'

This time it was her turn to quirk an eyebrow. 'You don't think it would suit a blonde better?'

'No,' he said, with the amusement she always aroused in him. 'And I'm no longer on any kind of terms with a blonde. Blondes bore me.'

Their little tête-à-tête was interrupted by Baba, who said in a low undertone, 'David's wearing his kilt. It means we'll be enduring the pipes ritual after dinner.'

Kyle shuddered. He found the sound of bagpipes agonizing even when they were being played by experienced pipers. What they would sound like when played by the Prince he couldn't even begin to imagine. As they entered the dining room he saw Thea's full-lipped mouth tug into a wide grin and knew she'd read his reaction perfectly.

The table seating ensured they could have no more privately snatched words together. Princess Marina was seated on Kyle's left, Edwina on his right. Thea was diagonally across from him on the other side of the table, seated between Fruity Metcalfe and Chips Channon.

Over a first course of oysters the conversation turned almost immediately, as it always did when Edwina and Dickie were present, to Hollywood stars and Hollywood movies.

'Why has your sister abandoned Hollywood for Berlin?' Edwina demanded of Thea, in her habitually abrupt manner. 'Charlie thinks she'd make a perfect gamine.'

Everyone around the table knew that 'Charlie' was the Mountbattens' good friend, Charlie Chaplin.

'Violet only does talkies,' Thea said, 'and so far Charlie hasn't made one. Besides, I'm not sure Violet would relish playing the part of one of Charlie's lost little urchins. She's more of a Sheba and Cleopatra type of girl.'

'I wouldn't have thought there'd be much demand for a Sheba/Cleopatra type in Hitler's new Nazi Germany,' Wallis rasped tartly, to much laughter.

The conversation moved from Violet to Rozalind who, with the exception of Princess Marina, everyone knew, and of the splendid photographs she had taken of the Yorks and their children, and of how she was now in Spain photographing the civil unrest taking place there.

Kyle listened with only half an ear, unable to draw his attention away from Wallis. For the mistress of a man who was heir to the greatest throne in the world, she was not only middle-aged – somewhere in her late-thirties – but was also remarkably plain. Whippet-thin, her hair-style severe, her only claim to beauty was her eyes, which were a remarkable violet-blue. If other people couldn't see what attracted Edward to her, Kyle could. Quite simply, because she was an American, Wallis didn't treat Edward with stultifying deference. She dared to disagree with him. She even teased him. It was obvious to Kyle that Edward loved her forthright manner, sheer vitality and the way she so easily made him laugh. She was making him laugh now, saying in a southern drawl to something he had asked of her, 'Of course I will. God willing and the creek don't rise!'

Her head was tilted towards Edward's and the emeralds in her ears and at her throat caught in the candlelight. Jewels of such sumptuous size and quality couldn't possibly have been bought for her by her husband, and he wondered how Ernest felt at his wife being given such gifts. He also wondered if the Simpsons had the remotest idea that Edward was fantasizing about them divorcing one day so that, when his father died, he could marry Wallis.

By now roast beef, with all its trimmings, had

441

followed the oysters, and a sweet had followed the roast beef. Kyle looked down at his watch, trying to estimate how much longer it would be before the evening came to a close and everyone retired to bed.

Not that he would be retiring to his own bed, and neither would he be reduced to corridor-creeping. When a couple were known to be having an affair their bedrooms were always thoughtfully allocated close to each other. His bedroom and Thea's would, he knew, be adjoining.

As white-gloved footmen served a savoury, he looked down the length of the candlelit table towards her. Whereas every other woman in the room was boasting sleek Marcel waves, Thea's curly, chestnut hair was as short and boyish as when she had first had it bobbed a decade ago. It should have made her look a lot less chic than the women seated so close to her, but it didn't. It merely made her look distinctively natural, and distinctively different.

He wanted to take her in his arms so badly it was a physical pain.

Once again he looked down at his watch. The meal was coming to a close, but after it there would be coffee in the drawing room and, if his previous weekend at the Fort was anything to go by, cards for those who wanted to play followed by late-night dancing to records.

He smiled at something Princess Marina had said to him, mentally calculating that it would be another three hours at least before he and Thea would at last be alone. Somehow he would get through the evening and, when he had, when he

442

and Thea were again in each other's arms, he would ask her – for the third time – if she would marry him, his reasoning being that there could be no better place for another shot at a proposal than a royal residence.

Having come to such a major decision, he felt almost buoyant.

The moment was fleeting.

'Let me,' his host said, rising eagerly to his feet, 'play a little tune on the bagpipes that I composed myself.'

Chapter Twenty-Nine

NOVEMBER 1935

'And so I th-thought, what better place for the weekend than G-Gorton Hall.'

Gilbert was at Mount Street, and the person he had answered the telephone to was the Duke of York.

'This summer's Jubilee celebrations have quite taken it out of Elizabeth and she is v-very under the weather,' Bertie continued. 'She's always wanted to visit Gorton and so I thought we would propose ourselves this coming weekend. No need for f-fancy arrangements, old chap. No other guests, you know. Just a quiet weekend *en famille*. Elizabeth is so fond of your girls.'

Gilbert said goodbye to him, his mind racing. The first difficulty was that he was in London, not

443

Yorkshire, and Parliament was sitting. Other difficulties came thick and fast. Zephiniah was in Aix-
les-Bains. Thea was in London, thank God, but
Olivia was in Berlin. And Violet... Usually quite
imperturbable, Gilbert ran a hand distractedly
through his hair. Violet could be anywhere, but
was most likely in Berlin. Wherever she was, the
chances of his contacting her were so remote as to
be negligible.

There was one thing he could accomplish immediately and that was to notify his household
staff at Gorton that the Duke and Duchess of
York would be staying over the weekend, as
would the family.

He picked up the telephone receiver again and
began making phone calls. It was a time-consuming task. Gorton could only be reached via
three different telephone exchanges and, when
he finally spoke to Mrs Huntley, Gorton's latest
housekeeper – under Zephiniah's reign few
members of the domestic staff stayed at Gorton
for long – she sounded anything but confident at
the prospect of having the house ready at such
short notice for royal guests.

Next he tried to contact Zephiniah. If a telephone connection to Yorkshire had been time-
consuming, the connection to Aix-les-Bains was
a nightmare. When he finally got through to the
hotel that he understood Zephiniah to be staying
at, it was to discover she wasn't a guest there. He
severed the connection, tight-lipped.

That his marriage had deteriorated to the point
where he didn't even know his wife's where-
abouts was a matter of deep shame to him –

444

shame because he cared so little about where she was and who her companions were, when she was out of the country. He had married her as a young fool of a boy might have married: out of lust, not love. Whether she had ever loved him was something he very much doubted.

The sham that his marriage had become wasn't something that could be paraded in front of the Yorks, and it wouldn't be, for he had no intention of denying Zephiniah the heady pleasure she would take in finally having royal guests beneath Gorton's roof.

Pausing only long enough to pour himself a stiff whiskey, he embarked on the long drawn-out process of contacting International Enquiries and obtaining the telephone numbers of all the hotels in Aix-les-Bains; then he embarked on the even longer process of telephoning them.

When he eventually tracked her down, Zephiniah went through the pretence of being apologetic that she hadn't let him know she'd changed hotels. He cut her short, saying merely, 'The Yorks have proposed themselves for this coming weekend. I'm assuming you will be with me at Gorton to greet them.'

'Good God! Whyever...? But of course I'll be there! But who else are we going to be able to invite at such short notice? Would the Baldwins, d'you think? Or the Coopers?'

'Bertie has expressly asked that the weekend is family only. Elizabeth is what he describes as being "under the weather". She wants rest, not entertainment.'

Despite her elation at finally having royalty beneath her roof, Zephiniah couldn't help being waspish. 'Then he's certainly chosen the right place for her,' was the last thing he heard her say before their connection, through no fault of either of them, was abruptly severed.

'How exciting!' Olivia said when, over a lot of static, he told her that Bertie and Elizabeth were to be guests at Gorton that weekend. 'We'll both be there, Papa. It's so helpful to Dieter's career to be able to converse with members of our royal family on casual, intimate terms. Dieter's friend, Ulrich von Ribbentrop, will be delighted. He's to take over as Germany's ambassador to Great Britain in a few months' time.' A little giggle of happy anticipation came over the line. 'With luck, Dieter will eventually step into his shoes.'

With very mixed feelings Gilbert gave her his love and said goodbye. Ribbentrop was a businessman who often visited London and Gilbert had met him a couple of times, though only at large functions where he'd done no more than exchange a few polite words with him. Unlike most of the men who found favour with the Führer, Ribbentrop was a sophisticated man with excellent English and Gilbert was aware that Hitler had made a good choice. Ribbentrop would fit seamlessly into British high-society circles – and always, of course, with his ear to the ground.

That his son-in-law would also have his ear to the ground was something he was also painfully aware of anything beneficial obtained by Hitler's rise to power as German's leader – the reduction of unemployment, the curbing of communism – had long since been overshadowed by his obvious determination to plunge the world into another war. Only a day ago the Führer had declared that all men between the ages of eighteen and forty-five were to be called up as army reservists and, in typical crackpot fashion, that non-belief in Nazism was now to be grounds for divorce.

In the many private conversations Gilbert had had with his son-in-law, Dieter had clung fiercely to his belief that over and above the anti-Semitic laws that had been brought into place – and which Dieter believed were not of any real importance – Hitler's greatness was in the way he was making Germans proud to be German again.

In the early days of their conversations Gilbert had been able to sympathize with Dieter's resentment at the Versailles Treaty. What he wasn't able to sympathize with was the way in which Hitler was defiantly breaking it. He had broken the clause about non-rearmament, increasing the size of his armed forces and creating an air force. Defensively Dieter had stressed that in all of Hitler's speeches he proclaimed a desire for peace and spoke of the folly of war. Gilbert, a good judge of men, had believed Dieter sincere in his opinion that Hitler wasn't a warmonger, but he didn't share it, and it grieved him that not only Dieter, but Olivia too, should be so blind.

He poured himself another whiskey, reassured by the knowledge that Dieter was unlikely to overhear anything from Bertie and Elizabeth that it would be better he didn't. Neither of the Yorks was political. The weekend was going to be exactly as Bertie wished it to be. A jolly, friendly, unpretentious, restful weekend *en famille* – or at least it would be, if he could rustle up enough members of his family.

'How sensible of Bertie to think of Gorton as a restful weekend haven,' Thea said, when she came home from her stint at the East End club for boys that she helped to run. She pulled a hat damp with rain from off her turbulent hair. 'However, I'm afraid I won't be part of the Fenton welcome party. Not if Olivia and Dieter are to be there.'

Her response was exactly as Gilbert had feared it would be. Taking a deep breath, he said, 'I know there are great divisions between you and Olivia politically, but for my sake, just for three days, would you both try and forget them? From what Bertie said, Elizabeth is particularly looking forward to meeting up with the two of you again. She would also like to meet up with Violet, but I don't even know which country she is in. One minute it's America, the next it's Germany.'

Thea shrugged herself out of her coat. 'My advice is not even to try and locate her. Violet is too racy for the Yorks, and as she's so brain-dead as to be spending time in Nazi Germany when she doesn't need to, then I've no desire to see her – not now and not at any time in the future.'

Wearily Gilbert pinched the top of his nose and then said sombrely, 'This isn't how a family is supposed to be, Thea. If your mother could see you three girls now, all at odds with each other, it would break her heart.'

'If we are at odds with each other, Papa, it isn't

my fault. If Olivia hadn't married a German – or, having married one, had kept a mind of her own – then we'd get along perfectly well together. I can't say the same for Violet.' She was about to say that Violet was absolutely impossible, and then saw the deep unhappiness written in every line of her father's face.

She checked herself, aware of how much more the deep divide between herself and Olivia meant to him than it did to her, and of how painful it must be to him that Violet travelled between Germany and America and yet so seldom spent time with him – or with anyone else in the family. It wasn't as if he even had the comfort of a happy relationship with Zephiniah. The family life that meant so much to him, and that they had all enjoyed when her mother was alive, was nothing but a much-loved memory. His hopes of re-creating it with Zephiniah had failed and now, when he needed a show of support from her, she was letting him down badly.

Overcome with remorse, she slid her arm through his and hugged it. 'Sorry, Papa. I didn't mean to upset you. Of course I can be civil to the family's two Nazis for three days. I'll even be civil to Zephiniah.' She paused, adding as an afterthought, 'Have you contacted her? She is going to be at Gorton, isn't she?'

'Yes.' He patted her hand, knowing how hard it always was for her to go back on any decision she had taken, and grateful for the effort she was making. 'It's a shame Rozalind is still in Spain. I believe both Bertie and Elizabeth took to her when she had her photographic session with them.'

'She shouldn't still be there. Did you see the piece Hal wrote about the civil disturbances taking place in Madrid and Granada? If she stays much longer she's going to find herself there as a war photographer – and, unlike the war we seem to be heading towards, Spain's war will be a civil war, the most hideous kind of war of all.'

Three days later, travelling by train with Thea to Yorkshire, Gilbert had plenty of time to ponder the depressing political situation in Europe. Earlier in the year, and in defiance of the League of Nations, Italy had invaded Abyssinia. Spain was in deep crisis and, like Thea, he could foresee the military's determination to overthrow the government ending in disaster. Germany, of course, was the chief anxiety. Baldwin believed that appeasement and the League of Nations would contain Hitler. Gilbert gravely doubted it, and had frankly told the prime minister that if Mussolini had got away with riding roughshod over the League, then there was little possibility of Hitler taking any notice of it.

As the train neared Darlington he put all thoughts of fascist dictators and would-be dictators to the back of his mind. The weekend ahead was going to be a relaxing one full of jollity – how could it not be, if Elizabeth was to be there – and, because of the Yorks' presence, there would, for once, be family harmony.

Zephiniah would be so full of triumph that she would be virtually exploding with it. Olivia would be her usual lovely self, totally oblivious to why her acceptance of the political situation in Germany

450

should be such a cause of concern to anyone. Thea had vowed not to bring up the subject of Germany with either Olivia or Dieter and, having arranged by telephone to meet up with Carrie on the Sunday afternoon, was looking forward to the weekend, instead of viewing it as a duty that had to be undergone.

The thought of how much he, too, would have liked to be meeting up with Carrie overwhelmed him and he was still thinking of her as they changed trains at Darlington for a connection to Richmond.

At Richmond his chauffeured Rolls was waiting to meet them.

'Lady Fenton arrived yesterday, and Count and Countess von Starhemberg arrived an hour or so after her,' his chauffeur said in answer to his immediate query.

Gilbert stepped into the car and leaned back against the grey leather upholstery with a sigh of satisfaction. Without Violet and Rozalind they would be a very small family group, but that couldn't be helped. What was important was that Zephiniah, Olivia and Dieter were already at Gorton.

The minute he stepped into the drawing room Zephiniah greeted him with a mixture of euphoria and agitation. Euphoria at the prospect of the Yorks returning the hospitality, and agitation because a veto on other guests meant the word wouldn't spread that she had become part of the Yorks' royal circle.

'Dieter's out with Tom Long,' Olivia said as she

451

gave her father a warm hug. 'They both have shotguns with them.'

Before he could ask what his gamekeeper and Dieter intended shooting on a late, dark autumn afternoon, Zephiniah said, unusually and persistently at his elbow, 'I do think we could at least ask Lady Markham to join us for the weekend. She lives close enough to be regarded as part of the family.'

'But she isn't.' That was Thea with her usual bluntness.

Gilbert was just about to tell Zephiniah that the Duke of York's request that there be no other guests was one he was going to adhere to scrupulously, when there was a knock on the drawing-room door and Mrs Huntley entered.

One look at her face and he groaned inwardly, knowing that relaxation was still on hold and that there was a domestic problem he was going to have to sort.

'What is it, Mrs Huntley?' he asked, fervently hoping the problem wouldn't be a serious one. 'Whatever it is, can we speak about it later, after dinner?'

'I'm afraid this won't wait, sir.' Her voice was unsteady, her face so distressed that even Zephiniah, Thea and Olivia were now paying attention. 'I've had a telegram.' The keys hanging from her belt rattled as she withdrew the telegram from her skirt pocket. 'It's my daughter.' There was a barely suppressed sob in her voice. 'She's been run over by a tram and is in Leeds Infirmary. She must be near to death's door, sir.' Tears flooded her eyes and began coursing down her cheeks. 'The in-

452

firmary wouldn't have sent me a telegram otherwise, would they?'

Gilbert read the telegram. 'No,' he said gravely, handing it back to her. 'I don't think they would, Mrs Huntley. You must leave for Leeds immediately, of course.'

'Thank you, sir.' Her relief at the manner in which her news had been taken was vast. 'I've already packed a bag and I'll telephone for a taxi. It should get me into Outhwaite in time for the five o'clock bus to Leeds and Bradford.'

'But she can't leave!' Zephiniah's horror had been growing by the second. 'How can we entertain royal guests if we have no housekeeper?' She spun to face Mrs Huntley. 'You will remain at Gorton, Huntley, until the Duke and Duchess say their goodbyes. Is that understood?'

Before a white-faced Mrs Huntley could speak, Gilbert said with steel in his voice, and as if Zephiniah hadn't spoken, 'The bus will take an age to reach Leeds, Mrs Huntley. Bennett will take you there. He won't have put the Rolls away yet, and I shall have no further need of it this evening.'

Zephiniah drew her breath in with a hiss.

Watching her, Thea was certain that a row to end all rows was about to erupt.

Mrs Huntley was equally certain of it and, before it could take place, possibly delaying her departure, she said with deep sincerity, 'Thank you, Lord Fenton. I'm very grateful,' and scurried from the room to put on her hat and coat and pick up her hastily packed bag.

Uncaring of Thea and Olivia's presence,

453

Zephiniah rounded on Gilbert, so incandescent with fury that Thea thought she was going to strike him. 'Are you completely insane? How am I to manage the weekend with no housekeeper? It can't be done, and you must tell her so!'

'I shall do no such thing. If I did so, and her daughter died without her being at her side, I would never forgive myself.'

'She *has* to stay until the Yorks leave! She *has* to!'

Turning away from him, Zephiniah headed at a near-run for the door, clearly intent on catching up with Mrs Huntley.

Gilbert didn't hesitate. In swift strides he caught up with her, seized her by the arm and, ignoring her cry of shock and pain, swung her round to face him, his own face white with the kind of anger neither Thea nor Olivia had thought him capable of.

'That's enough!' he thundered. 'I've made a decision and you're going to have to make the best of things, Zephiniah. Is that understood?'

She wrenched herself from his grasp. 'Then what are we going to do?' She shot back. 'The house won't run like clockwork without a house-keeper! No house this size ever does. And if I'm to make a suitable impression on the Yorks, everything has to be absolutely perfect!'

Olivia said tentatively, 'Is it too late to contact a staffing agency for a temporary housekeeper, Papa?'

'Far too late. The Yorks arrive tomorrow after-noon.'

Thea shrugged. 'Then if Zephiniah feels unable to face the thought of entertaining them without

454

a housekeeper, the visit can't take place.'

'It has to take place!' Zephiniah's protest was immediate. 'For it not to take place would be to ruin any chance of my forming an intimate friendship with them. It's all right for you and for Olivia. You have both been on intimate terms with them for years. I haven't.'

Thea walked across to the cocktail cabinet and began mixing herself a pink gin. 'Then if you want the weekend to go ahead with no anxieties concerning the smooth running of things, there is only one solution.'

'And that is?'

'That Papa asks Lady Markham if Monkswood can manage without Carrie for a long weekend.'

Zephiniah's near-black eyes were incredulous. 'Carrie Thornton? The girl from Outhwaite with whom you persist in having such an unsuitable friendship? The suggestion is not only ridiculous – it's impertinent!'

Thea turned to face her, her glass of pink gin in one hand, her free arm pressed hard across her waist. 'Then you have no housekeeper, Zephiniah. Your choice.'

Gilbert said in a voice brooking no argument, 'Carrie is an excellent idea. I'm going to telephone Monkswood immediately.'

He strode from the room and Olivia said, her forehead creasing with a fresh anxiety, 'Papa has already promised Mrs Huntley a lift to Leeds with Bennett – and, considering the hurry she was in, they have probably already left. Carrie is going to have to come on the bus in the morning. By the time she arrives here she won't have much time to get to grips with things.'

'Papa will send a taxi for her.' At the thought of Carrie acting as Gorton's housekeeper, Thea wanted to punch the air with jubilation.

Zephiniah rounded on her, beside herself with frustration and fury. 'You do realize you've made a bad situation even worse? How can Carrie Thornton parade herself as an experienced house-keeper? She's going to make the weekend an absolute unmitigated disaster.'

'No, she isn't,' Olivia said before Thea could respond. 'Carrie has been under-housekeeper at Monkswood for nearly seven years. And her "under-housekeeper" title is one she only keeps out of respect for Mrs Appleby, who, though she hasn't been well enough to leave her room for the last five years, still lives at Monkswood, thanks to Lydia Markham's kindness.'

'Though if you really think Carrie would be a disaster, Zephiniah, we could always combine forces and persuade Papa not to go through with his telephone call,' Thea added, knowing that she was indulging in malicious amusement, but unable to help herself.

Sucking in her breath and knowing she was stalemated, Zephiniah shot Thea a look that would have turned a lesser woman to stone.

Thea merely grinned. 'That's it then,' she said with deep satisfaction. 'Carrie always wanted to be in service at Gorton. Now she's going to be its housekeeper when royalty is staying. Nothing, lately, has given me so much pleasure – and do you know, Zephiniah, I rather think Papa feels the same way.'

Chapter Thirty

Carrie's immediate response when Lady Markham explained why Gilbert was at Monkswood, and why she had been summoned to the drawing room to speak with him, was concern for Mrs Huntley's daughter – and for Mrs Huntley herself.

'A tram accident?' she said. 'But how dreadful! Poor Mrs Huntley. How worried she must be.'

'She's very worried, Carrie,' Gilbert said, not at all surprised that this had been Carrie's first reaction; not elation at being asked temporarily to step into Mrs Huntley's shoes. 'However, Bennett will soon have her at the hospital – that is, if he hasn't done so already. What I need to know from you, Carrie, is if you are happy to act as Gorton's housekeeper this weekend?'

'Bearing in mind,' Lydia Markham interjected, 'that Lord Fenton's guests are the Duke and Duchess of York.'

'I'm happy to help out in any way I can,' Carrie said to both Gilbert and her employer, so unflustered at the prospect of doing so – and so unfazed at the thought of royal guests – that Gilbert had to hide his amusement.

'Thank you, Carrie,' he said gravely, 'I have a taxi waiting for us.'

Carrie looked towards Lydia for a nod of dismissal.

She was given it – and fifteen minutes later,

wearing a hat and coat and with her small suitcase stowed in the taxi's trunk, she was seated beside Gilbert as the taxi sped down Monkswood's mile-long drive.

In a lifetime of knowing Lord Fenton, it was the first time she had ever been alone with him in a situation of such unnerving intimacy. When she had been a regular visitor to Gorton, Thea and/or Olivia had always been present whenever he had spoken to her. In the very early days the person present had sometimes been Blanche and, in later years, it had often been Violet. Since his marriage to Zephiniah there had been a whole host of occasions when he had stopped to chat with her in Outhwaite or in Richmond, but their friendly chats had always taken place in a public place.

The taxi was most definitely not a public place. It was small and, as it was now a little after six o'clock and sunset had been at four, it was also dark. Carrie was grateful for the darkness. The rear seat of the taxi was not very wide, and that his body was a mere couple of inches away from hers was not only causing her heart to beat faster, but her cheeks were flying scarlet banners that she didn't want him to see.

'I left Gorton for Monkswood in such a hurry I didn't check on just what arrangements Mrs Huntley has already made for the weekend,' Gilbert said, as aware of her presence as she was of his, though, unlike Carrie, not betraying any physical signs of it. 'With luck, most of the preparations have already been made.'

'Please don't worry, Lord Fenton. I'm sure Mrs

Huntley was wonderfully efficient until the telegram arrived. As soon as we reach Gorton I'll have a private meeting with the butler and with Cook, and then I'll have a quick meeting with the rest of the staff to introduce myself to them and let them know what I expect from them.'

Her quiet confidence aroused such a rush of affection in Gilbert that it took all his willpower not to squeeze hold of her hand. Instead he said, 'Olivia and Dieter arrived yesterday. Thea came up with me by train earlier today. The Duke of York specifically asked that the weekend should be *en famille*, as he says the Duchess is feeling under the weather and wants to rest, not socialize.'

'Then that makes things much easier.'

He smiled across at her. 'It does indeed, Carrie,' he said, amazed at how happy he was at the thought of her being at Gorton once again.

The taxi was by now speeding across moorland and the only thing visible was the section of road in front of them, lit by the car's headlights.

Carrie cleared her throat and asked, 'Is Lady Fenton at Gorton, Lord Fenton?'

'Yes. She arrived yesterday.' He wondered if he should prepare Carrie for the rudeness she was likely to receive from Zephiniah when neither he nor Thea or Olivia was around, and couldn't bring himself to do so. What he would do, though, was threaten Zephiniah with a fate worse than death if she was ever anything other than scrupulously polite to Carrie.

He wasn't a man of complicated emotions, but he was feeling complicated emotions now. Carrie had a way of spreading happiness around her. No

459

matter what her circumstances, she made the best of them, and her attitude to life – and her inner serenity – was contagious. In the last hour his sense of wellbeing had soared into the stratosphere. He wished it would be correct for her to be on first-name terms with him, but there was no way he could suggest such a thing – and certainly not under the present circumstances, when she was to be at Gorton as his housekeeper.

He smiled wryly in the darkness, reflecting that his feelings, where the class gulf was concerned, were beginning to coincide with Hal Crosby's.

It wasn't only class, though, that prevented a more equal friendship between him and Carrie. He was twenty-two years older than her and, in his experience, people didn't tend to make friends with people a couple of decades their senior. Making such a friendship even more unlikely was his having known Carrie since she was eight years old. If she viewed him as anything at all, he was certain it was as a father figure.

The kind of easy, equal-terms friendship he would like to have with her was simply not possible – and any other kind of relationship, when he cared about her so deeply, was so out of the question that he didn't even allow it to enter his head.

The taxi swept through Outhwaite, and Carrie's hands tightened in her lap, her mind racing with thoughts of what she would have to check on when she arrived and what else she would have to do.

What staff, for instance, would the Duke and

Duchess be bringing with them? For long week-ends at Monkswood most couples arrived with a lady's maid and a valet. Unpretentious as Thea and Olivia had led her to believe the Yorks were, they were royal. That they would arrive with just two servants with them was unlikely. The Prince of Wales, for instance, never travelled anywhere without an equerry. The Duke of York might similarly arrive with an equerry as well as his valet, and an equerry would have to be accommodated as a guest, not as a servant.

She was still musing over things it was impossible to be sure about, and wondering what kind of menus Mrs Huntley had arranged for the weekend with Cook, when Gilbert propelled her into the drawing room at Gorton and both Thea and Olivia rushed towards her and almost hugged her to death.

'Isn't this a hoot, your being housekeeper at Gorton when all you wanted to be here was a tweeny?' Thea exclaimed, her narrow green eyes alight with satisfaction at the way things had turned out.

'Come and sit down and tell us what it is you will have to do,' Olivia said, trying to drag her towards a sofa.

Laughingly, Carrie disentangled herself from their hugs. 'You are a goose, Olivia. I'm here to work, not sit in the drawing room on a sofa! I'm going to have a meeting now with Mr Jennings and Cook, and until the Duke and Duchess leave you probably won't see me again. So goodbye – but don't forget that, if we do meet in the house, I'm Mrs Thornton.'

461

It was a reminder to Thea and Olivia that her being at Gorton as its housekeeper was not play-acting and had to be viewed with the appropriate seriousness. Glad that she had that matter sorted, Carrie turned all her thoughts to the reason she was there. First a meeting with the butler and the cook; then a general meeting of all the maids and male staff; then an inspection of the Yorks' guest suite, and the bedrooms set aside for whatever staff were accompanying them. There wasn't much time, and she couldn't afford to waste another minute.

The next afternoon, when Elizabeth and Bertie arrived at Gorton, Carrie, Mr Jennings and all the impeccably uniformed members of staff were lined up in the vast circular hall in order to greet them.

Gilbert introduced both Carrie and Mr Jennings by name.

Carrie dropped into a curtsey. Bertie gave her a brief nod, but Elizabeth, swathed in fur, paused long enough to give her a very sweet smile.

As Gilbert escorted the Yorks up the grand staircase to their rooms, Carrie had to bite her lip to contain her elation. She had not only *seen* the Duchess of York; she had been presented to her by name and the Duchess had actually smiled at her! When she went back to her duties, she was dancing on air.

Late that evening, after the entire day had gone flawlessly and she was seated alone in the house-keeper's room, deeply thankful that there had not been even the tiniest hiccup, there was a knock on her door. She opened it, expecting to come face-to-face with an equally thankful Mr Jennings.

'You don't mind, do you, Carrie?' Olivia, still wearing an evening gown, was carrying a bottle of white wine in one hand and two wine glasses in the other. 'I just can't bear not being able to chat to you, when we are both under the same roof, and I wanted to let you know how happy Elizabeth and Bertie are with everything. The poor things have had such a busy time lately, what with it being King George and Queen Mary's Silver Jubilee celebrations and Prince Henry's wedding. Last week they had a full three-day programme in Paris representing Britain at the annual banquet of the Caledonian Society of France – whatever that may be.'

With a welcoming smile Carrie closed the door behind Olivia, took the bottle and glasses from her and, as Olivia made herself comfy in one of two armchairs, said as she uncorked the bottle, 'Is your father pleased with how the Yorks' visit is going?'

'Ecstatic! You should know by now, Carrie, that in Papa's eyes you can do no wrong.'

Carrie's habit of blushing embarrassed her again, but her head was bent over the glasses as she poured the wine, and so Olivia didn't notice.

'Elizabeth kept the table in a roar at dinner,' Olivia said as Carrie handed her a glass of wine. 'She was telling us how, when in Paris, an enormous Frenchman dropped to his knees in front of her and said fervently that he wished France possessed people like her and Bertie – though he didn't use Bertie's Christian name, of course.

She said she pretended that it was perfectly normal to have a huge Frenchman with a *Légion d'honneur* in his buttonhole kneeling at her feet. Even Dieter chuckled.'

Carrie seated herself in the opposite armchair. 'And was the table service perfect at dinner? Mr Jennings said it was, but he may simply not have wanted me to get into a pickle of worry.'

'Everything went as smoothly as clockwork. The only slight dampener on the evening was Elizabeth retiring to bed early. Ever since Paris she's felt as if she was coming down with flu, hence her wanting to rest up as much as possible this weekend. She's hoping to stave it off.'

She leaned her head against the back of the armchair. 'It's wonderful to have you at Gorton again, Carrie.'

'It's wonderful to be here. Just before you knocked at the door I was remembering the first day I came here. I was very nervous and your mother made everything all right within minutes.'

'And then you introduced us to Hal, and Thea was rude about him, and you and Thea fell out over it. I remember that day so well, Carrie. We had happy childhoods playing by the river, didn't we?' The expression in her hazel eyes changed and became suddenly sad. 'I always hoped I'd see my children playing on the river-bank and watching the voles, just as we used to, but I don't think I'm going to have any children, Carrie – and you can't imagine how ghastly it is to want a baby and not be able to start one.'

Carrie couldn't and so, although her tender

heart ached for Olivia, she remained sensitively silent.

Olivia bit her lip. 'There's something else that's ghastly as well, Carrie. Though I know Dieter loves me, I think he's sometimes unfaithful to me. Lots of my friends' husbands are unfaithful. Their wives accept it as just being part of life, but I can't. I think of how happy Papa and Mama were and I want a marriage like that.' Her voice shook, and unshed tears glittered on her eyelashes. 'I want Dieter to be as true to me as I am to him. It isn't too much to ask, Carrie, is it?'

'No,' Carrie said fiercely. 'Of course it isn't.' She leant forward, taking Olivia's hands in hers, her eyes dark with concern. 'But I can't imagine it to be true, Olivia. Dieter always looks so happy to be with you – and sometimes, when you are in the same room as him, he hardly lets you out of his sight. I can't believe that, feeling as he so obviously does about you, he would be unfaithful. How silly would that be?'

'But men *are* sometimes silly.' Remembering that Carrie had had very little experience of men – and that whatever experience she may have had, it would not have been with sophisticated men like Dieter – she said, 'Have you ever had a boyfriend, Carrie? You've never said.'

For once Carrie didn't blush. Releasing hold of Olivia's hands and leaning back in her chair, she said, 'I'm twenty-eight, Olivia. Of course I've had boyfriends.'

Entranced, Olivia forgot her dark thoughts where Dieter was concerned. 'Who were they? What were their names? Do tell!'

Carrie's eyes danced in amusement. 'One of them was John Size, a farmer from Skeeby, on the other side of Richmond. And Ted Ramsden asked me to marry him, but I turned him down.'

'Ted Ramsden? The Ted who was Monkswood's gamekeeper and who went to work for Lord Rochdale?'

Carrie nodded.

Knowing how few opportunities there were for anyone in service to be able to conduct a courtship that ended in a proposal, Olivia's eyes were the size of saucers. 'You turned him down? But why, Carrie?'

This time, knowing she couldn't possibly tell Olivia the real answer, Carrie did blush. 'He wasn't the one,' she said simply. And then, thinking that now she'd begun saying things about herself that she'd never told anyone before, she might as well be in for a penny as a pound, she went on, 'That wasn't the only proposal I received.'

'Goodness gracious! Who did your second proposal come from?'

Carrie tilted her head a little to one side, paused only fractionally and then said, 'Hal.'

Olivia stared at her, opened her mouth to speak and couldn't.

'I don't know why you're so speechless with amazement, Olivia.' There was genuine surprise in Carrie's voice. 'Both Hal and I know it's what you, Thea and practically the whole of Outhwaite have always expected would happen.'

'Yes, but... But for you not to have told us...'

'There was nothing to tell. He loves me – but in the same way I love him, which is as a friend. He

466

isn't *in* love with me. He's still obsessed by Thea. I think he thought that if he married me it would put an end to his temptation, where Thea is concerned.'

Olivia's forehead furrowed in a frown. 'Temptation? I don't know what you mean, Carrie.'

Carrie suppressed a sigh. Olivia had one of the nicest natures of anyone she knew and she always looked breathtakingly sophisticated – so sophisticated that you had to know her really well before you realized that she sometimes failed to understand things that were, to other people, quite obvious.

She said patiently, 'Just because Hal made a decision years ago that he wasn't going to compromise his socialist principles by marrying a member of the aristocracy – or even having a long-term love affair with a member of it – doesn't mean to say he isn't constantly tempted to go back on that decision.'

'Oh, Carrie. Wouldn't it be wonderful for Thea if he did? Kyle has given up on her. It happened last year, when they were guests of Prince Edward at the Fort. He again asked Thea to marry him. She said she couldn't, when she still cared for Hal so much, and he told her that she was a fool and his patience had run out.'

Carrie, who knew this – she had had a telephone call from Thea the day after it happened – said, 'Thea's obstinacy in clinging to the hope that there's a future for her with Hal is equal to Hal's obstinacy in being determined that her hopes will never be fulfilled.' She rose to her feet. 'I hate to bring this to an end, Olivia love, but you can lie in in the morning. I can't. I need to go to bed.'

'Oh, of course!' All concern, Olivia leapt immediately to her feet. 'I think Bertie will probably go out with Papa and Dieter tomorrow shooting pheasants, and that Elizabeth will stay at Gorton, cosily tucked up in front of a fire, eating chocolates and drinking sherry and chatting with me and Thea.'

'It sounds blissful,' Carrie said, amused at how different her own day was going to be. 'Goodnight – God bless, Olivia. Pleasant dreams.'

Carrie's own dreams were rudely shattered three hours later by a sharp, urgent knocking on her sitting-room door.

Instantly wide awake, she swung her legs from the bed, grabbed hold of her dressing gown and, as she hurried out of the bedroom and through the sitting room, pulled it on.

She opened the door to an ashen-faced Mr Jennings. 'We have an emergency, Mrs Thornton.' There was nervous perspiration on his forehead. 'The Duchess has been taken ill. I don't know what her temperature is, but her maid says it's dangerously high. Lord Fenton has telephoned Dr Todd and he's on his way here now.'

Carrie didn't waste time in any expressions of shock. She said swiftly, 'Please return to Lord Fenton. I'll be with the two of you in just a couple of minutes.'

She was accustomed to handling dramas and emergencies at Monkswood, but none of them had included the sudden illness of a royal duchess.

With hands that were slightly unsteady, she dressed, coiled her long plait of wheat-gold hair into its usual neat bun, washed her face and was outside the door of the Yorks' guest suite, if not in a couple of minutes, then certainly within ten minutes.

Gilbert said, 'Todd will be here any second. The Duke is with the Duchess, as is her maid.'

'If the Duchess has a high temperature she'll need plenty of fresh lemon barley water to help bring her temperature down. I don't think there's any need to disturb Cook's sleep, but I'll wake a couple of the kitchen staff, two of the house-maids and a footman.'

Again she didn't waste time talking unnecessarily. Leaving Gilbert and Jennings waiting for Dr Todd's arrival, Carrie roused the minimum number of servants that she thought would be required to see to the Duchess's comfort during the night and instructed that the guest bedroom adjoining the suite occupied by the Yorks should be made ready for the Duke, so that his sleep would not be disturbed by the medical care being given to his wife. Then she went into the kitchen and instructed one of the kitchen maids to begin making fresh lemon barley water.

Twenty minutes later, when Dr Todd emerged from the Duchess's bedside to the room where Gilbert was anxiously waiting for news, Carrie was with him.

'Bed rest and nursing care are what is needed, Lord Fenton. The Duchess's temperature is one hundred and two degrees. My advice is that she doesn't consider a return to London until it is back to normal.'

'But she's not in danger?' Panic of any kind was alien to Gilbert, but the prospect of a royal guest dying beneath his roof was decidedly unnerving.

'No. If I thought she was in the remotest danger I would be informing her personal doctor and demanding that he travel north forthwith. That, thank God, isn't the case. However, there is a difficulty.'

'Which is?'

'The Duchess's maid is similarly indisposed.'

Gilbert uttered an oath he'd never before in his life uttered in front of a woman.

Carrie didn't flinch. She understood only too well how he was feeling.

'And the Duchess most definitely needs a nurse,' Dr Todd continued. 'I don't have one at my beck and call, but there's a clinic in Richmond that may be able to supply someone. I won't be able to arrange it until the morning of course, and her lady's maid should be in bed immediately. I wouldn't like to answer for the consequences if she isn't.'

'I can nurse the Duchess,' Carrie said. 'In my years at Monkswood I've nursed members of staff – and Lady Markham – through several illnesses.'

'Splendid!' Dr Todd hadn't the least anxiety about leaving anyone – no matter what their rank – in Carrie's tender, and obviously efficient, care. 'Then my advice to you both is to ensure the Duchess's lady's maid is put straight to bed and, like the Duchess, given plenty of liquids and plenty of rest. I'll be back first thing in the morning.' He began walking away from them and then

470

paused. Turning, he said as an afterthought, 'The Duke has a nervous disposition and isn't a man who is of any use in a sickroom. I advise that you encourage him to leave it and get some sleep.' And, with that, he continued on his way out of the house.

Gilbert's amber-brown eyes held Carrie's. 'Thank you,' he said simply. 'Let us now apprise the Duke of how his wife is to be cared for.'

With Carrie by his side, the back of his hand almost brushing hers, he entered the guest suite, taking comfort from her presence, just as he had once taken comfort from Blanche's.

'Thank you, Mrs...?' Elizabeth said dazedly as she accepted the glass of lemon barley water Carrie offered her.

'Mrs Thornton, Your Grace.'

'And you are?' Elizabeth asked, disorientated by her high temperature and forgetting their earlier introduction.

'The housekeeper, Your Grace. I am caring for you, as your maid is ill also.'

Elizabeth closed her eyes, fatigued by the effort of talking, and Carrie carefully laid a cold, lavender-scented compress against her sweating forehead in an effort to begin bringing down her temperature.

When morning broke and she went into the adjoining sitting room to speak to the Duke of York, Lord Fenton and Dr Todd, Carrie said, 'The Duchess has had an uncomfortable, disturbed night, but her condition hasn't worsened.'

'Nor has it, Carrie,' Dr Todd said. He had

known Carrie – for years and had no intention of addressing her as Mrs Thornton. 'Her temperature is still at one hundred and two, but if you keep doing what you have been doing – encouraging her to drink plenty of lemon barley water and continually applying cold compresses to her forehead – I think we will see an improvement by this evening.'

'I s-s-sincerely hope so,' Bertie said fervently. 'In the past, her fevers have s-s-sometimes continued for days.'

Throughout the morning Carrie got the kitchen staff to supplement the lemon barley water by regularly bringing up to the bedroom a drink that had been her granny's solution for fevers and flu: grated ginger added to boiled water, strained, with a liberal spoonful of honey added.

'That's very comforting and soothing, Mrs Thornton,' Elizabeth said weakly as she sipped it. 'Thank you.'

By late afternoon Elizabeth, though still weak, was no longer disorientated and Carrie judged it safe to suggest to her that she had a bath in lukewarm water, to aid the process of lowering her temperature.

Elizabeth, seeing the sense of it, agreed. Later, back in bed again, this time drinking an infusion of hot water, lemon juice and honey to which half a teaspoon of saffron had been added, she said, 'Did you say it was your grandmother, Mrs Thornton, who told you about adding saffron to lemon and honey?'

'Yes, Your Grace.' Carrie was sitting by Elizabeth's bedside, from where she could regularly apply cold compresses to her forehead. 'My granny was very good at nursing people. She was Lord Fenton's nanny and nursed him through many childhood illnesses.'

'Your grandmother was Lord Fenton's nanny?' Elizabeth's eyes widened. 'But how extraordinary!'

Though she thought it was probably inappropriate to explain, Carrie felt an explanation was needed. 'When Lord Fenton was too old to need a nanny any more, she acted as nanny for other members of his family, and then Lord Fenton retired her into a tied cottage in the village. That was where I grew up. So, you see, I've known Gorton – and the family – all my life.'

Gently she laid another cold compress on Elizabeth's forehead.

'And so when you left school you immediately came into service here?'

'No, Your Grace. I couldn't come here as a tweeny because I had become friends with Miss Thea and Miss Olivia – and with Miss Violet as well. Lady Fenton – the first Lady Fenton – thought it best if I went into service for a friend of hers, Lady Markham, over at Richmond.'

Elizabeth pushed herself up against her pillows, wondering if she was still a little delirious. 'But how did that all come about, Mrs Thornton? It sounds most unusual.'

'Yes, I think it was.' Carrie removed the compress and replaced the glass of lemon, honey and saffron with a tall glass of lemon barley water. 'When I was eight my father was killed in the

473

Great War at the battle of Hooge. His company commander was Lord Fenton, and he suggested to Lady Fenton that it might help me get over my grief if I came to Gorton and played with Thea and Olivia. Olivia is my age, and Thea a year older. I did, and we've been as close as sisters ever since.'

'What a very nice story.' Elizabeth was aware she was beginning to feel fractionally better. 'And so was it when you were in service with Lady Markham that you met your husband?'

Carrie smiled. 'I'm not married, Your Grace. "Mrs" is a courtesy title. And I'm still in service with Lady Markham. I'm her under-housekeeper, and I'm only at Gorton this weekend because Mrs Huntley, Lord Fenton's housekeeper, has had to dash to Leeds Infirmary, where her daughter has been taken after being in a traffic accident.'

'I'm beginning to feel as if I'm in a Hollywood movie.' There was amusement in Elizabeth's voice. 'A dash to a hospital. A sick house-guest. A Mrs Thornton who is a Miss Thornton. A house-keeper who isn't actually the housekeeper at all. What else is going to turn out to be not what it seems?'

Carrie, aware that Elizabeth had turned a corner and was now on the way to recovery, said, 'If you are beginning to feel a little better, would you like to try some clear chicken soup, Your Grace?'

Elizabeth nodded.

When Carrie came back into the room after giving the order for the chicken soup to be brought upstairs, Elizabeth said, 'What is your Christian name, Miss Thornton?'

474

'Caroline, but everyone calls me Carrie. I don't think I've ever been called Caroline in my life.'

'You must have had a nice childhood, growing up in such a pretty part of the Yorkshire Dales.'

'I did. Together with Thea and Olivia and another friend of mine, Hal, we would play down by the river and, in summer, paddle and swim in it. Sometimes we would watch the voles that live in the river-bank, and when it was blackberry and bilberry time we would pick quarts and quarts of them for Cook to make jam and tarts with.'

Elizabeth said, 'When I was a little girl we lived at St Paul's Walden Bury, and my best friend was my brother David. In the summer we would get up very early to let our six silver-blue Persian cats out. After that we would go and say good morning to the ponies, feed the chickens – there were more than three hundred of them – and collect eggs for our breakfast. Like your childhood, doing simple country things was the best part of my childhood also.'

In the early evening Elizabeth had another luke-warm bath, but by then she, Carrie, and Dr Todd knew there would be no need of another one, and that her temperature was fast returning to normal and a serious bout of influenza had been averted.

Carrie still kept up with the regime of cooling compresses, regular glasses of lemon barley water, and hot lemon, honey and saffron on the hour every hour.

Late in the evening Elizabeth said, 'I'm beginning to feel much better, Carrie. Usually when I have a fever it's days and days before I feel well again, so I'm very grateful to you.' She paused, and then said, 'Will you be returning to Lady Markham next week?'

'I expect so, Your Grace. Lord Fenton received a telephone call from Mrs Huntley at teatime saying that although her daughter has been badly injured, she no longer has a life-threatening condition, and so I imagine she will be back by tomorrow, or the day after at the latest.'

'Is my maid recovering at the same speed that I am?'

'Yes, Your Grace.'

Elizabeth's eyes, the same midsummer-blue as Carrie's, twinkled. 'Then that must be because she's having the same infusions and diligent care as I am receiving. Tell me some more about your childhood, Carrie. Did you have other friends besides Lord Fenton's daughters and Hal? When I was eight every friend I had was either a brother or a sister or a cousin.'

Carrie handed her another glass of hot lemon, honey and saffron and began to tell her about Charlie and Jim, Hermione and Miss Calvert.

Elizabeth told her about another of her childhood homes, Glamis Castle in Scotland. 'I remember once, when I was about ten,' she said, in a room that was now lamplit, 'when, with a coachman by my side, I was driving a pair of horses and they started to run away with me. We were hanging on, making straight for the gates – which were shut – and I said to our coachman, "What are we going to do?" and he took his bowler hat off and said, "We must trust in the Lord, Lady Elizabeth." And with that we hung on and, do you know, as we got nearer the gates they opened, and we flew through them at great speed. Wasn't that amazing? I've trusted in the Lord ever since.'

Carrie told Elizabeth about Charlie. About how she and Violet had been in the post office when he was being name-called by the women queuing up in it, and of how Blanche had taken her in the silver Rolls-Royce to Charlie's home and offered him employment at Gorton. She told her of how Lord Fenton had arranged for Charlie to be treated by the great Mr Gillies, and of the silver mask Charlie had worn in between his many facial reconstruction operations, and of how it had made him famous all over their part of the Dales.

That night Elizabeth slept soundly and in the morning, when Dr Todd came to see her, he announced that her temperature was back to normal.

'I had a very good nurse,' Elizabeth said to him.

'I'm grateful to hear it, Your Grace,' he said, with a smile in Carrie's direction. 'You are completely fit enough to travel, and may I take the liberty of wishing you and your husband a safe journey.'

Assuming the role now of a lady's maid, not a nurse, Carrie helped Elizabeth to dress. Standing behind Elizabeth as she sat at the dressing table, Carrie fastened the duchess's three-strand pearl necklace for her.

Elizabeth smiled at her through the mirror. 'In

all the times in my life that I have been unwell, I can never remember a happy side to it, as there has been this time. Talking to you brought back so many good memories of my childhood, and I so enjoyed hearing all about Hal, and the voles, and men in silver masks.' She lifted her hand, taking hold of Carrie's. 'Thank you so much for these last forty-eight hours, Carrie. When the day comes when you can legitimately be addressed as "Mrs", please let me know so that I may send you my good wishes.'

Chapter Thirty-One

JULY 1936

'*In Spain the government has asked France for assistance in suppressing the Nationalist insurgents led by General Franco. The Nationalists have, in turn, asked for assistance from Italy and Germany.*'
Thea was in Mount Street, listening to the early-morning BBC news.
'*Opinion at home is that the Republican government is unlikely to receive help from France, which is opposed to any intervention in Spain's internal affairs. It remains to be seen what the Nationalist emissaries will bring back from Rome and Berlin.*'There was a slight pause and then, in a different tone, '*King Edward's coronation is to take place on May the twelfth next year.*'
Thea turned the wireless off. King George had

died in January and, incredible though it still seemed to her, her friend, Prince Edward, was now King Edward VIII.

She wondered if she would receive an invitation to the coronation. She wondered just what kind of status would be accorded at the coronation to Wallis. Most of all, though, she wondered what help would be given to Spain's left-wing government by Britain's Labour Party and Communist Party.

The only person who would know what – if anything – was being planned was Hal. She had his telephone number, though pride ensured that she seldom rang it. She hesitated long enough to smoke a cigarette, then dialled his number.

He was still living in his little flat in Orange Street at the back of the National Gallery and she could visualize the telephone ringing in his minute hallway, and Hal coming to answer it, from where? The bedroom? The sitting room? The equally small kitchen?

'Hal Crosby,' he said abruptly, when he finally answered its insistent ringing.

Her stomach muscles tightened as they always did when she heard his voice. She wondered if he was dressed and, if so, what he was wearing. She wondered if his hair was still wet with the water he used every morning in an effort to tame it.

'It's me, Thea,' she said, when she knew she could trust her voice to sound steady. 'I've just been listening to the early-morning news. There's no longer any pretending Spain isn't in a state of full-out civil war. I'd like to know what help the left in Britain will be giving the Republican forces. Can we meet and talk?'

'I'll see you in the Hand and Racquet in half an hour's time.' The line went dead.

It was the terse way Hal handled all telephone calls and, knowing it, she replaced the receiver on its rest, unfazed.

The Hand and Racquet in Whitcomb Street was Hal's local, and the kind of traditional pub he liked best. Licensing hours in Soho bore little relation to those in the rest of London, and it didn't surprise her that Hal would be using the Hand and Racquet as a meeting place long before the time when it officially opened its doors.

Pausing only long enough to put on a bright-red jacket and snatch up her handbag, she was out of the house in under five minutes. From Mount Street to Whitcomb Street was a twenty-minute walk. She would easily be there on time.

When she entered the pub it was to find it deserted, apart from an elderly Mrs Mop sweeping the wooden floor, and Hal. He was seated at a corner table, nursing a pint of Guinness.

'Do you want a drink?' he asked.

There was no one behind the bar serving and Thea said, wondering if Hal had been given free run of the bar, 'An orange juice would be nice.'

'D'you hear that, Elsie?' Hal called across to the cleaning lady. 'An orange juice, if you can manage one.'

The cleaning lady gave a near-toothless grin. 'Only for you, Mr Crosby. I wouldn't do it for any other bugger.'

Hal cracked with laughter and Thea said, 'Spain, Hal. What's the latest news you have?'

480

'The latest news is that the Civil Guard has joined ranks with the Nationalists, as have a good half of the Assault Guard.'

The Assault Guard comprised special police units that had been created by the government five years earlier, to deal with urban violence. That they were so divided in loyalty showed just how dire the situation was.

'It looks as if the Nationalists are receiving support in huge swathes of the north, from Vigo to Burgos and down to Salamanca, and that they have support in a smaller section of the south, around Cadiz and Seville. The problem is that there aren't enough British reporters in Spain sending back reliable news.'

'And what help are left-wing organizations giving the Republicans? There must be something you and I can actively do, to help keep the government in power.'

'There's talk of international brigades being formed to fight on the Republican side, but so far nothing has been set up.'

'If there is, will you join one of them?'

'No.'

It was so not the response she had expected that Thea's eyes widened. 'But why not? Surely none of us can sit idly by, while a fascist like Franco is threatening to put an end to a left-wing government?'

Until now Hal's demeanour had been as serious as hers. Now, however, he grinned. 'What's the matter, Thea love? Disappointed in me?'

'Yes,' she said unhesitatingly. 'Socialists and communists in Spain – men, women and children

– are being shelled from the ground and bombed from the air by fellow countrymen who are right-wing fascists and want a military dictatorship; and even if there is an opportunity of helping them, you say you aren't going to!'

'I didn't say I wasn't going to help them. I said I wouldn't be doing it by picking up a rifle.'

'Then how?'

'By being what I am. A reporter. I'm going out to Spain as a war correspondent. I'm just waiting for my visa.'

He drained his glass of Guinness and then held her eyes with his. 'Instead of simply spouting off about things from the safety of London, you could do something else, Thea.'

'What?'

There was a sudden flexing of the muscles along his jawline. 'You could come with me.'

For Thea it was so unexpected, so momentous, that the world seemed to stand still.

She didn't ask him if he meant what he'd said. She didn't need to. The look in his gold-flecked eyes told her he had.

She said simply, 'Yes.' And a beat of a second later. 'Why?'

'Why now?' he asked, a raw edge to his voice, not misunderstanding the question. 'Because twelve years of being tormented by loving you and never holding you, kissing you, making love to you, is twelve years too bloody long. Because I thought you'd marry within your own class. Become Mrs Kyle Anderson and be happy. Because I asked Carrie to marry me and she very sensibly turned me down, saying that although she was sure I loved her, I wasn't *in* love with her, that I was in love with you. Because as usual she's right – Carrie's always right about everything – and because I was thirty in February and you'll be thirty in a week's time and life is too short to waste any more of it. And last, but by no means least, because when I go to Spain, I'd like to bloody well have you with me.'

'I'll have to have a visa.'

After all the years of waiting for Hal to come to his senses eventually and realize that, no matter how hard he tried to live without her, doing so was not only pointless, but impossible, it was a response so mundane she could hardly believe she'd made it.

The pub was empty except for them and, at the far end of the public bar, Elsie, swabbing down tables. Sunlight streamed in golden shafts through the Hand and Racquet's windows. Thea had never felt happier and was certain she never could be happier, no matter how long she lived.

'I love you,' she said thickly as he pulled her roughly towards him, and the next moment his hair was coarse beneath her fingers, his hands were hard upon her body and his mouth was dry as her tongue slipped past his lips.

That evening, in Berlin, Olivia was dining with Dieter in the elegant dining room of the Goldener Frieden, one of the city's most exclusive restaurants. A small band was playing romantic music. A sea of chandeliers sparkled. Dieter's fellow male diners were all wearing white tie and tails or high-ranking Nazi uniforms. The women were in lavish

483

evening gowns, their ears, throats and wrists ablaze with jewels.

It was a rarity for them to be dining alone and not with friends, and Olivia had been looking forward to the occasion for several days.

'To us, *meine Liebling*,' Dieter said, raising his champagne flute to hers.

Olivia was just about to say something loving to him across the table when she became aware that the American wife of one of Dieter's friends was making an angry beeline towards them.

'What on earth...?' she began, putting her champagne flute down.

Dieter swung his head round to see what had startled her and immediately jackknifed to his feet, saying in a strangled voice as the woman, enveloped in a cloud of Mitsouko perfume, reached their table, 'For the love of God, Connie! Not here!'

'Why not?'

In a slinky green lamé gown that left one shoulder bare and slithered over her slender curves, Connie Foxton was a woman on the warpath. Her blonde hair was held away from her face on one side, falling on the other in a long, smooth, shoulder-length wave. The blazing rage in her eyes was that of a woman scorned.

'Why not?' she demanded again. 'It's as good a place as any. And you can have this back!' She wrenched a bracelet from her wrist and flung it down on the table. 'And these!' She yanked a pair of long earrings from her ears and sent them skittering across the starched white tablecloth.

Around them diners had stopped eating and

were staring. A waiter who had been approaching Dieter and Olivia's table with hors d'oeuvres backed away.

Still not understanding just what was taking place, Olivia stared wide-eyed from Connie Foxton to Dieter.

Dieter said tautly, his face bloodless, 'You're making an exhibition of yourself, Connie.' Then he said to Olivia, who was still seated, 'I'm going outside to speak with Mrs Foxton.'

'Oh no, you're not,' Connie flashed back. 'I'm staying right here! And I didn't come here to talk to you – you two-timing Kraut bastard! I came here to tell your wife some home truths about you.'

Olivia pushed her chair away from the table and tried to stand, but her legs had turned to jelly and wouldn't take her weight. She knew Connie was drunk, but that wasn't explanation enough for her behaviour. She didn't want to hear what Connie was about to say. She didn't want to know. She felt as if she was standing on a precipice and that any minute she would be over the edge and falling.

'Connie, *please!*' she heard Dieter say in a low, urgent voice.

Ignoring him, Connie said to Olivia, 'You think he's wonderful, don't you? Well, let me tell you a few home truths, honey. He's as faithless to you as a buck-rabbit on heat.'

Understanding now only too well, Olivia somehow found the strength to rise to her feet. 'I don't believe you,' she said, aware that every last person in the large restaurant was riveted by the scene taking place. 'Would you take me home

485

please, Dieter?'

There was nothing Dieter wanted more than to be outside the restaurant and no longer the object of all those prurient eyes.

But Connie barred their way, swaying unsteadily on her feet. 'D'you want to know who else he's screwed around with over the years? Well, even if you don't want to know, I'm going to tell you. Frau Reni Tillich. Countess Marianne Thimm. Clarita von Strempel.'

'Don't listen to her!' There was desperation in Dieter's voice. 'She's drunk and vicious and out of her mind!'

'I may be drunk, and I may be vicious, but I'm not out of my mind, and your wife knows I'm not, don't you, honey?'

The manager of the restaurant was making his way to their table with a backup of waiters.

Dieter grasped hold of Olivia's arm. 'Start walking for the door,' he hissed at her. 'Start walking *now!*'

Olivia didn't move. 'But Reni and Marianne and Clarita are my friends!' She looked from Connie to Dieter. 'They're my *friends*, Dieter! How could you?'

He was cornered, too close to losing all dignity by being publicly manhandled out of the city's most exclusive restaurant to even attempt a denial.

'You think that's bad enough?' Connie persisted. 'That's nothing. He's also spent years bedding your sister on and off.'

'My sister?' There was incredulity in Olivia's voice. 'Thea?' For one brief blissful moment she was certain Dieter was right and that Connie Foxton was truly out of her mind. No one in a million years could imagine Thea doing anything so despicable.

'Thea?' Connie looked blank. 'Who's Thea? I mean your Nazi-loving tart of a sister. I mean that so-called Queen of Babelsberg, Violet Fenton.'

'Violet?'

Olivia was over the edge of the precipice now and falling into an unimaginable abyss. Slowly, and with a face like parchment, she turned to Dieter.

'Is it true?' The question was unnecessary. The agony on his face showed her it was true. 'Oh my God!' she whispered as the restaurant spun dizzily around her. 'Oh my dear, dear *God!*'

She wrenched her arm from his hold, snatched her evening bag from the table and pushed blindly past Connie Foxton. Her entire world had caved in, and in a way that was so horrendous, so sickening, so almost beyond belief that she didn't know how she was going to survive it.

Without pausing to retrieve her fur, she rushed out of the restaurant into the street. Taxicabs were lined up outside and, despite perilously high heels, Olivia sprinted for the nearest one, yanking the door open and saying breathlessly to the driver, 'Number nine Bellevuestrasse. Fast!'

As he pulled away from the kerb she saw Dieter race out of the restaurant after her, come to a floundering halt in the taxi's wake and then turn, running towards the taxi rank.

There was nowhere else for her to go but home, but at home, if she reached there before Dieter, she would be able to lock herself in their bedroom. She would be able to pack a suitcase and in the morning she would leave him, and Germany. She would catch the first train possible to Ostend and she would go home to Gorton.

'Please drive even faster!' she said to the driver, fumbling in her evening bag for money. 'I have to get home before my husband.'

Her distress was so obvious that he didn't need telling twice. He sped up the Kurfürstendamm, made a sharp left and another sharp left into the street skirting the Tiergarten, the city's park. They skirted the zoo, and then embassies flashed past: the Czech Embassy, the Swedish Embassy, the Italian Embassy. Then a sharp right and they were entering Bellevuestrasse.

As he squealed to a halt outside number nine, Olivia kicked off her shoes, threw all the money she had in her purse into his lap and, with her shoes in her hand, ran barefoot into the home that had, until that evening, meant so much to her.

'*Gräfin! Was ist los?*' the night-maid called out to her in alarm.

Olivia ignored her. Through the door she'd left open behind her she could hear Dieter's taxi squealing to a halt.

Hiking her ankle-length gown above her knees, she took the stairs two at a time, running for their bedroom. By the time she reached the door, he was in the house.

'Olivia!' he shouted as he began pounding up the stairs. '*Lieber Christ!* Wait and listen to me!'

Before he'd reached the landing she had slammed the door shut and turned the key in its lock. Then, shivering violently with shock, cold and anguish, she sank down in a huddle against it.

That Dieter was sometimes unfaithful was something she had suspected for a long time. It was something she had closed her heart and mind to. However, thanks to Connie Foxton, she could do so no longer.

Reni Tillich was one of the first friends she had made when she and Dieter had returned to Berlin. Only five days ago Reni had rung Olivia, asking if she would like to see a film with her. They had gone to a cinema in the Ku'damm to see *Das Mädchen Johanna,* a film about Joan of Arc. Afterwards they'd had tea and cakes at Cafe Kranzler.

Countess Marianne Thimm was married to one of Dieter's fellow diplomats at the Foreign Office. Though she wasn't as close a friend as Reni, she was still a friend. They met on almost a weekly basis at various embassy parties. They dined regularly at the Thimms', and the Thimms dined regularly at 9 Bellevuestrasse.

Clarita von Strempel was an older woman, somewhere in her mid- to late thirties, very beautiful, very elegant. In Olivia's first few weeks in Berlin as a diplomat's wife, Clarita had taken her under her wing, steering her through a minefield of strict Prussian etiquette.

The knowledge that all three women had betrayed her in such a way was almost more than Olivia could comprehend. She was in such pain that she was blind, deaf and dumb with it.

Violet's betrayal was, though, by far the worst. Violet's behaviour was monstrous – was beyond

489

being monstrous.

'Olivia!' Dieter was on the other side of the door, twisting the crystal door knob violently. 'Olivia, *meine Liebe!* For the love of God, unlock the door! I have to speak to you. I have to explain!'

'There can't *be* any explanation!' Hot, scalding tears poured down her cheeks. 'You slept with women I thought were my friends! You slept with my *sister!* Or are you still sleeping with her? Is that why Violet came to work at Babelsberg? So that the two of you could see each other more easily?'

'*Lieber Gott in Himmel!*' Dieter was almost out of his mind with distress.

What was happening to his marriage now was something he had thought would never happen. Though he'd been unfaithful to Olivia several times, he had never indulged in a full-scale, full-on love affair. He'd never had any desire to, because when it came to loving someone, he loved Olivia. In his own mind, all he had been doing was having a little bit of harmless fun – the kind of fun all red-blooded men occasionally indulged in.

As for Violet... He felt violently ill. He'd certainly never had any desire to leave Olivia for Violet. The very thought brought him out in a cold sweat. And since Violet had begun living and working in Berlin, he hadn't even met up with her for drinks. Violet had other, far more important fish to fry. Gossip was that she'd become Goebbels' mistress almost from her first week at Babelsberg and when she wasn't being squired around by Goebbels, she was being squired by the second most important man in Germany, the commander-in-chief of the Luftwaffe, Hermann Göring.

'Violet was ... was an aberration, Olivia,' he said through the still-locked door. 'It happened years ago, when she was filming at Beaconsfield. It meant nothing, Olivia darling. You know how Violet is...'

'I'm leaving you. I'm going home to Gorton, and I'm going to file for divorce on the grounds of your adultery with my sister.'

Dieter thought of the scandal. He thought of how he would be regarded by the family he had married into – the family that meant so much to him. He thought of the expression he would meet in the eyes of his father-in-law and Thea and Rozalind.

His hands were slippery on the knob of the door as he tried vainly to force the lock.

'I love you, Olivia darling,' he said, knowing that what he said now would affect the rest of his life. 'I've never loved anyone else. I never will love anyone else. I don't know why I behaved as I did, except that men don't think the same way about things as women do. Please believe me when I say it will never happen again.'

'How can I believe you?' The tears coursing down her face dripped onto her hands and the skirt of her gown. 'Reni, Marianne, Clarita, the Foxton woman and Violet – oh God, most of all Violet – know things about you that no one should know but me.' Her words came between heart-racked sobs. 'They know what you look like naked. They know how you kiss. They know how you make love.'

She was crying so hard she couldn't continue.

Dieter gave up the fruitless effort of trying to open a locked door. Ashen-faced, he leaned against the wall, his eyes closed. Then, in a quiet, flat, defeated voice, he said, 'I don't want you to go back to Gorton. I don't want you to leave me. Despite the way I've behaved, you are my life, Olivia. You must believe me. I love you, and I need you. Please, *meine Liebe*, give me another chance.'

Olivia's sobs gave way to shuddering, gasping breaths of air.

She was visualizing her life at Gorton without him. Who else would she ever find to love, the way she loved Dieter? Who else would there be who, just by looking at him, would make her heart leap for joy? Dieter hadn't loved, as he loved her, any of the women he'd been unfaithful with. He'd promised it would never happen again.

She supposed that all faithless men, when caught out by their wives, promised the same thing. But Dieter wasn't all men; his total panic at the prospect of her leaving him and returning to Gorton was real. He'd played fast and loose with something infinitely precious – their trust and total commitment to each other – but now he had been brought face-to-face with the consequences of doing so she doubted that he would ever do so again.

He needed her, just as she needed him.

To punish him, by leaving him, would only make her own grief and pain more unendurable.

She leaned her head against the back of the

door and knuckled the remaining tears from her eyes.

'Do you promise, utterly promise me,' she said unsteadily, 'that you will never again be unfaithful to me?'

'I promise you, Olivia darling.' His relief was so vast that there was a sob in his throat. 'Unlock the door, *meine Liebe*. I've been such a fool – and I'm never going to be foolish again. Please believe me. Please tell me you still love me.'

On legs that were weak, she rose to her feet and unlocked and opened the door.

His handsome face was so anguished that, as he took her in his arms, she went into them without a moment's hesitation. Their marriage had been within a hair's breadth of foundering, but it hadn't done so.

As his mouth came down on hers, she knew their marriage would never fail; that she was strong enough never to allow it to.

She knew something else as well. She would never speak to Violet – or willingly see her – ever again.

And she would never again smell the scent of Mitsouko without her stomach heaving.

Chapter Thirty-Two

SEPTEMBER 1937

Rozalind was in Berlin again. It was a city she would no longer have gone anywhere near, had it not been for the exceptional photographs she could take – photographs that her press agency was always hungry for.

In two days' time Mussolini and Hitler, who, after an agreement signed in October the previous year, were now in a formal military and political alliance with each other, were to appear together before massed crowds in the Field of May, the setting of the 1936 Olympic Games.

It was a photographic opportunity Rozalind had no intention of missing.

Having emerged from the Friedrichstrasse station, she was walking down the street of the same name, with a large bag holding the essential clothing and toilet items she travelled with over one shoulder, her up-to-the-minute Leica over the other shoulder. Friedrichstrasse was a major thoroughfare and, like all Berlin's major streets, its entire length was hung with immense scarlet banners bearing giant black swastikas on circles of white. They fluttered in the breeze from every public building, allowing no one to forget that Berlin – just like every other city, town and village in Germany – was Hitler's fiefdom.

Roz gritted her teeth. Every time she returned to Berlin the atmosphere was darker, more oppressive, more hysterically fevered – and it was this atmosphere that she constantly tried to capture on film, in the hope of bringing home to newspaper readers in Britain and America the nature of the time-bomb ticking away in Berlin's Reichstag: the time-bomb that was Adolf Hitler.

Her difficulty was in maintaining relationships with Violet, Olivia and Dieter which ensured that she had access to the kind of events denied other foreign press photographers. It helped that she viewed Violet and Olivia more as her sisters than as cousins and that, like Gilbert, she was certain Dieter's admiration for Hitler would eventually turn into something very different; and that when it did, Olivia, too, would cease singing from the Nazi song-sheet. Her cousins were important to her, far too important to let political differences – no matter how extreme – spoil her relationship with them.

It was Violet, not Thea or Olivia, who was a constant mystery to her. She couldn't for the life of her figure out why Violet – who had never previously been seen with any man not handsome enough to commit suicide for – was allowing herself to be squired around by a man as ox-like as General Göring, and by Joseph Goebbels, who had a club foot, walked with a limp and was so slightly built that he looked as if a puff of wind would blow him over.

Though she was staying, as she always did, with Olivia and Dieter, Roz was first meeting up with Violet in a cafe close to Friedrichstrasse's junction

495

with Unter den Linden.

Violet was there before her, her torrent of fox-red hair tamed into an upswept chignon beneath a white cap worn at a jaunty angle. She was wearing white bell-bottomed trousers, a white and navy striped sweater, and there was a white blazer slung carelessly around her shoulders.

'You're looking very nautical, Violet,' she said in amusement. 'Where is the yacht to go with the clothes?'

'Kiel,' Violet said deadpan, her tawny eyes full of delight at catching up with Roz once again. 'How long are you going to be in Berlin – and are you still after an introduction to Goebbels and Göring?'

'The answer to the first question is for as long as it's worth my while.' Rozalind swung her bag to the floor and slid onto a seat on the opposite side of the table from Violet. 'My answer to the second question is yes – but only in the hope of the kind of photographs that other foreign press photographers can't get. Why on earth are you still in Berlin, Violet? More to the point, why are you allowing yourself to be romanced by men as slimy and obscene as Goebbels and Göring?'

Violet shrugged. 'They're very powerful men, Roz.'

A waiter came up and Rozalind ordered a Martini.

Violet, already drinking a Martini, took a sip of it and tilted her head to one side, 'What is the latest news from home?'

'From Outhwaite? Charlie and Hermione's little boy is six and a little imp who is running

496

them both ragged. Not that they mind. Their sun rises and sets around him. Jim Crosby has got the latest Pig and Whistle barmaid in the family way, and the pressure is on for him to do the right thing and put a ring on her finger. Miss Calvert has found a new project: a young boy from the other side of Outhwaite who has university ambitions and needs all the extra coaching he can get.'

'And do you have news of Thea and Hal?'

Rozalind's natural exuberance ebbed. 'Only via the occasional letters that get through to your father, and which he then shares with me.'

She thought of the little information the family had had of Thea and Hal since their arrival in Spain a little over a year ago. Hal had obtained press accreditation immediately, and Thea's visa had been granted under the belief that she was his secretary. At first they had been in the north-west of the country, in Corunna and Vigo, both Nationalist strongholds. At the beginning of the current year they'd managed to make their way further east, into Republican-held Basque country. In the last letter Gilbert had received – which had been at the beginning of July – Thea had written that with the International Brigades now in Spain, they had joined a British unit that was heading towards Madrid to help in the defence of the city.

'And that was the latest news,' she said now to Violet, 'but the long silence is not as sinister as it may seem – not considering the way the country is being torn apart.'

'And all with the help of German planes and German pilots.' Violet's distinctive amber eyes narrowed. 'Without Hitler's help, Guernica could never have happened.'

The comment, and the way it was said – coming from a woman who was so frequently seen in the company of the man who commanded the pilots and planes that had pounded Guernica with explosives, set it alight with incendiary bombs and strafed it with machine-gun fire – was breathtaking.

Roz said slowly, 'I don't understand you, Violet. Unlike Olivia, you're not married to a Berliner and you don't have to be in Berlin, and unlike me you don't have a professional reason for appearing to condone the terrible things happening here so that the world outside Germany can see what is going on inside it. So why are you still at Babelsberg when you could be in Hollywood, or in London, filming at Elstree or Pinewood?'

'I have a reason, but it's my secret. One day I'll tell you.'

'And is the reason why Olivia's no longer having anything to do with you a secret as well?'

'No. Thanks to Connie Foxton, half of Berlin knows why Olivia isn't having anything to do with me.'

'Which is?'

Violet gave a Gallic, dismissive shrug of her shoulders, 'Because of a little naughtiness I indulged in years ago with Dieter. It was nothing important, and I can't imagine why Olivia is making such a fuss about it.'

'I can,' Roz said drily, imagining only a heavy flirtation.

Violet shrugged and shot her one of her

dazzling smiles. 'Let's have another Martini while you tell me all the latest gossip about Max. Is it true that since the Republicans did so badly in last year's presidential election he's said he won't be a contender next time around?'

'That was the quote printed in the *Washington Post* – and presumably you read it in the *International Herald*. That being the case, it must be true.'

'And is it true he's getting a divorce?'

Feigning an indifference she was far from feeling, Roz said, 'As several newspapers have printed in their gossip columns the news that he and Myrtle are divorcing, I'm assuming that's true also.'

'And?' Violet said impatiently. 'Come on, Roz. Don't keep secrets from me. Are the two of you back together again? Are you the reason for the divorce?'

'Absolutely not. No. Zippo. Zilch.' Roz was beginning to regret arranging to meet up with Violet. The last thing she wanted to do was talk about Max. 'I haven't seen or spoken to him since I decided our affair was going nowhere and broke things off with him.'

Her fingers tightened around the stem of her Martini glass – the tension not because it was still difficult for her to give a false account of why she had broken off her affair with Max, but because she knew exactly how long it was since she had last seen him. In two weeks' time it would have been exactly four years. If anyone had asked, she would probably have been able to give them the days and hours as well.

Four years in which no one had replaced him in her life, though heaven knows she'd tried hard enough. She'd had so many brief affairs – and even briefer flings – that she hadn't fingers enough to count them. The only constant in her life had been Barty, but in the end even Barty had realized he was wasting his time and had become engaged to a debutante whose father not only owned 1,000 acres of Perthshire, but a Scottish island as well.

Violet was now chattering about the film she was presently making. Every now and then Roz made a polite, interested noise, but her thoughts were on Max. Why was he risking potential harm to his political career by divorcing Myrtle? She could think of only one possible reason, and the reason made her feel physically ill. It had to be that he wanted to remarry. It had to be that he was having an affair, and that the new woman he was in love with was so important to him, so utterly necessary to him, that he wanted to make her his wife.

As she continued feigning interest in what it was Violet was telling her, she didn't know which emotion she was battling the hardest: a searing, crucifying hurt or rampant, raging jealousy.

Later that day, after dinner and when she was sitting with Olivia and Dieter in the library of their Bellevuestrasse home, Max's name was again brought into the conversation.

'It's a shame Max didn't make it to the White House,' Dieter said, one leg across the other, his right ankle resting on his left knee, a glass of grape-brandy in his hand. 'His disappointment must have been colossal.'

Roz thought of the way she had sacrificed her own and Max's happiness so that Max could enter the running for the presidency and knew that, if Max's disappointment had been colossal, then her own had been – and still was – off the Richter scale.

Struggling to keep the strain from her voice, and aware that some response was needed, she said, 'I'm sure you're right, Dieter. But it was all over for Max quite early on. Governor Landon pipped him to the post in the primaries and then was unable to make inroads into Roosevelt's popularity. A sitting president nearly always has an advantage, and Roosevelt's New Deal policies ensured he had enormous overall support. Every rancher and farmer in the country was totally behind him. Big-city political machines were behind him, as were the Labour unions. I doubt if Max being the Republican nominee would have made any difference to the final outcome.'

American politics didn't interest Olivia and she changed the subject. 'You must have been hugely disappointed Thea wasn't around last November, Roz, when all the drama of the abdication was going on.'

Roz, grateful the conversation had been steered away from Max, smiled wryly. 'I don't think even Thea's long-standing friendship with Edward would have been enough to have given me special access to him, Olivia. I was in London on the off-chance of getting something emotive, but the entire thing was announced, over and done with so quickly that all I managed was a couple of

501

shots taken when Edward's car was speeding between 10 Downing Street and the Palace.'

'And the coronation?' Olivia's eyes glowed. 'Wasn't it wonderful? I was in the Abbey with Papa, and I kept having to pinch myself to make sure I was awake and not dreaming. Even now I find it hard to believe that Bertie's now King, and that Edward is the Duke of Windsor and doesn't even live in England any more.'

Rozalind's amusement was vast. 'But you were heartbroken at the thought of Edward giving up his throne for love of Wallis. When did the sea-change take place?'

There was a giggle in Olivia's voice 'When I realized that if Bertie was King, then my friend, Elizabeth, would be Queen.'

Dieter finished off his brandy and, making no attempt to refill his glass, said, 'Thea still being in Spain when Edward married Wallis must have been as big a blow to you professionally as when she wasn't around at the time of the abdication.'

'Oh, bigger,' Roz said with deep feeling. 'Far bigger. If Thea had been around when the wedding at Candé took place, she would most certainly have been one of the handful of guests who risked the Palace's displeasure by attending it – and just as certainly she would have suggested to Edward that I take the wedding photographs. If I had, it would have been the most spectacular photographic coup of my career.'

'I might be able to put another coup your way, Roz. Perhaps not quite so historic, but a coup nevertheless.' Dieter put his now-empty brandy balloon down on the small table next to his armchair and rose to his feet.

He crossed to the fireplace and leaned against the corner of it, his arms folded, his head down, as if debating whether or not to continue with what he'd begun to say.

Olivia, too, was suddenly tense, her hands clasped tightly in her lap.

'What is it?' Roz asked, intrigued. 'What's bugging you both?'

'Hitler is what is bugging us both,' Dieter said tautly. 'Things have become even grimmer in Germany than they were the last time you were here. The Security Police take the law into their own hands without going through the courts. Anyone can be arrested for nearly anything at all. And there are informers on every street and in every block of flats. Informing on people has become a way of repaying old grudges. As for the poor benighted Jews... There are so many laws now prohibiting their movements and personal freedoms that it's virtually impossible for them to breathe without being marched off to a camp.'

'A forced-labour camp?'

'We don't have any of those now,' said Olivia quietly. 'And there are no more detention camps. Everything has been centralized into larger camps, called concentration camps.'

'And there are four of them.' A lock of pale-blond hair fell low over Dieter's forehead. 'Dachau, north-west of Munich. Buchenwald, near Weimar. Lichtenburg – which is solely for female prisoners – in Saxony. And Sachsenhausen, on the outskirts of Berlin.'

Roz, vastly relieved at hearing Dieter speak in a

503

way that was no longer admiring of what was going on in Germany, said drily, 'So you're no longer a fan, Dieter?'

'Of the Nazi creed and the Führer? No, I'm not. In the beginning I thought Hitler was the best thing that had happened to Germany in a long time. You have to remember the state Germany was in when he began his rise to power, Roz. The country was in such a mess, and in two, three, years all the things that had made it a mess were there no longer. There were no more communist agitators; no more street fighting. There was no more unemployment – even Britain and America were envious of that. There was no more inflation. We began to feel proud of ourselves as Germans once again, after all the indignities of Versailles. We even dared to begin feeling moderately prosperous again. I never liked everything about Hitler's regime, but for a time it seemed a great improvement on what had gone before, and Hitler spoke of bringing the Kaiser back from Holland – of restoring the monarchy.'

'And now?' Roz asked.

'And now?' Dieter opened his arms in a gesture of despair. 'Now I know Hitler never had the slightest intention of restoring the monarchy. It was simply part of his plan to be everything to everybody, until he had sufficient power not to have to please those he didn't want to please. And we Germans, God help us, gave him that power. So much power that we are now living in a country where no one dares publicly express any criticism of him; where even making fun of him can end in the perpetrator facing a death-sentence. Telephones are tapped. The mail is no longer sacrosanct. For the slightest infringement of any one of the scores of new laws constantly being brought into being, all citizens – Aryan as well as Jewish – face arrest and imprisonment without the benefit of a trial.'

'But for the Jews it's much worse.' It was a flat statement of fact that Roz wanted to hear Dieter admit.

He flushed. 'Yes, for the Jews it's much worse. In the beginning I thought the Jew-baiting and Jew-hating were a craziness that would come to an end when Hitler gained control of the hooligan elements amongst his followers. Only slowly did I realize that he was always in control of them; that Jew-hating wasn't an aberration, but a policy.'

For a long moment the room was silent, and then Roz said, 'What will you do? You're in the Foreign Office. You must be aware, as the British government is, that despite all his avowals to the contrary, Hitler is intent on war. What are you, and anyone who thinks like you, going to do when that time arrives?'

It was a rhetorical question. She was certain that neither he nor anyone else could do anything.

Dieter crossed the room, checked that the door was firmly closed and then said, 'Because there is no freedom of speech or action in Germany now, only the army has any power – and there are certain high-ranking figures in the army who feel the same way I do, and the same way many other high-ranking Foreign Office officials feel.'

Roz felt her heart almost cease to beat. 'You're

part of a secret opposition group?'

He nodded.

She knew better than to ask for any more details. The less she knew, the safer it would be for both of them – and for Olivia. Instead she said, 'Can I tell Gilbert?'

'Yes. The British government needs to know – and Gilbert will know how much to say, and what not to say.'

'I'm assuming that because of her liaisons with men like Göring and Goebbels, Violet knows nothing about this?'

'God, no!'

The mere suggestion had robbed Dieter's face of blood and, judging that it was time the subject was changed, Roz said, 'When you started this conversation, Dieter, you began it by saying that you could put a photographic coup my way. How does that connect to anything that's just been said?'

'The Führer likes to present the image of being so totally committed to Germany that romantic relationships never intrude upon his time. It isn't strictly true, though the term "romantic" may be a little excessive.'

Olivia said, speaking Violet's name for the first time that evening, 'Violet met Hitler not long after she first came to Berlin. She said he was a neuter – and, when it comes to masculine sexuality, if anyone's instincts can be trusted, Violet's can.'

She was looking at Dieter as she spoke and he flushed, saying, 'Rumour has it that several years ago Hitler was inordinately fond of his half-niece, Geli Raubal.'

'Geli shot herself,' Olivia said, in a tone indicating that in such a situation any woman in her right mind would have done the same thing.

'And now?' Roz asked, intrigued.

'And now, for more than six years, a young woman named Eva Braun has been Hitler's companion, though he doesn't publicly acknowledge her as such. She lives with him at the Berghof, his private residence at Berchtesgaden, on the Austrian frontier, though when he entertains there she only rarely makes an appearance. When he comes back from Berchtesgaden to Berlin in two days' time for the mammoth rally at the Field of May, he's bringing Eva with him – but she won't be one of the million or so people in the Olympic Stadium. She will be out of sight, as usual; and, because Olivia is one of the few people Eva has met socially, and because she and Eva got on so well together, she's asked if Olivia will keep her company that evening in her suite at the Adlon Hotel.'

'And you're suggesting that I go along with my camera?'

'I'm suggesting that if you are in the hotel at the same time, and if Olivia mentions this fact to Eva, Eva is certainly going to want to meet you.'

Roz hesitated. 'I came here to take photographs of Hitler and Mussolini together on the same platform. Why should I forgo photographs that my agency will certainly place for photographs of a young woman that no one in America or Britain has heard of?'

Dieter smoothed his hair back, away from his forehead. 'Because one day Hitler will marry her

– and when he does, photographs taken by you, when the bride was totally unknown to the world, will be photographs that are unique. There's only one proviso. Even if the press should show an interest, the photographs can't be published now. Hitler's fury would be so great that you would never be allowed into the country again. And, for her part in it, Olivia would most likely find herself in Lichtenburg.'

Roz hesitated, but she didn't hesitate for long. She had always trusted her instincts and was going to trust them now. She was going to forgo the shots of Hitler with Mussolini for photographs of Eva, not because she felt any certainty about such photographs one day being of any value, but because of curiosity.

She wanted to meet the woman who, for several years, had been – and still was – Adolf Hitler's mistress.

She wanted to know what kind of a woman Eva Braun was.

Chapter Thirty-Three

APRIL 1938

It was early evening as Thea walked down La Rambla, Barcelona's main thoroughfare. She had just finished a long shift at one of the local clinics and was en route to the small room she rented above a tobacconist's. Her thoughts were on Hal, who was a hundred miles or so further down the coast, where Franco's troops had succeeded in driving a wedge through what had once been Republican-held territory. All the reports reaching Barcelona indicated that the fighting had been desperate, and Thea, who knew Hal would have been in the thick of it, still had no news of him.

She came to a halt in the middle of the broad pavement, not wanting to reach her room, where she would only have grim thoughts for company. La Rambla was lined with cafes and she sat down at the first outdoor table she came to.

'*Una cerveza, por favor*,' she said when a waiter came up to her.

Her grey trousers and grey blouse – the blouse sporting a Red Cross badge on one shoulder – ensured that she was as much a part of the street scene as everyone else. Once, fashionable clothes were de rigueur in the La Rambla cafes. Now people who possessed fashionable clothes no longer chose to wear them. Barcelona had become a city of workers. The streets were a sea of proudly worn militia uniforms and blue overalls. And there were other, very obvious signs of the revolution. Nearly all private cars had been commandeered and people got around the city by tram and taxi. The words '*Señor*' and '*Señorita*' were no longer uttered – everyone called everyone else 'Comrade'. Service workers, such as her waiter, were no longer deferential, for everyone was equal. Tipping was forbidden by law.

It was the kind of classlessness of which Thea had always dreamed. Nothing else, though, was as either she or Hal had imagined it would be. Within Republican ranks there was unity between members of the International Brigades, no matter what country they came from, but that was as far as the unity went. Elsewhere in Republican ranks communists, Marxists and anarchists were as deeply divided between themselves as they were from the Nationalists. The sense of solidarity that she and Hal had believed they would find was totally lacking. Marxists said the anarchists were undisciplined and would not obey orders. Stalinists refused to supply arms received from Russia to any units but their own. Republican government forces were at loggerheads with voluntary militia units. Orders were given, countermanded and then given again. Chaos and confusion reigned.

It was a nightmare that both she and Hal fervently hoped would be resolved when Franco and fascism were finally defeated. At the moment, though, it was Franco and his Nationalists who looked to be winning the war.

She sipped her beer, staring at a wall on the other side of the wide boulevard, on which a giant hammer and sickle had been painted. By driving a wedge between Republican forces on the coast, General Franco had successfully split Republican Spain in two. There were rumours that the government was trying to sue for peace; that Franco was now turning his attention once more to Madrid and that the Republican cause was lost. There were further rumours that the International Brigades were about to be recalled, in the hope that this would encourage the Italians and

Germans fighting for the Nationalists to withdraw also.

Thea's hand tightened around her glass. Many men from Barcelona militias who had fought to try and stop the Nationalist push to the coast had managed to somehow make their way back to the city – but so far not Hal. As she absolutely refused to consider him either dead or captured, where was he? Was he now fighting somewhere else? Or was he too injured to make the attempt to return to Barcelona, and was he lying low with fellow Republicans until fit enough to make what would, she knew, be a difficult and dangerous journey through Nationalist-held country?

No answer came to her and, heavy-hearted, she rose to her feet. All she could do was remain where Hal could find her, but inaction had always been difficult for Thea, and never more difficult than it was now.

The evening was getting into its stride and the pavement cafes were packed with workers relaxing after a long day. The noise level was high, with music from cafe radios vying with loudspeakers bellowing revolutionary songs. A gale of laughter came from the table she was walking past and, not for the first time, Thea marvelled at the Barcelonians' ability not to be crushed by the horrors hurled at them.

Mussolini was Franco's ally, and only a month ago Italian planes had conducted a non-stop three-day bombing raid on the city. There had been no attempt to single out military targets. Bombs had been dropped indiscriminately. Whole swathes of working-class areas had been

511

decimated; schools had been hit. The images of the small children she had ferried, screaming and bleeding, between the schools and the city's hospitals would, she knew, stay with her for as long as she lived.

She turned off into another busy street, wondering whether to have some fresh sardines for her evening meal or make an onion-and-tomato omelette instead. Of necessity she lived cheaply. It didn't trouble her. In comparison to the thousands made homeless and destitute by the war, she knew she lived well.

She bit her lip hard, wondering what Hal would be eating that evening; where he would be eating. Far worse, she wondered *if* he would eating. The light had smoked to a spangled blue dusk. On a nearby balcony, laundry hung limply. From somewhere close at hand a baby cried.

A tram rattled down the centre of the dusty street. Still deep in thoughts of Hal, she didn't look towards it, barely registered it.

There came an ear-splitting whistle.

It was a whistle that, in Outhwaite, had called the cows in to be milked and the pigs to be fed. In London it had brought taxis to a screeching kerbside halt.

Her heart slammed so hard in her chest that she thought it was going to stop. Her eyes flew in the direction the whistle had come from. The tram was now twenty yards or so past her and was travelling further away with every second. He was standing on its platform, a wide grin on a face that was bearded and as grimy as when he'd been tending the pigs and cows. His militia uniform was filthy and sweat-stained. His hair had grown so long that his thick tangle of curls was anchored at the nape of his neck by a red neckerchief that had originally been around his throat. A rifle was slung over one shoulder. There were no bandages in sight. No slings. No crutches.

Careless of how fast the tram was moving, he leapt from it.

With blazing joy on her face, she broke into a sprint, dodging around stray dogs and workers enjoying an early evening stroll, hurtling into his arms.

'Hal! *Hal!* I've been worried out of my mind!'

She didn't get a chance to say any more. His lips came down hard and hot on hers in a fierce, deep kiss. Her arms were as tightly round him as a drowning man's to a lifebelt. She never wanted to let him go. Since they had been in Spain every separation had been an agony, but this last one had been by far the worst. As their passionate embrace went on and on, no one stared at them. In a world where lovers were separated and reunited – often only to be separated again, and for good – such scenes were commonplace.

When finally he raised his head from hers, Hal said thickly, 'I need a bath and food, Thea love.'

As she looked up into his face she saw how the face-splitting grin that he had shot her from the tram had hidden how truly exhausted he was.

'Sardines on toast, or an onion-and-tomato omelette?' she asked, wishing she'd made a stew the previous evening; wishing she'd bought fresh bread that morning.

'Both,' he said as, arms around each other's

waists, they turned off the street into the warren of smaller streets that made up the working-class area where, when Hal was in the city, the two of them lived together and where, when he wasn't in the city, Thea lived alone.

It was an area that had suffered badly in the March bombing and, with so many houses now uninhabitable, what had once been a bustling area was now near-deserted. The local church still stood, but as the Catholic Church was fiercely on the side of the Nationalists, it no longer had a congregation. With all priests being viewed as the enemy, it was rare in Barcelona to see one now, but a little way in front of them an elderly priest was heading towards the church, a shopping bag in either hand.

As they drew a little nearer to him Hal said, holding Thea as close to his side as was possible while still walking, 'I've never missed you as much as I have these last few weeks, Thea love. It's changed my mind about a lot of things.'

She leaned her head lovingly on his shoulder. 'Such as?' A lorry full of soldiers wearing anarchist neckerchiefs roared into the street and Hal said, 'Oh, things like marriage and–'

He broke off abruptly as in front of them the priest stopped walking, shook his fist at the soldiers and spat at them.

The lorry skidded to a halt. The soldiers spilled out of it. Hal said, 'Christ Almighty!' and then dropped his arm from around her waist and broke into a run.

For a second Thea was too stupefied with horror to react and then, as amid shouts of *'Cerdo*

514

Nacionalista!' the priest was ringed by eight or ten men and knocked to the ground, she broke into a sprint in Hal's wake.

Booted feet kicked the old man; a rifle butt came down on him hard.

Already in the middle of the melee Hal was yelling at the soldiers to stop.

For a second Thea thought they were going to, for one of the men hauled the priest to his feet – and then he put a gun to the priest's head.

'No! No Ya basta!' Hal shouted, leaping towards him and knocking the gun so that it fired upwards.

Then, as she saw the reactions of the soldiers, Thea too was within the ring of them, shouting, 'No! *No! NO!'*

Chapter Thirty-Four

JUNE 1938

Zephiniah stood by one of the full-length windows of her suite at the Dorchester. Her view looked out across Park Lane and into the majestic glory of Hyde Park. If she had wanted to, she could have enjoyed the early summer sunshine by stepping out through the sitting room's French windows onto a private balcony, only she didn't want to do so. She didn't want to be resident at the Dorchester, even though her suite was one of the hotel's largest and most luxurious. She didn't want to be in London full stop – and wouldn't have been, had it not been for the necessity of being in London for her divorce hearing.

She bit the corner of her lip, knowing that, as usual, she had been her own worst enemy. Her frequent meetings with Roberto at French and Swiss spas had been too flagrantly reckless. A little bit of discretion would have gone a long way and, if she had been discreet, she wouldn't now be in the process of being divorced.

That she was being divorced had come as a very nasty shock. She simply hadn't thought Gilbert would ever go to such lengths.

'Our marriage obviously brings you no happiness, Zephiniah,' he had said, sadness, resignation and a deep weariness in his voice. 'As a consequence, apart from the first few months of our marriage – when you weren't yet bored with it – our marriage has brought me no happiness, either. A divorce is for the best, and at least Señor Di Stéfano hasn't a wife to be distressed by his being named.'

She had thrown hysterics, but it had all been in vain. A private detective had followed her on two of her trips to France. Gilbert had all the evidence he needed to divorce her and, despite his position as a government minister, a divorce was what he'd been set on obtaining.

She hadn't understood it. Unless they wanted to marry again, members of the peerage usually ignored a wife's adulteries, got on with committing their own and, even if they spent all their time with a mistress and very little with their wife, behaved publicly as if their marriage was one of perfect

516

probity. Or at least they did so once they had first fathered an heir that was indisputably their child.

Was that why Gilbert was prepared to be the first Fenton ever to divorce? Was it because, if she became pregnant, he would have no certainty the child was his? She was forty-four, an age when he might have been expected to have no such fears, but even if he had, she could have put his mind at rest. Though she'd seen no need to tell him so, her periods had stopped two years ago.

When they had, she had thought she was pregnant – and by Roberto – and had immediately sought medical confirmation. The only confirmation she had received was that, like 10 per cent of women, her menopause had begun earlier than might have been expected. It was news she had kept to herself.

So why was she still keeping it to herself?

She crossed to a small table and took a cigarette from a silver cigarette-case studded in one corner with a pleasingly large diamond. There was another diamond, albeit a little smaller, in the corner of the lighter she lit the cigarette with.

The diamonds, and the lifestyle that went with them, would continue after the divorce. Gilbert had assured her of that and, as he was a man whose word could be trusted utterly, she would never have financial worries.

She blew a plume of smoke into the air. Since Gilbert had dropped his bombshell and put divorce proceedings in hand, she'd had time to reconsider her first hysterical reaction to no longer being Viscountess Fenton. For one thing, her title would change only slightly. Instead of

517

being *The* Viscountess Fenton (which Gilbert's third wife would hold, if he were to marry again), she would be Zephiniah, Viscountess Fenton – a courtesy title.

A further realization, though, had been the clincher.

As Gilbert's divorced wife, she would never again have to suffer being bored out of her mind. There would be no more interminably tedious stays at Gorton. No more staring out of windows at nothing but sheep and moorland. No more having to face the future that Gilbert was so looking forward to – a future where, after he ceased being active in politics, he would live permanently at Gorton.

None of the things she had hoped to gain by marrying Gilbert – apart from her title and financial security – had come to pass. Other than with his political friends, he hated socializing. She'd had dreams of becoming part of a glamorous royal circle – as her stepdaughters, each in different ways, had been; and as Olivia, if she lived in London and not Berlin, still would be.

It had never happened.

Another thing that had never happened was Gilbert becoming prime minister.

When she had first met him, the prospect had been spoken of so often, by so many people, that in her naivety she had thought it an event bound to happen.

It hadn't.

The first general election after their marriage had been in 1929 and, to her surprise and intense disappointment, he'd made no attempt to stand

518

for office. Instead of returning a Conservative government, the great British public had voted for Labour in their droves. She had wondered if, anticipating such a result, Gilbert had decided to keep his powder dry until the next general election when the public would, presumably, be disillusioned with Labour and anxious to vote Conservative once again.

Zephiniah had been right in assuming there would be enough disillusionment with Labour to vote a Conservative government back into office, but that government hadn't been headed by Gilbert. Instead Stanley Baldwin had bounced back like an indestructible rubber ball and had stayed in office long enough to ensure that, instead of Edward making Wallis his queen, he was doomed to a life of exile as the Duke of Windsor.

The last general election had been a year ago. By then she'd long ago realized that Gilbert had no desire – and not enough ruthlessness – ever to want to lead his party. More to the point, she'd also learned that British prime ministers led from the Commons, not the House of Lords, and that for him to be prime minister he would have had to renounce his peerage.

She walked back to the window, aware that her major disappointments with Gilbert wouldn't have been so impossible to overcome, if it hadn't been for the shoal of smaller, daily disappointments and irritations.

Top of her list was that no force on Earth could tempt him into a nightclub. He could dance – in fact he was a very good dancer – but he danced only in the ballrooms of private houses, and then

519

not very often. It was the same with casinos, which were meat and drink to her.

The excitement and adrenalin-filled rush of gambling was totally lost on Gilbert. Rather than playing roulette, blackjack and baccarat in Monte Carlo, he preferred being in Yorkshire, tramping the moors with a shotgun under his arm and his spaniels at his heels.

She couldn't even enjoy a furious row with him, because he was always so God-damned reasonable and, unless the issues were cruelty and injustice – when he became white-lipped with anger – he rarely lost his temper.

She, on the other hand, was so mercurial that she lost her temper at the drop of a hat, and enjoyed doing so. Her spectacular and frequent rows with Roberto often progressed into physical fights – and always ended with the two of them making frantic, passionate love.

She was roused from her thoughts, and her present longing for Roberto, by a knock on her door. She wasn't expecting a visitor, though it was just possible that her visitor was her lawyer.

Crushing her cigarette out in the nearest ashtray she walked swiftly across the sitting room and into the small, wood-panelled hall. When she opened the door, it was to a bellboy.

'Post, Lady Fenton,' he said respectfully.

Without much interest she took the envelope from the silver salver and walked back into the sitting room. It had been forwarded from Mount Street, as most of her post was these days.

Without bothering to sit down she opened the envelope. Inside was a short letter and another envelope, one bearing foreign stamps. Stamps that looked to be German. Or Austrian.

The envelope had been opened and was addressed to the long-dead aunt with whom, a lifetime ago, she had travelled to Vienna.

Sucking in her breath, Zephiniah's eyes flew to the accompanying letter. It was short and to the point:

Dear Lady Fenton (I see no reason to address you as Zephiniah or Cousin, as there has been no family contact since your return from Vienna, with my now-late mother, twenty-six years ago)

The accompanying letter may, or may not, be of interest to you, but because of its contents it is one that, in all conscience, I have felt obliged to forward.
Cynthia Crane

Slowly Zephiniah sat down, stupefyingly aware that the long-ago past was about to tumble around her. With a fast-beating heart she withdrew a letter from the envelope. A photograph fell out of it onto her lap.

It was a photograph of a young woman. She was slim and petite and looked very much as Zephiniah herself had looked in her mid-twenties. The photograph had been taken in a park. In the distance she could see Vienna's famous Ferris wheel.

She knew without reading the letter that the photograph was of her daughter. It was the first photograph of her she had ever seen.

She stared down at it for a long time and then, at last, she began to read the letter Judith had written:

521

Schülerstrasse 25
Vienna

Dear Lady Crane,
  My name is Judith Zimmermann. My adoptive parents were Erwin and Annaliese Zimmermann. My birth mother was the Honourable Zephiniah Colefax. I was born in Vienna on the tenth of April 1911. I write to you because you accompanied my mother to Vienna for my birth and because your address, and not my birth mother's, was on my adoption papers. I write to you, dear Lady Crane, because I am in most terrible distress. I need very, very badly to leave my country. Since Hitler decreed two months ago that Austria is now part of the German Reich, terrible things have happened to my people. My beloved adoptive parents are dead, executed when they protested at the Gestapo's confiscation of their property and the appropriation of our home. The doors of the hospital where I was a junior doctor have been closed to me. Jews can no longer work in the professions or study at university. I have no money, as my late parents' bank accounts, and my own bank account, have been confiscated. I live in a small apartment with friends who are all in the same dreadful position. I cannot emigrate without a sponsor – someone who will vouch that I will not be a burden on the country I am entering. I write in the hope that my British birth family can help me. I am educated, a doctor who is fluent in English. Surely there is room for me in the country of my birth mother? And please assure my mother, dear Lady Crane, that I will never be an embarrassment to her; that though I long to know her,

522

I will respect her wishes whatever they might be.
Yours, in deepest and most fervent hope,
Judith Zimmermann

With a trembling hand Zephiniah laid the letter down even more slowly than she had picked it up, aware that she was experiencing an epiphany. For twenty-seven years she had barely spared the child she had given birth to a thought and, when she had thought about it, it had only been in connection with the way it had ruined not only her debutante year but, in her opinion, her, life.

She had never thought of the baby as being a person. She had never marked the tenth of April in a diary, or been aware each year of how old the child would be. She had never, until now, even thought of the child by the name she had chosen for it.

Judith.

She looked down at the photograph. The young woman in it – her daughter – was lovely; and not only lovely, but fiercely intelligent. She had to be fiercely intelligent if, at twenty-seven, she was a qualified doctor.

She thought of Thea, running off to Spain with the son of one of Gilbert's tenant farmers; of Olivia, married to a Nazi; of Violet, consorting with the likes of the Nazi hierarchy. And she experienced an emotion she had never felt before. She experienced a deep, overwhelming upsurge of maternal pride.

Unlike the stepdaughters with whom she had never been able to forge satisfactory relationships, Judith was a daughter to be proud of.

She looked down at the letter again. How could she not have realized how drastically the German annexation of Austria would affect Judith's adoptive parents, and Judith herself? What was going on in Austria that people could be executed for objecting to having their property and home taken away from them, for no other reason than that they were Jews?

Gilbert would know, of course. And Gilbert would know exactly how to go about arranging for Judith's immigration to Britain.

An hour later, in the drawing room at Mount Street, Gilbert stared at his estranged wife in stupefaction.

'You have a *daughter*? God in heaven, Zephiniah! Why did you never tell me? Why was she adopted? Where is she now?'

'I never told you because it was something I never thought about.' Even though she was about to ask him for a vitally important favour, Zephiniah couldn't help being short-tempered with him. 'She was born in 1911, fourteen years before we met. Why would I have told you? As for why she was adopted, I would have thought that was obvious. I was seventeen, unmarried and, as the father had no intention of putting a ring on my finger, adoption was the only viable solution.'

Gilbert ran a hand over hair that was no longer quite as fierce a red as it had once been. 'But why are you telling me now, Zephiniah? And where is your daughter? What's her name?'

'I'll tell you when we both have a strong drink in our hands.'

A strong drink was exactly what Gilbert was in need of. He crossed the room to the drinks cabinet and poured two generous whiskey and sodas.

He handed her one of them, saying, 'I don't see that where she lives can be more of a shock than the one you've already delivered.'

Zephiniah, certain the shock was going to be a good deal greater, took a sip of her drink and then said, 'She lives in Vienna. Her name is Judith.'

'*Vienna?* But why on earth...?'

'She's Jewish, and so it was thought best that her adopted parents should also be Jewish.'

Gilbert wondered if he was suffering from the onset of early dementia. Surely what Zephiniah had just said couldn't be what she'd really said.

'I'm sorry, Zephiniah. I've obviously misunderstood you. Who is it that's Jewish?'

'I am. By right of having a Jewish mother. And if Jewishness is passed down in the female line, then so, I presume, is Judith. Whether I'm right or not, she believes herself to be Jewish. She's been brought up as a Jew and is being treated by the Nazis as a Jew.'

With a kid-gloved hand she held out the letter Judith had sent to her late aunt, the photograph that had accompanied it and the covering letter sent by her cousin.

Hardly able to believe she'd kept two such major secrets from him, Gilbert took them from her. One glance at the photograph was enough to convince him that Zephiniah was speaking the truth.

He read the covering letter. Then, his jaw

hardening, he read Judith's letter.

When he had finished he looked up, his brown-gold eyes holding hers. 'And so you want me to provide Judith with the written assurance she needs in order to enter Britain?'

Zephiniah nodded.

His face was grimmer than she had ever seen it. 'I wish to God you'd told me about her existence in the months leading up to the *Anschluss*. You must have realized the kind of treatment she and her adoptive parents would receive when Hitler got his way over Austria?'

'I dare say if I was interested in world events and politics, I would have realized, but I'm not, and I didn't. As I've already made clear, there has never been any contact between me and the Zimmermanns. Everything was all so long ago that there were years and years when I didn't even remember I'd once had a baby. I've never been one to live in the past, and she was way back in my past.'

'And now?'

'And now she isn't.'

Their eyes continued to hold, both of them aware it was the frankest, most truthful conversation they'd ever had.

'I will provide the necessary financial guarantee for Judith,' he said, 'of course I will, but I have to warn you, Zephiniah, that even though I will put things in hand immediately, her application for admission to Britain will take some time. Thousands of Jews – German and Austrian – are fighting for admission to Britain. There will be a yearly quota, though I don't know what it is.

There will also be different types of entry visas, some of which will be looked on more favourably than others. In Vienna there could well be a long wait for a document approving her departure, and other types of obstructions – obstructions that we in Britain can't begin to imagine.'

'You'll put things in hand immediately, though? This afternoon?'

Her frantic concern on behalf of the daughter she had never met was so unexpected that he said with a surge of affection for her, 'Of course I will. I'm leaving for Whitehall straight away. Will you write to Judith, or shall I?'

'I will.' There was no hesitation in her voice. 'I will, because I want to.'

With Gilbert pausing only long enough to pick up a homburg and a pair of pigskin gloves, they walked together out of the house. On the pavement he flagged down a taxi and, before he stepped into it and she walked the short distance out of Mount Street and down Park Lane to the Dorchester, Zephiniah said emotionally, 'Thank you, Gilbert. I knew, despite the hurt I've caused you, that you would help her.'

Before he could respond the taxi door had slammed behind him and she was walking away, a handkerchief to her nose – or was it to her eyes? He couldn't tell, but as he asked the cabbie to take him to the Home Office, he was filled with the extraordinary realization that, out of the fiasco of their marriage, affection and friendship had finally been born.

Once at the Home Office, his own ministerial

position ensured that he waited barely ten minutes before being shown into the office of Sir Samuel Hoare, the Home Secretary.

'Fenton, my dear chap!' Samuel Hoare rose, tall and thin from behind a massive Biedermeier desk, to greet him. 'I hope you're not here with news from the House that's going to keep me awake all night?'

'I'm not here on official business at all – so I hope you are going to forgive me. I'm here to request a favour.'

They shook hands. Gilbert had known Samuel Hoare for nearly twenty years. Like himself, he was a man who had held more than one Cabinet post and they had always enjoyed a cordial relationship.

He sat down, saying, 'My estranged wife's daughter, Judith Zimmermann, is a doctor in Vienna. She's Jewish. I have all her details with me. Date of birth – she was born in Vienna – address, et cetera. Needless to say, she needs to emigrate from Austria as soon as possible. I, of course, will vouch for the fact that Miss Zimmermann will not be a financial liability to this country, once she arrives in it. I realize her application will have to go through the normal channels, but would appreciate any tips on how this can best be done in the shortest possible time.'

Samuel Hoare looked startled. Gilbert didn't blame him for being so. It wasn't every day that a peer and a fellow Cabinet minister announced he was – at least until his divorce became final – the stepfather of a Jewish girl seeking to flee the terror of Hitler's Reich.

Keeping his curiosity concerning the circumstances of Judith Zimmermann's birth to himself only with the greatest difficulty, he said, 'The sponsorship aspect will be plain sailing. Visas are a little trickier.'

'Why? She's a doctor.'

'And therein lies the problem.'

It was Gilbert's turn to look startled.

Samuel Hoare took off rimless spectacles and rubbed the bridge of his nose with a thumb and forefinger. 'The number of immigration applications from German and Austrian Jews is astronomical. It's impossible to accept every application, and there is a weeding-out process. Different categories of applicants are granted different visas – and many more visas are granted to certain categories than they are to other categories.'

'But Judith is a professional person.'

'And professional bodies in Britain – doctors, architects, lawyers, et cetera – have no desire to see a huge tide of people, those as qualified as themselves, coming into this country, flooding their own professions and damaging work opportunities. To avoid this, the number of visas being issued to professional Jews – unless they are particularly distinguished – is lower than the number of visas being issued to, for instance, agricultural workers or domestic servants.'

'Then let her be issued with a domestic-service visa. Anything to get her out of Austria and into Britain before she finds herself in a concentration camp!'

Samuel Hoare flinched, unused to being brought face-to-face with the painful realities he usually only dealt with on paper.

'As I assume you will want to keep this letter, I'll have my secretary transcribe a copy of it. I'm sure everything will work out for the best, Fenton.'

Gilbert said his goodbyes, hoping fervently that in this case everything would, indeed, work out for the best. Things certainly weren't doing so where Thea, Olivia and Violet were concerned.

In the short taxi ride back to Mount Street he gave free rein to his deep anxieties about each one of his daughters. He'd heard nothing from Thea for more than three months, at which point she had still been in Madrid, driving an ambulance. It had been even longer since some kind of contact had been maintained by being able to read Hal's despatches in the *Evening News*. All Thea's last letter had said was that Hal no longer had any means of filing news reports and that he had headed back north, towards Barcelona, as a fighting member in a unit of the 11th International Brigade.

Olivia's position in Berlin was almost as much of a nightmare for him. Thanks to Roz, he knew now of Olivia and Dieter's change of heart where Hitler's Third Reich was concerned – and for that he was profoundly grateful. The knowledge that Roz had brought him of Dieter's involvement with those seeking to rid Germany of Hitler had, however, filled him with fear for his safety, and for Olivia's.

As for Violet... Words failed him when he thought of Violet having become an intimate of men like Joseph Goebbels and Hermann Göring.

Never had he believed he would have become grateful that Blanche was no longer alive, but when he thought of how devastated she would have been by Violet's lifestyle, he found himself thanking God she was no longer beside him to witness it.

It was evening by the time he walked, heavy-hearted, up the shallow steps of his Mount Street home and let himself in. The first thing he became aware of was that his butler hadn't hurried into the hall to greet him and relieve him of his hat and gloves.

The second thing he became aware of was that there was a huddled figure on the bottom tread of the central staircase, where no huddled figure should have been.

He stepped forward and, as he did so, Thea lifted her head. She was agonizingly thin and looked tired unto death. 'Papa?' she said, as if she couldn't believe he was real.

Gilbert, who was having just as much difficulty in believing he was awake and not dreaming, closed the distance between them in swift strides. 'Thea, my darling girl!' He dropped to his knees beside her. 'Why didn't you let me know you were on your way back to England? Are you ill, Thea? Are you hurt?'

She shook her head and, as he put his arms around her, holding her close, thanking God for her safe return, she said in a cracked, broken voice, 'Hal's dead, Papa. He's dead, and I was with him and I couldn't save him.' And then she started sobbing; sobbing as if she was never, ever going to stop.

Chapter Thirty-Five

DECEMBER 1938

It was the first week of December and Gilbert was walking down Pall Mall in the direction of Trafalgar Square. He'd just come from a meeting with the prime minister, a meeting that had filled him with nothing but despair. Neville Chamberlain was a man who yearned for peace in Europe and was prepared to go to any lengths – as long as they were not confrontational – to achieve it.

In September, with Hitler shouting that the Sudetenland was the last territorial demand he would make, Chamberlain had flown to Munich. He had come back carrying an agreement signed by himself, Hitler, Mussolini and the French prime minister Monsieur Daladier, that in exchange for the largely German-speaking Sudeten region of Czechoslovakia being incorporated into the Third Reich, there would be no aggression by Germany where the rest of Czechoslovakia was concerned. On his arrival back in Britain, Chamberlain had waved the agreement victoriously, declaring that he had secured 'Peace in our time'.

Gilbert, and the political friends who thought like him – Winston Churchill, Duff Cooper, Anthony Eden – were certain he had done no such thing. Chamberlain, though, as had been clear from the meeting Gilbert that was just coming from, was still naively convinced that Hitler's word could be trusted.

Gilbert was just approaching the Renaissance palace facade of the Travellers Club when he saw Max Bradley walking towards it from the other direction. They came to an awkward halt in front of each other at the foot of the club's steps.

Gilbert had neither seen nor spoken to Max since the time Max and Rozalind had split up, shortly before Max announced he was to be a contender in the 1936 presidential election.

It was Max who breached the awkwardness first. 'It's good to see you, Gilbert. You're looking well.'

It was a lie. Gilbert's handsome, strong-boned face looked positively haggard. Considering the perilous state of relations between Britain and Germany, Max wasn't surprised. Then he thought of Violet in Berlin, and of his responsibility for her being there. He thought of Gilbert believing her to be a Nazi-lover, in every sense of the word, and experienced such a burning attack of conscience that he knew he was going to have to put Gilbert in the picture.

'I'm staying here,' he said, indicating the club with a nod of his head. 'How about we have a drink?'

'That's fine by me.' Gilbert, curious as to what it was that had brought Max to London, walked with him into the familiar opulence of the club's entrance hall.

Instead of going into the bar, Max led the way into the Outer Morning Room, a large drawing room where a certain amount of privacy could usually be guaranteed. They sat in leather button-back chairs close to a window looking out over the street.

'It's been a while, Max,' Gilbert said after Max had asked an attentive member of staff for two Glenfiddich single malts. 'A little over five years, I think.'

'And a lot has happened since then,' Max responded, adding drily, 'For one thing, I'm not President of the United States.'

'Indeed, no.' Gilbert chuckled and the little ice left to be broken did so. 'And I am not prime minister.'

Max, wanting to bring up the subject of Violet and not sure of the best way of going about it, said, with one leg crossed over the other, 'So give me an update on Fenton family matters, Gilbert.'

For a long moment Gilbert didn't respond. His family matters were so dire there hadn't been one male friend he'd felt able to unburden himself to. Max, however, was different, for Max knew all the family – including Carrie – and that put him in a position no one else was in.

He said at last, 'The good news – the only good news – is that Thea is home. She went with Hal to Spain in the summer of '36. For well over a year he sent despatches on the war back to his paper, the *Evening News*. Then the despatches stopped and by the early months of this year he was south of Barcelona, fighting with a unit of the 11th International Brigade. Thea was in intermittent contact with him, driving ambulances for the Red Cross.'

He paused as the waiter served them their drinks.

'And Hal?' Max prompted, fearing the worst. 'Is he back in London, too?'

'No,' Gilbert said bleakly. 'He's dead. He and Thea were together at the time. They ran into a street fracas and he was shot in front of her.'

Max's jaw tightened. 'Where is Thea now? London or Gorton?'

'Gorton – she wanted to be near Carrie.' Gilbert took a swallow of his single malt and then said, 'But it's Violet who is of most concern to me, Max. You'll know from the gossip columns that she left Hollywood for the Babelsberg studios in Berlin four years ago. And you no doubt also know the kind of company she is keeping there. There's been enough "Government minister's daughter continues to date both Goebbels and Göring" headlines in the British press. How I've kept my position within the Cabinet is nothing short of a miracle.'

He put his drink down and leaned forward, his hands clasped between his knees, his grief over Violet so deep it was almost beyond bearing.

'She was such an adorable child, Max. So affectionate, so full of fun. Always reckless, and heedless of any consequences her actions might bring, of course. But I could never have envisaged ... never ever imagined that she would form friendships with men such as these.'

Max uncrossed his legs, drained his glass, took a deep breath and said, 'She hasn't, Gilbert. Or at least, not in the way you think.'

'But of course she has! I don't know what has

535

been in the American press, but surely you're up to date with what has been in the British press?'

Max cast a quick look around the drawing room. The couple of men who had been seated in it when they had arrived had left. Apart from themselves, the room was empty. Seeing no way of leading gently up to what he was about to say, Max plunged straight in.

'Four years ago, Gilbert, I had a meeting with Violet at the Beverly Hills Hotel in Hollywood. It wasn't a chance meeting. A man called Kirby, in the European intelligence and research section, had asked me to make contact with her.'

Gilbert froze.

Max, realizing that Gilbert had instantly made the connection between the US intelligence services and Violet being about to leave for Berlin, said succinctly, 'It was thought her position at Babelsberg – newly under the control of Joseph Goebbels – would put her in an ideal position to pick up gossip that could be useful to America and Britain.'

Gilbert felt as if his heart had stopped beating. 'The United States recruited my daughter as a spy!' He rose to his feet, trembling and white with rage. 'And you, Max? You facilitated it?'

Max thought Gilbert was about to punch him.

'The original belief was that she'd be in Berlin only for a short period of time – long enough to make whatever film it was she had gone there to make – and the arrangement was that she'd meet up socially and regularly with a contact in the US Embassy and pass on whatever gossip could prove useful. No one anticipated her turning into a fully fledged spy, or that four years down the line she would still be there.'

'But good God, Max! If the Gestapo get even a whiff of a suspicion as to what she's up to – and considering who she's spending her time with, they must have her within their sights all the time – she'll lose her life!'

Unsteadily he turned on his heel, heading to one of the many windows looking down into Pall Mall. He leaned his arm against it, his head against his arm, shuddering with the raging emotions he was trying to contain. If even a tad of suspicion fell on Violet she would be questioned by the Gestapo. Her relationships within the Nazi hierarchy might protect her a little, but nothing would be any protection if the truth as to why she had cultivated those relationships came to light. She would be tortured until she revealed what information she had passed on to the Americans. And when she had given that information, she would be executed.

He lifted his head from his arm, his forehead sheened with perspiration. It was Göring who, shortly after Violet had gone to Babelsberg, had revived beheading as a preferred method of execution.

For a moment Gilbert thought he was going to vomit. Behind him Max, now also on his feet, said, 'Every piece of information Violet has passed on to us has been passed on to British Intelligence. In the beginning what she gave us was useful, but not earth-shattering.'

'And now?' Still ashen, Gilbert turned away from the window.

'And now it's become of vital importance.'

'Does MI6 know Violet is the source of the information being passed on?'

Max shook his head. 'No. Only three people know she is the source. Me. Tom Kirby. And her US Embassy contact in Berlin.'

Gilbert experienced a stab of relief. The thought of his own government having such knowledge about Violet – and keeping it secret from him – would have been something he would have found impossible to handle.

Turning back to what really mattered, he said, 'No matter how important the information Violet is passing on, she can't be allowed to continue doing so. Though listening to Chamberlain you wouldn't think it, Britain and Germany will be at war within months, perhaps even less. Violet *has* to leave Germany. She has to leave now, before she's trapped there.'

The door opened and Clement Attlee, leader of the Labour Party, entered. Sensing the tension in the room he paused, looked towards the two of them and then, aware that a very private and heated discussion was under way, exited, closing the door behind him.

Max said tersely, 'I agree with you that she has to leave. Only she won't.'

'What the devil do you mean?' Even as he spoke, Gilbert's mind was racing. If he left immediately he could be in Berlin by early morning. Violet could be in London by late tomorrow night, and the entire nightmare scenario would be over.

'She's been ordered to leave and she hasn't.'

Max kept to himself that the order had been

538

his, and his alone: that Washington was too desperate for the information it was receiving from Violet to want it to come to an end.

Now that he had grappled with the initial shock, Gilbert was clear-headed and decisive. 'I'm going down to the front desk to book a seat on the late-night ferry to Ostend. I'll be in Berlin by morning. We'll finish talking when I've made the arrangement.'

Max nodded, and as Gilbert strode from the room he thought of the other person he wanted to talk to Gilbert about. He thought about Roz. He was still thinking about her twenty minutes later when Gilbert returned.

'Sorted?' he asked him.

'Yes. This isn't the Travellers Club for nothing. I've taken the liberty of ordering tea and coffee to be sent in. Tea for me, coffee for you.'

Max would secretly have far preferred another tumbler of Glenfiddich, but didn't say so. Instead he said, 'What is the latest news re Roz? We are no longer in contact, as you no doubt know.'

A waiter came in with the tea and coffee.

Gilbert waited until both had been poured, and then, adding a slice of lemon to his tea, he said, 'She's well. In fact she's arriving on the *Aquitania* at Southampton tomorrow morning and intends remaining in England until after Christmas – which she will be spending at Gorton. As will Thea and Carrie.'

'Carrie?' Even though Max had long ago accustomed himself to Fenton family eccentricities, Carrie spending time at Gorton over Christmas sounded a little odd. The last Max had heard of

539

her, she was a housekeeper at a stately home just outside Richmond. 'Won't Carrie be needed at her place of work?'

'Lydia Markham is spending Christmas in Madeira.'

Gilbert interlinked his fingers and stared down at them, sorely tempted to say more. And why not? There was very little age difference between himself and Max – and Max knew better than most what it was like to be in love with someone a couple of decades younger than himself. If he was ever going to unburden himself of his inner conflict, then Max was probably the best possible choice to unburden himself to.

He said, 'I see as much of Carrie as I can, Max. She's been the only person I've been able to speak to with regard to my many family anxieties – and I like being in her company. I always have.'

Max, immediately sensing all that Gilbert wasn't saying but wanted to say, commented encouragingly, 'Knowing Carrie, I find that perfectly understandable, Max. When does your divorce from Zephiniah become final?'

'In a month's time.'

'Then in a month's time you have no problem.'

Gilbert gave a mirthless laugh. 'Only an American would think there was no problem in a peer of the realm – and a government minister into the bargain – wanting to marry a woman who is his late nanny's granddaughter and the housekeeper to a friend of his first wife, a situation without problems.'

'Marry?' It wasn't often Max was almost robbed of speech.

'Well, of course marry! Where a young woman like Carrie is concerned, how could any honourable man consider anything else?'

Max thought of what he knew of Carrie, and what he knew of Gilbert, and could see the problem.

He said tentatively, 'What are Carrie's thoughts, where you and she are concerned?'

Gilbert looked at him as if he was mad.

'She doesn't have any thoughts, because she doesn't know how I feel! Dear God, Max. If she knew, she'd probably be appalled. To Carrie, I'm Lord Fenton. I'm someone she's known all her life and whom she thinks of much as she would a well-respected uncle who has always had her welfare at heart. Why should she feel any differently? I'm twenty-two years older than she is. I have – or soon will have had – two previous wives. Of course she doesn't know how I feel!'

Max, remembering how happy he and Roz had once been, despite a similar age difference, said, 'I think you're a fool for not giving her some indication. What harm can it do? And you might find you get a very nice surprise.'

'And if I did?' Gilbert's blue eyes blazed with frustration. 'This is England, not America. Class divides are written in stone.'

'Do you care?'

'I care, if it means Carrie not fitting in anywhere and being unhappy!'

'Britain's class system may have been written in stone up to now, but if you're right in predicting that Britain will soon be at war with Germany – and I think you are – then it won't be long before people will have more on their minds than class. If I were in your shoes, Gilbert, I'd make sure Carrie knew the nature of my feelings. Life is too short to miss out on happiness that could well be within your grasp.'

There was such naked feeling in his voice that Gilbert momentarily forgot about his own situation and thought of Max's.

'You're thinking of Roz,' he said perceptively.

Max nodded. 'I never have understood why she ended our relationship as abruptly and inexplicably as she did, and as she isn't married or engaged, it's about time I took the advice I've just given you and found out. The minute I leave here I'm heading off to Waterloo station. No matter what the outcome of my doing so, when Roz disembarks tomorrow at Southampton, I'm going to be there to meet her.'

Chapter Thirty-Six

There was a lump in Max's throat as he watched the *Aquitania* dock the next morning. The ship had played such an initial part in his and Roz's love story that he couldn't help hoping that Roz having sailed on it was a good omen. Since the day he had received her letter, posted from England and categorically breaking off her relationship with him, there had been no contact between them. His assumption at the time had been that she had met someone else: someone

542

younger; someone who was free to marry her.

She hadn't married, though. She hadn't even become engaged. She was still living as she had lived when they had been lovers. She was still an independent spirit, travelling the world with her Leica and beholden to no one.

As the gangplanks were lowered and disembarkation began, he felt a rising tension in his chest. He was taking a huge gamble. What if she walked off the ship arm-in-arm with someone? Someone Gilbert knew nothing about and hadn't been able to forewarn him about? What if, even if she wasn't with someone, Roz didn't want to have anything to do to with him? How was he going to deal with that situation?

He had secured himself a place in the arrivals hall where, hopefully, he wouldn't be able to miss her when she entered it. All around him were joyful greetings, as other passengers rushed eagerly into the arms of family and friends.

There was such a crush that he began to feel an edge of panic. What if he missed her? What if his journey had been all for nothing? Then, with a stab of relief, he saw her – and wondered how he'd ever thought it possible Roz could have been lost in a crowd.

She was head and shoulders taller than most of the women stepping into the arrivals hall – and three times as distinctive. Beneath a trilby worn at a provocative angle, her night-black hair swung sleekly forward at cheekbone level. A cherry-red, square-shouldered clutch coat was slung carelessly around her shoulders and beneath it she was wearing a grey grosgrain suit. Her heels were high and she was carrying just two items of luggage: a small suitcase and the camera-case she never travelled without.

In that moment he knew, beyond any shadow of doubt, that all his life his priorities had been wrong. He'd been single when he had met Roz. He could have married her, and he hadn't. Instead, because Myrtle possessed qualities making her the ideal wife for an ambitious Congressman, he had married Myrtle.

It was no wonder Roz had finally broken all ties between them and that, when his presidential ambitions had ended in failure, so had his marriage.

He didn't blame Roz for her actions, or a disillusioned Myrtle for hers.

The mistakes he had made were huge, but given another chance they were mistakes he would never make again. He knew now what mattered most in his life, and it wasn't what he had always thought.

It wasn't the greasy pole of Washington politics. It was Roz.

With his heart in his mouth he moved swiftly, manoeuvring a way through the crowd so that, though still some distance from her, he was standing directly in her line of sight.

She saw him almost immediately and stopped dead.

Feeling as if he was taking his life in his hands, Max walked towards her, came to a halt and said, 'Gilbert told me you were arriving this morning. I hope you don't mind my coming to meet you?'

'No.' Her eyes held his, wide with shock.

He took the suitcase from her hand. 'I've a lot I want to say to you, Roz, and the arrivals hall

544

isn't the place for it. How about we go over to the Grand Hotel for breakfast?'

'I've had breakfast. It was served on the ship.'

'Elevenses then.'

She nodded, and he still couldn't tell whether she was pleased to see him or appalled.

Together, side by side, but not touching, just as they had so often walked after their first meeting on the *Aquitania,* they walked out of the arrivals hall.

When they were in a taxi, he said, 'Gilbert tells me you will be spending Christmas at Gorton.'

'Yes.' Roz felt sick with nerves and bewilderment. After five years of absolutely no contact at all, surely Max had more important things to say to her than merely to comment on her Christmas holiday arrangements. She went on, 'I'm sorry you were knocked out of the presidential race so early on.'

Her throat was so tight the words came out stiffly and politely formal.

He said, still not able to gauge her reaction to him, 'So was I. I'm not sorry now, though. Roosevelt is going to have a nightmare of a time keeping America out of a war, if Hitler continues unchecked for much longer. The scenario in 1935 was a lot different from the scenario now.'

Roz could easily have got into a heated debate as to whether America's isolationist policy was the one the country should be pursuing, but she didn't want to talk politics. She wanted to know why Max hadn't engineered a meeting with her when his divorce from Myrtle had become final; she wanted to know if he knew the reason she

545

had broken off their affair; and, most of all, she wanted to know if he still loved her.

She said, unable to bear the stilted, awkward conversation a moment longer, and her voice no longer stiff and polite, but throbbing with emotion, 'Why didn't you get in touch after you were knocked out of the running for president, and after you and Myrtle divorced?'

He turned towards her on the taxi's shabby leather seat. 'It never in a million years occurred to me that you would want me to.' He took her hands in his. 'Your letter to me was so utterly final. The only thing I could assume was that you'd met someone else and – for all I knew, until I accidentally met up with Gilbert yesterday – that you were still with the person you'd left me for.'

'There was never anyone else. There never has been anyone else.'

'Then for the love of God, Roz! Why did you do what you did?'

The taxi had come to a halt outside the hotel. Neither of them was aware of it. Neither of them moved.

She said, knowing the answer to her question even as she asked it, 'Myrtle didn't tell you, then?'

The atmosphere in the taxi was now so charged that the driver made no attempt to remind them they were at their destination. Without turning his head, he put his meter onto extra waiting time.

With blood thudding in his ears, Max said, 'Myrtle didn't tell me *what*, Roz?'

'The last day we were together – at the apartment in New York – Myrtle came to see me. She told me you had been asked to stand as a nominee in the primaries. She said that accepting the nomination would mean you ending your affair with me and that, because you weren't prepared to do that, you had turned the invitation down. And she begged me to do what you wouldn't: to end our affair, so that you could fulfil your life's ambition of having a shot at running for the presidency.'

His hands crushed hers so tightly she thought her fingers were going to break. 'I didn't know, Roz. Please believe me when I say I didn't know.'

'When I read that you and Myrtle were divorcing, I was sure she would tell you, and when I still didn't hear from you…' The memory of the pain was so great, she flinched. 'When I still didn't hear from you I thought it was because you didn't want to step back into the past. That you'd moved on and there was someone else – someone new – in your life.'

'There isn't.' His voice cracked and broke. 'There never will be anyone new. The only person I want in my life, Roz, is you.'

The taxi driver coughed.

They both ignored him.

Roz said carefully, 'Before this goes any further, Max, you have to know that for me nothing has changed. I wasn't Washington political-wife material when you opted to marry Myrtle, and I'm still not Washington political-wife material. I do what I do. I'm a news photographer, and I'm vain enough to think that my work is important – that it brings the brutal truth of situations home

547

to people in a way more vivid than words alone. A month ago I was in Berlin, photographing fashionably dressed Berliners on the Ku'damm, screaming with laughter as Stormtroopers beat Jews senseless. In October I was in Czechoslovakia, photographing Sudeten Germans welcoming the monster that is Hitler as if he were the Messiah. Next month I don't know where I'll be. Probably Spain, because General Franco looks set to gain control of both Barcelona and Madrid and, when he's done that, it will be endgame for the Republicans. I'm nearly always going to be somewhere other than where you are – and I don't want the solution to the problem being the same as last time. I don't want there to be anyone else in your life but me.'

'It's not going to be like last time, Roz.'

Her hands were still trapped in his, his thigh was hard against hers and her mouth was a tantalizing few inches away.

He said fiercely, 'There's not going to be anyone else in my life, because I'm not going to marry anyone else. I'm going to marry you. You're right, in that you don't have one single good qualification for being the wife of a Congressman, but that doesn't matter any more. It doesn't matter because I'm not going to stand for re-election. I'm going to work in a new intelligence section that's being set up – and I don't have to be a Congressman to be an intelligence officer.'

It had started to rain. Roz could hear the raindrops pattering down on the taxi's roof. It was a sound she knew she would remember forever.

She said unsteadily, 'If you're going to marry

me, you have to propose to me.'

'In a taxicab?' There was amusement, monumental relief and bone-deep thankfulness in his voice. For every minute of his journey down to Southampton he had been terrified that Roz would want nothing to do with him; that she would regard him as being history, and would want him to stay history.

Now, in a few cataclysmic moments, he knew she loved him still, just as he still loved her. The fact that his life was back on track, though in a far different and better way than it had ever previously been, was a miracle he found almost too great to grasp.

Uncaring of how undignified it was for a man of his age to drop to one knee in the cramped back of a taxi, he did so.

'Dearest, darling Roz, will you marry me?' he asked. 'Will you marry me in the very soonest time possible?'

'Yes.' There wasn't the slightest hesitation in Roz's voice. Almost from the first moment they had met, she had known Max was the only man she was ever going to love. Though outwardly she had never let it show, the years without him had been an agony. She'd had affairs and had ended all of them without the least pang of regret. Now, coming completely out of the blue and in the space of half an hour, everything had changed. She was dazzled by happiness. And she knew exactly what kind of a wedding she wanted.

Because of his being divorced, it would have to be at a register office – and she wanted it to be just the two of them, and two witnesses. That way it wouldn't matter that Violet and Olivia were in Berlin, and it would spare Thea from attending a wedding when she was still in such deep grief over Hal's death.

'I think sixteen days' notice is necessary for a register-office wedding,' she said huskily, as he sat back on the seat and took her in his arms. 'That means it will be a Christmas wedding.'

It was the last thing she said for quite a while, for his kiss was deep and passionate and lasted a long, long time.

When at last he raised his head from hers, the taxi driver cleared his throat. 'Excuse me for interrupting the two of you,' he said, 'but I have a living to earn. So if you don't mind...'

Still with an arm around Roz, Max reached into an inside pocket for money and the driver jumped out of the taxi and opened the nearside rear door, saying as they stepped onto the pavement, 'Let me be the first to congratulate you both – and if you want a wedding car on the big day, I could put silver ribbons on the bonnet and do the job for half-price.'

Max gave a shout of laughter.

Still laughing and giggling – and with their arms round each other's waist – they ran in the rain up the steps of Southampton's Grand Hotel, the world a very different place for both of them from the one they had woken up to only a few hours earlier.

Chapter Thirty-Seven

It was a bitterly cold night as the last ferry of the day left Dover for Ostend, and only a few passengers were on deck as the ship slid out into the English Channel. Gilbert was one of them. With the collar of his overcoat pulled up high, a homburg crammed hard down on his head and gloved hands shoved deep into his coat pockets, he watched as beneath a star-studded sky Dover's cliffs faded ghost-like into the darkness.

Ever since 1066 the white cliffs that he could no longer see had stood inviolate. No foreign invader – not the Spanish in the sixteenth century, or the French in the eighteenth century – had succeeded in landing an army and storming inland. England's moat had been her protection.

But that had been before the days of air power. He thought of Hitler's Luftwaffe, brought into being against the terms of the Versailles Treaty, and of the way, as an ally of General Franco, it had flexed its muscles by bombing the little Basque town of Guernica into extinction.

At the thought of towns in Britain suffering a similar fate, fear squeezed his heart. He crushed the sensation. If Hitler created a situation in which Britain had no option but to go to war, it wasn't fear that would be needed. It was courage.

The kind of courage that Violet had, unknown to him, been displaying for more than four years. The kind of courage Dieter and Olivia maintained on a daily basis, as they networked with others who wanted to see a return to sanity for Germany and an end to Hitler. The kind of courage Judith would be having to find, in a city that no longer respected the life of anyone Jewish, or believed to be Jewish.

At last, knowing he should get as much sleep as possible, Gilbert made his way to his cabin, but his dreams were troubled, full of the images of burning towns and rampant swastikas.

By the time he was on a train, travelling through Belgium into Germany, it was early dawn. He ordered coffee and croissants from the steward and focused his thoughts on Violet. She was living in Dahlem, an affluent residential district in south-west Berlin. The train he was on terminated at Berlin's central railway station, and from there it was only a short cab ride to Dahlem. Only when Violet had packed her bags, closed her apartment and was with him was Gilbert going to head towards Olivia and Dieter's home in Bellevue-strasse, near the zoo.

That he now knew why Violet had for so long cultivated relationships with members of the Nazi hierarchy was a relief so great that in private he had wept. With the relief had come a terror that was overwhelming. Reckless and courageous as she was, that her motives for her friendships had gone for so long undiscovered could only have been down to the most phenomenal luck – and it was luck that could run out at any moment.

If it did, would it have any repercussions for Olivia and Dieter? At the very least it would raise doubts as to their loyalty – and if once there was a sliver of doubt and attention was focused on Dieter, the result, where he and his fellow plotters were concerned, would be catastrophic.

Snow was falling as the train approached the German border. Gilbert took his passport out of his breast pocket. Violet was a heroine on a mega-scale, but so too, in her own quiet way, was Olivia. He didn't, though, want to be the father of heroines – for heroines too often became dead heroines. What he was hoping, on this trip, was that he would be returning to England not only with Violet, but with Olivia as well.

He didn't want Olivia trapped in Germany when war was finally declared – and he was as certain as his friends Winston Churchill and Anthony Eden were that the Sudetenland was not going to be the last of Hitler's territorial demands and that war with Germany was inevitable.

The train came to a halt. Along with everyone else he disembarked in order to have his passport inspected and stamped, reflecting that if he returned with two out of three of his major anxieties taken care of, he would be profoundly grateful. It would, though, still leave an anxiety that was growing bigger with every passing day – and that anxiety was Judith Zimmermann.

'*Danke,*' he said as his passport was stamped and handed back to him.

It was six months now since his visit to the Home Office. Within twenty-four hours of that visit he had signed legal forms naming him as Judith Zimmermann's sponsor and guaranteeing that she would be no financial burden on the state. Copies of his guarantee had been sent to the British Embassy in Vienna. Judith had been notified. All the paperwork that could be done had been done. And still Judith was without an exit visa.

He stepped back into the train, wondering if Dieter would be able to cut through whatever red tape was holding up Judith's emigration. Even as the thought came to him, he realized how inadvisable it would be for Dieter to be seen to have a Jewess's welfare at heart. His safety lay in his apparent total loyalty as a Nazi. As a senior Foreign Office official, he even sported a much-coveted gold swastika lapel pin that was given only to the favoured and had Hitler's initials engraved on the back of it.

If anyone was going to have to wrestle with German officialdom over why no exit visa had yet been granted, then he, and not Dieter, was going to have to be the one doing the wrestling.

It would mean his travelling from Berlin to Vienna – and that would mean a delay in getting Violet out of the country. Much as he hated the thought of it, it was something that couldn't be avoided. He couldn't be so close to Vienna and not make personal contact with Judith, and with the officials who were stonewalling her visa application.

As the train eased away from the border halt and steamed into the Third Reich, Gilbert remembered travelling through the same country-side with Olivia, fourteen years earlier. The difference between the Germany of then and the Germany of now was so great – and so monstrous – as to seem almost unbelievable to him. In 1924 it had been a country he'd had great hopes for. Now it was a country that filled him with repugnance and despair.

At Berlin's cathedral-like central station a mammoth, impossible-to-ignore poster of Hitler looked down from a wall, eyes glittering and arms folded. Everywhere that could be draped with a flag was draped with one. There were so many swastikas everywhere that his head spun.

Ignoring Hitler's piercing gaze, he made straight for the taxi rank. The queue was long and, as he waited, he bitterly regretted not having realized that though it wasn't snowing in London, it most certainly would be in Berlin. He was wearing an overcoat over a three-piece Harris tweed suit and was warm enough, but his leather-soled shoes weren't the best kind of footwear for the icy, snow-covered streets.

Aching for strong coffee, he made his way slowly up the queue. He'd been travelling for fourteen hours and had been awake – apart from the couple of hours' sleep he'd managed to snatch on the ferry – for twenty-eight hours, and he was tired now, as well as anxious. What if Violet wasn't at home? What if she was at the studios? If he took a taxi to the film studios, would they let him in? And if they did let him in, would there be anywhere private where they could have the kind of conversation he'd come to Berlin to have with her?

Finally, with relief, he stepped into a taxi.

'*Gartenstrasse dreiundzwanzig, Dahlem, bitte,*' he said to the driver, knowing he wouldn't be having to ask himself all these questions if he'd telephoned Violet before he'd left Dover, but that to have let her know he was travelling in such haste to see her would have given her too much prior warning of why he was doing so; and that, Violet being Violet, she might no longer even have been in Berlin by the time he'd arrived. It was better this way, but as the taxi headed out of the centre of the city in a south-westerly direction, he was fervently praying he would find her at home.

The villas in Dahlem bordered on being mansions, and number twenty-three, though with smaller grounds than some of its neighbours, was still a preposterously large house for a single young woman to occupy alone.

That was, of course, if she *was* occupying it alone.

As he paid off the driver and stepped out of the taxi there was a sheen of perspiration on his forehead. Whenever he had visited previously there had never been a trace of any other occupant, but whenever he had visited previously Violet had always had plenty of advance warning.

With compacted snow scrunching beneath his feet, he walked up the steps to the door and rang the bell.

A maid, neatly dressed in black and wearing a dainty lace-edged apron, opened the door.

'*Guten Tag,*' he said, removing his hat. '*Informieren Sie bitte Fraülein Fenton dass ihr Vater mit ihr sprechen möchte?*'

The maid, whom he judged to be no more than sixteen or seventeen, bobbed a curtsey and opened the door wide.

He stepped inside, his relief vast that Violet was obviously at home. As the door closed behind him, he heard Violet call out from a nearby room, *'Wer ist es, Irmgard?'*

'Ihr Vater!' Irmgard called back.

From a room on the left-hand side of the large hall came a loud shriek. Gilbert couldn't tell if it was delighted or horrified.

In the brief seconds before Violet hurtled out of the drawing room and into his arms, he was filled with horror at the prospect of the commander-in-chief of the Luftwaffe, or the Reich Minister for Public Enlightenment and Propaganda, striding out of the drawing room in her wake.

'Papa! How lovely! Why didn't you tell me you were coming?'

She was wearing grey flannel trousers and a shocking-pink sweater that should have clashed with her torrent of red hair, but didn't.

After he had hugged her fiercely, she held onto his arm, propelling him into a drawing room that was blessedly empty.

'Are you in Berlin on government business?' she asked as he shrugged himself out of his coat, handing it, and his hat, to her maid.

'Goodness, no. I have not the slightest thing to do with foreign affairs. That's Halifax's department.'

Viscount Halifax, a fellow Yorkshireman, had been Foreign Secretary ever since Anthony Eden had resigned in protest over the prime minister's appeasement policy.

'When did you arrive? Are you staying with Olivia and Dieter?' As he sat down on a comfortable sofa, Violet slipped her feet out of her shoes and curled up beside him, her arm still hugging his.

'I travelled on yesterday's late-night ferry to Ostend and I've come straight here.'

'But why on earth...?' The delight in her eyes vanished, to be replaced by alarm. 'There's nothing wrong, is there, Papa? It isn't Thea, is it? Or Roz, or Carrie?'

'No, sweetheart. Everyone is fine. I'm not bringing bad news from home.'

She stared at him in bewilderment. 'Then I don't understand, Papa.'

His eyes held hers, so much love in his heart that it hurt. 'There's a lot I want to say to you, Violet, but before I do I'd like some coffee – black with no sugar.'

'But with a slug of cognac?' she asked, realizing for the first time just how tired and drawn he looked.

Cognac in midday coffee wasn't a habit with him, but he nodded, grateful for the suggestion.

Violet jumped to her feet and pressed a wall bell for Irmgard.

When the maid entered, Violet said in German, 'A huge pot of coffee, please, Irmgard. And the Rémy Martin.'

When he judged Irmgard to be well on her way to the kitchen, he said, 'Is your telephone safe, Violet?'

'No, in Berlin no one's telephone is safe. Consequently my telephone lives in a small cubicle to the left of the hall.'

He took her hands in his, saying emotionally, 'I

spoke with Max yesterday. He told me the reason for your being in Berlin. The reason for your friendships...'

He choked up, unable to continue.

She squeezed his hands tightly, her eyes as suspiciously bright as his. 'Please don't be upset, Papa. I can't bear to see you upset.'

'You've been very courageous, Violet. I'm very, very proud of you. But you have been here – doing what you've been doing – for too long. Max urgently wants you to leave.'

'His superiors in Washington don't want me to leave.'

'To his superiors in Washington you are expendable.'

To put such an unpalatable truth into words cost him a lot.

Violet flashed him a sudden wide smile. 'Well, now I know why you're here, let me make you some breakfast, before we make necessary arrangements. What would you like, Papa? Bacon and eggs or an omelette?'

'An omelette,' he said, sagging with relief that his mission had been so easily accomplished.

She rose to her feet and he said, startled, 'You're not really going to make my breakfast yourself, are you? Surely in a house this size you have kitchen staff?'

Violet giggled. 'You'd think so, wouldn't you? But I don't. I only have Irmgard.'

'But why?'

He was looking so perplexed that she felt a surge of protectiveness towards him.

'Dear Papa, in Berlin everyone is an informer.

559

To pass on tittle-tattle about neighbours or employers has become the accepted way of showing loyalty to the party. I don't want someone under my roof who is polite to my face and behind my back is watching and reporting on what music I play, what books I read. I know without a shadow of doubt that Irmgard doesn't do so. I have a cleaning lady come in twice a week for a couple of hours, and I can just about suffer that. Would you like some cheese in your omelette? I have some nice Emmentaler cheese, very mild and nutty.'

She left the room as Irmgard, carrying a tea-tray with coffee cups, percolator and a bottle of Rémy Martin, entered. With a shy smile she put the tray down on a low table and poured his coffee.

When he had the room to himself once again he poured a generous amount of cognac into the coffee and felt relaxation seeping through his bones. If the task he had set himself in Vienna went as smoothly as the one he had set himself in Berlin, he would be able to begin sleeping easily again.

He looked around the room. The furnishings were very modern; very Violet. The carpet was white with black zebra-like markings running through it. The long low table that the tea-tray was resting on had chromium legs and a glass top. The sofa he was sitting on was covered in white leather, as were the chairs in the room. Over a pale marble fireplace was a large abstract painting, and in a corner was a Christmas tree, looking unlike any Christmas tree he had ever seen before. Though the tree was unmistakably real, it had been sprayed silver and all the baubles on it were silver.

With a catch in his throat he saw that the angel on the top of the tree was as near a replica as Violet had been able to get of the angel that decorated the top of the tree at Gorton every year.

Violet popped her head round the corner of the door. 'Your omelette is ready, Papa. It's going to be on the dining table the minute you sit down.'

He drank the last of his cognac-laden coffee and rose to his feet. In contrast to the way he had felt when he arrived at the house, as he walked out of the drawing room and into the dining room he did so a very happy man.

There was a fresh percolator of coffee on the table and Violet sat opposite him, every now and then passing him a fresh roll, or the butter dish.

'The painting in the drawing room,' he said. 'It's Nazi doctrine that abstract art is degenerate and not to be tolerated, so how do you get away with having a Kandinsky-type painting so prominently displayed?'

Violet clasped her hands in front of her on the table. 'First of all, Papa, the painting isn't a Kandinsky-type painting. It *is* a Kandinsky. And second, I get away with it because no one apart from my cleaning lady and Irmgard – ever steps across the threshold.'

He laid down his knife and fork.

'But surely – the people you see ... Goebbels and Göring...'

'They don't come here, Papa. This house is my sanctuary. It is what keeps me sane, and is why I

561

have been able to do what I have been doing for so long.'

'Then is what the foreign press has led us to believe... The photographs of you accompanying...' His voice tailed off. It was beyond him to utter the names again.

Seeing his distress, she said gently, 'I think it's about time I told you about the relationships that trouble you so much. First of all, Paul Goebbels.'

'Paul? But I thought his Christian name was Joseph?'

'His full Christian name is Paul Joseph. He likes me to call him Paul. I don't sleep with him, Papa. He doesn't want me to sleep with him. I'm just window-dressing.'

Gilbert stared at her. 'You mean Goebbels is homosexual?'

Violet giggled. 'Heavens, no. He's notorious for his extra-marital affairs, but our relationship is a little different.'

She unclasped her hands and poured herself another cup of coffee. 'One of the first people I became friendly with when I arrived at Babelsberg was another actress, Lída Baarová. Goebbels was crazy about her, but she's a Czech, and as Czechs are Slavs – and therefore members of an inferior race, in Nazi eyes – Goebbels tried to keep the affair from Hitler for as long as he could. His being seen out and about with me was a smokescreen, nothing more.'

She took a drink of her coffee and then said, 'It worked quite well for a year or two, but when Goebbels asked his wife for a divorce, his wife went straight to Hitler, and Hitler's reaction was instant. Divorce was *verboten,* and so was a Slav mistress. Lída fled to Prague, and Goebbels maintained his dignity by continuing to be seen out and about with me, which means that I still circulate in the very highest of Nazi circles.'

'And Field Marshal Göring?'

'Ah, well. Hermann Göring is a slightly different matter.' Violet took a deep drink of her coffee.

Gilbert waited.

When she put her cup down she said, 'What you have to understand, Papa, is that there is great rivalry between Goebbels and Göring. Göring believes I am Goebbels's mistress and that, by his being seen in public with me, he is plunging the man he loathes into frenzies of jealousy. In actual fact Göring is devoted to his wife, who understands the game being played.'

She paused, a shiver running down her back. Other men in the Nazi hierarchy, men like Luther Schultz, second-incommand at Kripo, the criminal investigative branch of the country's police force, most certainly did not understand the game being played, and his not doing so resulted in the kind of unpleasant situations she had no intention of telling her father about. Her refusal to become his mistress had made Schultz into an enemy – the kind of enemy no sane woman wanted.

With great effort she pushed the thought of Luther Schultz to the back of her mind. What she was trying to do at the moment was reassure her father, not give him even more cause for concern.

'So you see, Papa,' she continued, 'where Paul Goebbels and Hermann Göring are concerned,

563

nothing is as it seems.'

'Except that every time you passed on inform-ation to the Americans you risked your life.'

She pushed her chair away from the table and walked across to one of the room's long windows. Looking out of it, and with her arms folded tightly across her chest, she said, 'I know you, and the rest of the world, are aware of what happened in Germany a month ago, Papa, but cold facts will not give you any idea of the horror of it – and, for the Jews, the terror.'

'Kristallnacht,' he said, knowing only too well to what she was referring. 'Crystal night. The Night of the Broken Glass.'

It had been the night when, thanks to the instant reporting of it by foreign journalists, any lingering trust he might have had in the policy of appeasement had been snuffed out like a candle-flame.

In retaliation for the shooting of a German Embassy official by a Polish Jew, Hitler had ordered full-scale coordinated attacks on Jews throughout Germany. Jewish homes, hospitals and schools were ransacked and looted by both paramilitary forces and non-Jewish citizens. Nationwide, in an orgy of hate and destruction, the windows of Jewish shops were smashed with axes and sledgehammers, the shards of broken glass in the streets giving birth to the name Kristallnacht. In towns the length and breadth of the country synagogues burned; businesses were looted; Jews were beaten on the streets, and thousands were arrested and taken to concentra-tion camps.

It had been as if the entire non-Jewish German nation had been convulsed with a sickness: a dark and savage and brutal insanity.

In America, President Roosevelt had told reporters, 'I can scarcely believe that such a thing could have occurred in twentieth-century civilization.'

It had been a statement that Gilbert was in complete agreement with.

Violet hugged her arms a little tighter against her chest. 'If the information I have gleaned, and passed on, has done anything to make the American government rethink its isolationist policy, and to impress on Britain's government that Hitler has no intention of keeping any promise or any treaty that he makes, and that the sooner Britain is on a war footing the better, then the risks were necessary.'

She turned to face him and the sun streaming through the window caught her torrent of red hair, making it glitter like fire.

'Hitler is a madman, Papa. He's a megalomaniac. His telling Britain and France that the Sudetenland is the last of his territorial demands is a lie, as is his constant claim that all he wants is peace.'

She came back to the table, this time sitting down next to him.

Slipping her hand in his she said, 'Only hours after he had signed the Munich Agreement, Hitler told Goebbels that Chamberlain's backing down over the Sudetenland crisis had shown him how powerful he himself was. Hitler told him that, because of his other plans for territorial expansion, a war with Britain and France would be inevitable, but that he was master of the situation; that Germany's military situation was excellent and that the country could fearlessly face a war with the great democracies. This, Papa, while at the same time Prime Minister Chamberlain was waving his piece of white paper at Heston Aerodrome declaring it was an agreement, signed by Hitler, promising that Britain and Germany would never again go to war with each other!'

Ashen-faced, Gilbert stood up, saying, 'That Goebbels would tell you such things only makes me more vastly relieved that you will soon be out of the country. I'd return to London with you today, if I could, but I have a vital task to see to first in Vienna. While I'm there it will give you time to pack what you are going to bring with you and close up the house.'

'Vienna? But why? Since the *Anschluss* things are even more horrendous there than they are here.'

'Zephiniah has a twenty-seven-year-old daughter living in Vienna. Her name is Judith Zimmermann and she believes herself to be Jewish – and may even be Jewish. I'm acting as her sponsor so that she can emigrate to Britain, but things aren't moving along very fast. I'm going to Vienna to find out why.'

Violet had a score of questions she would have liked to ask about a stepsister she had never heard of, but uppermost was her need to disabuse her father of the impression he was under.

'I shan't be packing, or closing up the house,

Papa. At least not yet.'

He opened his mouth to protest and she said swiftly, 'Hitler isn't only planning to break the agreement he made at Munich and to march into the rest of Czechoslovakia; he's planning an invasion of Poland. I can pass on this information till I'm blue in the face, but what is needed for America and Britain to treat it as hard fact and for Chamberlain to put Britain on a full-scale war footing – is documentary evidence. The very second I've got that, Papa, I'll be on a train to Ostend as fast as light.'

Their extraordinary-coloured amber eyes held, hers fierce with determination, his filled with the horror of knowing that the stakes were so high that he had no choice but to give way to her.

'Promise me,' he said unsteadily, 'promise me that you will keep your word.'

'I promise, Papa.' She stood on tiptoe to kiss his cheek. 'Darling Papa, what a worry I've always been to you, haven't I? But I promise I won't be, once I'm safely back in England. I do so long to be in Outhwaite again and to see Hermione and Miss Calvert and Jim and Charlie. Do you know I haven't yet seen little Charlie junior? We'll have to have the most *enormous* Gorton party, and it's all going to be the most splendid fun.'

They walked arm-in-arm into the hall and she didn't ring for Irmgard to fetch him his hat and coat. She went for them herself, and helped him on with his coat.

The drawing-room door was open, the Christmas tree clearly visible.

He said, 'Did you have a long search to find an

angel so like the one you grew up with at Gorton?'

'No. The Christmas markets in Berlin are flooded with Christmas-tree angels in all shapes and sizes.' Her eyes grew misty with remembrance. 'I used to love decorating the tree with Mama and Thea and Olivia. Some years Roz spent Christmas with us and helped as well, and Carrie was always there, holding the ladder steady for whoever was placing the angel on top of the tree. When I was little Thea and Olivia never had much time for me, but Carrie always did. In all the years I have lived away from home the person I have always missed most – apart from you, of course – has been Carrie.'

Gilbert, who missed Carrie every second of every day that he wasn't with her, said with deep feeling, 'When I'm away from Carrie, I miss her too.'

Violet tilted her head to one side, regarding him intently.

At last she said perceptively, 'Then when your divorce is finalized, why don't you marry her?'

'I'm going to,' he said as she handed him his homburg. 'At least I am if, when I pluck up the courage to ask her, she says yes.'

Chapter Thirty-Eight

Olivia was as surprised and delighted to see him as Violet had been.

'You should have let us know you were coming,' she said, ushering him into a drawing room furnished in a style reminiscent of Gorton Hall when Blanche had been alive. 'I would have met you at the station.'

'Is Dieter home?'

'Not for another two or three hours. The Foreign Office workload is manic at the moment. Have I to ring for some plum-cake and English tea?'

'That sounds grand.'

He had decided before he'd arrived at the house that he was going to say nothing about the purpose of his trip until Dieter was with them. Talking about Judith wasn't something he wanted to do twice and, unless Olivia brought Violet into the conversation, he wasn't going to mention her name to Olivia, either. To put Olivia in more danger than she was already in would be insanity, and what she didn't know she couldn't, if she was ever questioned, tell.

He was going to tell Dieter, though. There could well be a time when Violet would need his help.

The thought made him shudder and Olivia said in immediate concern, 'Poor darling Papa. You're not used to Berlin's fierce cold weather, are you? Let's get cosy in front of the fire with cake and tea, and I'll tell you all about the most amazing experience I had a little while ago.'

He'd always found Olivia the easiest of his children to be with. She didn't possess Violet's unnerving ability to shatter his peace of mind, or Thea's political left-wing intensity. Nor did she possess their fierce intelligence and perceptiveness. Thea would have realized instantly that something was dreadfully wrong for him to have arrived in Berlin so suddenly without warning, and would have questioned him, just as Violet had questioned him.

That Olivia hadn't, and that they were about to have tea and cakes in front of a log fire while she chattered away happily, was something for which he was thankful.

The minute he was seated Olivia said, 'The Führer has a secret known only to a handful of people – I'm one of them, and Roz is another.'

His relaxation vanished in an instant. 'Tell me,' he said, fearful of what he was about to hear.

Olivia kicked off her shoes and curled her feet beneath her on the sofa. 'He has a mistress – and he's had her for several years now. She's twenty-three years younger than he is, and he never takes her out and about in public. He hides her away at the Berghof, his home in the Alps at Berchtesgaden.'

Gilbert let out a cautious sigh of relief. It was certainly an interesting secret to know, but hardly one that would bring the Gestapo down on Olivia's head – not, that is, unless it was openly chatted about.

'You don't talk to friends about it, do you?'

'Lord! Of course not, Papa. It's fascinating, though, isn't it? And the most fascinating thing is that she isn't at all as you might imagine a mistress of Hitler's would be. Both Roz and I rather liked her.'

The blood left Gilbert's face.

'You've *met* her?' he asked incredulously.

Olivia bubbled with laughter. 'I met her for the first time when Dieter, along with other high-ranking members of the Foreign Office, was invited to the Berghof and wives were invited also. She was fascinated by the fact that I was English, and we got on rather well together. Then, in October, she accompanied Hitler to Berlin when he was giving a major speech in the Olympic stadium. True to form, Hitler didn't want her presence noted and, as she was going to be on her own in a hotel room that evening, she asked if I would keep her company. And so I did.'

'And Rozalind?' he demanded, wondering when the many shocks he'd received over the-last thirty-six hours would come to a merciful end. 'How on earth did Rozalind come to meet her?'

'She came with me to the hotel and, when I went up to Eva's room, she remained in the hotel lounge. After a little while I mentioned that my American cousin was downstairs, and Eva immediately suggested that she join us.'

'Dear God! Where were the SS officers when this was happening? There must have been some in the hotel with her?'

'There were. Two of them were seated outside

her room all the time we were there, but they'd been told to expect me and so I wasn't a surprise to them, and they accepted Roz as being just another foreigner Eva wanted to meet.'

'And there have been no repercussions?'

'No. None. Don't look so worried, Papa. We were simply three young women, all approximately the same age, having a very jolly time together.'

He came back to the sofa, sitting beside her once again. 'And so this young woman you say is Hitler's mistress? Who is she? What did you say her name was?'

'Eva. Eva Braun. And she wasn't at all what we had expected. Knowing how formal Germans always are, Roz and I were wearing evening gowns and we arrived to find Eva wearing shorts.'

'Good grief! Why on earth...?'

'She was in the middle of an exercise routine. She's very slender, very athletic. Despite our wearing very unsuitable clothes, we joined in the routine with her and we all laughed ourselves silly. She's pretty, but not at all glamorous or sophisticated. When we'd exhausted ourselves and were sitting drinking wine and eating pretzels she told us that she loves swimming, skiing and American films. She only spoke of Hitler once, and that was when she was talking about his dog and of how fond she is of dogs. Roz said afterwards that she doubts if Eva is even remotely politically aware. There was absolutely no Nazi talk. None at all. She was bright enough, and very bubbly, but certainly not an intellectual. Her main interest –

which I understand completely – is clothes. Can you imagine Hitler chatting about clothes? I can't.'

Neither could Gilbert.

Not until four hours later, when Dieter was with them and they were having dinner – with the dining-room door firmly closed and no telephone in sight – did Gilbert bring up the subject of Judith.

Olivia's jaw dropped. 'But that's incredible, Papa. It's more than incredible, it's unbelievable.'

'Unbelievable or not, it's a fact – as is Zephiniah having Jewish blood, and the baby having been given to a Jewish family for adoption.'

Dieter said slowly, 'And as far as you know, her papers are all in order and there is no problem about her entry to Britain?'

Gilbert nodded. 'The delay can only be at the Vienna end of things.' He laid his knife and fork down. 'I'm travelling there tomorrow, in the hope of finding out what the hiccup is and getting things moving.'

His words were greeted with a long silence.

Olivia and Dieter exchanged looks that indicated neither of them thought it likely his trip would meet with success.

At last Dieter said gravely, 'I doubt it is, as you say in your understated English way, a "hiccup" that is the problem. If you think things in Berlin are bad for Jews, they are far worse in Vienna. If Judith Zimmermann's home, family possessions and bank account have been appropriated, then the next action is most likely to be her imprisonment in Mauthausen, than the satisfactory handling of her exit visa.'

573

'Mauthausen?'

'A newly opened concentration camp near Vienna. The transportation of thousands of Austrian Jews to German camps such as Sachsenhausen and Dachau was deemed to be too costly and time-consuming.'

The self-loathing in his voice was oceans deep. He said bitterly, 'There was a time when Hitler made us proud to be German, but it's hard now to remember that far back. Now I am so ashamed, Gilbert, that there are times when I find it hard to breathe.'

His hand tightened around the stem of his wine glass until the knuckles were white.

Olivia said to him tentatively, 'Now that Austria is merely another region of Germany, would it be possible for Papa to bring Judith back with him to Berlin? She would be safer here, with us, than she is at the moment in Vienna.'

'No matter how distant the connection, it couldn't be known that a Jewish girl is part of our extended family. If nothing else, it would label us as Jew-lovers. My work at the Foreign Office would come to a very swift end and I would come under the kind of scrutiny that could endanger all the people in *die Gruppe*.'

He didn't have to specify what group he meant. Gilbert, as well as Olivia, knew very well to whom he was referring.

Olivia said, 'Aryans are still allowed to employ Jews for menial work. She could work here in the kitchen until she gets clearance to leave for Britain.'

'That's true.' Dieter paused thoughtfully and

then said, 'And that way there could be no speculation – not even from our existing household
staff.' He looked across the table at Gilbert. 'There
is still a problem, though. The usual method of
travelling to Berlin from Vienna is through
Czechoslovakia. Judith's passport would have to
be shown and, unless it already bears a stamp
signifying that she has emigrant status, she would
be turned back. A safer option would be to take a
train from Vienna to Munich, and then from
Munich to Berlin. And whichever way you travel,
don't travel openly together. You are too obviously
English, Gilbert. It will attract attention to her.
Once she's here with us she will, as Olivia has said,
be far safer than she is at present. Just make sure
she brings every scrap of documentation she has,
with regard to her emigration and entry into
Britain.'

'And the train times tomorrow from Berlin to
Vienna?'

'I don't know the times of trains through the
day. The most usual train to catch is the night-
sleeper. It leaves Berlin at midnight and arrives in
Vienna at ten in the morning.'

'Then that is the train I shall leave on.'

'Before you do, I'd like you to take a short
night-time walk with me in the Tiergarten.'

Gilbert, knowing Dieter wanted to update him
on his fellow conspirators' plans, said, as the door
opened and a maid came in to clear the table,
'Thank you, Dieter. There's nothing I'd like
better than to see the Tiergarten under snow and
by the light of the moon.'

'Things are not progressing,' Dieter said tautly as, with overcoat collars turned up against the bitter cold, gloved hands deep in their pockets, they crossed Bellevuestrasse and entered the park. 'There is too much difference of opinion as to the best way to proceed. Those in *die Gruppe* who, like me, are in the Foreign Office think the only sure way to be free of Hitler is assassination. Men with an army background – the generals who are with us, but who have sworn an oath of loyalty to him – think the solution is a *coup d'état*. The result is stalemate.'

Snow crunched beneath their feet as they began walking along one of the park's narrow pathways.

'And although I am most firmly with those who wish to kill Hitler, I am also beset by other questions. For instance, once he is dead, who steps into his shoes? Göring? Goebbels? You see the problem we have, Gilbert? A simple assassination is not enough. There has to be a complete, new, non-Nazi government ready to take over. The task we face is monumental.'

Gilbert could well see the problem Dieter and his fellow conspirators faced, but it wasn't one with which he could usefully help. Mindful of how little time there was before he needed to leave for the railway station, he said coming to a halt, 'There's something I must tell you before I leave. Something it is best Olivia does not know – at least not yet.'

Dieter turned to face him. Taking a hand out of his pocket to hold his coat collar together against his throat, he said, 'Everything these days is a

576

secret. One more will make no difference to me.'

'It's with regard to Violet.'

Dieter tensed. 'Olivia and I no longer spend time with Violet. A long time ago I was ... over-friendly with Violet. Olivia has forgiven me, but she can't forgive Violet. It's something I deeply regret, but I've always known the day would come when I would have to tell you why Olivia no longer has a loving relationship with her.'

Gilbert drew in a deep, steadying breath. He'd known Olivia and Violet were no longer on close sisterly terms, but had thought it had been down to Violet's lifestyle.

The truth was a huge blow; not so much where Violet was concerned – at the moment he could forgive Violet anything – but where Dieter was concerned. He'd always had a great deal of affection for his son-in-law and, since knowing of his involvement in the conspiracy to topple Hitler, a great deal of respect as well.

Now he didn't know what he felt.

Dieter said awkwardly, 'There were other things as well, Gilbert. Violet's affairs with men like Goebbels and Göring...'

'She's had no such affairs.'

Dieter gave a disbelieving laugh.

Gilbert said bluntly, 'Ever since Violet came to Babelsberg she's been spying for the Americans. She loathes and detests the Nazis just as much as you do. I'm telling you because I think the day may come when she will need your help – or when you may need hers.'

Dieter stared at him in incredulity and then understanding dawned, to be followed by horror as he realized how gravely both he and Olivia had misjudged Violet – and then horror followed horror as he thought of the constant danger Violet was in.

He said, his voice raw, 'But why for the Americans? I don't understand.'

'The suggestion that, as a high-profile film actress at Babelsberg, Violet was in a unique position to mix with Nazis close to Hitler and pick up useful information was made to Max Bradley. And it was Max who recruited her. I doubt she needed much persuasion, but what clinched it was when he told her that whatever information she passed on would also be passed on to British intelligence.'

Cloud covered the moon, and the snow-covered pathway was suddenly barely visible. Without speaking they turned, beginning to retrace their steps, aware that all that had needed to be said had been, and that tomorrow, for both of them, was going to be another long, stressful day.

At five past ten the next morning Gilbert walked out of Vienna's Westbahnhof station. When he had been a student he had spent a holiday in Vienna, but the city that now greeted him was changed beyond recognition. There were uniforms everywhere: the brown uniforms of Stormtroopers; the black uniforms of the SS; the field-grey of regular army men. As for swastikas – there were even more, if that was possible, than in Berlin.

He took the underground to Stephansplatz, in the centre of the city, wondering what it must be like for Judith and her fellow Jews, living with the fear that those uniforms and swastikas created.

578

The things that were *verboten* to Jews in Vienna and the rest of Austria were just as numerous as – if not more so than – the things that were *verboten* to them in Germany.

They couldn't go into cafes or restaurants without being humiliatingly refused service. If they tried to travel by tram, they were unceremoniously ejected, no matter what their sex or age. Public parks and libraries were closed to them. Treatment was refused them at state hospitals. Pharmacies would not sell drugs or medicine to them. Hotels wouldn't take bookings from them. They weren't even allowed to own a pet – and the pets they'd owned had been brutally taken from them.

Shops in Kärntner Strasse, which led off from Stephansplatz and was one of the city's main shopping streets, nearly all bore signs stipulating 'Jews Not Admitted'. The only shops without such signs were those with Jewish names, and all of these had had their windows smashed and their stock looted.

Five minutes later, still in Kärntner Strasse, Gilbert turned left and then left again.

For a moment, as he entered the cobbled Schulerstrasse, he thought a Christmas entertainment was taking place. A crowd of people was laughing and jostling to get a better view of something happening in the middle of the street. A couple of men had children high on their shoulders in order that they could see better. One of the children, rosy-cheeked and well muffled, was laughing so hard he could hardly keep his balance. Even Stormtroopers on the inner ring of spectators seemed to be enjoying themselves.

He drew nearer, passing number nine Schuler-strasse and then number eleven. As he drew abreast of the crowd he paused, curious to know what was giving so much fun. What he expected, he didn't know. Perhaps a man dressed as Father Christmas, or festive street jugglers.

What he saw, as the crowd momentarily parted, was neither of those things.

A handful of old people, both men, and women, were on their knees in the snow. There were placards on their backs with the words 'I AM A JEWISH PIG' written on them, and they were on their knees, shovelling the snow away from the centre of the road with bare, red-raw, arthritic hands while their former neighbours laughed, jeered and spat at them.

For a second the scene was so diabolical Gilbert couldn't register the reality of it.

When he did, he also registered his impotence. He couldn't do anything to stop what was happening. Any attempt he made would be halted instantly by the Stormtroopers and, if he was to be of any help to Judith, he couldn't risk attracting their attention.

With bile rising in his throat so that it was all he could do to stop himself from vomiting, he kept on walking. He passed numbers seventeen and nineteen, and then numbers twenty-one and twenty-three.

Then he reached his destination. Number twenty-five. The door was broken in. The windows smashed. He didn't even attempt to enter it.

He leaned against the wall, his head back, his

eyes closed, certain he had arrived too late and that Dieter had been right and Judith was now in Mauthausen. His sense of failure was total. How was he to go about getting a young Jewish woman out of a concentration camp? How could he possibly go back to Berlin without her?

He became aware of a woman's hurrying footsteps approaching from across the street. They came to a halt a few feet away from him.

Unwillingly he opened his eyes.

'Entschuldigen Sie mich, bitte. Sind Sie Englisch?' the woman asked.

She was middle-aged and, despite the bitter cold, had no coat on and was wearing an apron. He looked beyond her and saw that the door of the house directly opposite was ajar.

'Ja. Ich bin Englisch.'

She looked nervously up the street at the crowd and the Stormtroopers. Then, looking towards him once again, she said in fractured English, 'Are you Viscount Fenton?'

'Yes,' he said, hope flooding through him. 'I am Viscount Fenton.'

'You look for Fräulein Zimmermann?'

'Yes,' he said, every nerve in his body now taut. 'I am looking for Fräulein Zimmermann. Do you know where she is?'

The woman gave another swift look up the road towards the Stormtroopers, but none of them were looking in their direction.

'In my house,' she said. 'Come.'

She led him across the street and pushed the slightly open door further ajar. They stepped into a long, high-ceilinged, narrow hallway. There were closed doors opposite each other, and a little further down the corridor, on the right-hand side, another door. A door that led into a living room. A door that was open.

The woman stepped into it and, his heart hammering, Gilbert followed her.

It was a typical middle-class German living room. The furniture was heavy and dark and smelled of beeswax. There was a piano. A table filled with silver-framed photographs. Standing in the middle of the room, so tense with nerves that she looked as if she might snap into pieces, was a slender, dark-haired young woman with hazel eyes.

'I am Gilbert Fenton,' he said, stepping towards her, 'And I'm very pleased to meet you, Judith.'

She wasn't a blood relation. The correct thing to do would be for him to shake her hand.

He didn't do so. Instinct made him open his arms wide and, with a small cry, she fell into them.

The top of her head fitted neatly beneath his chin and, as his arms closed protectively around her, he said, his voice thick with emotion, 'I'm taking you to Berlin, Judith. My daughter and her husband live there and, until all your emigration papers are in order, you will be safer with them than you are here.'

He released his hold of her slightly so that he could look down into her face.

'Before we leave, is there anything you would like to ask me? Anything you want to know?'

'Yes.' Already tension and fear were ebbing from a face as fine-boned as Violet's. 'I would like you to tell me about my birth-mother, and I would like you to tell me about the haven that is England.'

Chapter Thirty-Nine

Two days after arriving in London from Berlin, Gilbert was on a train travelling north to Yorkshire. In the forty-eight hours that he'd been back in Britain he'd met the prime minister and had again urged him to rethink his present policy where Nazi Germany was concerned. Neville had thanked him with clipped courtesy and had given his opinion that Herr Hitler was simply gathering within the Reich the German-speaking peoples who had either been severed from it by the Versailles Treaty or who, like the Austrians, had always considered themselves to be ethnically part of a Greater Germany.

'And though he has agreed that Britain must rearm in the light of Germany's ferocious re-armament policy, his fundamental belief remains the same,' Churchill had growled when Gilbert had met up with him at the Travellers Club. 'He still holds to his conviction that conciliation and the avoidance of anything likely to offend Hitler are the best policy. The end result of such thinking will, I fear, put our green and pleasant land at great risk. Herr Hitler doesn't need the language of sweet reasonableness, Gilbert. In order to be reined in, he needs the language of a mailed fist.'

As the train rattled north Gilbert tried to visualize Chamberlain as a war leader, wielding a mailed fist. His imagination wouldn't stretch that far. With his slight build, turkey-neck, reedy voice and desiccated manner, what Neville reminded him of was a counter assistant in a haberdashery shop.

He thought back to the situation he had left behind in Berlin. Though Judith was safer living under the roof of a member of the German Foreign Office than she had been in the house of her defiantly brave Aryan neighbour, her basic situation hadn't changed. She was still missing the last piece of paperwork with which to leave the Reich and enter Britain.

Dieter, however, knew exactly the channels that had to be approached – and how, under his guidance, Judith should approach them. 'She will be in London within a week or two, perhaps less,' he had promised Gilbert. 'Trust me, *Schwiegervater.*'

It was rare that Dieter referred to him as 'father-in-law'.

Gilbert felt tension run down his spine. The risks Dieter was running in being part of a conspiracy to rid Germany of Hitler were enormous – and what would happen to Olivia, if Dieter was arrested? He comforted himself that Olivia was a British citizen and the daughter of a member of the British government and that, as she wasn't an active member of the conspiracy, there could surely be no question of her being arrested, too.

With his mind a little eased, he turned his

thoughts to the person who was never far from them.

Carrie.

Because ever since she had been a child he had always cared for her and been fond of her in a fatherly way, it had taken him a long time to acknowledge just how drastically his feelings for her had changed over the years. Now his emotions had become overwhelming. Carrie, with her sunny nature, inner calm and constant common sense, had become as necessary to him as Blanche had once been. Did she feel the same way towards him as he felt towards her? Certainly if she did, she would never have shown it. How could she have? He doubted if Carrie had ever done an inappropriate thing in her life, and she would be even more acutely aware than he had been of the difficulties that stood in the way of a romance between them.

Those difficulties, which had once seemed insurmountable, seemed insurmountable no longer. The twenty-two-year age difference, once huge, didn't seem so now that Carrie was no longer a young girl in her early twenties, but a mature woman of thirty-one.

As for the other difference – the yawning gulf of the class difference between them – that was still there, but no one in his family would care about it; people in Outhwaite had been too long accustomed to Carrie's betwixt-and-between social status to suddenly take exception to it, if she definitively crossed the line by becoming Lady Fenton; and if his friends in government found his marriage socially objectionable, then that was just too bad. He didn't care. He only cared that Carrie wouldn't suffer on account of people's snobbishness and if, in London, she was made to feel uncomfortable, then he would simply resign his government position and live permanently at Gorton, which was, when all was said and done, the only place he really wanted to be.

That was if, when he proposed to her, she said yes.

By this time tomorrow he would, he hoped, be out of his misery.

As the train pulled into Darlington, which was as close to Outhwaite as the mainline trains went, and as he rose in readiness to step from his first-class carriage to the platform, he suddenly wondered what Blanche, if she could have seen into the future, would have thought of his being in love with Carrie and wanting to marry her.

Certainty flooded through him.

Blanche, whose affection for Carrie had been so deep; who had loved him with every fibre of her being, and who had always only wanted his happiness, would, he knew, have been happy for him and would have given them her blessing.

There was no chauffeured car waiting for him at the station. Ever since he and Zephiniah had first separated he had dispensed with a full-time chauffeur at Gorton – and the car kept there was no longer a Rolls-Royce. It was a dark-green Riley that he drove himself.

His London car was more imposing, and in the capital he was always chauffeured and would have been chauffeured all the way from Mount Street to Gorton, if his chauffeur hadn't slipped on London ice and broken his leg.

He settled himself on the rear seat of a taxi, anticipating the happy surprise on Thea and Rozalind's faces when he turned up several days before his planned Christmas Eve arrival. It was going to be a good Christmas. Max was spending it with them and, when he returned to America, Rozalind would be with him, entering her homeland for the first time as Mrs Maxwell Bradley.

Someone who would soon be entering Britain for the first time was Judith, if not by Christmas, then hopefully very soon in the New Year – and by then, God willing, Violet would also be home, and the only loved ones he would have left to worry about would be Olivia and Dieter.

The next morning, at breakfast, he said to Thea and Roz in as casual a voice as he could manage, 'I was thinking of telephoning Carrie and asking if she could take some time off today.'

'She's coming over here for part of Christmas Day and the whole of Boxing Day.' Thea helped herself to another slice of toast. 'I absolutely insisted she spend as much of Christmas as possible with us – especially as Lydia Markham is in Madeira and there is no Christmas entertaining taking place at Monkswood. And if she can take time off today, why don't you invite her to help us decorate the Christmas tree? Roz and I are going to Richmond this morning, Christmas shopping, but we'll be back by early afternoon.'

'And then, when we've done the tree, we can all have mince pies and mulled wine in front of the drawing-room fire,' Roz said, pouring herself more coffee.

Gilbert, aware that Thea and Roz had given him the perfect pretexts for telephoning Carrie and asking for her company, beamed across at them. 'A wonderful idea,' he said, rising to his feet. 'Absolutely grand'

'There's a telephone call for you in your office, Mrs Thornton,' Briggs, Monkswood's butler, said to Carrie.

Carrie, who had been checking the linen cupboard, stopped what she was doing. 'Thank you, Mr Briggs. I expect it's the butcher, checking on the turkey and ham order.'

She hurried off to take the phone call, well aware that the local butcher would be vastly disappointed at the size of his Christmas order from Monkswood. Normally, with Lady Markham at home and guests in the house, the order was huge. This year, with only the staff to be fed, it was considerably smaller.

A few moments later she said into the receiver, 'Mrs Thornton speaking.'

The voice that responded was not that of the local butcher, and was one she recognized instantly.

'Carrie?' Gilbert was always thrown by Carrie being addressed as 'Mrs' at Monkswood. 'It's Gilbert.' And then, aware she had never addressed him as anything other than Lord Fenton, added so as not to bewilder her, 'Lord Fenton.'

Carrie sat down swiftly, before her legs gave way. 'Good morning, Lord Fenton. There's nothing wrong, is there?'

Her mind raced as to what could possibly be wrong. If there had been a Fenton family calamity, then the perpetrator was bound to be Violet. Who on earth was she now consorting with in Germany? Goebbels and Göring were bad enough, but what if it was now Hitler? Where Violet was concerned, anything was possible.

'Nothing is wrong, Carrie. I was telephoning to see if you had any free time today? I thought you might like to come over to Gorton and help decorate the tree – and perhaps, beforehand, we could have a walk with the dogs. There's snow on the moors, but as yet only a light sprinkling and the sky is cloudless.'

'That would be ... lovely.' Carrie's heart was beating fast and light. Was Lord Fenton really suggesting they should take a morning walk together? They had done so often in Richmond, whenever they had met there accidentally. But this time would be different. This time it was something he had given thought to. 'And I can easily take the time off. With Lady Markham away, there is nothing pressing for me to do here today.'

He was about to suggest that he called for her in the Riley, but Carrie forestalled him.

'I'll come to Outhwaite on the ten o'clock bus, if that is all right, Lord Fenton?'

'Yes.' He knew immediately why she had made the suggestion. His calling for her in person would have had Monkswood's entire household in a fever of speculation, and Carrie wasn't to know that, if she fulfilled all his hopes, such speculation would no longer matter. 'Yes,' he said, patting his waist-

589

coat pocket where a small satin-padded box lay next to his heart. 'I'll be at the bus stop to meet you, Carrie. And, Carrie, we've been friends for far too long for you to continue addressing me as Lord Fenton. I'd much prefer it if you began calling me by my first name.'

There was a beat of stunned silence at the other end of the line and then she said uncertainly, 'Yes, Lord Fenton. Of course. If that's what you would like.'

'Gilbert,' he corrected gently.

'Yes ... Gilbert.'

Even though he couldn't see her, he knew she was blushing furiously.

'This is a lovely surprise,' she said, as he walked her from the bus to where the Riley was parked outside the Pig and Whistle. 'I haven't been on the moors for ages and ages.'

'Me neither.' He smiled down at her – everything all right in his world simply because she was by his side.

He'd left his spaniels in the back seat of the car, and there was an outcry of frenzied barking as the dogs recognized Carrie.

'Silly things!' Carrie said affectionately, giving them a lavish fuss before settling down in the front passenger seat.

He closed the door on her, ignored the raised eyebrows of Mrs Mellor, who was on her way to the post office, then walked around the Riley and slid behind the wheel.

'I'm just back from Berlin,' he said, turning on the engine and putting the car into gear. 'Violet is coming home soon, perhaps within a couple of weeks.'

'For a holiday or for good?'

It felt strange sitting beside him in such close intimacy. She remembered the occasion when he had come to Monkswood for her in a taxi to ask her to stand in for Mrs Huntley, when Mrs Huntley had had to make an emergency dash to Leeds Infirmary to see her daughter.

Then it had been dark, and they had been seated even closer together in the rear of the car. She had been able to smell the lemon tang of the cologne he used, and had known that if she had moved her gloved hand by even a fraction, it would have brushed against the back of his.

Today, separated by the gearstick, they were seated a little further apart, but there was no third party with them, as there had been when they'd been in the taxi.

'For good,' he said in answer to her question as he drove out of the village. 'Though I doubt whether she will be at Gorton, or even London, for long. I rather think home, for Violet, means Hollywood.'

'I'd much rather think of her in Hollywood than in Berlin.'

'So would I,' he said fervently.

He glanced across at her, his eyes meeting hers. 'The stories about Violet and the Reich Minister for Information and Propaganda, and the commander of the Luftwaffe, are not as they seem, Carrie. Violet can't wait to put Berlin behind her – and neither can Olivia, though for Olivia, of course, it is a little more difficult, seeing as how

Berlin is her marital home.'

She understood perfectly how difficult things must be for Olivia, and she also understood why, in speaking of Goebbels and Göring, Gilbert had avoided speaking their names. Speaking their names would, she knew, have been more than he could easily bear.

She said sympathetically, 'You must miss them, Violet and Olivia.'

'I do.' He wanted to tell her how much he always missed her, too, but didn't want to lead up to a declaration of his feelings for her in the car – and particularly not when he was still driving it. 'Tell me about Monkswood,' he said, as the road out of Outhwaite began climbing up to the edge of the moors. 'It must be tediously quiet when Lydia is away and there are no weekend house-parties.'

'It is quiet, but not tediously so. Monkswood is a big house, even bigger than Gorton. There is always something to be done, and sometimes things are easier to do when – apart from the staff – the house is empty.'

The spaniels put their front paws on the back of Carrie's seat and began nuzzling the back of her neck.

'Down, Coco! Down, Leo!' Gilbert said, knowing that with the slightest encouragement the dogs would be in the front seat and on Carrie's knee.

Carrie knew it too, and would have rather liked it. There were no pet dogs at Monkswood and she missed the company and affection that dogs gave.

The narrow road merged into a rutted track feathered with snow, and beneath a wide sky the moors fanned out on either side of them, glittering under a blanket of pristine white.

Gilbert eased the Riley onto the verge and came to a halt, glad to see that as well as a warm coat and Fair Isle knitted beret and gloves, Carrie was wearing wellingtons.

'I like the view from here. It looks out over the valley towards the house,' he said, as he opened the back door of the car and, with frenzied barking and tails wagging, the dogs clambered out into crystalline air.

Side by side and with the dogs at their heels, they walked a short stretch of moor to where the land fell away and there was a view of the valley and the curving river and the bridge.

And beyond the bridge, sheltered by a backdrop of trees, Gorton Hall.

As they came to a halt, gazing down at it, Carrie said, 'This has always been a favourite place of mine. When I was eight years old I sat not far from where we are now standing, hugging my knees and grieving for my father and looking down at Gorton, sick with nerves because I was to go there later that day for the very first time.'

'To play with Thea and Olivia?'

She nodded, turning towards him. 'Though I didn't know it then, it was the most important day of my life.'

'Because our family became your family?'

She nodded again, her eyes overly bright. Snow had begun falling and flakes were beginning to rest on her Fair Isle beret and on her hair.

Gilbert's heart lurched in his chest. She shone with beauty, both inside and out, and he knew that if she said 'yes' when he proposed to her, he would be the luckiest man in God's creation.

He said, 'Just as that day was the most important day in your life, Carrie, so today could be the most important in mine. I'm going to ask you something on which all my future happiness depends.'

A stray snowflake landed on her cheek and he took his glove off, brushing it tenderly away. Then, as her eyes widened, he took her hands in his, his heart pounding like a piston. 'I love you, Carrie. I love you more than anything in the world and I want you to marry me. I know this is so unexpected you can't possibly give me an answer straight away–'

'Yes.'

'–and so, because I don't want to be given the wrong answer, I want you to think about it very carefully–'

'Yes.'

'–and if you could learn to love me just a little bit, I promise you I will make you happy.'

'Yes,' she said for the third time. 'Yes, I will marry you, Gilbert. And I don't have to think about it.'

Her eyes were shining, her rosy-cheeked face radiant. 'I've been in love with you ever since I was seventeen or eighteen. There is nothing I would like more in the world than to be your wife.'

Gilbert's head reeled. Whatever the response he had hoped for, her response exceeded it so immeasurably that he was momentarily stupefied.

Fleetingly he thought of the decades he had wasted; decades they could have been together, if only he had been more perceptive about her feelings, and more perceptive about his own.

The wasted decades didn't matter. What mattered was now.

'Will you mind very much being married in a register office?' he asked, taking her in his arms. 'Because of my divorce, a church wedding is out of the question.'

She said fiercely, so happy she felt as if she was flying, 'I'd marry you in a bus station.'

He burst into laughter, hugging her tight, the years that separated them melting away.

Then, his eyes darkening with heat, he lowered his head to hers.

He kissed her gently at first and then, as her lips opened like a flower beneath his, with increasing passion, not raising his head from hers until both of them were breathless.

Still holding her close, knowing that after twenty years he had found true love again, he said huskily, 'I have something for you, my darling.'

He felt inside his coat to his waistcoat, withdrew the ring-box that had been lying snug against his heart and lifted the lid.

Carrie drew in a deep, unsteady breath.

'It belonged to Blanche,' he said, of an exquisite antique garnet-and-pearl ring. 'I'm certain she would have wanted you to have it: as an engagement ring, if you would like, or – if you would prefer a different ring as an engagement ring – to wear as a dress ring, as she wore it.'

Barely able to speak, her throat was so constricted with emotion, Carrie said, 'I should very much like to wear it as my engagement ring, Gilbert.'

As snow began falling thickly around them, he removed the glove from her left hand and slid the ring onto her wedding finger.

She gazed down at it with a mixture of wonderment and joy and then, as his arms tightened around her and he lowered his head once more to hers, she parted her lips for more of the kisses she had waited for, for so long.

Snow was also falling in Richmond.

'I think that's enough Christmas shopping for now, don't you?' Roz said to Thea as they stepped out of a bookshop after buying a copy of the worldwide bestselling novel *Gone with the Wind* for Carrie. 'For one thing, we've come to the bottom of our list, and for another, even if we hadn't, I simply can't carry any more parcels. My arms are giving out.'

'Home then?'

'Home,' Roz agreed, looking forward to the warmth of Gorton's roaring log fires.

The taxicab office was on the opposite side of the market place and, as they walked gingerly towards it over the icy cobbles, Thea said suddenly, 'I'm trying really hard to be full of Christmas spirit, Roz, but the truth is it's all pretend. I don't have an ounce of it inside me.'

Roz came to a halt, uncaring that the snow was coming in ever thickening flurries. 'Because of Hal?'

Thea nodded, her narrow dark-lashed eyes

bright with tears.

Roz moved a heavy parcel from one arm to the other. 'Let's go into a cafe for a pot of tea before getting a cab. I've never asked about Hal's death, because you've so obviously not wanted to talk about it, but for you to talk about it now might come as a relief.'

'Yes.' The blood had drained from Thea's face. 'I need to talk about it – and Hal would want me to tell you how he died. Until now, though, I've felt talking about it would undo me completely; and if that happened, I might never get the pieces of myself back together again.'

'And now you think you might?'

'I don't know, Roz.' There was despair in her voice. 'But I can't keep silent about if forever, can I?'

They went into a small teashop only yards away from the taxicab office. It was packed with people taking a breather from Christmas shopping, but they managed to get a corner table, and Thea seated herself so that her back was to the room and she was facing Roz and, on the wall, a faded print of Jervaulx Abbey.

Roz ordered a pot of tea and Thea drew in a deep, unsteady breath. 'Spain was a nightmare, Roz. Nothing was as either Hal or I had thought it would be. The shortage of weapons was un-believable. None of the Barcelona militias received weapons from the government. Their arms were hunting rifles, worn-out Mausers that jammed, and shotguns previously used for shooting rabbits and hares. Worse than that, though, was the way that atrocities by the Nationalists would be answered by atrocities from our fellow Republicans.'

She came to a halt, unable to continue.

The waitress brought them their pot of tea. Roz poured it and added milk and a spoonful of sugar to each cup.

After a little while Thea said unsteadily, 'Hal and I hadn't seen each other for months. I was in Barcelona, driving ambulances for the Red Cross and helping out in the city's clinics. Hal had been fighting with other members of the International Brigades further down the coast.

From outside the cafe came the sound of carollers singing 'Away in a Manger'.

Thea put her hands around her cup of tea, but made no effort to lift it to her lips.

'The fighting ended in overwhelming defeat, but Hal was not horribly wounded and neither was he captured. Somehow he made his way back to Barcelona and – oh, Roz – it was so bloody marvellous to know he was still alive and to be together again!' She closed her eyes, reliving the moment when Hal had leapt down from the moving tram; when they had raced towards each other in the crowded street and he had kissed her, for what neither of them had known was the last time.

It was a long time before she opened her eyes and spoke again.

'We were walking towards our flat, and a few yards in front of us there was an elderly priest. A lorry with men in the back of it wearing anarchist neckerchiefs rounded a corner, heading towards us. Because the Catholic Church is on the side of the Nationalists, priests in Barcelona keep low profiles. This priest didn't. As the lorry drew level with him, he shook his fist at the soldiers and spat. The lorry skidded to a halt.'

Her face was as white as the cloth on the table in front of them.

'The men jumped down from it and raced towards the old man. It all happened so fast, Roz. They were shouting "Nationalist pig!" And the next minute the old man was on the ground being kicked and beaten, and Hal had raced to protect him. Then one of the men hauled the priest to his feet and put a gun to his head.'

She stopped and opened eyes so full of grief and pain that Roz felt her heart turn over.

Thea's voice sank to a whisper. 'Hal leapt towards him, knocking the gun so that it fired upwards, and in the same split second there were other shots. I saw parts of the priest's skull fly into the air, and Hal buckled at the knees, blood pouring from his chest.' She made a helpless, hopeless movement with her hand. 'I rushed towards him and the men headed back to their lorry. Hal was still alive and, as the lorry drove off and I held Hal in my arms, he said ... he said...' She struggled to continue, tears pouring down her face. 'He said, "I love you, Thea. I always have." And then, as the blood pumping from his chest spilled over my hands and into the ground, he said, "This is a bugger of a way to die, love." And died.'

For a long time neither of them spoke again: Roz because she couldn't think of anything she could possibly say that would bring Thea a shred of comfort, and Thea because for her there was nothing left to be said.

At last Roz said gently, 'Let's go home, Thea. Carrie will be there by now, waiting for us to decorate the tree.'

Thea nodded, saying as she rose to her feet, 'I wish Carrie was always at Gorton, Roz. It's where she belongs.'

Then, her face etched with grief and loss, she followed Roz out of the cafe and into the snow-covered market place.

Chapter Forty

The Christmas party at Carinhall, Hermann Göring's vast estate an hour's drive north of Berlin, was in full swing. Though Hitler was not present, all other members of the Nazi hierarchy were, some accompanied by a wife, others by a mistress or girlfriend, others – as Göring's parties were famous for the number of glamorous actresses that attended them – merely on the prowl for a new mistress or girlfriend.

Carinhall parties were always mammoth pro-ductions. At this one, the baby lions kept by Göring as pets frolicked in an outdoor enclosure, with red ribbons tied around their necks. Reindeer with silver-painted antlers roamed in the grounds nearest to the house. In the forested part of the estate horse-drawn sleighs raced along snowy paths, bells tinkling.

Violet wasn't in the mood for a sleigh-ride, or

for a party at which the guests were so numerous they could have filled a football stadium. Her day had been spent on a film set at Babelsberg and she had a vile headache. Making her headache worse was Luther Schultz. He had been stalking her since the moment she arrived and, no matter how hard she tried to lose herself in the throng; she could feel his hard, lascivious eyes always on her.

It was Margarete Himmler, wife of the chief of Germany's police force, who enabled her to shake free of Schultz. Seeing Kripo's second-in-command standing in an island of isolation, she made a beeline for him and Schultz had no option but to transfer his full attention to her.

Aware that she was no longer under Schultz's scrutiny, Violet did a swift about-turn, not wanting him to be able to find her easily again. She also needed a quiet, dark room in which to recover from her headache, and she had been a guest often enough at Carinhall to know where she would find one.

Threading her way through the crush of guests, she made her way up the opulent staircase and along a corridor, until she came to the door of a room too far from the head of the stairs to be a magnet for couples seeking a little privacy.

The room was dark, the curtains drawn. Gratefully Violet felt her way towards the bed and lay down on it, closing her eyes. Under normal circumstances at a party such as this she would have been circulating, listening for careless gossip about the Führer's plans.

She had already furnished her contact at the US

Embassy with the information that, in March, Hitler intended marching his armies into what remained of Czechoslovakia. Goebbels had told her that, with Czechoslovakia under his belt, Hitler was then going to invade Poland – and that was why Violet was still in Berlin, for if she could get documentary proof, it would, she knew, finally put an end to the British government's disastrous appeasement policy.

There came the sound of footsteps weaving unsteadily down the corridor, and of feminine giggles.

Violet held her breath, but the footsteps came to a halt not at her door, but at the door of the room next to hers.

She sat up and swung her legs from the bed. Listening to two people making love was not, in her book, the best way to defeat a headache.

There came the sound of someone stumbling, and then a woman's voice said, *'Es ist hier dunkel. Wo ist der Lichtschalter?'*

There came a click as the light-switch was found, and then another voice, also female, said, *'Dieses Kokain ist das beste, Hedda. Vertau mir.'*

Aware now that the privacy of the room had been sought in order to snort cocaine, Violet lay down again. If that was what Hedda and her friend wanted to do, it was fine by her. All she wanted was to be left in peace.

There was more giggling from next door and the faint sound of a line of coke being cut on a clear surface.

Then she heard a different voice – Hedda's voice – say, *'Warum wurden die Verräter im Auswärtigen*

Amt nicht verhaftet?'

Violet's eyes shot wide open, every nerve-ending in her body jangling. What Hedda was asking was why certain criminals at the Foreign Office were not being immediately arrested for treason.

There came the sound of one of the women snorting coke, and then the woman who was in the know said, *'Der Führer will wissen, ob irgendwelche Genërale in der Verschwörung verwickelt sind. Es soll keine Verhaftungen geben, bis das volle Ausmaß der Verschwörung bekannt ist.'*

Perspiration beaded Violet's forehead. Because the Führer wanted to know if members of the army were also in the plot, there were to be no arrests until the full extent of the plot was known. What the woman hadn't said, but what was obvious, was that the men in the Foreign Office were being used as small fish to catch much bigger fish.

Hedda's next question was to ask if all the plotters would then be beheaded.

'Ja. Natürlich,' was the answer.

Feeling as if iced water had been poured down her spine, Violet rose unsteadily to her feet. Somehow she had to leave the room without the women being aware they had been overheard – and she had leave Carinhall immediately and speak to Dieter.

Twenty minutes later she was at the wheel of her little BMZ Roadster, speeding south in the darkness through low-lying, thickly wooded countryside, her brain teeming with questions.

Would Dieter know who the plotters in the Foreign Office were? If he didn't, how could he warn them? Was Dieter perhaps one of the plotters himself? If he was, then not only was he in grave danger, but so was Olivia.

An hour later, thinking of first one plan of action that Dieter and Olivia might have to take and then another, she entered the northern outskirts of Berlin, heading for the Tiergarten and Bellevuestrasse.

It was ten-thirty when she drew up outside the house. Though the curtains were drawn, chinks of light indicated that at least one of the downstairs rooms was occupied, and the hall light was on. There were no other cars in the street: no Gestapo black Mercedes sedans; no sign of any surveillance.

Her fur coat had a hood and she pulled it up over her distinctive hair before stepping out of the car. Then, praying that Dieter would be home, she ran up to the colonnaded front door and rang the bell.

It was two or three minutes before the door was opened and, when it was, it was opened by Dieter himself.

He stared at her in complete stupefaction.

She didn't wait for him to recover his power of speech and, as he was making no move to invite her in, she pushed past him.

'Do you have staff within earshot?' she demanded as the door closed behind her.

'No. What's this about, Violet? Are you in trouble?'

'I'm not. Colleagues of yours at the Foreign Office are – and it's quite possible you are as well.'

He sucked in his breath, his nostrils whitening.

It was a reaction that told her just as clearly as words that he was one of the men of whom Hedda's friend had been speaking.

'Let's talk in the library,' he said. 'There's no telephone to worry about in there.'

Both of them had momentarily forgotten about Olivia, and when she opened the drawing-room door and stepped into the hall they spun to face her, as if caught in a romantic assignation.

Olivia was just as stunned at seeing Violet in her home as Dieter had been when he opened the door to her, but she recovered her power of speech far more speedily.

'You *bitch!*' Sobs rose in her throat. 'How *dare* you desecrate my home by coming into it? Dieter doesn't want to speak to you! He never wants to see you or speak to you again, and neither do I!'

Dieter swung round, gripping her tightly by the arm. 'This isn't what you think, Olivia. Violet is here with information.'

'Information?' Olivia stared disbelievingly from Dieter to Violet and back again. 'What kind of information? The only thing Violet is carrying with her is the scent of Hitler's henchmen!'

'My scent is Mitsouko,' Violet snapped. 'And I'm not here for the good of my health, Olivia. I'm here for the good of yours!'

Aware that a sister-versus-sister fight of mega-proportions was about to break out, Dieter said curtly, 'Let's go to the library. And not another word until we get there.'

Still holding Olivia so firmly by the arm that she was bruised for days, he marched her, with Violet hard on their heels, across the marble-floored hall

605

and into a book-lined room furnished with a sofa, two matching wing armchairs and a large desk.

'Now,' he said when the door was firmly closed behind them. 'What the devil is all this about, Violet?'

Still in her fur coat, and without sitting down, Violet said swiftly, 'The Gestapo know there are traitors in the Foreign Office. They have names – but in the conversation I overheard the names weren't given. The reason for no arrests as yet is that Hitler wants to know who else is in the conspiracy: he especially wants to know if any army generals are also plotting against him.'

'Christus!' Dieter thought of the army generals in the conspiracy: General Halder, General Beck, General von Witzleben, who was commander of the Berlin Garrison, General von Brockdorff, who was commander of the Potsdam Garrison. He sought strength from the fact that so far none of their names were known to Hitler. Somehow every army member in the plot had to be warned, as had his two superiors in the Foreign Office.

'I don't understand.' As if her legs would no longer support her, Olivia sank onto the sofa and looked bewilderedly towards Dieter. 'Why are you letting her know there is a conspiracy? Don't you see she's just fishing for information? Don't give her any names. If you give her names, the Gestapo will know them within an hour of her leaving here.'

'I'm not here to be told names,' Violet said curtly. 'I'm here so that Dieter can warn whoever in the army needs to be warned and so that he and the others in the conspiracy at the Foreign

Office can get out of the country before they are arrested.'

Olivia, who was always slow to see where a conversation was leading, gave a cry of alarm.

Dieter said grimly, 'I'm not the only one who is going to have to leave the country. Olivia is going to have to leave with me. Your father thinks her British passport will protect her, but it won't. If I'm arrested on a charge of treason, she will be treated as being guilty by association.'

Aware it was going to be a long night of plan-making, Violet shrugged herself out of her fur and sat down in one of the wing armchairs. 'You are already under surveillance, Dieter. The chances of both of you successfully leaving the country together are as close to nil as it's possible to get.'

'But if, as you say, I'm already under surveil-lance, won't Olivia leaving for England alert the Gestapo that I'm about to follow her?'

'Not if she doesn't leave for England. If she leaves only with a weekend-case for a shopping trip to Paris, the same suspicions won't be aroused.'

'And then would I catch a train to Calais and cross the Channel from there?' Olivia asked, still not understanding quite how Violet had suddenly become someone to trust again.

It was a question so obvious that Violet didn't even bother answering it.

Another thought struck Olivia and she said suddenly, 'Dieter and I can't leave without taking Judith with us, and we are still waiting for the final piece of documentation that will allow her to travel and enter Britain.'

'Judith is here? With you?'

Dieter nodded. 'And Olivia is right, Violet. Leaving without her would be passing a death-sentence on her.'

'Where is she now?'

'In bed,' Olivia said. 'Have I to go and get her?'

'Considering the added danger she's now in, I think that would be a very good idea.'

When Olivia had left the room, Dieter said bluntly, 'This is exile for me, isn't it?'

'For now. Where will you go? London? Yorkshire?'

He buried his head in his hands. He had enjoyed his time at the German Embassy in London, but that had been when it had simply been a foreign posting. He had never wanted to live permanently in England – and he didn't want to live permanently in England now: not in London, not in Yorkshire, not anywhere. He was German. And Germany was his home.

He dropped his hands, saying bleakly, 'Germany will soon be at war with England. You know that. I know that. If I'm living in England when war is declared I will be interned – possibly for years. And if the end of the war is in Germany's favour, I'll be shot by my own countrymen.'

Violet closed her eyes for a moment, thinking. Then she said, 'There is a possible solution.'

'What solution? I'm damned if I can see one.'

'When it comes to war, I doubt if the Republic of Ireland will pitch in with Britain – and neither is it likely to pitch in with Germany. My guess is that southern Ireland will remain neutral. It's a beautiful country, Dieter. Parts of it are reminiscent of the Yorkshire Dales. Olivia would love it there.'

'Ireland?' With every second, Dieter's respect for Violet's unexpected clarity of thought was deepening. Ireland would be near enough for Olivia not to feel totally cut off from Gorton. If he bought a small estate – and he could surely get enough of his money out via Switzerland to enable him to do that – he could become a gentleman farmer. They could enjoy a country life of horses and dogs, fishing and walking; and eventually, when Hitler was a thing of the past, they could return to Germany.

The library door opened and Olivia entered, with Judith a step or two behind her.

With vast relief Violet saw that Judith was showing no signs of panic or distress. She was perfectly composed, her face full of character, her eyes full of intelligence.

She was also, and this was the important thing as far as Violet was concerned, petite and fine-boned.

Olivia said, 'I've put Judith in the picture. She knows what has happened and what is under discussion.'

Violet rose to her feet. 'Violet Fenton,' she said, holding out her hand. *'Sprechen Sie Englisch?'*

'I speak it perfectly.'

'Good!' Violet flashed her a vivid smile. 'That's two obstacles out of the way.'

Once again she seated herself in the wing chair. Olivia and Judith sat down side by side on the sofa. Dieter remained standing.

'What are you thinking, Violet?' he asked, wondering what the first obstacle had been.

'I'm thinking that the minute you have warned everyone who has to be warned, you are going to have to leave the country fast – and that, as Judith can't possibly be left behind, neither can she wait even a few days more for the return of a passport that will enable her to leave Germany and enter Britain. She's going to have to leave immediately, with Olivia – and on my passport.'

'But you don't look anything alike!'

'We do in the things that matter. We are the same height, the same build. We are the same age, or near enough. We both have fine-boned faces. My eyes are amber. Judith's are hazel. And she speaks flawless English.'

'And hair colour?' Dieter looked from Violet to Judith and back again. 'I know Judith's hair can be dyed, but isn't it difficult to dye from a dark colour to a lighter colour? And your hair is the most extraordinary colour, Violet.'

Violet shrugged. 'I'm an actress. I have wigs for every occasion. I can be back here in less than an hour with a Titian wig from home that will utterly transform Judith.'

'But the risks!' Olivia grasped hold of Judith's hand tightly. 'If anything should go wrong...' She couldn't finish the sentence, because if anything were to go wrong it would be Sachsenhausen concentration camp for Judith – and maybe even for herself.

Dieter said gravely, 'The risks of not following Violet's suggestion are greater than those of following them, Olivia. Unless Judith has docu-

610

mentation to leave the country and enter Britain by the time I leave Germany, she will be arrested when the Gestapo arrive at the house searching for me. When it is discovered how short a time it is since she left Vienna, and how I immediately gave her employment here as a maid, it will be assumed that she, too, is somehow part of the conspiracy, or that at the very least she knows about it. And so she will be taken to Gestapo headquarters for questioning.'

He didn't have to spell out what that kind of questioning would entail.

His eyes held Judith's. 'The decision is yours, Judith. It's one you have to make for yourself.'

'I prefer the first risk.' Her voice was steady. She looked towards Violet. 'But it will leave you without a passport, Violet. When you need to leave the country, how will you do so?'

'Don't worry about me. The US Embassy owes me a very great favour. When it is time for me to leave, I'll have an American passport.'

'Then that's it!' Dieter looked down at his watch. It was just after midnight. Thanks to Violet, in less than an hour all the major decisions that had to be made had been taken. 'You and Judith will leave by train for Paris tomorrow,' he said to Olivia. 'Judith, give your identity card to Violet. You mustn't have it on you. You are Violet Fenton from now on, not Judith Zimmermann. Olivia, the minute you are out of the country, telephone me saying you are having a wonderful shopping trip. Say nothing else. Then, knowing you are safe, when I have done all that needs to be done in Berlin, I will join you.'

'What about our things?' The magnitude of what such a flight entailed was almost more than Olivia could comprehend. 'What will happen to all our clothes? To my jewellery? What will happen to the house and all our furniture?'

'I think it's safe to say that the house and furniture will be appropriated, as Judith's family home and furniture were appropriated. Clothes don't matter, *Liebchen*. Jewellery...' He paused, looking towards Violet. 'I think that even on a shopping trip to Paris, Countess von Starhemberg would be expected to have a jewellery-case with her, don't you, Violet? And as Judith will be travelling as Violet Fenton, the famous movie actress, then surely she would also have a jewellery-case with her?'

Violet nodded, knowing better than anyone that extravagance of all kinds was taken as normal behaviour where movie stars were concerned. 'It's also important that Judith is wearing a lavish fur – so that will be two fur coats out of your wardrobe, Olivia. Not just one.'

'Good.' Olivia's sincerity was deep. 'That means I'll get to keep both my sable and my mink.'

Despite the gravity of the situation, amusement twitched at the corners of Judith's mouth. 'I've dreamed of stepping on English soil for months and months, but I never dreamed I'd be doing so as a movie star, wearing a fur and carrying a jewellery-case!'

Violet laughed, aware that someone who could keep a sense of humour at such a time was someone she could become very good friends with. 'You're going to look wonderful. When I return with the wig, I'll come with my make-up

612

box as well. By the time I have made you up, not even my father would be able to tell the difference between us.'

Olivia's thoughts were now focused entirely on Dieter. 'When you leave, darling, will you leave as Judith and I are leaving? Will you take the train to Paris, and then to Calais?'

He shook his head. 'No. Leaving Berlin to join you in Paris would set all sorts of alarm bells ringing. I'll seek an excuse to travel to Munich, and then I'll shake off whatever surveillance I am under, cross into Switzerland and from there into France. My journey to England will take a little longer than yours, *Liebchen*, but we will be together again before too long.'

Olivia stifled the sobs of anxiety that were rising in her throat. Dieter was making his escape sound easy and danger-free, but she knew it was going to be neither. She also knew that, without Violet, there would have been no chance of escape for him; that within weeks, perhaps within days, he would have been arrested by the Gestapo and, along with everyone else known to be in the conspiracy plot, executed.

When Violet rose to leave, Olivia hugged her tightly, tears of gratitude and love on her cheeks. 'Promise me that as soon as you have a passport you'll leave Berlin,' she said fiercely. 'Promise me, Vi.'

Violet hugged her back. 'I'll be leaving just as soon as I've tidied up a loose end that needs tidying. There's nothing I want more than to be at Gorton again, with you, Papa, Thea, Roz and Carrie.'

'And Dieter and Judith.'

'And Dieter and Judith,' Violet said, wondering just when Dieter would tell her about the future he was planning for them both in southern Ireland.

Olivia gave a shaky smile. 'That's good. That makes me feel much better. Now I can set about doing what has to be done.'

'Which is?'

'Working out how many of my favourite dresses can be squeezed into two weekend cases.'

Chapter Forty-One

JANUARY 1939

Judith was walking across Grosvenor Square en route to Claridge's, where she was meeting her mother for lunch. Left to her own devices, she would have preferred to be heading towards the Corner House at Marble Arch, which was Thea's favourite eatery when meeting up with her socialist friends. Zephiniah, though, would not have been seen dead in a Lyons Corner House, and Judith, though she didn't share the same scruples, would never have asked it of her.

At the thought of Zephiniah, love, amusement and exasperation flooded through her. Her mother had not been at all the kind of person she had imagined her to be. For one thing, she wasn't happily married to Gilbert. She was newly divorced from him and intent on marrying an Argentinian, Roberto Di Stéfano.

'I've been in love with Roberto for years,' she had said with startling frankness when Judith had asked about him. 'From well before I met and married Gilbert – though we weren't still having an affair when I met Gilbert. Our affair began again later, when we met by accident in the casino at Aix-les-Bains.'

On her fraught-filled journey from Berlin to London – certain she was going to be stopped and arrested at every border check – Judith had tried to remain calm by imagining what her future life with her mother was going to be like. She had imagined countless different scenarios, and not one of them had come close to the reality. Though her mother had been overcome with emotion at meeting her – Thea had told her afterwards that she and Olivia had been utterly riveted by the sight of Zephiniah in floods of happy tears – her mother clearly hadn't envisaged the two of them living together.

'Roberto and I spend far too much time on the-move, darling,' she had said, after explaining to Judith that her home would be with Gilbert and Thea. 'We spend months and months in either France or Switzerland, and if Britain goes to war then we shall leave for Argentina.'

Something else Judith had never expected was how caustic Zephiniah could be whenever Thea, Olivia and Carrie's names came into the conversation. Her mother could barely speak about Thea – with whom Judith had bonded immediately – without shuddering. She wasn't quite as

615

hostile when it came to Olivia, though she never tired of saying what a fool she thought Olivia was for not making capital out of her friendship with Elizabeth Bowes-Lyon, now that Elizabeth was the queen consort.

It was when it came to Carrie, though, that she became truly incandescent. 'How can I take pride in the courtesy title of Zephiniah, Viscountess Fenton, when Lady Markham's former house-keeper will, when she marries Gilbert, have the title Viscountess Fenton? There will be jokes as to whether I, too, was a former housekeeper. I'm going to be a laughing-stock – as is he!'

Judith couldn't imagine Gilbert ever being a laughing-stock. He was far too well loved and respected – and certainly so by her. In the few short weeks since she had known him, he had become like a second father to her. He was as uptight and as honourable as her adoptive father had been. More, he had travelled to Vienna in order to save her from horrors that she knew her mother – and anyone else who hadn't lived in Hitler's Germany couldn't begin to imagine.

Exiting the square, she walked down a road blessedly free of black-uniformed, jackbooted SS officers and swastika-bedecked flags. The miracle of being in England – a sane, sensible country that had no time for maniacal, rabble-rousing, hate-filled dictators – was one she knew she would never take for granted, and every morning she prayed that the coming day would bring Violet to similar safety.

When she thought of what Violet had done for her, her heart filled with such gratitude she thought it was going to burst. Even Zephiniah had realized the enormity of Violet's action in enabling Judith to leave the Reich with Olivia. Whoever else Zephiniah spoke disparagingly about, she never did so about Violet.

Her mother also never had a cutting remark to make about Rozalind.

Two weeks ago Rozalind and her husband had spent Christmas at Gorton Hall. Rozalind's step-brother, Kyle, had driven up from London to spend Boxing Day with them, and Rozalind had told Judith there had once been a romance between Thea and Kyle and that she, Olivia and Carrie were all hoping it would spring into flower again. Despite still officially being Monkswood's housekeeper – a situation that wouldn't change until her employer, Lady Markham, arrived home from Madeira – Carrie had spent as much of Christmas as she could at Gorton, the garnet-and-pearl ring sparkling on the fourth finger of her left hand.

On Boxing Day evening it had been open house at Gorton, and Judith had met Miss Calvert, who had once been Carrie's teacher at Outhwaite village school; Jim Crosby, who had been Gorton's odd-job man and who now had a little business of his own, doing odd jobs for people far and wide; his wife, who was a barmaid at the Pig and Whistle; Hermione Hardwick, who had been Thea and Olivia's governess; Charlie, her husband, who was Gorton's head gardener and who wore a piratical black eye-patch and had a scarred face that was the most genial Judith had ever seen.

When she had met up with her mother – who

617

had spent Christmas in Monte Carlo with Roberto – she'd known that as well as having her birth mother back in her life again, she also had a family who, though not blood-related to her, might just as well have been, for their love and acceptance of her were so total.

Deeply grateful for them, she entered Claridge's dining room to find her mother already seated and waiting for her.

Seeing the roses in Judith's cheeks, Zephiniah said in immediate concern, 'Please don't tell me you've walked here in the freezing January weather all the way from Mount Street, darling?'

Judith, who in far worse weather had tramped Outhwaite's moors with Thea, Gilbert and two cocker spaniels, said with amusement, 'Mount Street is barely five minutes' walk away, Mother.'

'Nevertheless, you should have had Gilbert's chauffeur bring you.'

Zephiniah, who had never in her life fussed lovingly over anyone, took great pleasure in fussing over her beautiful newly acquired daughter and had staggered everyone by insisting that, as she was Judith's mother, Judith should address her as such.

Judith seated herself at the other side of the small table for two and Zephiniah said, 'Is Rozalind still in London? Perhaps I should have asked her to join us.'

'She is still in London, but this morning she's at a meeting at the Knightsbridge agency that handles her photographic work.' She broke off their conversation to ask the wine waiter for a dry sherry.

'And Olivia?'

'Olivia and Dieter are in Ireland, looking for a property to buy. They are going to live there, and finding a home has become a matter of some urgency.' Judith's mouth curved in a wide smile. 'On Christmas Day, Olivia announced she was having a baby.'

Zephiniah's response was typically tart. 'That news has been long enough in coming! They must have been married for at least ten years. Is Gilbert over the moon at the prospect of becoming a grandfather?'

'He's very happy for her. Everyone is.'

Out of the corner of her eye Judith saw a waiter hovering and gave her attention to the menu.

Zephiniah, who had already studied the menu, said, 'And was there any other announcement – such as an announcement of when Gilbert's marriage to his former nanny's granddaughter is to take place?'

Judith moved the menu to one side. 'Please don't speak so disparagingly about Carrie, Mother. She never speaks about you in that way. As for the wedding – neither Gilbert nor Carrie has any intention of it taking place until Violet is safely out of Germany.'

The waiter gave a discreet cough and there was a judicious pause in the conversation as they gave him their orders.

When they were again left in privacy, Zephiniah said, 'And Thea? Is it true she's standing as a Labour Party candidate in a North Yorkshire by-election?'

'It is. And as I can't apply for a position as a

619

junior hospital doctor until Violet is safely home and the tangle of how I entered the country is sorted, I'm going to help her with her election-eering.'

Zephiniah stared at her, aghast. 'But she's standing as a *Labour* Party candidate!'

'I know – and yes, I also know that Gilbert is a Conservative government minister, but he's fully supportive of Thea, and he's fully supportive of my wanting to help her. He's a quite extraordin-ary man, isn't he?'

There was no way, after Gilbert's actions when she had told him of Judith's existence and situ-ation, that Zephiniah could disagree with her.

'Yes,' she said. 'He is.' But as she reached for her wine-glass, it wasn't Gilbert she was thinking about. It was Roberto, a man not at all extra-ordinary in the way Gilbert undoubtedly was, but a man she had come to realize was her soul-mate.

The funeral of Lord Hubholme was taking place in the church that stood in the grounds of his Suffolk country estate. Gilbert had been at Eton with Henry Hubholme and had counted him a good friend for well over thirty years. It was a funeral he couldn't possibly have avoided attend-ing, but it was one he was finding it difficult to bear, for reasons other than Henry's far too early death.

From the moment he had decided to marry Carrie he had known that the social consequences would be profound. What he had not expected was that he would be made aware of them so soon.

He had travelled down from Gorton especially for the funeral, and it had been immediately obvious to him that news of his Christmas engagement was already common knowledge.

The reactions, though subtle, were just as he had anticipated. He could sense people's unease at being seen in conversation with him – especially because at his death Henry had been an equerry, and the King and Queen were fellow mourners.

Social ostracism was something his broad shoulders could easily bear, but he had no intention of exposing Carrie to it. Rather than do that, his plan was that the minute it became necessary he would resign from the Cabinet, close up the Mount Street house and retire to Yorkshire. None of which he would mind doing, not if it meant his own and Carrie's continuing happiness. He knew that Carrie, though, would mind for him, and that her unhappiness at being the cause of his changed lifestyle would be deep.

The thought of Carrie being caused unhappiness on his account was an agony to him, but as he filed out of the church with the rest of the mourners he couldn't for the life of him see how it was to be avoided, not when, among the upper classes, snobbishness and sense of caste were so deeply ingrained.

It was the Queen who, with great sensitivity and inborn kindness, removed all his anxieties.

'How nice to see you, Lord Fenton,' she said as, on the way to the royal Rolls, she paused to exchange a few words with him, 'though I must say I would rather have run into you at a wedding than a funeral.'

'My feelings entirely, Ma'am.'

She shot him her sweet, still-girlish smile. 'Speaking of weddings, I understand you are newly engaged?'

'Yes, Ma'am.' He hesitated, his tension showing. Did Elizabeth know the identity of his fiancée? Was she about to congratulate him, in ignorance of who it was he'd become engaged to?

Elizabeth adjusted the collar of her fur and tilted her head a little to one side. 'When, some years ago, I was taken ill at Gorton, your fiancée was extremely kind to me. I seem to remember asking her to let me know when she married, in order that I could send her my best wishes.'

'That was very kind of you, Ma'am.'

Periwinkle-blue eyes held his. 'I would hate to think of a girl as sweet-natured and kind as Miss Thornton meeting with social difficulties, and so I wonder if I might suggest something to you?'

'Please do, Ma'am. I would be grateful for anything you have to say.'

Even though Bertie and Elizabeth had now been King George VI and Queen Elizabeth for just over two years, Gilbert still found formality when speaking to them in public a little difficult to maintain.

The affection in the Queen's eyes showed him that she often had the same problem.

'I'm sure,' she said, 'that under the circumstances you felt a quiet engagement was more suitable than one celebrated with a large party – and a party in London, not at Gorton – but I think it a mistake.' Her gloved hand touched him lightly on the arm. 'A large party, with absolutely everyone you know in public life in attendance, would be much the best thing. The King and I will propose ourselves and, by being guests and so conspicuously giving your coming marriage our blessing, there will be none of the social unpleasantness the two of you might otherwise meet with.'

'Thank you, Ma'am.' The words came from the bottom of his heart, and were it not that clusters of other people were only yards away from them – and that she was now his queen – he would have given her an enormous hug and a smacking great kiss.

Elizabeth removed her hand from his arm, adjusted her fur one more time and said, before continuing to make her way to the waiting Rolls, 'And we shall propose ourselves to the wedding as well – no matter whether it be a London wedding or a Gorton Hall wedding.' Her blue eyes danced with laughter. 'Though a Gorton Hall wedding, with all of the very interesting Outhwaite friends Carrie told me about when we exchanged shared reminiscences, could very well prove to be far the most interesting option!'

Chapter Forty-Two

With a fast-beating heart Violet strolled into Berlin's most fashionable cafe, the Romanische. Able to hold more than 1,000 people, it was frequented by the famous and so had been her cafe of choice for years. Every fellow movie actor she knew – and by now she knew absolutely everyone employed at Babelsberg – could, at one time or another, be found there.

The waiter who, after her frantic telephone call to the safe number of her American contact, had been told to expect her, weaved his way towards her between tables thronged with the cafe's late-afternoon clientele.

'A table alone, as it is Wednesday?' he asked in English, as she had been told he would ask.

'Yes.' She didn't correct him by pointing out it was a Friday.

He seated her at a table placed discreetly against one of the far walls, and she ordered a coffee and a slice of chocolate Herrentorte.

In all the years she had been passing on information this was the first time she had done so in the Romanische, and it was the first time she wasn't passing information by word of mouth, but was handing over tangible top-secret evidence.

She glanced down at her watch. It was a minute or two after five o'clock and as dark as night outside. How long would it be before Goebbels realized that carbon paper had been removed from a memo he'd had with him on his visit to Babelsberg only an hour and a half earlier? If he did realize the carbon paper had been removed, he would know immediately who had taken it. His briefcase had been left in her dressing room when he had gone to look at uncut footage of propaganda film. Never before had he been so careless, and if there was in his briefcase documentary proof of Hitler's intentions towards

624

Poland as well as Czechoslovakia, then she'd known that never again would she have such an opportunity of obtaining it.

If such a document was in the briefcase.

If the briefcase wasn't full of unimportant material that it was not worth her risking her life for.

It hadn't been.

On official stationery, with carbon paper still attached, there had been a handwritten memo to Goebbels signed by Hitler. Dated two days earlier, it was short and to the point.

She had read it at speed, translating it with ease:

Poland's existence is intolerable and incompatible with the essential conditions of Germany's life. As a result of her own internal weaknesses, Poland must go and will go! The total obliteration of Poland must be one of the fundamental drives of German policy. In spring, the liquidation of the rump of Czechoslovakia. In autumn, the occupation of Poland.

Meanwhile, on my anniversary speech to the Reichstag next week, I will speak in warm terms of 'the friendship between Germany and Poland' and declare it to be 'one of the reassuring factors in the political life of Europe'. When we unleash a Blitzkrieg against Poland, Britain and France will be totally unprepared for our action. We will hold the upper hand and then be able to look even further east for yet greater living space.

The German word Hitler had used for 'living space' was *Lebensraum*. She'd stared at it, momentarily bewildered. What further 'living space' could there possibly be for the Reich further east? Further east from Poland and Czechoslovakia there was only Russia...

Russia.

She'd sucked in her breath, knowing that – whatever the risk – she had to get the document into American, and then into British, hands.

When Goebbels returned to her dressing room and found her gone he would assume she was on one of the film sets working, and as he'd made no arrangement for her to travel back into Berlin with him, or to have dinner with him that evening, he would, if luck was on her side, merely pick up his briefcase and continue on to wherever it was he was next going. And if God as well as luck was on her side, he wouldn't notice the carbon paper was missing until she had passed it on to the Americans and until, with the false passport already given to her, she was well out of Germany and halfway to Ostend and a ferry home.

The waiter returned with her coffee and slice of cake.

Neither of them made eye contact with the other.

The waiter carried on serving other tables. Violet unfolded a serviette, picked up a cake-fork and turned her attention to the sickly-sweet Herrentorte.

When she had finished the cake and her coffee she raised a hand, signalling for the bill, then reached into her handbag for her purse. She had folded the flimsy carbon paper into a neat, small square and withdrew it from her bag along with three Reichsmark banknotes.

When the waiter breezed up to her with the bill on a salver, she slid the carbon paper onto it, under cover of the banknotes.

Two minutes later he had disappeared into the kitchens and she was walking out of the Romanische and into Auguste-Viktoria-Platz, dizzy with relief. The deed was done. All she had to do now was retrieve the passport from her Gartenstrasse house and shake the dust of Berlin from her heels.

She'd parked her little Roadster in an alleyway off the square and she hesitated beside it. If Goebbels already realized what she had done, then it was quite possible the Gestapo were already in Gartenstrasse, waiting for her. If they were, she'd stand more chance of successfully escaping the area in a taxicab than she would in a car known to be hers.

She flagged down a cab, feverishly calculating what the odds were of Goebbels not realizing – of his never realizing.

When a carbon copy of any document had been taken, the most usual thing was for the flimsy, messy blue carbon paper to be removed and destroyed. Goebbels was fastidious about his personal cleanliness. He certainly would never want to risk getting carbon ink on his fingers, and it was more than likely he was accustomed to carbon paper being scrupulously removed from documents before he received them.

If he didn't remember that the carbon paper had still been attached to Hitler's memo, then she was in no danger whatsoever. However, if he did remember…

As the taxicab neared Gartenstrasse she sat on the edge of her seat, ready to shout instructions to the driver if, when they rounded the corner, there was even one sinister black Mercedes in sight.

There wasn't.

'*Warte auf mich*,' she said to the driver.

Feeling in his pocket for his cigarettes and a lighter, he nodded, quite happy to wait for as long as she wanted him to.

She raced down the path, ran up the steps to the front door, fumbled with her key in the lock and sprinted into the house

'Irmgard! *Irmgard!*' she shouted, taking the stairs to the first floor two at a time.

Once in her bedroom, she yanked open her bedside drawer and snatched up the passport, then wrenched open her wardrobe doors and grabbed a small travel-bag from a top shelf.

'*Was ist los?*' Irmgard demanded, rushing into the room, her eyes wide with fright.

As she slammed open drawers, throwing personal possessions into the travel-bag, Violet didn't tell her what was the matter. There wasn't time. What she did tell Irmgard was that she was to leave the house immediately and never come back to it.

She paused at that point, taking money out of the wallet she kept in her underwear drawer and stuffing it into Irmgard's hands.

'The Gestapo are probably coming for me,' she said in German. 'If you have relatives in the country, visit them, Irmgard. And take the Kandinsky with you.'

With a terrified Irmgard hard on her heels, she ran back downstairs and into the kitchen. Seizing a knife from the knife rack, she ran into the drawing room, yanked the Kandinsky from the wall and prised it out of its frame. Then she rolled the canvas into a tube and stuffed it beneath Irmgard's arm.

'It's yours, Irmgard,' she said. 'You'll be able to sell it for a lot of money, though not in Germany. Go to Switzerland to sell it. Or France. And thank you for being such an angel to me for so long. Now leave, Irmgard. Leave and don't look back.'

When Irmgard was safely out of the house, Violet gave a last, long look around. Throughout all her years of living in Berlin, the house had been important to her. It had been a refuge from the part she'd had to play whenever she left it. Now she was leaving it for the last time.

Vastly relieved that Irmgard, at least, wasn't going to be found at the house and questioned, she went back upstairs to retrieve her handbag and pick up her hastily packed travel-bag. As she stepped into her bedroom there came the distant sound of car tyres squealing as they rounded the corner into Gartenstrasse.

She sucked in her breath and closed her eyes, praying that the cars would continue on down the road: that they wouldn't come to a halt outside number twenty-three.

Her prayers went unheard.

One after another the cars screeched to a halt. Doors slammed open and then slammed shut.

Leather-gloved fists hammered on the door,

629

and then the door was broken in and jackbooted feet pounded up the stairs.

Seconds later a squad of men burst into the room.

Violet didn't flinch.

'I'm a British citizen,' she said icily as they laid hands on her, aware that even though the passport in her handbag would have served her well at border checkpoints, it was pointless trying to pass if off as genuine in the situation in which she now found herself.

Goebbels knew she wasn't American, and as she was being arrested for passing information to the Americans, the American Embassy would be in no position to help her. The only embassy that could possibly be of help was the British Embassy.

The men who had seized hold of her and who were dragging her out of the room were wearing the uniform of the criminal investigative police. An officer, waiting for her at her bedroom door, said tight-lipped in English, 'You're a German resident. You've been a German resident for years.'

'The British Ambassador will make a formal protest!' she shouted as she was dragged past him, and then, as she was manhandled down the stairs and knowing that she should at least be pretending outraged innocence, 'And why am I being arrested? What am I being charged with? Where is the proper warrant?'

Even as she shouted the words, she knew how pointless they were.

The police in Nazi Germany did not deal in proper warrants. Whatever the future held for her, it wasn't an appearance in a court of law.

What the future held for her was interrogation at the most-feared address in Berlin. Prinz-Albrecht-Strasse 8. Gestapo headquarters.

She was bundled into the back of one of the cars, her terror so great that her legs were weak. No one interrogated at Prinz Albrecht-Strasse ever emerged in the same physical condition in which they had entered.

That was, if they emerged at all.

And now she was being taken there and in ten minutes, perhaps less, she would be inside the building and beyond all help.

With her hands held tightly together on her knees, she looked out of the window and saw that they weren't heading for central Berlin; instead they were taking the road that skirted the city on the west and then headed north.

'Where are we going?' she demanded of the men she was sandwiched between, and then, as she received no answer, '*Wohin gehen wir?*'

The officer on her left grinned. '*Sachsenhausen.*'

Violet's pupils dilated in bewilderment. Sachsenhausen concentration camp wasn't somewhere people were taken for questioning. It was somewhere they were imprisoned; it was also somewhere they were executed.

She gripped her hands even tighter together.

Was that why she was being taken to Sachsenhausen? She'd known when she had taken the carbon paper, and asked her American contact how it should be handed over, what the penalty would be, if she didn't manage to flee the country before its loss was discovered.

She had known she would be executed. And she

had known how she would be executed. There were only two methods of execution for traitors in Nazi Germany: hanging and beheading. And for women, beheading was the favoured option.

At least, though, she was going to be spared the torture rooms of Prinz-Albrecht-Strasse 8's basement – and she had always known, if it came to having to pay the ultimate price, how she would handle that final, dreadful walk to the scaffold. She would pretend she was returning home to Gorton.

Drawing on all her skills as an actress, she would close her senses to the reality around her and imagine she was walking down the lane from Outhwaite towards the bridge over the river. She would cross the bridge and see Gorton Hall in front of her and know that all the people she loved most in the world were there, waiting to welcome her. Papa and Carrie. Thea, Olivia and Roz. Jim and Charlie. Hermione and Miss Calvert.

And that way, encircled by all the love she knew they had for her, there would be no place for terror. About to be reunited with her family and friends again, she would die without a shiver.

Chapter Forty-Three

FEBRUARY 1939

Tom Kirby's office in the Office of Public Affairs was a much bigger room than the room in which Max had met him in the summer of 1934. The view from the window was the same, though. A busy street: more public buildings, and the reassurance that the White House wasn't far distant.

Max had known the instant he'd received Kirby's message to meet him that, whatever news Kirby had for him, it wouldn't be good.

It wasn't. It was the worst possible news. News he'd prayed he would never have to hear.

'She was arrested *six weeks* ago?' he said disbelievingly. 'Dear God in heaven, Tom! How could it have taken her US contact in Berlin six fucking weeks before he knew of it?'

He'd been sitting, facing Tom across the seeming acres of Tom's desk. Now Max erupted to his feet, slamming his fists down hard on the desk, leaning over it towards Tom, the veins in his neck standing out like cords. *'Where the crucifying fuck did he think she was? On holiday in the fucking Alps?'*

Aware that Max was on the verge of grabbing hold of him and trying to strangle him, Tom Kirby put the castors on his chair into quick movement, sending his chair skidding backwards so that he was out of Max's reach.

'Take it easy, Max,' he said, raising a hand to warn him off. 'Violet often went for weeks without making contact. After she handed over the carbon of the Hitler memo, nothing happened to indicate that its loss had been realized. Her go-between – the courier who worked out of the Romanische cafe – wasn't arrested and there are no signs that he's come under any kind of suspicion. Our people in Berlin still consider Violet's obtaining such hard proof of Hitler's future intentions in Europe to be an absolutely perfect piece of information-gathering.'

'*How could it have been?*' Max thundered, feeling as if he was about to explode. '*If she was arrested six weeks ago, she was arrested the same – or practically the same – day that she handed over the carbon of the memo!*'

'I know.' Tom edged his chair a fraction further backwards. 'The embassy now knows that. The courier in question is no longer in Berlin, but is now working out of a restaurant in Paris.'

Max sank back down onto his chair. 'And Violet?' he asked, once more in control of himself, knowing that no amount of rage could improve such a nightmarish situation. 'Where is Violet?'

'We don't know. If it wasn't for her maid reporting Violet's arrest to the British Embassy, we wouldn't even know that she was arrested immediately after leaving the Romanische. Presumably she was taken to Prinz-Albrecht-Strasse.'

Max breathed in hard.

Tom Kirby rose to his feet. Rounding his desk, he put a hand on Max's shoulder. 'It's been six weeks, Max,' he said again. 'Her arrest had to be because Goebbels realized what she done. When you consider the nature of the memo, the assumption has to be that, after her arrest, she would not have lived long.'

Max's eyes held his, agony in their depths. 'And that is what I have to now tell her family – her family that is now my family?'

'Yes, Max. I'm afraid it is. And what you must also tell them is that her action in being able to put such concrete evidence of Hitler's intentions into the hands of her country's government has ensured a major change in Britain's policy towards Nazi Germany. Major changes where armaments production and land, sea and air defences are concerned are already in hand. Prime Minister Chamberlain's days of appeasement are over.'

Feeling a decade older than he had when he had woken that morning, Max rose heavily to his feet. It was only a little over two months since he and Roz had returned to Washington after spending Christmas at Gorton. Now they would be coming back to Yorkshire again – and with hideous news.

News that he had first to break to Roz.

As he stepped out of the building and onto the sidewalk he did so with a heart as heavy as lead, his sense of responsibility for having recruited Violet crippling.

Six days later, with an ashen-faced Roz at his side, he was walking out of Waterloo station.

'I'm going to ask the cabbie to drop you off at

635

Claridge's while I continue on to Mount Street,' he said as they headed for the taxi rank. 'I need to be on my own when I break the news to Gilbert, Roz. You understand, don't you?'

She nodded, her gloved hand hugging his arm a little tighter.

Over the five days they had spent crossing the Atlantic she had tried to convince him that what had happened to Violet would have happened even if he hadn't recruited her as an informer for American intelligence.

'If you had refused to approach her, Tom Kirby would have found someone else to approach her,' she had said, 'and the outcome would have been just the same.'

'If someone else had approached her, she wouldn't have done it,' he'd said bluntly. 'She did it because it was I who asked; because, even though you and I weren't a couple at the time, she regarded me as family.'

At Claridge's Roz got out of the cab, her heart filled with grief. It was hurting with her own grief, it was hurting on behalf of the grief that Gilbert, Thea, Olivia and Carrie would so soon be feeling; and it was hurting at the thought of the guilt she knew Max would carry with him until his dying day.

She went into the lounge and ordered coffee. The first thing Max had done when they had landed at Southampton had been to telephone Mount Street and tell Gilbert he was back in London and on his way to speak to him; which meant, as Mount Street was only just around the corner from Claridge's, that Max would already

be there.
When the coffee came she drank it black.
And then she asked for a brandy.

Though Max had said nothing more on the phone than that he was back in the country and wished to speak to him, Gilbert had known from the tone of Max's voice that his reason for wanting to do so was not a good one.

He opened the door himself to Max, took one look at Max's harrowed face and said, 'It's bad news, isn't it? Bad news about Violet?'

Once in the drawing room, Gilbert didn't sit down to hear what Max had to tell him; he simply closed the door behind them and said, 'Tell me.'

'Violet finally did what she'd been determined to do, Gilbert. Six weeks ago she supplied irrefutable proof of Hitler's future military intentions, which are not only occupying what remains of Czechoslovakia, but invading Poland and, after Poland, looking further east, towards Russia.'

'How, in God's name, did she get proof of such a thing?' Gilbert's voice was hoarse, the question an attempt to stave off the terrible denouement that he knew Max was leading up to.

'She removed carbon paper from a memo handwritten by Hitler that was in Josef Goebbels's briefcase. Her instructions for delivering it were to pass it to a courier working out of the Romanische cafe, which she did successfully.'

'And then?' The moment Gilbert had been dreading could be put off no longer. There was perspiration on his forehead and crippling coils of dread in his belly.

'Within an hour of doing so she was arrested at her home – and she hasn't been seen, or heard of, since.'

Gilbert's always pale skin drained to a bleached white.

Knowing there was no way of sparing him Tom Kirby's opinion of what had then happened, Max took a deep breath and said, 'It's Kirby's opinion – and the opinion of the US Embassy in Berlin – that, considering the nature of the memo and who had sent it, Violet would not have lived long after her arrest.'

'But if there's been no definite confirmation, those are only opinions, Max!' There was desperation in Gilbert's voice. 'Without confirmation, how can anyone know for a certainty that Violet is dead? She could well be still alive!'

Max said as levelly as he could manage, 'The briefcase Violet took the carbon from had been left by Goebbels in Violet's dressing room at Babelsberg. No one but Violet could have taken it. The contents of the memo were as top secret as it is possible to imagine, and the sender was Hitler. Taking all those things into account, it's impossible to think Violet is still alive. I'm sorry, Gilbert. More sorry than I am capable of saying.'

Gilbert sank down onto a sofa and buried his head in his hands, his shoulders shaking. When at last he could speak, he said thickly, 'Olivia and Dieter are back in Ireland. I'll have to break the news by phone. Thea and Carrie are at Gorton. I can't tell them on the phone. I must be with them when I tell them. You'll come with me?'

'Of course.' Max blew his nose heavily in an effort to regain his self-control. 'Roz is at Claridge's. I wanted to be on my own when I spoke to you.'

Gilbert nodded, made a despairing motion with his hands and then rose unsteadily to his feet. 'We'll leave for Yorkshire now – immediately. We'll pick up Roz on the way.' He stopped, unable to go on, and then, after a colossal inner struggle, said, 'No mention in front of Thea and Carrie as to the basements in Prinz-Albrecht-Strasse and of how death-sentences are carried out in Hitler's Reich. They won't know, and they don't need to know.'

Then, every line of his face etched with suffering, his broad shoulders bowed, he stumbled from the room as if he were a man of seventy, not a man in his fifties.

All three of them spent the four-hour-car journey from London to Gorton in almost total silence. As Gilbert's chauffeured Bentley ate up the miles, the only thing Roz said was, 'When I was at Claridge's I telephoned Kyle. I thought you would prefer that I did so, Uncle Gilbert, rather than having to break the news to him yourself.'

'Thank you, Roz.' There was gratitude in his voice. Unlike Roz, Kyle wasn't a blood relation, but being Roz's stepbrother made him extended family and he was someone Gilbert would have had to tell. That Roz had taken on the burden of doing so had been sensitive of her.

As they left the A1 and headed into the Dales, the narrow roadsides were peppered with primroses. In Outhwaite, thanks to a very mild spring, pale-lemon winter jasmine tumbled up and over the side of Hester Calvert's front door. There was a bush of golden-yellow forsythia at the war memorial corner and daffodils in every carefully tended front garden.

The approach to Gorton was thick with daffodils. Because they were wild, they were smaller and paler than the ones in Outhwaite's gardens, but they were beautiful, nonetheless.

Their beauty didn't comfort Roz. It only signalled that soon – within ten minutes – Gilbert would be breaking the news of Violet's arrest and certain fate to Thea, Carrie and Judith.

He did so as succinctly and as gently as he could, but it was beyond all possibility for him to break the news in a way that could be bearable.

'She can't be dead!' Thea had been sitting on the arm of a sofa and jumped to her feet, her eyes blazing, her face chalk-white. 'She can't be dead, Papa! It's impossible! No one is more alive than Violet!'

Gilbert tried to speak and, seeing that it was beyond him, Max said quietly, 'Under the circumstances, Thea, no alternative seems possible.'

Thea gave a cry of anguish, and Judith, tears streaming down her face, put an arm around her shoulders.

Barely able to comprehend the hideous enormity of what Gilbert had just told them, Carrie's immediate instinct was not to give vent to her own shock and grief, but to give Gilbert what comfort she could.

Crossing swiftly to his side, she slid her hand through his arm and hugged it tight. 'Maybe it isn't true,' she said fiercely. 'Until we know for definite, or until more time has passed, surely there's still hope?'

She'd known, as his hand had lovingly covered hers, that grateful as he was for the comfort she was trying to give, he didn't believe there was any hope – and she sensed that no one else in the room did, either.

There came the sound of a car coming down the quarter-mile-long drive. Sending gravel flying, it swerved to a halt in front of the house.

Roz crossed to one of the room's long windows. 'It's Kyle,' she said. 'He must have only been twenty miles or so behind us all the way from London.'

'Kyle? Oh, thank God!' The gratitude in Thea's voice was naked.

Breaking away from Judith, she rushed from the room, and moments later all that could be heard from the circular hall were her choked sobs and Kyle's voice, low and tender as he tried to soothe her.

When she re-entered the room his arm was around her waist and her head was on his shoulder, her face ravaged, but her sobs under control.

Still with his arm around her as if he was never, ever again going to let her go, Kyle said to Gilbert. 'What's the latest news? Roz told me the arrest was six weeks ago, but not the circumstances surrounding it.'

'The whole thing is a long story.' Gilbert looked towards Max. 'Would you fix brandies for everyone, Max? I've never in my life been more in need of one.'

Carrie had no need for brandy. What she needed was fresh air. 'I'm going outside, Gilbert,' she said. 'I'd like to be on my own for a little while.'

He patted her hand to show he understood, his throat so tight with grief that he didn't trust himself to speak.

More than anything in the world he wanted to leave the room with her. He didn't want to have to say again the words Tom Kirby had used to Max. Where Kyle was concerned, though, he had no choice. And Kyle was a diplomat. He knew as much as – if not more about Nazi Germany than – Max or Gilbert did. He would know that Violet would have either died under torture or on a scaffold, her head severed from her neck by a headsman wearing impeccable evening dress. The knowledge would be there in Kyle's eyes – and Gilbert didn't know how he was going to survive seeing it there.

Carrie went to the cloakroom for her jacket and then walked out of the house. For a long moment she stood beneath the pillared portico and then, slowly, she walked down the wide flight of steps. As she did so, the day in 1917 when Violet had been seven and she had been ten, and she'd walked down the steps on the way to post the officers' mail and had found Violet seated glumly on them, was as vivid in her memory as if it had happened yesterday.

She remembered the way they had bicycled into Outhwaite and how Violet had sung 'Tipperary' at the top of her lungs, and the way her torrent of fiery hair and the patriotic ribbons tied to her handlebars had streamed in the wind.

That she would never see her again was a monstrosity beyond all imagining – and so she refused to imagine it. Sinking down onto an ice-cold step, she clasped her hands tightly in her lap, knowing that she was the only person who still had hope – and, with typical Yorkshire stubbornness, refusing to relinquish it.

Chapter Forty-Four

In Sachsenhausen concentration camp August Groebler prepared for his day's work. He took pride in being an executioner and dressed carefully. A stiff-fronted white shirt. Black trousers with a broad stripe of braid down the side, the trousers shiny from daily usage. Black socks – wool because the temperature in the vast room where executions took place was frequently freezing cold.

He hooked a pair of braces over his shoulders, wondering how long a day lay ahead of him. Sometimes he had only three or four decapitations to carry out. Other days he worked until even his strong-muscled arms ached.

He fastened a celluloid wing-collar to his shirt. A short working day meant he would be able to meet his grandchildren from school, a task that his daughter appreciated.

With great care and peering close to the mirror, he fastened his white bow-tie, wondering about the age and sex of those he was about to behead. Strangely the young, who had so much more to lose, often behaved with more dignity than the old. Even more strangely, it was usually the women who showed the most courage.

He slid his arms into his low-cut white piqué waistcoat, fastening mother-of-pearl buttons over his gigantic girth.

There had been a time when executing a woman had been something of a rarity for him. Now it had become commonplace.

He put on his shoes, tying the laces in a double bow. A man's feet had to be firmly planted when wielding an axe, and the last thing he could risk was a shoelace coming undone. To trip over when bringing the axe down on someone's neck would be a very messy business.

As he shrugged himself into his tailcoat he had a strong feeling that his first beheading of the day was going to be a woman. Hopefully she wouldn't be too much trouble. Whatever the day ahead held, at the end of it he would be eighty marks and an extra ration of cigarettes better off.

He put his top hat on his head and picked up his regulation white gloves.

His axe, which he'd personalized by having a white lily engraved on it, was waiting for him.

And so was his first victim.

Violet lifted her head high as she started on the walk she had always known she would one day take. Nothing mattered any more but the scene around her. The lane leading down from Outh-waite was edged with flowering blackthorn and the meadows leading down to the river were starred with celandines. Soon she would come to the curve in the lane that led to the bridge and then, beyond the bridge, would be Gorton Hall.

It was a mild day for March – she had decided a long time ago that it would be a mild, gentle day when she made this walk. The breeze was soft against her face and in the branches of an alder a blackbird was singing.

In her mind's eye she peopled Gorton with the people she wanted to find there when she arrived. Her father, of course, and Carrie. Thea, Olivia, Roz and Judith. If Olivia and Roz were there, then Max and Dieter would be there too, and if it was to be a complete family gathering, then Kyle would be there as well.

It would be quite a crowd, and in the evening the crowd would be even bigger, for there would be a party – she was determined there would be a party – and at a party would be Jim and his wife, and Charlie and Hermione, Charlie junior and Miss Calvert.

When she reached the bridge she came to a halt, knowing that her journey was almost at an end and wanting it to last just a little bit longer.

Resting her arms on the stone parapet, she gazed down into the limpid depths of the slow-moving river, remembering all the other times she had stood in exactly the same place, doing exactly the same thing. Sometimes she had been alone, as she was today. Sometimes Carrie had been with her. Often it had been her father who had been with her and, when she had been a little girl, her mother. She could remember the feel of her mother's hand holding hers: the sense of safety it had given her.

With all the force of her vivid imagination she imagined she was holding her mother's hand now as, turning away from the parapet, she continued the walk towards the people she loved.

Chapter Forty-Five

Carrie had no idea how long she had been sitting on the steps, but what she did know was that, if she stayed where she was much longer, someone would come and try to persuade her to return indoors.

And she didn't want to do so. Not yet.

Plunging her hands deep in the pockets of her jacket, she walked down the remaining steps and then across the gravel to the drive. At the end of the drive, where it ran into the lane and the bridge came into view, she came to a halt.

A woman was walking from the bridge in the direction of the house. She was too far away for Carrie to see her clearly, but she could see that although the woman's hair was dark, not fiery, there was something familiar about her; so familiar that the breath stopped short in her chest.

Then she sucked air back into her lungs and began to run.

She ran as she had never run before. She ran

646

with a prayer on her lips and hope blazing in her heart.

Violet began running too.

As, with wings on their heels, they sprinted towards each other and all Carrie's hopes were confirmed, tears of joy streamed down her face.

'Oh, Violet!' she gasped as they hurtled into each other's arms. 'You're alive! I *knew* you were alive!'

They rocked together, hugging each other tight, and then Carrie pulled away from her a little, to look into Violet's face. 'Everyone else thinks you've been executed. Papa. Max. Thea. Everyone!'

Violet laughed, delighted at the sensation she'd caused. 'I would have been, if I'd been arrested for what I thought I was being arrested for, but I wasn't. I was arrested for being a prostitute.'

Carrie gaped at her.

'Don't look so horrified, Carrie darling. I wasn't one. I simply rejected a man who objected to being rejected, and he decided to revenge himself on me by having me arrested.'

She tucked her arm into Carrie's as they began walking towards the entrance of Gorton's long tree-lined drive.

'The bastard in question, Luther Schultz – more commonly known as *Schweinehund* Schultz – is Kripo's second-incommand. Kripo,' she said as she saw Carrie's bewilderment deepening by the second, 'is Nazi Germany's criminal police. In other words, *Schweinehund* Schultz can arrest anyone he wants, on any charge he wants. He was risking it a bit by arresting me, because I have friends in much higher positions than the one he holds, but I wasn't arrested under my name, only as a number.'

'Which meant that when you were finally released, your imprisonment could be put down to an error that he would appear to have no connection with?'

'Very sharp of you, Carrie love. What he didn't know was that he was doing me the most gigantic favour, because if he hadn't had me arrested, I would most certainly have been arrested on a charge of treason. As it was, being only a number in Sachsenhausen concentration camp, no matter how hard the Gestapo may have been looking for me, they couldn't have found me.'

'But what about when you were released? What then?'

'Oh, then I had a problem. I had to get out of Berlin fast, and I had no passport. That had been taken when I was arrested.'

They were in the drive now, walking between the avenue of beeches.

'Then how?'

'There was another passport. A passport at Berlin's Central Office for Jewish Emigration in the name of Judith Zimmerman.'

'So *that's* why you dyed your hair black!'

'And it's probably going to take weeks of washing to get back to its natural colour. Who will be there when we walk into Gorton, Carrie? Is everyone there? Is Roz there? Are Olivia and Dieter there?'

'Thea and Roz are there. Max is there, and so is Kyle. Olivia and Dieter are on their way from Ireland. They live there now, and Olivia is having a baby.'

'A baby?' Violet's eyes shone with delight. 'How wonderful! Do you think if it's a girl they'll name her after me?'

'I think if it's a girl they'll name her after your mother – but Olivia is going to be so over the moon at knowing you're still alive that she'll probably do anything you ask of her.'

'When is the baby due? I'll have to arrange to be home from America when it is.'

'America?' Carrie came to a shocked halt. 'But you've only just arrived home! How soon are you going to be leaving for America?'

'Quite soon, but not until after there's been the most glorious welcome-home party for me – and I wouldn't be leaving even then, if it wasn't for the screen test.'

'Screen test?' Carrie was beginning to wonder if she was dreaming the entire bizarre conversation.

'For *Gone with the Wind*. While I was on the train I read in a newspaper that although Vivien Leigh has been signed up for the part of Scarlett O'Hara, she hasn't started filming yet. And she's dark-haired and, as Scarlett O'Hara is Irish, she must have had red hair, mustn't she? I'm going to get Zsigmund to get me an introduction to David Selznick, who's producing. Once he sees me, I'm quite sure I'll replace Vivien as Scarlett. It's a part I was born to play.'

'You're going to have to do a lot of hair-washing first. And who is Zsigmund?'

'Zsigmund is Zsigmund Sárközy, a director who was once in love with me – as I now realize I was with him.'

649

Violet came to a halt. The house was now only a hundred yards away and she was savouring the moment.

With a deep, ecstatic sigh, she said, 'Let's hold hands, Carrie, and run all the way to the house.'

Carrie's smile was luminous as she thought of the expression she would see on Gilbert's dearly loved face when they walked into the drawing room together. 'Yes, let's,' she said, taking hold of Violet's hand and knowing they were about to run faster than they'd ever run in their lives before.

Epilogue

JUNE 1939

Luther Schultz was seated behind his desk in Police Headquarters in Alexanderplatz, his fists clenched, a newspaper laid out before him. The newspaper was the *International Herald Tribune*. On its front page was the headline 'Italy and Germany sign Pact of Steel', but it wasn't the front page he was looking at. It was one of the inner pages, and the photograph that was enraging him was a wedding photograph.

The photograph was credited to Rozalind Bradley and the caption read, 'Movie star Violet Fenton is bridesmaid at Father's wedding, with Britain's King and Queen in attendance'.

The photograph was a group shot, with King

George standing on one side of the happy couple and Queen Elizabeth on the other side of them. All of the family, apart from the traitor von Starhemberg, Starhemberg's wife and Violet, were unknown to him. Two spaniels sat immediately in front of the bride and bridegroom as if they, too, were guests.

Beneath the photograph was a short write-up of the wedding and where it had taken place, none of which held any interest for him. It was the concluding couple of sentences that had sent the blood roaring along his veins in a tide of white-hot frustrated fury:

Miss Fenton has recently returned from Berlin, where she has made many movies at the Babelsberg studios. Now recently married to movie director Zsigmund Sárközy, she is no longer disappointed at not replacing Vivien Leigh in the movie Gone with the Wind. *Instead she is to be Cathy to Hollywood heart-throb Tyrone Power's Heathcliffe in* Wuthering Heights, *a movie being directed by her husband.*

The consensus in Hollywood is that the new Mrs Sárközy is about to take the world by storm.

Savagely, Schultz tore out the page and screwed it into a ball.

An American movie would never get past Goebbels's Film Review Office – especially as it was rumoured that Goebbels would no longer even allow Violet's name to be spoken in his presence.

Not only was Schultz no longer able to stalk her; he wouldn't even be able to see her on-screen. He sucked in his breath, his lips flattening

651

against his teeth. How had she done it? How had she disappeared from Berlin within hours of being released from Sachsenhausen? Even more bewilderingly, how had she managed to leave the country when he held her passport? And why was her passport an American one and not a British one? He didn't understand it any more than he understood how people could look as happy as the people in the photograph looked.

Everyone, including Britain's king and queen, had radiant smiles on their faces.

A bizarre thought struck him. He seized hold of the sheet of balled-up paper and feverishly smoothed it flat to see if he was right, or not.

He was.

Even the spaniels looked to be smiling.

The publishers hope that this book has given you enjoyable reading. Large Print Books are especially designed to be as easy to see and hold as possible. If you wish a complete list of our books please ask at your local library or write directly to:

Magna Large Print Books
Magna House, Long Preston,
Skipton, North Yorkshire.
BD23 4ND

This Large Print Book for the partially sighted, who cannot read normal print, is published under the auspices of

THE ULVERSCROFT FOUNDATION

THE ULVERSCROFT FOUNDATION

... we hope that you have enjoyed this Large Print Book. Please think for a moment about those people who have worse eyesight problems than you ... and are unable to even read or enjoy Large Print, without great difficulty.

You can help them by sending a donation, large or small to:

**The Ulverscroft Foundation,
1, The Green, Bradgate Road,
Anstey, Leicestershire, LE7 7FU,
England.**
or request a copy of our brochure for more details.

The Foundation will use all your help to assist those people who are handicapped by various sight problems and need special attention.

Thank you very much for your help.